REIGN OF THE
DRAGON BORN

DEDICATED TO
Those who strive to be better.

Shadow Dragon Saga
Curse of the Dragon Shadow
Legend of the Dragon Soul
Rise of the Dragon Sworn
Blood of the Dragon Throne
Reign of the Dragon Born
Secret of the Dragon Crown

First Edition
Published by Fairies and Fantasy Pty Ltd 2024

ISBN: 978-1-922390-88-2 (paperback)
ISBN: 978-1-922390-89-9 (hardcover)

Reign of the Dragon Born copyright © 2024 Selina Fenech
Cover art and interior illustrations © 2024 Selina Fenech
Editing by Zero Alchemy

www.selinafenech.com

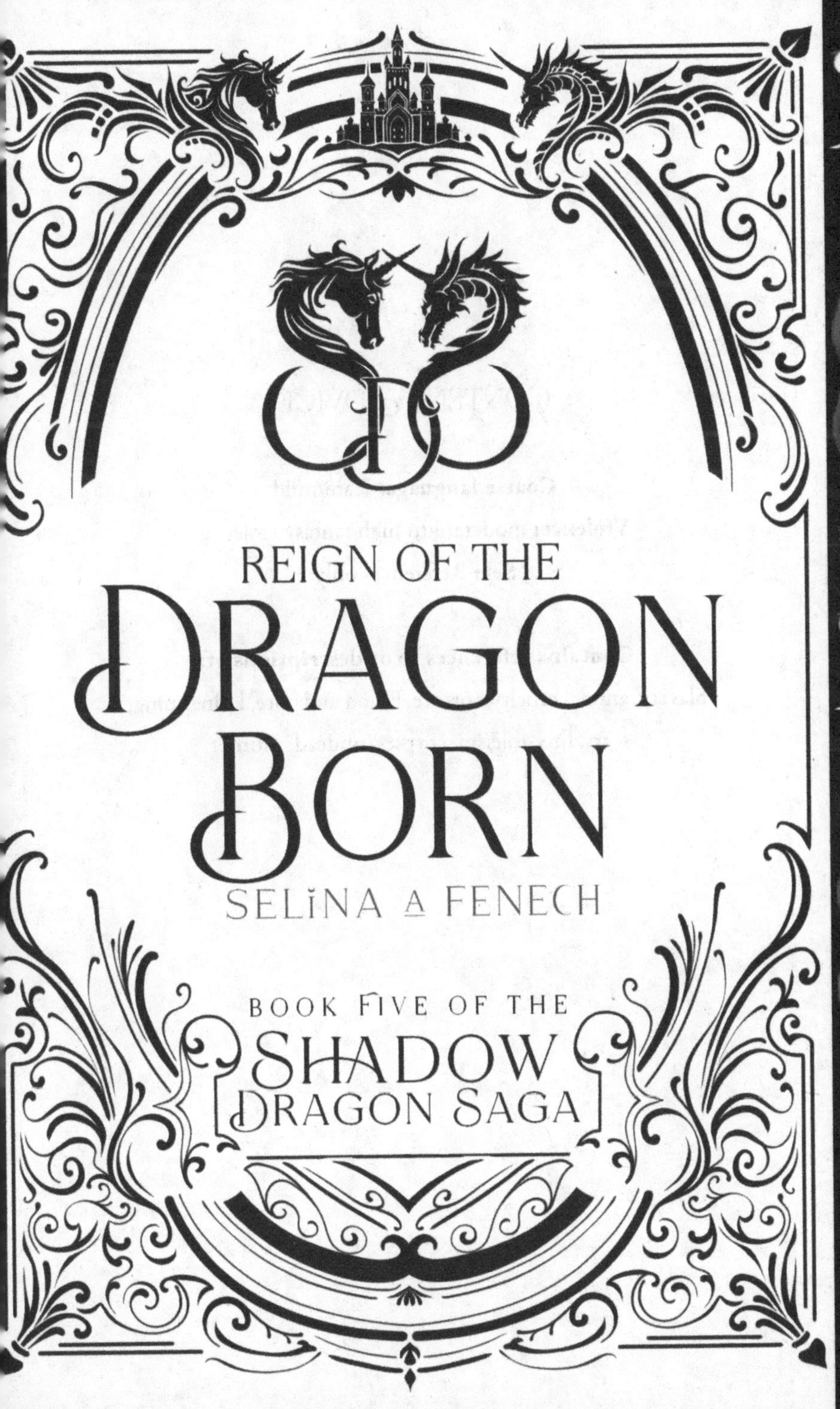

REIGN OF THE DRAGON BORN

SELINA A FENECH

BOOK FIVE OF THE

SHADOW DRAGON SAGA

CONTENT ADVICE

Coarse language: Rare/mild

Violence: moderate-to-high fantasy violence

Sex: References only

Contains references to or descriptions of:

Slavery, animal cruelty, torture, blood and gore, kidnapping, scars, fire, ableism, corpses/undead, murder.

CONTENTS

Dragon Keeps

1. Braigwenkeep (Trade Hub)
2. Nevrynkeep (Mining)
3. Ardahnkeep (Trade Harbor, Old Rolanian Capital)
4. Tjollaskeep (Mining)
5. Salixkeep (Fishing)
6. Ulfrenkeep (Mining)
7. Ylvakeep (Farming)
8. Leskakeep (Farming)
9. Pryshakeep (Farming)
10. Dastmyrkeep (Glass)
11. Tarrickeep (Mining)
12. Gerichkeep (Lumber)
13. Skaellakeep (Farming)
14. Idrakeep (Penal)
15. Hjelzahnkeep (Training)
16. Eslindekeep (Incomplete)

NORTHERN
ALDERKIN DEPTHS
(Nerruu Deemfret)
Gris Hofen
(15)
Sunborn Range
Stonewing Crest
(4)
CENTRAL
ALDERKIN DEPTHS
(Luns Deemfret)
Eishowl Peaks
(6)
Bovin Steppes
Unicorn Tears River
(13)
(5)
Erst Hofen
The Red Cliffs
SOUTHERN
ALDERKIN DEPTHS
(Sons Deemfret)
Talon Bluffs
Nord Myrr
Lorg Sesstra
(8)
Lorg Eldstrom
Lorg Draeka
(9)
Draeskull Crags
Starris River
(3)
Grand Hofen
DRAEKHANHELM
Etherflame Plains
(7)
Serpents Run
Seasong Shores
EYLE NORDCREST
(14)
Mestra's Horn
EASTERN
ALDERKIN DEPTHS
(Ilst Deemfret)
DRAEKHAN'S REST
SKYBREAK SEA

ALDERKIN
DEPTHS
Relic Lower
Wet Descent
Whisperwind Passage
UPSLOPE
DragonMaw Descent
Stores
Upper Flats
The Curtain
1.
2.
3.
12.
11.
9.
The Grand Arch
Relic Upper
Flowstone Steps
Delver's Circuit
Crystalline Reservoir
STONESHIELD GATE
Livestock
Roo Farm

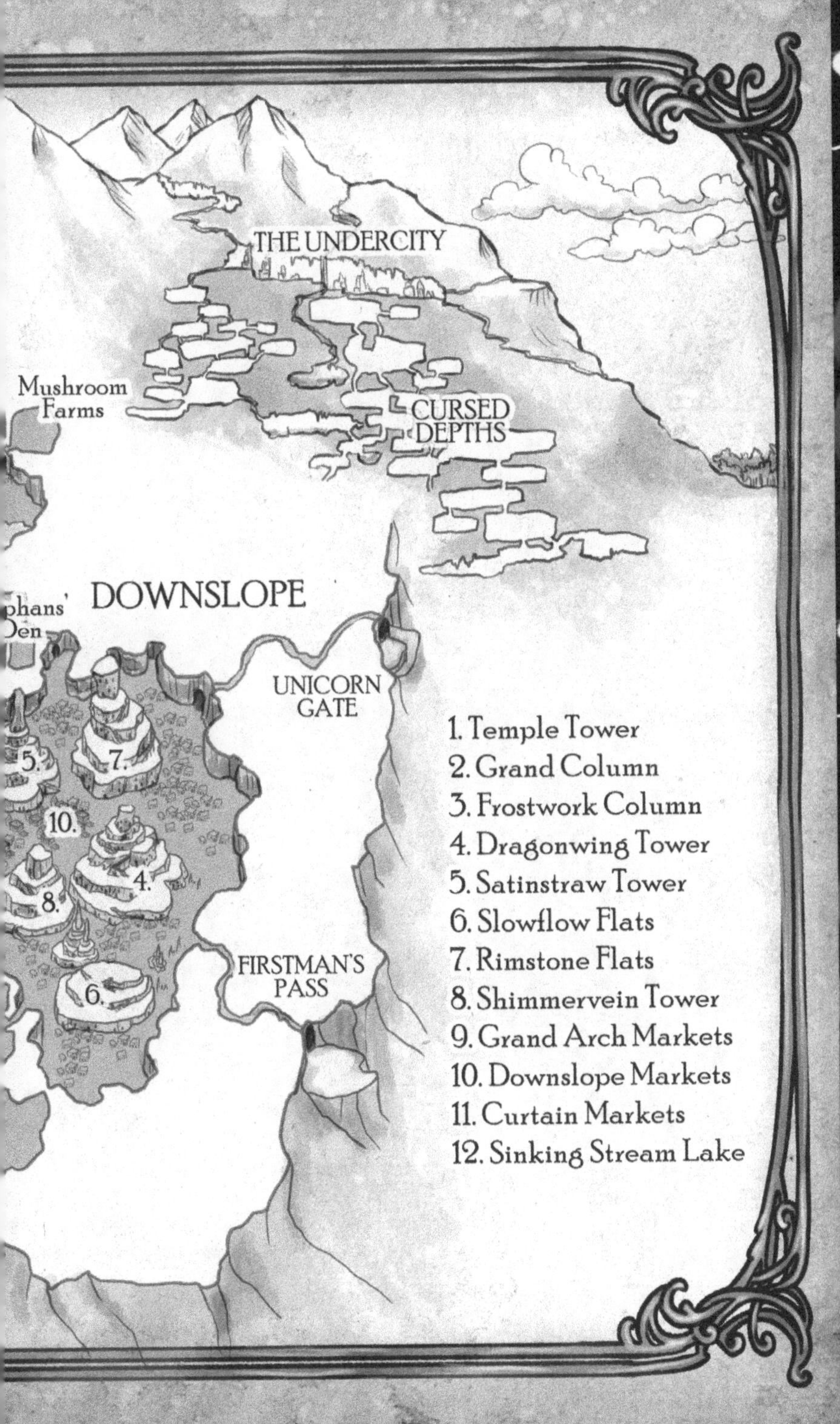

THE UNDERCITY
Mushroom Farms
CURSED DEPTHS
DOWNSLOPE
phans' Den
UNICORN GATE
5.
7.
10.
4.
8.
6.
FIRSTMAN'S PASS
1. Temple Tower
2. Grand Column
3. Frostwork Column
4. Dragonwing Tower
5. Satinstraw Tower
6. Slowflow Flats
7. Rimstone Flats
8. Shimmervein Tower
9. Grand Arch Markets
10. Downslope Markets
11. Curtain Markets
12. Sinking Stream Lake

ONE

Riony's heart raced in time to the heart stone lying against her chest—Lyrrin's pulse fluttering as she met her mother—and it felt like the world was ending.

She used to imagine what horrors might herald the end of days. Stars falling from the sky, birds crying like babies, rivers running with blood.

Nothing prepared her for what was surely the true harbinger of the end of the world which lay before her.

Kessara Heithorn ... pledging her undying loyalty.

What in the deepest cursed depths is going on?

Riony was still damp from the thunderstorm they'd flown through to escape the capital of Elundrae, still smelled the metallic tang of her blood that soaked her almost as thoroughly, her body still flushed with the energy of the silvernix Kess had used to heal them both.

Completely, sincerely, what the sparks?

Riony stared down, open-mouthed, at the nasty gremlin bowing at her feet.

She looked like she had been dressed as finely as she used to be at Heithorn estate, but her dress had been torn apart and muddied, her neat braids pulled and fraying, releasing windswept streaks of charcoal and white hair.

Kess looked up, and Riony snapped her mouth shut and stepped away. Of all the things she was prepared to handle when she set off with a wolf to find her old tormentor, she wasn't even slightly prepared to deal with *that*.

Riony turned away, only to be faced with the sight of Eslinde and Lyrrin, crouched together, talking tentatively, their intent expressions so, so similar.

Or that.

Riony turned again, pacing madly between the stars-damned *princess of Elundrae*, her grayglim, far too many dragons, a couple of dragonriders who looked almost as confused as her, and also a few living Alderkin.

Not prepared for any of that either.

A hand against her cheek stilled her, and she turned again to meet the warmth of Aishena's dark eyes.

"Slow down, take a breath, and then tell me why you have so much blood on you. Is it yours?" Her tone was flat and scolding.

"It might be?"

Aishena clicked her tongue and began searching for the wound.

"I'm fine, it's okay."

"Is that 'Riony fine' or *not*-just-about-to-die fine?"

From nearby, Niskina snorted a laugh.

Riony took Aishena's searching hands in hers to still them. "I mean really fine. Healed by silvernix again, by *her*."

They both glanced at Kess, and Aishena raised her eyebrows.

Riony flicked her chin at the crowd of powerful strangers surrounding them. "And right now, more worried about all of this."

Aishena withdrew her hands and rested them on her athames. Her eyeline targeted the grayglim. "It is … concerning."

Lyrrin's heartbeat still pattered rapidly, but she also smiled in a way that tore Riony's insides in three directions at once.

"I couldn't *not* reunite them, though. Even with the risks. Could I?"

Aishena's shrewd gaze softened, but she didn't answer, still looking over the strangers. Her sharply cropped hair, dyed a dark brown, swung at her jawline. She kept an eye on her brother, who in turn had taken up position as a guard, watching the skies with his seeing stone.

The cyan of Riony's glow crystal shimmered over Dracuni's moonlight-toned scales as the unidragon rested

her head on Riony's shoulder.

Little sister is happy. You brought lots of good things back with you. Maybe you should follow wolves more often.

Riony huffed and patted the silky tufts of hair between the spikes on Dracuni's neck.

She whispered, "We still have to be careful, with you. We don't know who we can trust."

Wolf girl said a lot to you. Is she a friend now?

Kess was upright again, sitting beside Griskin and leaning into his fur. At least she hadn't remained bowing to the ground, waiting for some kind of response. Riony's cheeks flushed hot, utterly mortified at the idea.

Kess had said a lot. The words still echoed through Riony.

I don't ask any forgiveness. I only ask that you let me serve you. I am yours.

Riony sighed out a long breath. "I *really* don't know what she is now."

You're the one who went off to save her.

"Only because she ... I mean ... I didn't think it would ... I just ..."

"Dragons! Incoming!" Benjin jumped off the stump he'd been standing on and ran their way. "Two at least."

Riony swung toward Kess. "What's going on? Is this some kind of trap? Did you say ... all of that *stuff* just to delay until the other dragons got here?"

Pulling herself up onto Griskin, Kess frowned. "If there was any trap being set, why would we wait for more dragons? We already have three."

The younger blond dragonrider jogged over beside them. "Umm, why would we be setting a trap on them? We're the ones with the princess and Alderkin. How do we know these people aren't setting a trap on us?"

"I'm sure *nobody is setting a trap*," Eslinde said, exasperated. "If there are dragons coming out of Draekhanhelm, they are coming after me because I stole the king's most valued prisoners."

Riony's mouth twisted. "I suppose that makes sense."

"The dragons are still a ways out." The older dragonrider eyed the sky, squinting at what was only a few small dots so far. "We have time to mount up and get ahead of them before they reach us."

Eslinde nodded firmly and began pointing between their party. "Dashiel, take the Alderkin again on the orange. Kess, take the snowflame and as many of the others as you can, their dragon is too small for all of them. Vance, I'll be on Viska with you and Yensen. We can take Lyrrin too."

Riony stepped between the princess and her sister. "You won't take Lyrrin. Also, Dracuni doesn't fly."

The younger rider, Dashiel, had already begun moving toward the orange dragon when they stopped and turned back. "What do you mean?"

Lyrrin pushed in front of Riony's guarding stance.

"She can't fly. We've got to take her through the gateway."

Dashiel eyed Dracuni. "She's so big. She should have been flying after a few months of age. Even Shiff can fly already."

The little ice-blue and muted-purple dragon puffed her chest and flapped her wings in response. Dracuni snorted, her head drooping and diaphanous wings tucking in tighter to her body.

"How have you been training her?" Dashiel asked.

"I've been training her to roast the asses of people who question her training." Riony put her hand on Lyrrin's shoulder, keeping her in place. "Lucky for you we don't have time, because those dragons are getting closer and we're going through the gateway with Dracuni."

"Our dragons won't fit through the gateway," Eslinde said.

"Then we're going to have to split up," Riony replied.

"Nooooo. Not now." Lyrrin looked up at Riony, her bright-blue eyes pleading.

Eslinde's lips pulled thin and she straightened up, barely up to Riony's shoulders but as imposing as a giant. She smoothed back her white hair.

"No. Your sister is right. We will split up. Those riders are coming for me and the Alderkin. We can lead them away. Dash and Vance are some of the best riders there are. I'm sure we can lose those two riders and meet up again soon."

Riony gave her a single, firm nod. "Fly southwest. There's a shrine at the end of the river in the Valley of Unicorn Tears. Find it, we'll be there."

The incoming dragons were now close enough that the beat of their wings through the air could be heard. Eslinde and her grayglim warden claimed the orange dragon, and Vance mounted the brilliant gold beast.

"Kessara, do you want the snowflame again?" Dashiel asked.

"No. I'm going with the others through the gateway." Kess moved Griskin to stand behind Riony's shoulder. "As long as Riony agrees."

"Sparks. Why me? I guess?" Riony's insides felt jumbled.

She was not equipped or willing to be the master of another human, let alone someone who used to lord over her.

"Are you sure?" Niskina asked. She had cold eyes on Kess and hadn't loosened her grip on her pole axe.

Riony wasn't at all sure. She'd saved Kess, but had done it more for Griskin, who was a very good boy, and for a chance to inflict pain upon Kife. Maybe also for that small glimmer of hope, brought about by Kess saving Riony with her silvernix after she'd cracked her skull open, that Kess might make some good decisions in her life for once.

But Riony still didn't like the idea of Kess being *around*.

Having Kess at her back sent a shiver running through Riony, reliving the sensation of a bone dagger sliding deep

in between her shoulders.

She knew it wasn't Kess who had stabbed her, and had for a while, but at the time, when her body wouldn't move, wouldn't breathe, and she felt death entwining her in darkness, she had believed it was the cruel wolf girl who had ended her, for no reason more than spite.

She'd been able to believe it all too easily. If it happened again now, she wouldn't be surprised. Only disappointed.

"Can we just get out of here and work the rest out later?" She herded her people toward the gateway, which Benjin had already activated.

"Should we take Lyrrin with us?" Yensen called from beside the orange as Eslinde climbed into the saddle.

"No," Riony snapped.

"No," Eslinde repeated. "It won't be safe for her in a chase. Will you look after the Alderkin for us, too?"

Riony nodded.

"And Shiff?" Dashiel asked from atop the snowflame.

"Sure, but if you don't catch up with us quickly, fair warning, Lyrrin will claim your dragonling as her new pet."

"Quickly now," Eslinde cried.

The incoming dragons were almost upon them, as their own three dragons spread their wings and one after another rushed upward into the sky.

The small campfire crackled as wind gusted it out, spreading embers like glowflies through the air.

"Everybody through, fast," Aishena called from beside

the glowing gateway.

Benjin and Niskina stepped back to allow the cloaked Alderkin through, then followed.

Lyrrin made a soft, whimpering sound as Riony pushed her toward the gateway, her eyes watery and on the sky. "What if they get caught? What if they can't find us? What if I lose her again, already?"

Riony swallowed her feelings, trying to come up with comforting words.

A voice at her back spoke first. "Eslinde's grayglim will protect her, and the Zarram siblings are excellent riders with excellent dragons. They'll be okay."

Kess, offering words of assurance.

Riony blinked at the awful girl three times. Could she have really changed? Riony's lips twisted in disbelief.

Do dragon's piss fire?

Giving Lyrrin a gentle push, Riony said, "Go on, go through. Your amma knows you're alive now. I'm sure she won't stop trying to find you."

Lyrrin pouted but stepped through the gateway.

The untamed dragonling looked to Dracuni, then the sky where her owner had gone, and went afterward.

"They're almost over us," Aishena called out, gesturing Dracuni through next.

Riony glared at the incoming dragons as they swooped low in the sooty sky. Two lilac shimmerdarts, small and swift, shot past, and a massive red etherflame trailed behind.

Riony held her breath as they went overhead, releasing it as they followed Eslinde and the others.

Dracuni was halfway through the gateway, glimmering light spilling around her as she wriggled her shoulders through.

"Do you need a hand?" Riony thought the words loudly as well, unsure whether Dracuni would hear her with her front half already in another location.

I can fit! Don't push me. The crystal is sharp.

"The dragons are turning!" Kess snapped.

"What? Why?" Riony turned her eyes upward again.

The faster two dragons did a loop over the exposed gateway, the riders looking down at them. And they must have seen something because they signaled the big red back toward them too.

Only Riony, Kess, Aishena, and half of Dracuni remained. Aishena's murderous mother still hadn't flown out to find them, so Riony scratched the idea it could be her seeking her children.

"Could they be after you?" she asked Kess.

Kess winced. "Maybe. There might be some people who think I killed a few first heirs. I'll go, see if I can lead them off."

The large red was over them now too, diving down from the dark sky, heading their way. Kess spurred Griskin into motion, running him up onto one of the broken walls of the shrine, pausing there in open sight before dashing away along the clearest stretch of ground.

But the red dragon remained on target, coming straight for Dracuni.

"It's not changing course!" Aishena yelled, drawing athames.

Kess and Griskin skidded to a stop.

Riony swore, reached back, and unsheathed her sword. The clearing lit up purple as it activated. She placed herself between Dracuni and the red etherflame's seeking talons and braced. A gray shape darted in the corner of her eyes, then Riony's vision filled with scarlet scales, spikes, and teeth.

At the last moment the dragon swerved, head jerking awkwardly. A cry of alarm came from the rider as a wolf came pouncing up the dragon's spine and slammed into him.

The dragon banked sharply, revealing its back to Riony as it swooped around. Griskin loosed a feral growl as his jaws closed around the rider's shoulder, and Kess slipped from her saddle in a fluid motion, hunting blade in hand.

She caught on to the rider and wrapped herself around him in a grapple, slicing in swift motions through his scale mail armor.

Riony gaped as the dragon flew unevenly away over the tangled woods. She was stunned stone-still by the sheer ferocity of the attack and the horrifying thought that followed.

That maybe, all the times she'd faced Kess and Griskin, they'd been pulling their punches.

What's happening? Dracuni shifted within the gateway, backing out slowly.

Riony shook herself and focused. "I think the dragons are coming after you. As for everything else, I'm understanding less and less with every second. Watch out!"

A smaller shimmerdart landed in a whoosh directly on Dracuni's tail. Its talons clasped around the scaled length and wings pumped as it caught and pulled the unidragon.

Sensations of pain and fear rushed from Dracuni through Riony, and she launched herself at the dragonrider, crashing into the flank of the smaller dragon.

Batting it with the full length of the crystal sword, Riony dodged swiping talons as they detached from Dracuni and turned on her. Dirt swirled all around as the shimmerdart pumped its wings, the rider directing it away from Riony's attack.

The second shimmerdart dove to join the fray, curving its path away from a glowing blue return athame thrown by Aishena. Then two more larger forms overshadowed them.

The gold dragon and snowflame crashed down over each of the smaller shimmerdarts like an avalanche of shimmering scales. Vance and Dashiel, the dragonriders that had come along with the princess, showed no hesitation in clashing against their attackers in midair.

The gold dragon caught their shimmerdart neatly,

wings and rider pinned together within clasped talons as Vance swept the dragon onward, away from the shrine. Blasts of flame and crackling energy followed.

The second shimmerdart had more time to react, and the rider turned the dragon over in a corkscrew maneuver, face-to-face with the similarly sized snowflame. The dragons tangled, claw to claw, turning over and over as their wings beat against each other's.

The orange, with Eslinde and her grayglim, hung back.

A burst of ball lightning shot from the shimmerdart and Riony ducked as it flew overhead.

Kess and Griskin raced into the clearing. A smudge of blood marked Kess's face below the constellation of moles on her cheekbone.

"The red is downed. What can I ... Dash, no!"

The shimmerdart had a claw around the snowflame's neck. Dashiel hadn't commanded their dragon to breathe yet, something Riony found a respect for, knowing how it shortened a snowflame's life, but no matter how they twisted and turned their dragon, the shimmerdart wasn't shaking loose.

A stream of liquid fire spilled from the snowflame's mouth, pouring over the shimmerdart beneath it. Splatters of burning dragon blood rained around the clearing. Riony hissed as a drop splashed over her arm.

The shimmerdart burned, its rider fallen, but still it didn't let go, unable even in its dying moments to take

action without a command. It crumpled, falling, and was taking Dashiel and the snowflame with it as it plummeted to the earth.

Kess's wiry body tensed, leaning close to Griskin, and the two of them launched toward the falling dragons. Then a flash of gold passed overhead.

Vance brought Viska in and plucked Dashiel from the fiery comet of dragons. A moment later, the shimmerdart and snowflame crashed down. Deafening cracks sounded as trees split and flames went up all around.

All the incoming dragons were down, and Vance brought the gold dragon in, dropping Dashiel off lightly before landing himself. Eslinde and her grayglim came in to ground beside them.

Are you okay? Dracuni had backed all the way out of the gateway, looking sadly toward the plume of smoke rising from the woods nearby.

Riony's heartbeat hammered in her ears. She wasn't the one who was injured.

"Those poor dragons!" Lyrrin was also through.

Then all those who had gone through the gateway returned, weapons readied and eyes searching for the fight. Except the Alderkin, whose bright eyes were all on Dracuni.

Eslinde dropped down from her saddle and approached. "I don't understand. They should have come after us. Unless they saw the Alderkin, but still, they should have ..."

Riony kept her sword raised, lifted toward Eslinde and

the dragonriders.

"What is this about? Why are you drawn against us?" Then Eslinde's gaze went over Riony's shoulder and landed on Dracuni as well.

In a ring around Dracuni's neck and shoulders, scratched through her scales by the gateway crystal, iridescent silver blood shimmered.

TWO

Lyrrin had spent so many hours of her life imagining the moment she and her birth parents were reunited. But she'd never imagined it like this, with Riony pointing a sword at her mother. A low whine built in her throat, and she swallowed it away.

Eslinde took a step forward, drawn to the sight of the silvernix bleeding from Dracuni's scratches. The droplets gleamed like moonlight in the cyan glow.

"Stay back," Riony growled.

Eslinde's grayglim and the older dragonrider, Vance, moved to flank Eslinde.

In response, Aishena, Niskina, and Benjin formed up into an opposing line beside Riony.

Lyrrin remained frozen between.

Taking a respectful step away, Eslinde gestured for the two men at her side to remain still.

Her eyes remained on Dracuni. "What is that? It can't be ..."

"It's nothing." Riony shrugged but kept her sword level. "We could all agree it's a trick of the light and go about our business as though this had never happened."

Behind Lyrrin, the Alderkin murmured between themselves in a melodious, susurrus language.

"That is silvernix, isn't it? That's ..." Eslinde turned narrowed eyes to Kess, who stalked up behind Riony and took a guarding position at her shoulder.

A flash of something between hurt and pride twisted Eslinde's pale brow. "You knew! Didn't you? This is what you were keeping from me all that time."

Lyrrin noticed Riony flinch as she turned to see Kess behind her. Riony and the wolf girl locked eyes for a long moment, and Kess said nothing.

Eslinde tilted her head. "I understand your loyalties, but I think it's clear, whether you confirm or deny it. This is ... this is ..."

Riony sighed. "Yeah. You and your Alderkin may not have been the biggest secret in Elundrae after all. I had been hoping to keep this one a bit longer, though."

Dracuni bowed her head and Riony whispered, "It wasn't your fault."

Eslinde muttered under her breath, staring round-eyed

at the bleeding dragon. The wounds were already closed, the shimmer of silvernix starting to fade.

Behind Dracuni, the gateway remained open. Riony glanced toward the unidragon and it, then back to the princess. "I'd like to know that you aren't going to do anything evil and stupid, now that you know what you know. The last thing I want is anyone attempting to one-up Kess's efforts."

Lyrrin's face twitched and crumpled with a flurry of emotions, and she stepped closer to her mother. "It's okay. You're not going to hurt Dracuni, are you? We don't have to fight."

Eslinde shoulders dropped, and she batted her hand again at Yensen and Vance, pushing them back. "Of course not. Lyrrin, I won't ever hurt you, your sister, or your ... dragon? I don't understand how this could be possible, though."

Lyrrin tried to respond, tried to reassure Riony that her mother could be trusted, or that at least she desperately wanted to believe her mother could be trusted, but her sister spoke over her.

"You don't need to understand; you just need to keep to your word and understand that I'll do *anything* to make sure you do."

"That, I can confirm," Kess added.

The Alderkin with hair the color of Lyrrin's removed his hood and bowed his head. "You have our word that we will not harm Dracuni and will do all we can to prevent others from harming her too."

Lyrrin was awed every time she looked at Yrik. Her grandfather, Eslinde had said. She had also told her that her father had died before Lyrrin was born.

Lyrrin had always known that was a possibility. Growing up in this world, many people lost family one way or another. Lyrrin tried to be happy to have found any family, to have had her theories confirmed about how similar she was to the depictions of Alderkin in the depths.

But it still hurt, as well, to know the truth.

Riony didn't look entirely convinced by the Alderkin's declaration, but still turned the tip of her sword toward Vance and Dashiel. "And what about you two dragonriders?"

"We're with Eslinde, however she commands," Vance said.

Dashiel exhaled through a lopsided grin. "Honestly, I just want to know how you bred her! She's amazing, I mean, apart from that she can't fly. Is that part of her breed too? What is she? Did you choose not to tame her or did the taming not take because—"

Vance put a heavy hand onto Dashiel's shoulder, stilling the flow of questions.

Sighing, Eslinde straightened her expression and her muddy dress. "I understand you barely know us and that we may seem intimidating to you—"

"Actually, I sort of think they're beating us in terms of

intimidation." Dashiel gave a wry smile toward the glowing array of Alderkin weapons wielded by the other group.

"However, we must work together now to keep your special dragon safe. Because it seems to me somebody else out there knows about Dracuni."

Riony groaned and glared at Kess.

"Kife," they said together.

"Your brother?" Eslinde asked.

Kess nodded, her lips twisted in disgust. "That's why I was trying to keep him out of the palace, away from meeting the Dragon King. He knows, and he was determined to share that information with just one other person."

Eslinde turned her face up and eastward. "Considering the three riders who attacked were all in my father's colors and that we have more dragons incoming again, I would hazard a guess that your brother finally got his wish."

Riony lowered her sword but left it activated. She ran one hand over her face. "Sparks, I was really hoping he didn't survive the mob. Why did I have to be the idiot that left him alive?"

Niskina's dark glare was directed solely at Kess. "If your brother told the Dragon King ... if the Dragon King knows ..."

Riony turned toward the dark spots flying in on the horizon. "There may be nowhere safe in Elundrae for us now."

"We could move shrine to shrine, like we did when

Kife was after us on his dragon," Lyrrin suggested.

Aishena shook her head. "The Dragon King has enough riders that he could keep multiple on watch at every shrine."

Lyrrin shivered. It had been scary when it was just one dragon chasing them. She asked hopefully, "Undercity?"

"I can't see how we'd keep Dracuni fed and hidden there," Riony replied.

The unidragon bowed her head and Riony gave her neck a comforting pat.

"We could steal a boat, leave Elundrae, and live as pirates," Benjin said, eyes twinkling.

Aishena batted him softly on the back of the head. "That isn't funny."

"I wasn't joking."

Lyrrin turned on the spot, taking in all the people around her. Her sister, looking ready for battle but also like she hadn't slept in weeks. Her mother, so new in her life. Aishena and Benjin, still with a bounty out from their mother. Dracuni, too big to hide and too small to fly. Niskina, giving Kess murderous looks while Kess only looked at Riony. And all the new people and dragons they'd somehow have to hide and keep alive too.

Lyrrin slipped her hand into Riony's. "What do we do?"

"I ... I don't know," Riony whispered.

Eslinde cleared her throat. "Actually, I might know somewhere safe."

It took a lot of convincing to get Riony to agree to Eslinde's suggestion. She challenged all the minutiae of their plan, and it hurt Lyrrin to see how much Riony didn't trust her mother.

Do I trust her? She's the Dragon King's daughter.

Lyrrin only knew that she wanted to trust her. She wanted her mother to be someone who could also be family.

Their group had to split up again, with Dracuni unable to fly, and the two remaining dragons too big for the gateways. Riony refused to allow the two dragonriders to go alone on those dragons, in case they flew off to spread the knowledge of Dracuni.

Aishena volunteered to fly the orange dragon—Ambri, the riders called him—with Dashiel taking Viska. Vance preferred to remain with Eslinde.

Eslinde hesitated before the glowing gateway. "You're sure it is safe?"

Yrik raised his eyebrows at her.

Lyrrin offered her a hand to hold as she went through. "It's fine. We use them all the time."

Eslinde took her hand, her thin fingers cold and stiff. "I don't mean the Alderkin magic. I mean the encampment you're taking us to. Reports to the capital say they are filled with marauders and cannibals. And I'm sure that's an exaggeration, but how well can we trust anyone outside of dragonkeeps?"

Lyrrin raised her eyebrows then, matching her grandfather's expression. "Like us?"

"Oh no, not like you. I meant people who choose to be out ... here." Eslinde eyed the twisted and bare trees nearby, as though expecting revenants or criminals to burst from the shadowed forest.

Lyrrin smiled softly. Although she'd grown up in an aboveground village until a few years ago, she had still been terrified when she was taken aboveground again after years of safety in the undercity. Taken by slavers, attacked by revenants, dragonriders, and the shadow dragon itself.

Everything she'd feared had come to pass. But she survived. And she'd since learned that not everything aboveground was monstrous.

"You don't need to be scared."

Eslinde looked down at her, silver eyes glittering.

Most of the others had gone through. Riony remained, waiting on Lyrrin, with Kess and Niskina at her back. Yensen and Vance in turn waited on Eslinde.

Riony stood beside the gateway, her eyes on where Eslinde and Lyrrin's hands were joined. "It will be a quick visit. We need to let our friends know what's happening, that we won't be around for a while, then we can get where we're going."

"Come on. You're going to like it." Lyrrin tugged at Eslinde's hand, and they both stepped through the wavering portal.

On the other side, the Alderkin remained hooded and within the shrine building, close to the gateway. Dracuni sat by the doorway out, and Lyrrin gave her a pat on the neck as she took Eslinde through.

Myrwa's enclave was calm and quiet. A few people moved around as the final cooking for the day was being shared, but many had already retired for the evening to their makeshift homes.

Soft cyan light filled the sanctuary within the standing stones—glow crystals, provided by Lyrrin, hung like stars between the fabric and hide huts. The path between the homes wound between vegetable patches, vibrant with an abundance of winter greens and rampant beanstalks.

A few children giggled and chatted near the communal fire, men stood nearby, singing as they wove netting on a hanging frame, and some women sorted through a jumble of torn fabric, stones, and metal poles.

"It's nice, isn't it?" Lyrrin looked up expectantly.

Eslinde blinked as she turned around, taking it in. "Are they all like this? The encampments around shrines?"

Lyrrin shrugged. "Not really. This one has been here the longest and has the most people. But they're all nice in their own way."

Myrwa stood up from a seat near the fire and pulled Riony into an embrace, her long shawl swaying around them, faded crimson like her graying red hair.

Then as she stepped back again, her expression turned cold. "Back again? Who is this you've brought with you? Last I saw that wolf girl, she seemed intent on murdering you."

Kess, hovering near Riony's shoulder, quietly moved Griskin a few steps back.

Riony spoke softly, "Don't worry, I'm keeping an eye on her."

She had Aishena's pack and began pulling bundles from it. She handed them to Myrwa and others who came to take the items their group had been collecting on their travels. Tools and crafts from other enclaves mostly.

If it were a normal day, they would take back trade from Myrwa's camp with them. But it wasn't a normal day, and Lyrrin didn't know when they'd be visiting the other shrines again.

"What about these other folk?" Myrwa sucked at her teeth as she glared at Eslinde's silver hair and her uniformed grayglim lurking nearby. "They look a lot like dragonlords and riders to me. Didn't think you'd mix with that type."

Her scolding expression made Lyrrin's chest ache.

"Come over here, you can warm up." She pulled on Eslinde's hand, dragging her out of earshot of Riony and Myrwa's conversation.

The grayglim followed closely, eyes wary and alert. Vance also kept his eyes on mother and daughter, but from a distance that made Lyrrin more comfortable.

She wondered what Eslinde's life must have been like, growing up as a princess in a palace, under guard and with everything she wanted.

Eslinde the First. Lyrrin could still hardly believe it.

Does that mean my name is really Lyrrin Eslinde? Like Aishena and Benjin and all their family get their last name Hjelzahn from Hjelzahn the First?

Lyrrin wasn't sure she liked that. She liked being Lyrrin Eyfarr. The name she and Riony had chosen for themselves together, when they were no longer owned by anyone, a name that reminded her of the parents who raised her.

As they approached the fire, a willowy older man, Haled, stood up and offered them a couple of bowls of steaming vegetables and flatbread. Eslinde reached into a pocket of her gown and pulled out a small purse.

"Will this do?" She held a silver sov on the palm of her hand.

Haled waved her away with a twiglike arm, chuckling to himself as he returned to rolling out dough.

Lyrrin flushed. Even a silver sov had been more than she and Riony ever had in the undercity. She hadn't seen currency at all since traveling aboveground.

"You don't need to pay," she said in a hush, then a little louder, "Haled, we aren't staying long. Can we have some food to take with us, please?"

Haled reached for a nearby basket and began filling it with stacked freshly cooked bread, jars of preserves, and bundles of fresh, snakelike beans, tied with string. "Of course, Lil Moon."

Once, only once, Riony had called her that in front of Myrwa, and now everyone there used the nickname for Lyrrin. It both warmed her heart and hurt it at the same time.

Eslinde put her coins away and bowed her thanks.

Under her breath, she said, "He's very kind."

Lyrrin chewed on some soft, smoky bread. "Not really. We all share out here."

Eslinde nibbled on the end of a green stalk from her bowl, watching as Benjin and Niskina also moved about the camp, doling out items from their bags.

"And they have no dragons at all here? How do they survive?"

Lyrrin pointed toward the large ring of towering crystals at the edges of the shrine enclave. "It's safe from revenants within the standing stones."

"What about dragons for other uses? Hard labor, manufacturing, protection from enemies?"

Myrwa drifted in beside them, making Eslinde jump when she snapped, "Only enemies we need to worry about are the blighted dragonriders. They come by every now and then, yelling at us and our 'rebellion,' before smashing something and seeing what they can take from us."

She flicked her chin at where Riony had joined the women picking through the broken hut. Riony hefted a large metal beam while the others propped it up again. Kellae stood to the side, bouncing her baby on her hip and chatting.

Eslinde frowned. "It's clearly a misunderstanding. I'm sure if the riders knew what this place really was—"

"Ha!" Myrwa shook her head and wandered away again, muttering about marauders and cannibals.

Eslinde's pale cheeks went as red as Riony's hair.

Lyrrin bit her lip. She had wanted this to all go differently. In all the times she'd dreamed of meeting her mother, she'd never imagined it would be quite so ... embarrassing.

"It's okay. I'm sure there are lots of things I don't know about where you lived, too," she said.

Eslinde smiled down at her with watery eyes.

Over near the central shrine building, Riony whistled softly and signaled it was time to go. Their group gathered up again, and Eslinde offered her gratitude with royal formality as she took the basket of food from Haled.

Back near the shrine, the grayglim stood close, watching as Benjin traced the activation rune. Giving the man a sharp look, Benjin leaned further over it, obscuring his work from view.

Eslinde turned back to the people waving goodbye.

"The others here, do they know how to use the gateways too?"

Lyrrin's lips pursed. "We haven't taught anyone else how to. I think we should. Sometimes revs hang around the boundaries for too long, making it hard for people to go out hunting and foraging. And sometimes the dragonriders hurt people."

"I'm sorry," Eslinde said, sounding as though it were directly her fault.

"We move around the shrines, visiting them all as often as we can to help out." Lyrrin dropped her voice low. "But the others say it's too dangerous to let anyone else use the gateways too. Because of Dracuni."

The gateway illuminated, and one after another, they all stepped through.

The shrine on the other side had no encampment around it. Perched on a barren, rocky hillock and blasted by the frigid winds off the southern coast, it hadn't been used for more than temporary stops in their travels. Lyrrin pulled her hood up and her gloves back on.

Benjin took the lead, trying to strike up a conversation with the Alderkin just behind him, but they remained quiet.

Dracuni trotted along beside the dragonrider's hatchling, both deep in some silent, enthusiastic conversation.

Eslinde and Lyrrin had split up along the way, with

the princess assisting the dragonrider who's gait grew more and more pained the farther they walked.

Kess and Griskin wove back and forth along the group, sometimes scouting ahead, other times guarding the rear. Niskina kept her eyes on Kess and her hand on her pole axe, using it as a walking cane. Her mouth was drawn down in a scowl.

It was a long walk, and Lyrrin was yawning and shuffling her feet when their destination still wasn't within sight.

"Big day, huh?" Riony said.

She moved up behind Lyrrin, scooping her under the armpits and lifting her onto her shoulders.

"Whatever do you mean? Pretty normal, really." Lyrrin slouched, leaning on Riony's head.

"Speak for yourself! I got chased by a rioting mob, found out Alderkin were alive, and had one of the worst people in the world pledge themselves to me. I'd say it was fairly eventful."

Lyrrin yawned again as she bumped along on her perch. "That was weird, what Kess said."

"Right? What do I do with that?"

"I think she likes you."

"Dear sister, why would you say something so hurtful to me?"

Lyrrin smirked and sighed. Her sister's hair smelled of smoke and blood. Even with Riony checking in with them as often as possible, Lyrrin had been worried the entire time her sister had been gone with the wolf.

"You know, I thought you were the biggest tamebrain ever for going to find Kess."

Riony shrugged, making Lyrrin lift and drop. "Fair. But also, you were the one who was all 'you're being so mean, give her a chance!' after Kess helped us save Dracuni. I blame your influence."

"Fair. But still, I'm glad you went and found her."

Riony's hands were warm where they held Lyrrin's shins, and she squeezed her gently. "How is it? Being around your amma?"

"She seems really nice. You know, for a dragonlord."

"Yeah, I think so too. Just ... Don't get too attached. Just in case. Bonds of blood don't always mean you can trust someone." Riony's head turned toward where Kess rode on Griskin, not far ahead.

Lyrrin shivered.

The moon cast its color-stealing light down over them and the cold of the winter night seeped into Lyrrin's bones as their destination came into view.

The looming walls of a dragonkeep.

THREE

Walking into a dragonkeep set every nerve within Riony on edge. Even if the place was only partially completed, abandoned to weeds and rodents. The immense walls encircled only halfway around where a city was meant to be, craggy and unfinished along the top.

Rising against the night sky, the wall seemed to bare its teeth at them, turning Eslindekeep into a shadowed monster in the night.

"Aishena and the other rider should have been here by now." Riony's jaw ached from tension.

Eslinde led the way around the outer wall until they could pass it. Within, a smaller temporary wall that had probably protected the builders undulated, its still standing and crumbled sections curving up and down, serpentlike.

Loose stones shifted under Riony's feet as they climbed in through a broken gap.

"There," Kess said, pointing upward.

Benjin had the seeing stone on his staff activated before his face, following Kess's direction. "I can't see anything."

Riony squinted into the night sky but saw no winged shapes moving against the stars. She nudged Dracuni beside her.

Can't hear any other dragons except Shiff. Shiff likes to talk a lot.

Kess stared as well, then shook her head. "Sorry, I thought I saw a dragon."

Niskina gave Kess a cold look. "Did you or not? If it wasn't Aishena and Dashiel, we might have a problem. More of a problem than *you* already pose to us."

Benjin, by her side, nodded fiercely.

They all paused, watching the sky, but nothing more moved above them.

Eslinde said, "It might have been a great owl. They get very big around here, almost treedart size."

Riony shuddered. She could barely handle a pocket-sized owlette. She'd never told Lyrrin she was secretly glad when that pet got away.

"And there's plenty around for them to be hunting." Eslinde nodded toward the abandoned construction, where bantam ferrets scurried across the brushy ground between roads that went nowhere, empty foundations, and piles of rusting steel.

Gasping, Lyrrin shifted her weight on Riony's shoulders, indicating she was climbing down, and Riony bent over to help her.

Lyrrin went chasing over to a stack of cut stone where a flurry of furry forms escaped into the gaps.

She crouched and made kissy noises, trying to reach her fingers in. "They are sooo cute!"

"No more pets," Riony snapped.

They moved forward again, more hesitant now, over the uneven road. The cobbled paving, having never seen use or maintenance, had shifted over the years, pushed out of place by burrowing creatures and roots. It took them through the outlined edge of the unbuilt city toward a flat structure on a low peak in the center.

Vance grunted softly and bent to rub one of his knees.

Riony turned to him. "I haven't seen many Rolanian dragonriders before."

"Rolanian *dragonlords*," he corrected.

"You say that as though it's somehow better. And yet my estimation of you just dropped significantly."

Straightening up, Vance looked her in the eyes. "Or at least we were before we disobeyed our father, refused to tame Shiff, and fled the burning remains of our dragonhold."

"Okay, that's sounding better again."

Vance huffed, but his eyes were sad. "You don't like dragonriders?"

Riony returned a humorless smile. "Never met one I would trust not to skin me alive if I blinked at them wrong. Aishena had better get here safely."

"Same for Dashiel."

Turning back to them from up ahead, Eslinde tutted. "They're probably just being careful, flying low to avoid being followed. I'm sure both are safe and will be here soon."

Riony wanted to stay positive, but everything around her felt like a trap. The way the Alderkin continued to stare at Dracuni, conversing in low tones in their own language. The grayglim trailing after Eslinde like a bound spirit. The dragonrider, keeping as much of an eye on Riony as she was on him.

And Kess, at her back.

"Would you stop lurking behind me?" Riony rasped.

Kess's shoulders lifted, and sadness flashed over her eyes before her expression set calm and firm again. "Of course. Whatever you wish."

Griskin trotted faster, moving ahead of Riony.

She ran a hand up into her hair, scrunching the red curls in her fist. "And just in case you were wondering, yes. You have made things exceptionally awkward and weird. Things haven't been this awkward and weird since the last time I bedded your amma."

Riony waited, but there was no bite in return.

She sighed. "So ... thanks for that. I might have preferred

it if you'd stayed mean."

Kess half turned and quirked an eyebrow. "Do you want me to be mean to you?"

Heat rushed up Riony's neck. "No. Stop it. You're taking things even further in the weird and awkward direction. I just want you to be yourself again, doing whatever selfish thing you want to do."

Kess's ice-blue eyes held Riony for a long moment, then she nodded slowly. "The selfish thing I want to do now is look after you. Good luck stopping me."

"You're failing to understand the meaning of selfish!" Riony snapped.

The slightest smirk rose on Kess's lips as she turned away, prowling ahead like a guard on patrol.

Riony was relieved to be distracted from the wolf-riding gremlin when Eslinde brought them to a stop at the base of solid, sprawling foundations.

"This is what was to be my palace." Eslinde stared dully at the stone wall before them, marked with archway niches all along the base, the flat top spreading across the crest of the low hill.

"Would have been nice if it had a little something more. Like walls or a roof," Riony said.

"My keep had been under construction before Lyrrin was born, but unfortunately all progress on that front ceased when my parents discovered my pregnancy. They decided that me having my own dragonkeep was no longer a good idea."

Riony searched the area with her eyes. There were certainly enough building supplies left about to set up a somewhat protective area, set camp, but with all trees cleared during construction and only a few smaller ones sprouting through, they would be very exposed.

"And why is it a good idea for us to be here? We're open to rev attacks, and wouldn't the first place the Dragon King looks for you be your keep?"

"They won't look for us here because they would also assume it's not a secure location, but that's because they don't know about this." Eslinde reached into the niche before her, pushed a stone aside, and pulled a lever.

The wall within the archway swung aside, revealing a gaping tunnel within. It sloped smoothly down into the earth, solid stone on every side and large enough for even their biggest dragon to enter.

Vance chuckled softly. "You and your rebellious ways. What have you got down there?"

Eslinde smiled softly in reply, her silver eyes sparkling.

Riony planted her feet and folded her arms. "Whatever is down there, we can wait until the others arrive to find out. I'm not going in there until I know Aishena is safe."

Benjin climbed the nearby slope to get up on top of the foundations, above the open tunnel, watching the dark skies. "They're coming now!"

Flying in from the south, the gold and orange dragons

approached fast, as though in a race.

"Nothing on their tail?" Kess asked in a growl.

Benjin squinted through the seeing stone on his staff. "Not that I can see."

As the two dragons passed over the half-made outer wall, Viska put on another burst of speed, breaking ahead. Riony tensed, one hand reaching up to wrap around the hilt of her sword at her shoulder.

Then she heard laughing.

The gold dragon came to a sliding halt along the road nearby, talons scraping across the stone. Dashiel leaped down, grinning and panting.

"I told you I'd win!" Dashiel yelled up at the orange that glided in to land beside them.

Aishena brought the dragon to an elegant stop. She remained in the saddle, peering down. "Considering I had the lesser dragon and haven't flown for years, I wouldn't be so cocky about winning by such a small margin."

Dashiel beamed. "Maybe I went easy on you."

"Maybe I went easy on you," Aishena replied.

The tension across Riony's back eased at seeing Aishena there, in one piece, and even enjoying herself, despite her ever-blank expression. But with all the time they'd spent together since leaving the undercity, Riony could translate even the smallest flicker of emotion from the stern young woman.

Although Aishena required no assistance, Riony moved

beside the dragon and caught her about the waist as she climbed down from the saddle.

Gently lowering her to the ground, Riony grinned and murmured in her ear, "Took your time. Run into some trouble, or were you just too busy flirting?"

Aishena pressed a hand to Riony's arm, her way of offering unspoken gratitude. She spoke back equally low. "We went out over Eyersunn Sea to lose some riders that were after us. Also, as I have never flirted in your presence, I'd be surprised if you could recognize it."

"There was that one time you got super drunk and tried to kiss me."

Aishena's hand around Riony's arm squeezed and released. "And I do enjoy being the better person for still being friends with you despite how you keep bringing it up. But I certainly hope that you don't think *that* is how *I* would flirt."

"It honestly took me far too long to realize you weren't flirting with me every time you glared my way."

Aishena offered a rare smile. "You've grown so much."

"So you weren't flirting with the pretty blond dragonrider?"

Aishena shrugged and took her pack which Riony had carried for her when they split up. "I didn't say that. I'll just point out that some of us can flirt and stay on task at the same time."

Across the paved area, Dashiel's laugh rang out, from something either Vance or Kess had said to them.

Riony wasn't sure either Kess or the stoic dragonrider could say something that would make someone laugh like that, but they were the only options in proximity.

It seemed everyone was happy to have the riders and dragons back.

"Come on then, now we're all here. Inside, everybody." Eslinde gestured to the tunnel. "Some help with the torches, Vance?"

Vance led his golden dragon into the tunnel, then brought her head to an alcove at the side that Eslinde directed them to.

The etherflame breathed a rush of fire into a channel on the wall, and all the way along the length of the tunnel small puffs of flame flickered from gaps beside the torches, setting them alight.

Despite the abundance of lighting, the passage still seemed stark and cold compared to the underground world Riony was familiar with. The undercity, with its glow stones, and luminous, waxy limestone flows, and ever-present scent of spiced mushroom or roasting rope worms.

A pang ached in her chest. She hadn't realized just how much she missed it.

Vance and Dashiel led the two tamed dragons in first, followed by Eslinde, her grayglim, and the Alderkin.

Kess kept ahead of Riony now, closer to Dashiel's side,

chatting amiably in a way Riony found disconcerting.

Riony kept her group with her—Lyrrin, Aishena, Benjin, and Niskina, with Dracuni behind them, in case they needed to get out fast. Riony clenched her teeth as the heavy doorway sealed behind them.

Dashiel's dragonling remained trotting along at Dracuni's side, watching the unidragon with an awed expression and no doubt also chatting away.

Eslinde spoke from the front, her voice echoing between the hard stone walls. "Every first heir designs and oversees construction of their own dragonkeep. And I had such big plans for mine."

She paused, showing them a hallway of smaller rooms and private dormitories to one side. "I was in complete control over construction, and it was before my parents became suspicious of my motivations and kept me monitored, so I'm certain they're unaware this exists."

They passed another hallway with rows and rows of bedding, a barracks, stretching far into the darkness. The next room was stacked floor to ceiling with metal crates.

"Arms and armor," Eslinde said.

The spaces were eerie, unused, a fine layer of dust lying over every surface and making the air dry and grimy on Riony's tongue.

"Luckily, the underground section was completed and sealed before my pregnancy was discovered and

construction ceased. I doubt my parents had any reason to suspect what I built here, that these foundations contain anything other than the usual basements and dungeons."

They passed a vast mess hall with long bench seating, and the adjoining kitchens, with multiple ovens, each as large as a room in the stalagmite apartment Riony once called home.

Within the kitchens and the bathing room they passed next, metal water pumps jutted from the ground, their curved handles the most decorative thing in the stark spaces.

Eslinde came to a stop at an intersection to another tunnel as tall and wide as the main one. She gestured inside. "Housing for dragons."

Vance and Dashiel led the tamed dragons in. Riony stepped in after them, checking the space. The huge square-cut room looked ready to stable scores of dragons, with walled bays furnished only with troughs. More water pumps stood at the end of each row.

Riony tried one, giving the handle a couple of quick pumps. Water splashed out at her feet. There must be an underground reservoir.

Shiff galloped in, sticking her nose into a trough, then snorting loudly.

"She's hungry," Dashiel said while settling the orange dragon into a stall.

Eslinde shook her head. "I hadn't reached the stages

of stocking food stores, I'm afraid. And even if I had, it would have spoiled between then and now."

Dracuni had followed Riony in and inspected one of the stalls with a huff. **No blankets?**

"I'll find you a blanket." Riony patted her on the nose. "Food is something we're going to have to work out—if we stay here. Dracuni's a big eater still too."

"But we can stay here, can't we? It's so good!" Lyrrin asked, having run the length of the stables and back.

"You're just hoping to catch one of those bantam ferrets," Riony accused.

"Maybe."

Eslinde raised her voice over the growing chatter. "I know it's late, but we still have a lot to discuss. Find a room you prefer to be yours, settle the children and dragons in, then join me in the meeting chamber up ahead."

Riony eyed the tamed dragons, left still and unmoving in their stalls. "I'd feel better if Dracuni stays with me."

"Unfortunately, the hallways ahead are only designed for humans. Dracuni will have to stay here with the others." Eslinde gave an apologetic look, then swept away with her grayglim behind her.

Lyrrin and Benjin, smiling and wide-eyed, raced off to claim the very best room for themselves.

Kess followed, stalking out on Griskin.

Riony's gaze trailed after, and as the girl and wolf

disappeared around the corner, a worried shiver rocked Riony's shoulders.

Niskina shared a grim look with Riony. "Don't worry, I'll keep an eye on her. I know she saved your life, but I don't trust her."

Hands on weapons, Niskina and Aishena left the stables.

Dracuni moved into the same stall as the dragonling. *I can stay here. Shiff is nice, I trust her.*

"It's not Shiff I'm worried about," Riony whispered. "If someone tries to hurt you, you can't exactly flame them."

Dracuni lifted her shoulders in an almost human shrug. *Shiff says Dashiel and Vance are good. That they didn't tame her, even though it got them in trouble.*

"But they still have two tamed dragons with them."

Dracuni looked over at the gold and orange beasts, her lilac eyes shimmering and sad. *They are silent, as though not even there. Shiff says she's never gotten to speak with another dragon much before. They're all silent where she came from.*

A breath sighed out of Riony at the thought of growing up alone amid beings who were only the ghosts of the real thing.

Dashiel appeared beside Riony, startling her. "Tamed dragons ... I know. I wish we could untame all of them. Kess showed us how. Amazing, right?"

"Yeah ... amazing," Riony muttered.

"Maybe we could untame Viska and Ambri soon and—"

"I can't see that being a good idea." Vance stepped beside his sibling, folding arms across a wide chest. "Having a couple of dragons that can fly and fight is too valuable to lose right now, when we're out in these rev-blighted wastes with the Dragon King's forces after us."

Dashiel winced. "It's something we can at least think about."

Vance slapped a hand down over their shoulder, directing them out of the room.

"Maybe one at a time? I'm sure Viska will still like you ..." Their voice drifted away as they left the stables.

Dracuni snorted softly. *See? Nice people.*

"They're still dragonriders and dragonlords." Riony sighed.

She adjusted a strap on her bag and fidgeted in her armor, feeling the weight of them. She was looking forward to putting it all down and resting. It had been a long day.

"Are you sure you'll be fine in here?"

If I need you, you'll hear me. Dracuni pressed her cheek against Riony's.

It took a few more moments before Riony was willing to step away, and as she moved out into the hall, she was met with the haunting vision of the three Alderkin, tall and cloaked, standing in wait.

Her hand went to her sword on instinct, and their eyes

followed, glinting in the torchlight.

"Where did you get that blade?" Lyrrin's grandfather spoke in a voice like crumbling stone.

As tempted as Riony was to give him the same answer she'd once given to Kess when asked how she'd acquired a weapon, she figured it was too early to be making ass jokes with an ancient and magical race who were the last of their kind.

"I found it. In the Alderkin depths. In a tomb," Riony winced, apologetic. "I only took it because I needed a weapon, because I was lost and shackled to a monster who was *really* getting on my nerves, and I didn't think at the time … I'm sorry."

Riony held her breath, praying to her ancestors in the stars that the Alderkin wouldn't take her sword off her.

Priyune nodded, her eyes soft and glittering green. "The tomb of one of our greatest warriors, a mighty protector of unicorns from another war with humans, centuries before the dragon enslavers came."

Shael traced a mysterious shape in the air and bowed her head. "It was said she flew above the world and tore lightning from the sky to cast at those who sought to capture unicorns for themselves."

Yrik moved closer, assessing Riony with eyes the precise color of Lyrrin's. "It is a sword worthy only of one dedicated to protecting the sacred lifebringers. And it seems, although the unicorns are gone, the dragon you call Dracuni is of the same blood and magic."

"And I'm dedicated to protecting her," Riony said.

Yrik's eyes narrowed. "Are you? How long did you travel away from her to find the wolf-riding girl? How long did you leave Dracuni unguarded?"

"I ... She wasn't unguarded." Riony's mouth went dry.

There was no one she trusted more than Lyrrin, Aishena, Benjin, and Niskina to keep Dracuni safe. But she had felt guilty every moment she was away. She'd questioned every step she'd taken following Griskin. Even now, she wasn't sure it had been worth it.

Having Kess around left Riony's insides constantly churning.

She'd meant what she said, before getting stabbed in the back. She wanted the world to be better, to live kindly, to start by finding peace between herself and Kess.

But now, even with the apologies and promises Kess had vowed, Riony wasn't sure she could ever trust her.

Bringing Kess in had brought so many others with her, all of which now knew about Dracuni, all of which could be a threat.

Yrik held Riony in his sapphire gaze as though he could read every doubt passing through her mind. "Nothing is more important than keeping Dracuni safe. Nothing. If you wish to be worthy of wielding that sword, you need to accept that."

47

FOUR

Kess hadn't even found a room to settle in before she was ambushed.

Niskina stomped the end of her pole axe on the ground and then leaned against it.

She tossed her tumbling curls back and glowered thickly at Kess. "I don't know what you think you're going to achieve from this game you're playing with Riony."

The clank of the weapon against stone echoed down the long corridor. Aishena was there too, standing coolly at ease and all the more threatening for it.

Kess turned Griskin slowly to face them. "I feel I've made my intentions clear. Embarrassingly so, apparently."

"Then let me make something clear to you." Niskina stepped fearlessly beside the wolf. "Riony might have decided to give you another chance, but I haven't. Your actions, your betrayal, led to my father's death. I won't forget that, and I won't ever forgive that."

Kess turned cold, as though plunged into an icy lake. "I know, I'm sorry, I—"

"I don't want to hear it. I don't trust it, and I don't believe you won't do worse again. You're only alive right now because Riony, for some depths-cursed, inconceivable reason, wills it." A full-body shudder of revulsion shook Niskina as she held Kess's gaze.

Then, as though she was unable to stand her presence a moment longer, she spun and left.

Aishena remained, a casual stillness to her like she was a statue of a soldier.

"Are you going to threaten me too?" Kess asked.

"Indeed." A glint flickered in Aishena's dark eyes. "Because Riony is a better person than all of us, in allowing you here. So, if you hurt her again, in any way, *any way*, you can expect that pain returned upon you tenfold."

Kess wanted to argue that she wouldn't hurt Riony, that keeping her from ever being harmed again was what she wanted more than anything. But she was also scared that she would fail. That through the simple fact of who she was, who she'd been, that she would be the cause of more pain.

Kess smirked off the rattle of fear. "Did nobody listen to what I said before? Was I too low to the ground? Could you not hear me?"

"*Everybody* heard you. *Nobody* believed you."

"So, it was both mortifying and futile. Wonderful." Kess's fingers twitched to hold a dagger, to have a weapon in hand, ready to defend herself.

She fought off the instinct. She refused to be cowed or give the grayglim-trained young woman a reason to strike.

Sighing, she steadied herself. "But my intentions are the same, whether you believe it or not."

"We'll see." Aishena remained statue-still, holding Kess in her dark gaze for a long moment before she vanished into the shadows.

Kess shrugged off the ache in her chest.

Griskin turned his head back to Kess and whined softly.

Kess leaned into his fur and rubbed his ears. "It's okay. Even if it's still you and me against the world, it's okay."

She held him for a long moment, inhaling the smoky musk of his fur and listening to his breaths as he panted nervously. She still could hardly believe he had come for her, had brought help for her, hadn't abandoned her. He was the only reason she was alive, a hundred times over.

And he made her feel like remaining alive was something she wanted, maybe even deserved.

She wrapped her arms around his neck in a hug. "I missed you so much. I'm sorry that I was ever cruel to you. You're one of the best things in my life and I owe you everything."

Kess decided not to bother finding a room to make her own. The most she could do anyway would be unpack some bags from Griskin, but it seemed better to keep everything on them.

A time would come when the others would decide they were done with allowing her to stay, with tolerating her presence, and she didn't want to have to leave anything behind when she was expelled.

Griskin padded down the expansive corridor, ghostly quiet. He didn't like the echoing tunnels and stone walls. At least the air was free of fungus spores.

They were the first to join Eslinde and Yensen in the meeting room.

Torches flickered along the walls, and an imposing granite table sat heavily in the center of the space.

The princess was pale with exhaustion, her eyes rimmed in pink, but she met Kess with a warm smile.

Kess found her lips turned upward in response. "Secret underground chambers? Seems as though you learned some things from your father."

Eslinde scoffed. "I'm sure the Alderkin's claim to secret underground chambers predates Yeonard Draekhan by centuries."

Kess pulled Eslinde's earring from her pocket and handed the now empty vessel to the princess. "Thank you, for this, and for ... caring whether I survived. I wouldn't have made it without you."

And if I wasn't healed enough to fly, Riony might not have made it either.

Eslinde's fingers closed around the earring and around Kess's hands, holding them. "I noticed your leg no longer troubled you. I'm glad you rejoined us, Kessara, not only for what you brought with you."

"What I brought?"

"My daughter! And not only that, but this unidragon creature they have! Such a resource. This ... this gives us hope."

Kess pulled her hands free from Eslinde's. "Dracuni isn't a resource. She's a living, feeling creature."

Eslinde tilted her head. "Of course. But we have to consider what can be done now with her, that we couldn't have done before."

Lyrrin jogged in then, jostling the large basket of food. "It's good we stopped at Myrwa's. I'm starving!"

"Same," Benjin followed close behind, and snatched a handful of green beans and a flatbread the moment Lyrrin put the basket down on the meeting table.

Riony and her friends came in next, with the Alderkin, Dashiel, and Vance following.

Eslinde gestured a little awkwardly to the children. "I thought, perhaps, they might need to sleep by now? This should be a meeting for grown-ups."

Lyrrin gaped, then pouted.

Riony had removed some of her armor but left the

harness on for the sword on her back. She unsheathed it to sit down, and Kess noted how, even though the magic wasn't activated, Riony hefted it easily as she leaned it against the table beside her. She noticed how Riony did it in a way like she wanted people to notice.

"Everyone's hungry," Riony said. "I'm not sending them kids to bed on an empty stomach. And they should be included. They're some of our best strategists—don't look at me with pity! They're better than a lot of adults. They have good ideas."

"Like becoming pirates?" Eslinde muttered.

"It wasn't necessarily a *bad* idea." Riony shrugged and chewed on some bread covered in pickles passed to her by Lyrrin.

Aishena and Niskina took seats on either side, and Riony leaned into Aishena, whispering, then offering a bite of her food which Aishena declined tersely, which only made Riony grin wider.

Niskina reached over and pinched some of the bread, and Riony elbowed her, chuckling.

Kess wasn't clear on whether Riony was in a more romantic relationship with either of them—or both—but the familiarity and depth of care they each had for one another was obvious, and it left Kess feeling brittle and aching.

In all the years she and Riony had been confined to each other's company, they'd never had that sort of easy closeness. There had been closeness, but the kind that hurt them both more than it brought any comfort. And Kess knew why. She understood exactly why, and that only hurt more.

Eslinde cleared her throat from where she remained standing at the head of the table. "I wanted to speak with you all tonight, because I hope we can all be allies in our important cause moving forward."

Riony leaned back in her chair. "And what cause is that?"

Eslinde gestured to Kess. "I've heard from Kessara that you have suspicions about the true cause of the shadow dragon curse."

Riony also eyed Kess. "Tamed dragons?"

Eslinde nodded. "Consider your suspicions confirmed. Which then leads us to the bigger question. What are we going to do about it?"

Kess slid from Griskin into her chair, and he curled up behind it. "We're going to try to do something about it? With the Dragon King himself hunting Dracuni? Seems risky to do anything more than stay hidden and safe right now."

Eslinde had found a moment to pull her tangled hair back into a tight bun, but she shook her head with such vehemence that silver strands escaped around her face. "We must do something! The alternative is the ruination of all of Elundrae."

Niskina put together her meal, then passed the basket of food along. "What do you expect us to do?"

"You untamed one dragon. We could untame more. Enough to put an end to the curse."

Riony downed the last of her bread and leaned forward on her elbows. "Hold on. It's not all that easy. We haven't exactly got dragonriders lining up saying, 'oh please, turn my faithfully mind-wiped steed into a wild beast.' Even your friends here won't give up theirs."

"You really want to be out here without any dragons to protect us?" Vance growled.

"Managed it well enough so far." Riony picked her teeth. "Besides, even if we did have a supply of dragons to be untamed, you need silvernix."

There was a pause as Eslinde hesitated over her words. "Yes, and I had thought we'd have to find a supply, perhaps steal some."

Kess shot a look at Eslinde's remaining earring. She assumed it contained another dose. One wasn't enough for her plan, but still, she didn't share the information.

Gesturing back toward the stables, Eslinde said, "But with Dracuni—"

"*Nope*." Riony rose to her feet. "And that's where I'm out. Typical that your very first thought is to use Dracuni for her blood."

"Even for the greater good? Even if it could heal our entire land? We would be sure to bleed her humanely—"

"And that's an even bigger *NOPE*." Riony grasped the hilt of her sword.

Lyrrin straightened in her seat, but her chest was still level with the tabletop. "What Riony means, is that only Dracuni gets to decide what happens with her blood. Not us. We all agreed that's how it should be."

"This is also how it was with the unicorns." Yrik bowed his head to Lyrrin.

Benjin tapped his fingers on the table, stirring up dust. "How many dragons are we talking about? How many would need to be untamed to make a difference, to stop the shadow dragon from raising the dead? Ten? A hundred? A thousand? All of them?"

Aishena gazed at him thoughtfully. "We saw a mural in the Alderkin depths—that was one of our first clues about the true cause—that suggested the shadow dragon manifested even from the very first tamed dragon."

"This is true," Priyune replied. "I had the tragic misfortune of being witness to the event."

"The first taming? That was over eighty years ago! You don't look that old." Benjin's eyes narrowed.

"Alderkin age differently. We grow slower but live much longer."

Lyrrin grasped the edge of the table fervently. "Does that mean I'm going to get *taller*?"

"You're fine at any size, little spitfire," Riony said. "I think the more important part was that Priyune here has been alive the entire time the shadow dragon has."

Priyune offered Lyrrin a sly wink, then continued. "We saw the first dragon spirit enslaved, saw its tormented soul separated from its body. But it was decades later before humans began replicating that event in large numbers."

Eslinde nodded confirmation. "It was fifty years ago that my father's method of dragon taming was leaked, dragonglass was in wide production for storing silvernix, and everyone who was able tried to capture and tame their own dragons, and then began breeding them. That is when the first stories of the shadow dragon raising dead began."

Kess didn't know a lot of the wider history, but she knew tales from the Heithorn line. Her family had been some of the first Taens who hunted and tamed full-grown wild dragons.

It was what they had become famous for, and they considered those who sourced their dragons through breeding as dishonorable.

Until those who bred their dragons gained a financial edge over them, and the Heithorns began breeding dragons the same as all other dragonlords.

Yrik held his hands in front of him, staring at his blue-clawed fingers. "The Alderkin tried to understand it, tried to find our own way to stop the curse. But it was too powerful. The use of the life-giver's magic to subjugate such powerful souls ... Each broken spirit has only made the shadow dragon stronger, all merging into that single mourning, vengeful entity."

"How many dragons were around back then? Before everyone started taming them?" Benjin asked.

"Only the king and his heirs had them before that. A few dozen, definitely less than one hundred," Eslinde replied.

Vance puffed his cheeks and blew out a breath. "There's no way we can untame that many, to get the numbers even close to that low."

Benjin chewed his thumbnail. "But maybe we don't have to. If we can even get the numbers down to what they were a year or two ago, back when revs stayed dead when you killed them, that would make a huge difference."

Eslinde's mouth opened into a neat *O* shape. "That ... that might be feasible."

Riony folded her arms and smirked at Eslinde. "Told you. The kids have good ideas."

Benjin lifted his chin smugly. "So, how many would that be?"

Eslinde tipped her head side to side, lips moving silently as though counting in her head. "Tamings have slowed down a lot in recent years. Many minor dragonlords have run out of silvernix, but the greater households and heirs have not, and each is still taming dragons for riders and industry. Reports are that around eighty dragons were tamed in the last two years. I have been keeping an eye on numbers."

Benjin's smile dropped. "That's a lot. Even if we did have silvernix for them all."

"Which is up to Dracuni," Riony reiterated.

"But it's not impossible," Lyrrin offered. "And if the dragonlords saw the difference that made, maybe they would voluntarily untame their own dragons."

Kess scoffed under her breath.

Eslinde smiled thinly at her daughter. "Maybe they would."

"What other options do we have?" Dashiel brushed crumbs from their hands. "Couldn't we just wait for all the silvernix to run out? Then there would be no new tamed dragons."

Eslinde sighed and finally settled herself down into her chair. "My father has already found a way to tame without silvernix. Although I have removed that option from him, for now."

She gestured to the Alderkin. "I wouldn't put it past him to find a way again. And besides, he still has a vast store of silvernix, by his account. Enough to last decades. And then if he were to ever capture Dracuni ..."

"We're not going to let that happen," Riony said in a low, hard voice.

"Can't we tell everybody about the curse? Spread the truth?" Lyrrin asked. "If everyone knew, they'd do something, wouldn't they?"

Kess remembered their time in the palace, trying to persuade dragonlords to join their cause, to offer even a portion of their dragons up for untaming to attempt to weaken the shadow dragon curse.

But none of them wanted to hear it. None of them would give up the conveniences and luxuries dragons brought them, no matter the cost.

Even now, with two tamed dragons under their roof, there was always a reason why it couldn't be done. Always an excuse, even as all the world was blighted by fire and the undead.

The hopelessness of it all left Kess feeling hollow and numb.

Eslinde's shoulders drooped. "I've tried for years to share the truth, until people thought me and my ramblings mad. My father is entirely in control of the narrative, the silvernix, the power."

Drawing herself back up, Eslinde took a slow breath and looked about the room, holding each person's gaze in turn. "If we cannot untame enough dragons, the only other option I see to make a difference in the world, is to remove the Dragon King himself."

FIVE

Asilence fell over the table. Kess rubbed her tired eyes, her head shaking. "You're suggesting we overthrow the king?"

"No," Eslinde said with a sad finality. "I'm suggesting we kill him."

Murmurs of shock rippled around the room. Lyrrin, particularly, paled.

Eslinde offered her an apologetic look, then continued. "He is the only person who knows where his silvernix stores are held. If nobody else can find it, and nobody has, then without him, it is as good as gone."

Aishena raised her eyebrows. "No more silvernix, no new tamed dragons."

"I would estimate less than a year before all other sources are used up, give or take." Eslinde tilted her hand side to side in the air.

Kess cringed at what she was about to say, but it needed considering. "Dracuni counts as another source, potentially as large, or larger, than the king's supply, as she grows bigger."

Riony's expression in response could have melted the skin right off Kess's bones.

"All the more reason to end Yeonard Draekhan." There was no love in Eslinde's voice as she spoke her father's name. "I doubt he would have shared Kife's information to anyone else. If we can remove both the king and your brother, only the people in this room know about Dracuni's silvernix blood, yes?"

"As much as I adore the idea of seeing Kife lifeless on a pyre, making any attack against the Dragon King himself feels too reckless. Even for me. Which is saying something." Riony returned to her chair.

She looked tired as she leaned forward, scrubbing her face with her hands. "It's going to be hard enough to stay safe and hidden with the king's riders out there after us. It's more important right now to keep Dracuni safe as best as we can, not rush out on some kind of royal assassination mission."

The Alderkin all nodded in agreement.

There was worry in Riony's eyes as she looked over

them, her lips pulling in.

Lyrrin leaned toward where Riony sat across the table, as though drawn that way. "I'm not sure I like the idea of aiming to kill people either. Protecting the people we care about is what do, helping people get to the shrine enclaves, building those communities. And it has made everything so much better."

Kess shivered. She hadn't yet changed from the remains of her ripped gown, and Eslinde's underground was chilled in a way that the undercity hadn't been. But the rattle in her bones had nothing to do with the cold.

Riony and her friends had been doing all those heroic things while Kess had hunted them. How did she think she had any place now among them?

Protecting people we care about. I can do that. At least I can do that.

"We only fight in self-defense," Benjin added. "Choosing people for death feels icky."

Riony waved a finger around the room, pointing at everyone. "Also, as glorious as we are in battle, I'm not sure our little group is really up to the task of taking down the immortal king of all of Elundrae."

"Perhaps not," Eslinde agreed. "Which is why I had planned to bring the Rebel Riders in to help us. Or at least hope to, once I can gain their trust enough to receive an invitation to meet."

Silence again, as Riony and her friends exchanged

glances.

Eslinde sighed. "I know you may believe them only to be from stories, however—"

"It's not that," Riony said almost bashfully. "It's just, we *have* received an invitation from them."

"It says they were impressed by what we've been doing around Elundrae!" Benjin puffed out his chest.

Kess felt a twang of jealousy. If she hadn't betrayed them in the caves, if she hadn't brought her brother into the hunt so he could stab Riony in the back, maybe she also could have been the kind of person who received invitations from heroic Rebel Riders.

She asked, a little roughly, "So, you've met with them already?"

"No. We haven't followed it up yet," Niskina said, pouting.

"The invitation seemed entirely suspicious!" Riony waved a dismissive hand at her. "Remember what happened last time we accepted an invitation to meet up with rebels? I never want to see broken glass again in my life."

A wash of red flashed through Kess's memory. Riony covered in blood. Riony in pain. Pain Kess had caused. She flinched and tried to make herself small and invisible in her chair.

Riony frowned her way, then sniffed. "Besides, the invitation was sort of weird and vague anyway. Along with those other dodgy messages coming into the shrine enclaves, trying to lure us out, I wasn't trusting any of it."

Eslinde raised a hand timidly. "Oh, those messages were from me. After Kess told me about Lyrrin, I was trying to get in contact with you, but without arousing any suspicions."

Kess smirked. "Told you they'd think they were a trap."

Eslinde pinched the bridge of her nose briefly before regaining composure. "I would still like to follow up on the Rebel Rider invitation. It's somewhere to start."

Riony huffed and leaned into Niskina. "Looks like you'll finally get your wish."

The curvy young woman frowned over a soft smile. "Maybe not. As much as meeting Rider Jaym in person, or whoever the Rebel Riders really are, sounds like a dream come true, I made a decision a while ago. While you were away, Ri. I decided that once you were back, I would leave."

"Nisk?" Riony lowered her voice, but not enough. "Is this because of Kess?"

"No." Niskina's gaze flickered over Kess as though over a stinking carcass. "Not entirely."

Raising her voice, Niskina addressed her friends, despite the larger audience. "It's because it's time for me to stop being selfish. I've been thinking for a while about what more I can do, for everyone. And my thoughts keep going back to the Alderkin depths."

Aishena's hard gaze softened ever so slightly. "You want to go back there? I thought you hated it, that you only stayed because of your father making you?"

Niskina's smile in reply was sharp-toothed and wry. "Yeah, well, maybe my pabba had the right idea after all. That place is worth working on, to make it better for everyone. There's so much I can do there, sharing produce and supplies between the undercity and the shrines."

Benjin leaned halfway over the table with enthusiastic momentum. "The crystals Lyrrin has been sharing have made a huge difference to the people at the shrines. Imagine if you could share even more!"

The Alderkin muttered between themselves at this.

Niskina's eyes twinkled. "Exactly. Also bringing items from the undercity to the shrines will recharge them. This is what I want to go and do. I have the strength and knowledge now to really make a difference."

Riony's jaw worked, and she gave Niskina a pained look. "We won't be able to go with you. Not the Hjelzahns, not Dracuni, or any of these royal fugitives. Are you sure?"

"I am. I never wanted to be a delver. Pabba fled his grayglim duties to marry my Rolanian amma—"

Yensen's eye twitched at this revelation.

"—only to take her to die as a delver, and I rebelled against him every moment since. But now that I know I don't have to be a delver to do what needs to be done, I want to go back."

Riony reached both arms around Niskina, murmuring to her softly. The tattoo on her arm, four rings, two blades, one candle, disappeared under the tumbling fall of Niskina's curls.

Kess turned away, finding her eyes had flushed hot and teary.

All the mistakes she'd made. All the cost others have had to pay for them. She wasn't sure if anyone could ever forgive her. She wasn't sure whether she could ever forgive herself.

"Well," Eslinde said softly into the quiet room. "It seems we have come to a plan. Rest well, everyone. Tomorrow, we begin."

Kess didn't rest well. Despite it being long into the early hours of tomorrow's morning, despite the yesterday that felt as though it had spanned a year, despite having Griskin with her again, curled beside her in a way that felt perfectly like home, Kess couldn't sleep.

Instead, she decided she would continue her own plan of protecting Riony. She stalked Griskin silently along the cold tunnels of the base as the torches guttered away the last of their fuel.

All the others had found their own rooms, and those who had belongings unpacked them. A lot of the private room doors were closed. Kess didn't know which one Riony was behind. Maybe one along with Aishena.

Eslinde had kept Aishena and Benjin aside after the meeting, telling them about their encounter with their mother, explaining what they knew of the possession. The two Hjelzahn siblings listened silently and at attention, but the edge of tension was visible on Aishena's neck and jaw.

Would Riony be comforting her now?

Kess's chest felt heavy, and she rubbed tired eyes.

Movement up ahead set her every nerve alert. The large shape of a dragon, being led toward the exit as quietly as one can lead a dragon.

Picking up her pace, Kess snuck up to identify who had the dragon under their command and why.

Yensen. He turned quickly, having heard Griskin despite how soft-footed they'd approached.

"Kessara. You're still awake?" he said.

"Thought I'd do a patrol."

He nodded. "I had the same idea. To keep an eye on the skies."

He had the reins of the orange dragon, Ambri, in his hand. A good pick, much less recognizable than Viska.

They hadn't left any signs of their passage around the entrance aboveground from what Kess could see, but if anyone did come checking, Kess didn't like the idea of getting trapped down there without warning.

"Good idea. Tomorrow we should set up shifts, keep someone on patrol all the time."

Yensen only nodded again, his silky black hair shining

like a pool in the darkness.

Kess smirked. "And if anyone spots you, don't lead them back to us."

He returned a twist of his own lips. "Of course not."

They went their separate directions. Kess headed to the stables, hoping that if she could see that Dracuni was still safe, that would give her the reassurance she needed to rest.

The vast room housing the dragons was dark, only one torch sputtering at the entrance. Kess and Griskin stalked silently along the stalls. In the closest, Viska slept, with Shiff curled near her neck. Ambri was gone with Yensen. Kess passed stall after stall down the cavernous room, her heart rate building as each remained empty.

Until she reached the final stall, in the darkest end of the stables, far out of reach of the single light source.

The moment Griskin stepped in front of that space, a bright-purple glow flared in Kess's eyes.

She held a hand across her face to shadow it until her sight adjusted.

In the stall, Dracuni lay curled on her side, sleeping.

And sitting on the ground in front of her, awake and alert, was Riony.

"Thought I heard someone moving around. Have you come to steal Dracuni in the night?" Her voice was low, with a biting edge of disappointment that stabbed right through Kess.

Rushing the words out, Kess stuttered, "I came to

check she was safe."

"And aren't I glad I decided to make sure she was safe, too." Riony had her sword, activated and bright, lying on her lap, with one hand on the hilt. "I thought to myself, I'll sleep in here, just in case, but surely none of my honorable new companions will try anything. I was trying to be sooo trusting. I even took my armor off."

Riony had a blanket over her shoulders and beneath wore only a tattered undershirt and braies. "Armor or not, I'll do whatever I need to do to protect Dracuni. Although I really don't want to have to fight you in my underwear."

"It's not what I want to do with you in your underwear either."

Riony's eyebrows crept up her forehead.

The air was warm from the bulk of sleeping dragon, and Kess swallowed a dry throat.

"I mean ... I don't want to fight you at all. I still intend what I said, even if nobody believes me. I am pledged to you and your service." Kess reached a hand to her neck, feeling the smooth wood of the acorn there.

"Feels like the kind of thing you might ask a girl if she even wants first?"

Kess clenched her teeth, trying to keep her chin up and still. "I know you don't want me around, that nobody does, but I can be valuable to you."

Riony muttered some curse under her breath. "Your *value* isn't the issue."

Kess tugged sharply on the acorn's string, pulling the knot at the back free. "Here. You should have this back."

She tossed it gently, and Riony snatched it one-handed.

Frowning, Riony checked the pendant over. Kess had found, in the time she kept it, how the top could come off and there was a carefully hollowed space inside. But whatever it once held was gone.

Riony tied the leather string around her neck next to another, then rubbed the acorn again with her thumb. "So ... How long after you left me for dead did you go back into the ice cave again?"

Kess shrugged. "About as long as it took you to come back to where you'd left me dangling on a ledge above a gargantuan mess of revenants."

"So many fond memories." Riony cooed, but not even her usual smirk brightened her face. "Now, turn around and leave already. This is going to be a long enough night as it is without having to spend it with you."

Riony settled back in against Dracuni's stomach but didn't close her eyes or deactivate her sword. And Kess skulked away on Griskin, exhausted and heart aching.

SIX

Standing outside the entrance to Eslinde's underground base, Riony felt like the farmer in the old riddle her father used to tell her. The farmer had a bale of hay, a lamb, and a wolf, and had to take them all across the river, but the boat could only fit two.

If the farmer left the hay with the lamb, the lamb would eat it, and if the lamb was left with the wolf, the wolf would eat the lamb, and the farmer had to be clever to make sure everything reached the other side safely.

Watching the gathering of family and strangers separated out before her, Riony hoped she wasn't leaving any lambs with wolves.

Or that she wasn't the unsuspecting lamb.

"Be careful out there." Aishena grasped Riony's hand

between their chests and pulled her in close.

Then she turned and farewelled Niskina the same way.

Riony and Niskina stood alongside Eslinde, her grayglim, the two dragonriders, and Kess.

Aishena, on the other side, with Lyrrin, Dracuni, Benjin, and the Alderkin.

Riony whispered to Aishena, "Keep an eye on Dracuni and Lyrrin. I'm not sure the Alderkin would do anything, but I'm sure they'd have the power if they chose to."

Riony had spent the last few days trying to get a feel for all the new people around her. But the Alderkin remained ominously secretive, and everyone else had spent most of their time resting, recovering, and for the Zarram siblings, grieving the loss of their father and home.

Which made Riony feel bad for pressing Vance on his dragonlord identity. She hadn't added up before that the burning building filled with rioters had been their home. That the man swarmed by the mob as they left was their father.

Eslinde, who knew all of that, still wanted to take action toward her goals right away. But the Rebel Rider invitation specified arriving only during a certain phase of the moon—just part of its frustrating ambiguity—which required a few days' wait.

There was a lot of tense debate about who would leave and who would stay, but then they all began digging into the supplies of arms and armor Eslinde had stored, and the mood lifted.

Aishena's delver armor had been worn beyond repair during the last year, but now she stood in gleaming gold dragonrider scale mail with blue accents. "You've got the riskier end of the bargain, I fear. Kess, dragonlords, and a grayglim warden."

All of them were also now out of their muddy clothing and wearing varying levels of armor in Eslinde's colors. Yensen, however, remained in his shadowy uniform.

Riony said, "Are you worried about having a grayglim around? Because I'm ready to go with your instincts if we need to lose him."

Aishena frowned, then shook the emotion off. "I don't like him. But I'm not sure I'd like any grayglim at this stage. Just ... watch your back."

"Much prefer you watched it for me." Riony grinned. "But unfortunately, I need you keeping Dracuni safe."

Even now, the Alderkin gazed at Riony with disapproval for leaving. But with Eslinde taking both their full-grown dragons on her mission, Riony refused to not have somebody keep an eye on the away team. It would be all too easy for the dragonlords to fly off and bring an army back to take Dracuni away.

Lyrrin, who had just said a somewhat awkward farewell to her mother, moved on to hug Niskina goodbye, then gave Riony a quick squeeze too. "Don't worry, I'll keep Dracuni safe, since you're running off on us again."

Riony ruffled Lyrrin's hair, seeing the blue sparkle near her scalp. "You know one of the reasons I'm going is to make sure your mother stays safe. Besides, I won't be long this time."

Lyrrin swatted her hand way and pulled her hood up. "I was just teasing. My grandfather said he would talk to me about Alderkin magic while you're gone, so you can stay away as long as you like."

"Love you too," Riony called after her sister as she headed back into the tunnel.

While Niskina continued her goodbyes, Riony turned to the orange dragon. Vance was flying Viska and wanted Eslinde with him, which meant Yensen too. So Riony got stuck with Kess on the dragon Dashiel would fly.

Because wherever Riony went, Kess apparently was going too.

Yay. Maybe Kess realized this was actually the best way she could torture me.

Before Riony reached the dragon, Eslinde came to her side. She wore the same dress as she had left the capital wearing but washed clean of the mud that had darkened it. It was a fine suede-like velvet in silver-gray, hemmed in elegant gold embroidery.

She had put on gleaming gold pauldrons over the long-sleeved gown, more as some sort of display of power than for utility. Her hair was wound up in a neat braided bun.

For the first time since they had met, she truly looked

like royalty.

Eslinde placed a soft hand on Riony's arm. "I haven't had a chance to say it yet. But thank you."

"For?" Riony swallowed.

It was so strange to have the ethereally beautiful woman, who was Lyrrin's mother and also a first heir, there with them. The rebellious attitude that had endeared Riony to her while she was the guest at Heithorn estate made sense now.

"For raising her. So well." Eslinde's silver eyes fluttered to Lyrrin.

Flashes of memories punctured Riony's thoughts. Her mother, teaching Riony about the wetnurse herbs she was taking in order to feed the infant they had run away with. Her father, sitting on the floor and singing counting rhymes to a clapping toddler.

Memories of both of Riony's parents, bringing Lyrrin into their family as though she were their own.

Riony sniffed. "I can't take much credit for that. It's only been the two of us for a few years. And she's been acting fully grown since she was five."

"She has?" Eslinde smiled beneath glassy, distant eyes, as though she were trying to imagine it. "I've missed so much."

"I'm sorry. If there had been any way we could have stayed and given your baby back without losing all our lives, we would have. But none of us thought the Heithorns would have taken kindly to me walking back in saying, oops, sorry I killed the guest's bodyguard."

"You?" Eslinde cocked her head, blinked at Riony, and then sighed. "No, it's not your fault. Even after your escape, my mother kept up the lie that you had all died. I had no reason to think otherwise until Kessara came to me."

"I'll have to hear that story someday."

They separated again, each moving to their dragons.

Wait. Dracuni fussed, trotting back and forth at the entrance of the base.

"You need something?" Riony called back.

They had already said goodbye earlier, but Riony felt Dracuni's nerves build the closer Riony got to the orange dragon.

I want to come too. I should.

Riony began her climb into the saddle. "You should do no such thing. You're the one the Dragon King is hunting."

Viska and Ambri had been saddled to fit them all, and Kess had developed a combination saddle and harness for herself and Griskin.

As they mounted up, Dracuni stepped out from base entrance, stretched her wings, and flapped them determinedly. The diaphanous webbing fluttered, gusting the wind around her, but she didn't lift from the ground at all.

Shiff chased after her, bouncing and soaring in small flapping jumps around her.

Riony couldn't tell if the dragonling was trying to encourage or tease.

Sparks! Dracuni hissed through her teeth and dug her claws into the paved ground, cracking the stone beneath her.

"It's okay. You'll work it out soon. But you have to stay in the base until we're back."

Dracuni continued to swear richly as she spun around, her tail flicking, and retreated into the tunnel. Shiff and Lyrrin both ran in after her.

Dashiel reached a hand down to Riony and helped pull her up the rest of the way. "I can help, if you want. Some dragonlings need a bit more guidance than others finding their wings."

Settling into the seat farthest back, with Kess and Griskin between them, Riony gave a thin-lipped smile as she pulled her flying goggles down. "Thanks."

A moment later, they were off. Niskina rode on Viska as they detoured to deliver her to the closest shrine. When they arrived, Niskina activated the gateway to the depths, put on a steely expression, and stepped through.

They hadn't opened the gateway directly to the Alderkin depths since the time Lyrrin went to collect crystals. Anytime they helped people travel there, they sent them to the shrine down the hill, where a small enclave had grown that helped people travel to the undercity.

But Niskina had made it clear where she wanted to go.

Riony waited beside the glowing portal, and a moment later, Niskina returned.

"There are still ropes and climbing gear in the hole leading up to the undercity. I think the delvers are using it as an access to new areas. I'll be able to make my way up."

"Are you sure?" Riony leaned in, taking Niskina's hand in hers and holding it tight between them. "You could come with us instead, meet your sexy Rebel Riders."

Niskina chuckled and rested her forehead against Riony's. "Don't tempt me away from doing something good. You know I'm easily tempted."

Riony took a deep breath, breathing in all the scents and being of the woman who was now as much her sister as Lyrrin. "No, you're easily one of the best people out here. Go on. Say hi to the rope worm guy for me. Warn the delvers about the revs in the pit. And stay in touch."

She stepped back, and Niskina nodded, then disappeared through the gateway. The rippling glow faded out.

Niskina's absence already left a hollow in Riony as she climbed back onto Ambri. She was glad they'd agreed to a contact system and would leave messages by the gateway regularly for each other.

In front of Riony, Kess had a dark expression on her face and her eyes had a flush of pink around them. "Her selflessness is ... inspiring. Those dark depths need somebody to do some good there."

"This isn't about your love life, Kess."

From the front, Dashiel snorted, and then they were in the air again.

It wasn't long before Riony spotted other dragons in the sky, blocking their way east. Patrols and hunters, spread regularly across the horizon. Riony, holding Lyrrin's seeing stone, pointed them out to Kess, and Kess passed it up the chain to Dashiel who signaled to the other dragon's riders.

After a sequence of hand gestures, both dragons banked steeply, heading south at speed. The winter air, already chilled, grew bitter and howling as they reached the Eyersunn Sea and glided out over the waves.

Riony was glad there had been plenty of goggles in Eslinde's supplies. She could imagine the icy air biting at her eyes without them. Even with a number of layers worn beneath her armor, the metal felt frozen.

She hadn't taken any of Eslinde's armor. It felt wrong wearing the armor of dragonriders and dragonlords. But she regretted it now, seeing how Kess and Dashiel, in theirs, weren't being frozen to the bone. The dragon scales didn't channel the cold the way steel did.

Riony leaned a little closer to Griskin, unashamedly stealing his warmth.

They flew until the coastline was a gray smudge on the horizon, then went east, following the line of land on their left until the ruddy heights of the Red Cliffs became visible.

Back over land again, the dragons flew higher and more cautiously, keeping watch for any other wings in the sky and for the destination described to them in the invitation.

Within three days after a dark full moon, meet us behind the staircase spire, where the clouds rise from the land.

Riony rolled her eyes.

Who talks like that?

Speaking in riddles didn't endear Riony to them. She preferred people who said what they meant. She hadn't been sure about chasing down the vague location in Snowshimmer Ridge before, and she wasn't sure about it now.

If the Rebel Riders were real, if they were anything worth finding, why didn't we ever hear more stories about them and their deeds outside of the books?

Stories of them actually helping people?

From their vantage point in the sky, it didn't take long to find the towering outcrop of stone, chipped away into even steps.

Would've taken us months to find on foot. Did they expect us to come in on dragon?

Maybe they assumed Dracuni could fly.

One short loop around the spire confirmed gusts of steam rising into the frigid air, and Vance and Dashiel brought them down into the cover of vapor.

The dragons landed with a soft splash, ankle-deep in pools of clear aqua water. The edges of the pool and surface of the mountain were limestone that had formed as slick and white as ice, and the air was cloyingly warm.

Riony scanned the small plateau. "Nobody here?"

"Anybody see anything?" Dashiel called across to the others riding Viska.

The gold dragon walked a circle through the warm water.

Eslinde called back, "Nothing. No signs of life, no symbols, or entrances. Maybe this isn't the right place?"

The spire loomed above them, the sun behind it, cutting its staircase shape in a clear silhouette. And the hot springs at their feet, defrosting Riony with their warmth, also brought to her a memory that flushed her from the inside as well.

She cleared her throat. "You don't think these are *the* hot springs?"

"What do you mean *the* hot springs?" Kess asked.

"I mean from the stories. Where Rider Jaym and his true love did things that I'm still not convinced are physically possible." And just to make sure it was clear, Riony added, "Sex things."

Kess's ears went red.

Dashiel shrugged. "I've only read a chapter or two of the stories. And I'm not entirely sure any of it was or could be real."

"Even if it was, what would it matter?" Kess asked.

"Well, for starters, I'd be both impressed and inspired by the passionate possibilities." Riony enjoyed seeing Kess's discomfort as her ears darkened further, to a deep maroon. "But more importantly, maybe this is supposed to be some sort of clue?"

Eslinde called across from Viska, "A clue? How?"

"You read the invitation. I bet this is some sort of test and the invitation is just the first step. Only people who've read the stories, who are really into the *Rebel Riders*, will be able to spot the markers and know what to do next."

Riony squinted through the mist. "Can you move us closer to that edge?"

Dashiel nodded, and Ambri sloshed through the hot water to the limestone crust that surrounded the pool.

"Look, down in that valley." Riony pointed over Griskin.

Between two close cliff faces, a bridge of stone dipped down, then up, an inverted archway.

"Do you know what that looks like to me? It looks like the cradle archway, where Rider Zeina kissed her true love for the first time. But then it ended on a cliffhanger and I didn't get the chapter after that to see if it went further." Riony sighed with deep lament.

"Are all of the scenes in these stories about sex?" Dashiel asked.

"All the best ones," Riony replied.

"Fine. Let's take a closer look, I suppose. Unless anyone has any better suggestions?" Eslinde asked in a resigned tone.

There were none. The two dragons spread their wings,

gusting swirls of mist around them and water streaming behind as they launched out of the hot springs.

Riony's stomach flew up into her throat as they dove toward the archway. The closer they got, the more Riony was sure this was the same cradle archway from the story.

Although it had only been words on a page, the landscape of limestone white and rusty-red earth, cracked down the center by a sharp gorge, was a vivid memory in Riony's mind, and matched perfectly to what she saw now.

And Rider Zeina was her favorite character, so she remembered the scene well.

"Where next?" Dashiel yelled back.

As they flew over the top of the archway, Riony cast about, unable to see their next heading. "I don't know."

Kess's shoulders sagged, and she pointed off to their right. "That zigzagging chasm. There was one like that in the books."

Riony's eyebrows popped up. "I haven't read that one. *Interesting* that you have."

Kess slouched farther over.

"And which character had an intimate encounter there?" Dashiel's lips turned up as they looked over their shoulder at Kess.

"They raced their dragons through there." Kess's voice sounded like it came out through gritted teeth.

Riony nodded sagely. "Sounds like something they'd do. But I bet you anything I know what they did afterward."

She took Kess's thick silence as an affirmative.

Dashiel's face lit up, and after a few hand motions toward Vance, they took off.

Apparently keen to recreate the entire experience, the two riders took them shooting downward into the chasm. The narrow walls were just wide enough to fit the dragons one after another, the outstretched wingtips barely fitting as they glided through.

The chasm cut sharply left, then right, and Riony held tight to the saddle and Griskin in front of her, who whined slightly as they dipped and turned in the air.

Darkness grew as the chasm went deeper into the earth, shadowed by the overhanging cliffs on each side.

Anticipation grew within Riony, imagining the entrance to an underground base up ahead as they went deeper.

Then Dashiel leaned back and Ambri's wings struck out, catching the air and slowing them abruptly. A moment later, they were on the ground.

Riony leaned to the side, trying to see what lay ahead.

"Dead end," Dashiel called back.

Vance brought Viska in to land behind them at a slower pace, having apparently decided not to join in the race.

"Nothing?" Eslinde called out, her voice high and clipped. "Any other clues?"

Riony couldn't see anything. "You're more up to date than me, Kess."

Kess pulled her googles up, squinting up into the sliver of light high above and frowning deeply.

Riony followed her gaze. They were a long way down with sheer walls cutting up from the ground on three sides. She shivered. They were boxed in, cornered.

"We should go. We need to get back into the air, now. This is—"

A shadow flickering over them cut off Riony's voice. Dragons. Five dragons, descending upon them.

This was a trap.

SEVEN

Lyrrin clutched her chest where the paired heart stone hung on a string. It thumped wildly with her sister's thundering pulse.

Biting her lip, she tried not to be scared.

"Don't worry, lots of things make my heart race, not just bad things," Riony had said before she left.

And that meeting the Rebel Riders was probably going to be one of those things. Riony didn't explain exactly why meeting the people from the stories she read was going to be so exciting.

All she said was to only worry if the heartbeat stopped.

Taking a deep breath, Lyrrin tried to relax. She adjusted her seating on the padded floor. The cold seeped up through the fabric beneath her. Extra blankets had been dragged into the dragon stables to create a comfortable, soft nest within view of Dracuni and Shiff.

The two young dragons seemed locked in some eager conversation nobody else could hear. Shiff would flutter her small wings, followed by Dracuni, followed by more silent back and forth and shaking heads, and then flapping wings again.

The room was lit with the cool cyan light of the glow stones, since the torches were out of fuel and Aishena had yet to find more in the vast stores of crated goods warehoused in the base that everyone had been helping themselves to.

Benjin danced across the floor in front of Lyrrin, wearing a too-large set of dragonrider armor, his staff clashing against Aishena's unlit athames.

They had been training together for a while, but Benjin had yet to land a blow on his sister. Generally, he came away happy as long as she hadn't knocked him down too many times.

Aishena had also been training Riony on better sword fighting technique, although Riony seemed to enjoy it when Aishena managed to toss her onto her back.

With a monosyllabic bark from Aishena, Benjin froze mid swing. Aishena stepped in, adjusting his stance, rotating his torso with her hands and tapping his feet into position with her own.

"Huut," she barked again, and they swung back into

motion as though time unfroze.

Lyrrin watched, jealous. She'd been given some basic instruction on how to wield a dagger, but she didn't have the reach or physical strength deemed worthy of learning more advanced melee fighting.

But she had her crystals.

A range of them were scattered on the blanket in front of her now, and in front of them lay her belt, stretched out long and straight. She worked on fixing a couple more pouches onto the belt.

She liked to keep a collection of the runed stones at hand, as easy to reach as possible. A glow stone, a couple of flash stones, and burst bombs.

She had one little crystal with float and burn runes on it, like Riony's sword. It had been the test she'd done before her sister allowed her to touch her beloved blade. She used the flaming crystal now for getting fires started.

There were a few crystals with combinations that hadn't worked out that she should probably discard, and the ten-stroke rune Riony had taken from the warrior's tomb which she still hadn't worked out, that she carried in her pack normally, but had in front of her now while she was organizing.

She was frowning at it when the Alderkin approached.

"May we sit with you, child?" Yrik asked in his voice like a gentle earthquake.

Lyrrin's breath hitched, and she squeaked, "Yes?"

It had been a lie when she'd told Riony that the Alderkin were going to teach her magic. Or maybe wishful thinking. They hadn't at that time made much of an effort at all to speak with her.

Now that they had come to talk to her, Lyrrin tried to contain her excitement.

She shuffled over on the blankets to make more room for the three Alderkin, an attempt to be respectful, or wary, or whatever she was supposed to be at that time. She wasn't sure.

But as Yrik, Priyune, and Shael joined her on the padded floor, sitting so close Lyrrin could smell the earthy autumn-rain scent of them, all Lyrrin could do was stare.

They were Alderkin, and so was she. At least in part. Their hands matched hers, as did the brightness of their eyes and hair.

It had been a while since Lyrrin had dyed hers. It hadn't seemed as important since leaving the undercity. There were less people around that she felt she had to fit in for, and the people of the shrine enclaves didn't seem to care. So they saved Riony's hennan harvests for Aishena.

There was an almost finger-length growth of blue from Lyrrin's scalp now, before older remnants of dye dulled the lower strands to a muddy gray.

The Alderkin's ears were different than hers, long and pointed. That seemed to be something Lyrrin had retained from her human mother. Her face was softer too, less hard

angles and sharp planes.

"You work with crystals?" Priyune leaned in, brushing fingers like blades across the stones laid out before them.

The forest-toned woman seemed to have recovered greatly since their arrival at Eslindekeep. The Alderkin had kept to themselves during that time, and there had been worry Priyune may succumb to her injury. But the Alderkin rejected any notion of using silvernix, even when Dracuni offered.

Lyrrin stuttered shyly, "I've loved them since we first got to the undercity. To the ... Alderkin depths?"

"Luns Deemfret." Yrik bowed his head. "That is our name for it."

"Do they sing to you?" Priyune asked, tapping the corner of a rune.

Lyrrin nodded, and Priyune gave her a twinkling smile in return that made Lyrrin's chest feel full and warm.

"You know more than a few runes, and you are mixing them. How did you learn?" Shael, who seemed the youngest, barely an adult by human standards, leaned in close.

Lyrrin knew she must be much older than she seemed, if Priyune, who had only the faint lines of wrinkling around her eyes was over eighty, and Yrik, who looked as though he could be her father, was really her grandfather.

"By myself, mostly. And with a few accidents," Lyrrin admitted.

"Careful with these ones." Shael pointed to the flash

and burst bombs.

"Oh yeah, we worked that out." Lyrrin chuckled nervously.

She reached over to the ten-stroke runed stone and lifted it in her hands for them to see. "I can't work this one out, though. Could you ... would you show me how it works?"

Yrik stared at it for a long moment. "No. No not that one. That is special magic only for Alderkin."

Isn't that what I am? Lyrrin couldn't voice the question out loud.

In a softer voice, Shael added, "If it was to work for you, it would sing to you."

The fullness and warmth inside Lyrrin vanished, replaced with a clenching, hollow chill. She may have Alderkin blood, but clearly, she wasn't Alderkin *enough*.

Having spent all her life growing up as not *human* enough, to find out the Alderkin didn't consider her one of them either made her feel like she'd swallowed one of her burst bombs.

Yrik's angular face remained emotionless, but his blue eyes shimmered. "And the humans, they know and use our magic too. Did you teach them?"

"They already knew, mostly. People in the under ... in Luns Deemfret, they've been working runes out for a while before we got there. I worked out the gateway rune, though. But we haven't taught anyone else that one."

The Alderkin shared looks between each other, and Lyrrin hoped it was in approval. She suddenly felt as though her every word and action was being judged.

Aishena and Benjin's combat had slowed, and it was clear Aishena was keeping as much of an eye on Lyrrin as she was the sparring.

There didn't seem to be any aggression or threat from the Alderkin, though. If anything, they seemed sad.

Are they disappointed with me?

Then she saw the way they eyed Aishena and Benjin, training in front of them. With crystals weapons in their hands.

Lyrrin spoke softly. "You don't like humans using the crystals?"

She felt stupid as soon as she said it. Of course they wouldn't like it. Why would they? Their magic, in the hands of the people who had destroyed their entire race.

Without waiting for an answer, she rambled on. "We're only using the magic to help us protect Dracuni. Mostly. And to protect each other, but that's important too."

It wasn't true, though. They had also been using the magic and sharing the magic to improve their lives in the blighted, undead infested landscape of Elundrae.

Was that so wrong? Lyrrin felt all mixed up inside, and the Alderkin had gone quiet.

There was so much Lyrrin wanted to ask, about her father, about where they had been all this time, what their lives were like before, but she felt small under their timeless gaze.

So she turned back to the sparkling stones in front of her. "Was it the unicorns that gave crystals their magic?"

Priyune inclined her head slightly. "It was their magic. It flowed everywhere, through the earth, and our people learned how to create sacred spaces in the locations the unicorns visited the most, and ring those areas in standing stones to contain and amplify that magic. To use it for ourselves."

Lyrrin glanced over at Dracuni and her long golden horn. "We worked out the crystals would charge at shrines, and we thought it had something to do with Dracuni, too."

Shael smiled, eyes twinkling. "Yes, your creature with the blood of magic. She has been bringing life back to the land she has traveled on."

Each of the Alderkin had changed out of the stinking rags they'd fled their prison wearing, now in clean, simple military uniforms. The flat gray fabric seemed so plain against their gemstone features.

But as they all turned to look at Dracuni, there seemed to be an energy in the air, humming and singing through Lyrrin the way the crystals did as she traced their runes.

A harmonization.

Something Lyrrin desperately wanted to be part of. But all she could do was say, "Yeah, Dracuni is pretty special. We hoped that just having her around would be enough to keep things charged, but we did need the shrines too."

Keeping her eyes on Dracuni, Shael said, "There's only one way that works without—"

"Shh!" Yrik snapped.

Lyrrin flinched.

Shael tutted and snapped back, "Her mother knows already. Alleem worked it out for her, to keep her safe. He would want that extended to his daughter."

Yrik shook his head, silky blue hair shivering in the cool light. "Alleem shared too much, and we've all suffered for it."

The two Alderkin locked eyes. Priyune leaned away, as though avoiding the argument entirely.

Lyrrin pulled her lips in tight, fighting off the hot swell of tears.

In a tiny voice, she asked into the tense silence, "Alleem, my father ... What happened to him?"

"He was killed by the unicorn slayer!" Yrik's head whipped toward her, his expression still sharp.

Lyrrin's voice trembled. "By ... Yeonard Draekhan?"

By my other grandfather. Lyrrin felt as though she should be torn in two.

Then Yrik blinked, as though remembering who he was looking at, and his eyes softened, drooping deeply. "I'm sorry. He ... My son. It was hard to lose him, after we'd already lost so much."

Movement shifted in front of Lyrrin. Aishena and

Benjin had stopped entirely, and Aishena was pushing her brother toward the door. With a knowing look to Lyrrin, she nodded once and left them to privacy.

Priyune leaned back in then. "He was taken away, around the same time Eslinde stopped visiting us. Which we now know is when she was growing you. We thought he had been taken and killed immediately, but some months later he was returned to our cell."

"Mortally injured," Yrik moaned the words. "Tortured beyond all sense."

"Shh yourself," Shael snapped softly. "The child needn't know—"

"She will know what happened to her father," Yrik responded. "How the unicorn slayer brought him back to us to die, declaring that he had fulfilled his part in some bargain in returning Alleem to his family. No matter that Alleem did not live to see the next day."

Lyrrin tried to imagine the man she had never known, to feel for him the way she'd felt when Riony had told her that the parents who raised them were never coming back.

There was a tight ache in her chest, but the sense of loss was different. It was the loss of something she'd never had. What ached the most was having seen the pure heartbreak in Eslinde and the Alderkin's eyes when they spoke of Alleem. Seeing how much he had been loved by others.

Lyrrin asked, "Do you think he knew about me?"

"None of us did, until recently," Priyune replied.

"No, don't you remember?" Shael folded her icy clawed fingers in her lap and closed her eyes.

Her voice was the low hush of old memory. "When he came back to us. His final words … ramblings about gateways, about how he wouldn't show the slayer their ways, even for the child. We thought he meant the slayer's child, for Eslinde, that something had happened to her."

Pale-blue eyes popped open again. "But he could have meant his own child. He could have known about you. It seemed the slayer did everything to pry our gateway magic from Alleem. But he said he never shared it. He found some other way to be brought back to his family."

To die. Lyrrin shivered, and a fat tear splashed from her eye.

"We haven't told anyone else, either," she felt the need to say again.

The Alderkin bowed their heads solemnly.

"That was wise." Priyune reached over and clasped Lyrrin's hand. "To keep Dracuni safe, to keep you safe, to keep our ways safe."

Lyrrin tried to smile, but she still felt bad for not sharing. She knew it would make life so much easier for so many.

In a flurry of marching steps, Aishena returned to the stables. "I stepped out to check for signs of the others returning and saw a dragon flying over."

"Was it them?" Lyrrin wiped her face and stood up.

"No. Just one dragon, high up. I couldn't identify it. It's gone now, but ..." Aishena glared dark eyes at the walls around them. "The entrance to this base is solid, impenetrable, but I don't like the idea of being trapped down here if our location is found. We don't have enough food for a siege."

The Alderkin rose to their feet around them as well.

Lyrrin frowned, thinking through their conversation. "Would it be possible to bring a gateway stone here? Would it still work if we moved one?"

Their hesitation was clear. The gateways and how they worked were something they would die to protect. But there was something even more important.

"If we had a gateway in here, with us, it would make it so much easier to make sure Dracuni stays safe," Lyrrin added.

"It would still work," Priyune said. "But without being within the standing stones, it would run out of charge at some point."

Aishena gave them all a shrewd look. "The one in the depths didn't have standing stones around it."

Shael nodded. "Deemfrets do not usually contain gateways, for that reason. That one was moved into Luns at the end of the great massacre, to evacuate out who we could. I'm surprised that stone still had any magic left in it."

"Some Alderkin were evacuated?" Lyrrin asked.

Luns Deemfret, the central Alderkin ruins, was the

last holdout of Alderkin fighting at the end of the war. But if some got out ...

Could that mean there are others out there? Somewhere?

Aishena's jaw moved as though chewing over the thought. "Even if we had a gateway in here with us, if we are trapped, only the humans could get out through it. The dragons are too large, except for Dashiel's little one. Even Dracuni won't fit soon."

Dracuni snorted.

"Still," she added, "it would buy us time. We could bring food in for the dragons, find some way to break the siege. It would give us options."

Options were something. Better than no way out. Lyrrin had spent most of the years she remembered living underground, but the Alderkin ruins felt like home. The cold square-cut tunnels of Eslindekeep felt like a trap, even without enemy dragons at the door.

She said as firmly as she could, "We should do it. One of the dragons could carry the gateway here. We would save its magic to only use in an emergency."

Then she added, a little pleading in her tone as she looked to the Alderkin for approval, "And we won't share how to use it with the others, the dragonriders."

Hesitation again, but then the approval came.

Lyrrin knew, beyond anything, they wanted to keep Dracuni safe. As did she and her friends.

But Lyrrin had also only just gotten Riony back, after

weeks with only infrequent visits. Lyrrin had only just found her mother and the people she was descended from.

She thought those things would bring her some peace, but she felt more in danger than ever.

And she had more to lose than ever.

EIGHT

It was too late to fly out of the chasm. They were down deep with nowhere to get a running start. All Riony could do was wait as five dragons descended upon them.

"Is this who we're looking for, or do we have a problem?" Dashiel asked.

Riony held up Lyrrin's seeing stone again. "The riders aren't in dragonlord colors. Whether or not that means we have a problem we'll find out shortly."

"Is that a razing *flamesong*?" Kess hissed, eyes locked on the largest black and gold dragon.

"The ones that spontaneously explode sometimes?" Riony watched it too, as it flew in behind the others, one red, one white, one aqua, and one bronze.

"And someone is riding it," Dashiel said, awed.

Kess's voice was low. "I thought it was an exaggeration, in the stories, saying one of them rode a flamesong. Just how much of the stories are real?"

Riony reached for her sword and brought it into her lap, activating the float rune in case she needed to move quickly. The dragons came within flaming distance, but didn't immediately roast them, which Riony considered a good sign.

They landed in a rush of wind and dust, their wings sending out whirling eddies that danced along the ground.

As the air cleared, the five dragons, ranging from a small shimmerdart to the massive flamesong, faced them from a wary distance away, cornering them against the cliff wall.

A gruff voice carried across the gap. "Riony? You're the one we sent an invitation to meet to. But it seems as though you've brought along more than a few uninvited people as well."

"Yeah, and it seems like your invitation has led us into a nice little trap," Riony yelled back.

The man on the bronze etherdart had a sharp jaw edged with a neat beard and handsome features that were weatherbeaten and marred by the wear and tear of battle.

He moved the dragon a step closer. "Just a little something we do to test for threats. We keep watch of the hot springs, and then if we decide those we invited weren't worthy after all, well ..."

He eyed the sheer cliff face behind Riony's group and

the dark marks on the stone there. Scorch marks.

"At what point do you decide we're worthy or not?" Riony asked.

He shrugged lazily. "How about we start with introductions and go from there."

Eslinde shifted then, climbing nimbly down from Viska. Both Vance and Yensen attempted to stop her, but she batted their hands away.

She moved herself between the two opposing lines of dragons and spoke with a clear voice. "Eslinde the First."

From atop the bronze dragon, the man's eyes narrowed.

Eslinde continued, gesturing to the others. "My grayglim and two trusted riders accompany me."

A pale Taenish woman with neatly braided black hair moved her shimmerdart closer. "And who's that one? And why do you have a wolf?"

Eslinde hesitated, as though unsure how to describe Kess and her place there.

Riony sighed and climbed out of the saddle, then jumped lightly to the ground beside Eslinde.

Riony rested her sword on her shoulder. "Look, you invited me, and I brought these people along. And I brought them for a good reason. If that's a problem, I'd love to stop dancing around it and start knocking people off their dragons."

The man's eyes narrowed again, but from over on the aqua dragon, a woman chuckled.

"Stars, she really is how the stories say she is!" Warm golden eyes looked down at Riony from a face so striking it made Riony's heart flip-flop.

The woman wore minimal armor and clothing despite the cold weather, showing off blushed sienna skin and a musculature that made Riony feel desperately inferior.

A thick scar twisted the skin near her full lips, accentuating their shape as she smirked.

That scar ... Riony had read about one like that.

Her mouth went dry. "You ... are you ...?"

The woman's eyes squeezed into sweeping lines as she smiled. "I'm Zeina."

Riony's hand shot out, grasping Eslinde's arm for support. "*Rider Zeina?* And she ... she's heard stories about *me*?"

Zeina's face brightened again with amusement, and she blinked slowly before trailing her eyes leisurely up and down Riony.

Tearing her eyes away from the beautiful woman, Riony looked over each of the other riders. "Wait, if she's real, I mean, if the stories are really based on you, then ..."

The man on the red etherflame had sun-kissed golden curls that fell in tousled waves around a tanned face, younger than Riony expected.

"Rider Jaym?" she guessed.

He offered her a winking salute.

Oh, sparks. Niskina would have loved this. Riony felt

a little faint.

On the flamesong, a giant of a man sat still and solemn. Short-cropped brown hair had a sparkle of gray at his temples. He fit no description other than that of the bold steed he rode.

"Rider Samor?"

He sniffed and lowered sad eyes.

The man on the bronze dragon who first greeted them, and the Taen on the shimmerdart …

"I don't know these two," Riony said with a shrug.

"Our noble leaders won't let me write them into the stories." Jaym's tone was one of utter heartbreak, despite his cheeky smile. "Probably because they are already coupled up and don't have anything exciting to include."

"*You write them?*" Riony's grip on Eslinde tightened.

The princess patted Riony's fingers. "It's called propaganda, love."

"Thallan," offered the man with gruff reluctance.

"Norallei," added the woman.

Kess appeared by Riony's side, having stalked up silently on Griskin.

"Hold on. I've heard of this one too." Zeina lifted her chin as she assessed them. "The wild wolf girl who's been giving smugglers trouble for years."

Riony pouted and side-eyed Kess, trying not to be put out that Rider Zeina had also heard of her. A blooming

hint of begrudging respect was also quickly tamped down.

The Zarram siblings and Yensen offered their names from their seats, and Kess grumbled hers, leaving off the Heithorn part. The full round of introductions were complete, but the Rebel Riders all remained on their dragons, and tension remained in the air.

Rider Jaym had his eyes on the sky, and Samor had a dagger in his hands that he cleaned his nails with. Only Zeina seemed unbothered, cracking nuts in the palm of her hand and popping them in her mouth.

In an unfriendly rasp, Thallan said, "Now that we're all friends, perhaps you can tell us why you've brought a First heir and her entourage with you?"

Before Riony could answer, a keening shriek pierced the air and the flutter of feathers rushed past her.

Riony startled and cringed again as the pocket-hawk circled her, then came to rest on Jaym's extended arm.

Sparks. Jaym didn't say anything about his pet in the stories. Breathing hard, Riony made every effort to not flinch away from the beady-eyed creature that preened its outstretched wings.

Thallan still awaited her answer.

Flustered, Riony couldn't take her eyes off the bird. What if it flew at her again?

I'm going to humiliate myself in front of the Rebel Riders. That's what.

Then a dark shape moved into Riony's vision. She refocused, finding Kess there. The girl and the wolf had taken a single step forward, putting themselves between Riony's eyeline and the hawk.

Kess knew of Riony's fear of birds. She'd teased her mercilessly about it when they were kids.

What is she doing?

Kess didn't turn or acknowledge the action at all. She remained straight-backed, angled to block as much of Riony's view in that direction as possible.

I pledge my life to you and your cause. For whatever good it can provide you.

Deep within Riony something cold and hard softened.

Blinking rapidly, she tore her eyes away from Kess and turned back to Thallan and the riders. She cleared her throat.

"Eslinde and the others came to us for a number of reasons, which all put together mean I'm fairly certain we can trust her and trust that she isn't going to go running back to Pabba," Riony said. "At least, half half-certain."

Eslinde fidgeted her fingers and seemed to be actively fighting to keep her mouth closed.

Riony huffed. "Yeah, you should probably take over. I never said I was some kind of diplomat. I'm just here to hit things with a sword in case it turned out there was something that needs hitting."

Offering a small smile, Eslinde stepped forward. "I am

here because I have defected, and I come to you with the aim of joining forces to bring down the Dragon King."

Norallei scoffed. "Want to take your fadda's throne for yourself? We're not getting caught up in any of that nonsense."

Unbothered, Eslinde said, "Then you should know I'm last in line and with no designs upon that power. We aim to assassinate Yeonard Draekhan as part of our goal to end the shadow dragon curse."

It only took Eslinde a few moments to succinctly sum up their knowledge of the curse and how they hoped to defeat it.

Definitely for the best I let her do the talking, Riony thought.

The Rebel Riders remained silent for a while, then Thallan scratched at his stubbled jaw. "If it's all true, it could work. That silvernix stash is hidden well. Or at least well enough we've never found it."

"You've been looking?" Eslinde asked.

Thallan's mouth twisted bitterly. "We've been after it for years ... spent far too long searching the capital, and even got into Draekhan's Rest a couple of times, chasing rumors. Don't think we've ever gotten close to finding it."

"You managed to infiltrate the king's private estate? Impressive," Eslinde conceded.

"But you didn't actually find anything." Riony frowned at the aged armor and heavily laden saddlebags of the riders

before her. "So, what have you been doing all this time? Other than failing to find the king's silvernix? Is it all just sleeping with each other and writing stories about it?"

Zeina's eyes crinkled, and she spoke through a full mouth. "It may be a large part of what we do."

"You don't believe the other parts of our daring tales?" Jaym sounded hurt.

Riony didn't attempt to look his way again. "I generally believe what I see, and in all my time aboveground, I haven't ever seen you all before, daring or otherwise."

The warm rush of having met the heroes of her favorite stories had worn off as Riony wondered again why she hadn't heard of them outside of those booklets. They'd heard of her exploits. They'd even heard of Kess.

But from all the people Riony had helped and met across Elundrae as they set up shrine enclaves or liberated slaves, none had mentioned stories of the Rebel Riders doing the same.

Thallan said, "We put our efforts mostly toward skirmishes with other riders, trying to keep the worst of them grounded. Making sure they don't think they are the only rulers of the sky."

Jaym sighed dramatically. "We used to harry dragonkeeps, just for the fun of it! But we lost some of our group, a while back ..."

He glanced across at Samor before continuing. "We've mostly been lying low since then, doing what we can to keep ourselves and our dragons alive while fighting off the ever-increasing number of revs."

Riony brought her sword down off her shoulder and deactivated it, letting the tip fall heavily before leaning on the cross guard. "So ... the same thing *non*-rebel riders do?"

Zeina's cool smirk faded, and she threw a nutshell at Jaym. "You're making us sound terrible."

Jaym muttered, "She's not wrong, though. We haven't done more than look after ourselves for years. Very dragonlord style behavior."

From the flamesong, Samor spoke up, his voice deep and soft. "*We* don't enslave people."

"You do enslave dragons, though," Kess said, a low tone of disappointment in her voice as she stared up at the bronze etherdart and white shimmerdart.

Riony noticed it then too. She'd been so fixated on the people she hadn't paid much attention to the dragons. *Trust that Kess did.*

Both of those dragons were motionless and solemn, unmoving without their rider's commands. Both had the cap of a steel spike visible on their foreheads.

The other three, Zeina's, Jaym's, and Samor's, were alert and mobile, taking in their surroundings and observing the conversation, and, Riony guessed, in their own silent conversations with their riders.

It sure was something, to see those three riding real wild dragons, but it was a disappointment that they didn't

all give their beasts that freedom.

"It's necessary," Thallan growled. "It takes years to raise a wild dragon and bond with it. It makes more sense to steal tamed dragons from our downed foes."

Riony remembered the three dragons that had tried to catch Dracuni after their escape from the keep.

Apart from the Zarrams' snowflame that died in the fight, all of the king's dragons had been left downed where they were. Alive, but unable to fend for themselves. They didn't have time to try to take them too and assumed they would be reclaimed by others.

Should we have kept them ourselves? Had more tamed dragons to fight on our side?

Riony felt a worming sick feeling inside. She was glad they didn't. It didn't feel right at all to take on more tamed creatures, the weapons of those that oppressed them and the very thing cursing their land.

"Besides, your dragons are no more free than mine," Thallan added, flicking his chin toward Viska and Ambri.

Riony said, "The princess and her entourage are fresh from the palace. I feel as though the *Rebel Riders* are the ones I expect more from."

Zeina threw a nut in the air and caught it in her mouth. She crunched it thoughtfully. "She's right. We could be doing more."

Shoulder to shoulder with Norallei, Thallan growled, "*We* have been more than willing to return to battle. It's

you three who haven't been ready."

"If you do want to be more involved again, if you do want to make a difference, you can join us," Eslinde's voice rang out. "You and ... are there more of you? I expect you didn't all come to the meeting location. Are they back at your base?"

"We don't really have a base," Zeina said wryly. "We keep on the move."

All of their saddles were stacked with bags and bundles, cooking pots and blankets.

"So this is ...?" Eslinde gestured to the five of them.

"This is all that's left of us." Samor's eyes were rimmed red. "There used to be more."

Jaym added in a singsong voice, "I may have exaggerated our number in the stories, if that's what you're going by."

"There are two other groups to our name, on the move as well." Thallan gestured to the sky. "But only a handful in each, like us."

"Oh." Eslinde slumped a little.

Riony leaned in, whispering not at all quietly, "This is fine, right? Five more dragons is definitely enough to take on the immortal king of all the land and his, what ... few dozen dragons?"

"Eighty-two riders under his direct control, another forty-five in lower-ranking city guards, his own private stable of thirty-three, which he allows use of to his grayglim when necessary. Not including factory dragons. Not including each heir's dragons and riders the king could call on. As of last count," Eslinde rattled out.

Riony smirked. "Sure. Easy."

Zeina winked at Riony. "I'm in if you are."

Riony didn't reply, sure that if she opened her mouth, she'd stumble her words as she focused on not spontaneously combusting, flamesong style.

"From what I understand, if your goal is to end the curse on our lands, there could be other ways." Thallan looked around at all the dragons there.

"We're pretty good at taking on other riders. What if we focus on bringing down as many as we can, in smaller skirmishes? Does a dead dragon work the same as an untamed one?"

"You'd just kill every tamed dragon you come across?" Kess hissed.

Griskin growled softly, taking a step forward, but with a slight glance over her shoulder toward Riony, Kess moved Griskin back where he was.

Eslinde lifted both hands in front of her. "We don't know for sure it works that way. Their deaths might not lessen the curse."

Thallan didn't seem convinced. "Well, we don't have any other way to get rid of a heap of tamed dragons. Not unless you have your own massive stores of silvernix somewhere."

Riony shot Eslinde a look, and Eslinde returned it

with a subtle nod.

"No, we don't," the princess said. "But these are all details we can work out as we go. All we need to know for now is whether our goals are aligned. Whether our mission is one you want to join."

Thallan grumbled gruffly, but before he could speak, Jaym spoke over him. "Helping to save the world sounds good to me. It'll give me lots to write about."

"Getting to know our new friends better sounds pretty good to me, too." Zeina popped another nut between her lips in a slow, sensual way that made Riony gulp.

"We decide together." Thallan gave a long-suffering look toward the two youngest of his group.

They excused themselves to discuss the matter in private. The Rebel Riders marched their dragons along the chasm until they were out of earshot, but the conversation didn't take long.

Not even long enough for Riony to raise her own fears that maybe they shouldn't be bringing these people in.

Harrying dragonkeeps for fun, fighting other dragonriders, and considering killing dragons en masse ... These were people who lived by violence.

And Riony knew that sometimes violence was justified, but she didn't want it to become their first choice, their normal.

The riders returned with their answer. They were in.

Putting her fears aside, Riony aimed for optimism.

Plus, she wouldn't mind getting to know Zeina a bit more either.

Rider Zeina. Sparks. And she winked at me!

Their group returned to their dragons, and soon they were flying back over the mountains toward the sea, leading the Rebel Riders back to Eslindekeep.

The ground below moved strangely, and it took a while for Riony to work out what she was seeing. It could have been old ash, juddering and swirling in the winter winds. It could have been a landslide.

But the gray, undulating mass below, covering the landscape, was a horde of revenants.

Bigger again than the one that had chased them and Myrwa's people to the shrine.

Riony shivered.

Could they really get rid of the revenants? And what would they be willing to do to achieve that?

The revenants knew nothing but violence, and Riony wasn't sure whether the dragonlords and dragonriders were much different. Maybe violence was needed.

Maybe the Rebel Riders were just what they needed.

Riony didn't know exactly what good they might bring, whether they would help or hurt them, but she already knew they weren't the heroes she read about.

Nine

Being outside in the open left Kess on edge. She glanced at the sky every other second, between keeping her eyes on Riony and sharpening new bone knives.

After a week cooped up inside, with nothing but bickering between the Rebel Riders, Eslinde, and Riony's groups as winter rains hammered the ground above, the first day of sun seemed like a good reason for a day out.

Riony had stopped complaining about Kess shadowing her, which Kess figured was progress. As long as she wasn't going to be expelled from the group, as long as she could be left to do what she needed to do to keep Riony safe, Kess was happy. That was all she needed.

Or at least, that's what she told herself, as she watched Riony move through a sword training sequence with her massive crystal blade. *Unlit.* And Kess's chest felt like it was being squeezed between dragon claws.

Riony caught Kess tracking her movements and frowned at whatever she saw on her face. "If I only use it with the float magic on, I'm going to get soft."

Kess could only nod and watch the strength in each swing, the tension in Riony's arms and shoulders, the tight grip on the hilt, the twitch of Riony's lips and nose as she pushed through.

Heat flushed through Kess and sweat prickled over her neck where a lump had formed and refused to dislodge.

That sun is too bright today for winter clothing. It's just the heat. It's not how impossibly razing beautiful she is. Get a grip.

Kess had already moved off Griskin. His dark fur soaked in the sunlight, and he lay on his belly beside her, panting. Kess leaned her back against a cool block of stone.

Two dragons patrolled overhead, one of the riders—*Zeina, ugh*—who Kess wasn't sure she trusted, and Yensen, who had earned her trust by his unflinching loyalty to Eslinde during their escape.

The patrol shifts had been going well, and Kess had even flown a few on her own, after a little more instruction from Dashiel on landing safely.

No signs yet that the king and his search had narrowed down their location to Eslindekeep.

But it was decided that there wasn't a lot of use knowing

an attack was incoming if they couldn't get Dracuni away quickly or safely. Another few weeks of growth and she wouldn't fit through the gateways anymore.

Dracuni needed to learn how to fly. And despite the risk of leaving the base, that training couldn't be done underground.

The half-built walls of the keep made a perfect practice ground, and Dracuni was currently perched on a section beside Shiff, both flapping their wings, Dracuni carefully mimicking Shiff's movements. Dashiel and Vance stood on the unfinished wall as well, calling out instructions.

Eslinde lounged on Viska below, keeping the gold dragon's wing stretched out, so that when Dracuni jumped, and fell, there was a soft landing.

Kess was surprised that Riony wasn't staying closer beside Dracuni to keep her safe. But from the way Kess's eyes weren't the only ones on Riony as she moved through her display of strength with her massive sword, she figured Riony's message to them all was clear.

Aishena and Benjin also trained nearby, and a yelp of celebration from the boy cut the air. Aishena was down, if only for a second, and up again fast enough to put her brother on his back as he preened and paraded his win.

Even Lyrrin remained separate, sitting on her own to the side on a stacked pyramid of stone blocks, hunched over and working on something small in her hands as she often did.

Shadows broke the bright glare of sunshine as the two dragons on patrol came in to land. Time to swap for the next shift.

Norallei and Thallan were already bringing their dragons out of the base and waved a signal to the incoming riders as they took off.

Zeina and her aqua seasong dragon, Gleem, hit the ground first. Gleem had a Bovin between her teeth, the massive beast old and boney, but big enough to feed all the dragons for a while.

The warrior woman didn't seem happy with the quarry, though. She leaped to the ground, her face darkened with a scowl. She flicked her head toward her dragon who nodded in reply and moved off toward the underground entrance without her.

Kess wondered what that would be like, to have the mental connection and communication with a dragon that a bond brought.

When Yensen brought his dragon to a stop, Zeina marched up to him.

"Where were you? You were meant to remain patrolling above the keep while I went farther out to hunt and check on nearby enclaves. That's the plan you and your princess set up. You'd think you could follow it."

Yensen's long eyes narrowed, and in a flat voice, he replied, "I was following game to hunt. I apologize that I ended up following it too far."

Zeina gestured to the empty mouth and claws of Ambri.

"I didn't say it was a fruitful hunt," Yensen muttered.

Riony paused mid swing and strode across to Zeina's side. "What's going on?"

Zeina's body swayed toward Riony's as though drawn like a magnet, and her expression softened. "Thankfully nothing. Thankfully you all weren't ambushed while this royal lapdog here abandoned his post. I thought grayglim were meant to be reliable."

"Yensen is," Kess called over.

The grayglim caught her eye and gave her a grateful nod.

She added, "And we need more food. If he had a chance to hunt, it was good he took it."

Zeina scoffed, but her attention was off Yensen now and on Riony.

She lazily rested an arm on Riony's shoulder. "I think we should take him off the patrol roster. Do you want to replace him?"

Yensen rolled his eyes and guided Ambri away into the base.

Riony laughed nervously. "Oh, I don't know the first thing about flying."

Zeina's voice dropped lower. "I could teach you. I'd love to take you for a ride, whenever you like."

Riony's cheeks matched her hair. Her eyes flickered, a flashing glance over to Kess, who turned around to pat

Griskin and pretend not to be listening in. But it was hard not to. The semicircle of walls surrounded them like an amphitheater and all sound within carried.

Riony murmured, "Okay, so, you need to be careful how you phrase things around me. I have misread situations and been disappointed in the past."

Zeina's voice was a deep rustle of dried leaves. "I won't disappoint you. I could not disappoint you *right now*, if you like."

Moving away, Zeina trailed her arm off Riony's shoulder and tilted her head for Riony to follow as she disappeared into the base.

Kess shot a look at Aishena, who didn't seem concerned at all about Zeina's blatant flirting or the starstruck look Riony returned the Rebel Rider.

The Hjelzahn girl had finished her training and joined Dashiel on the wall beside Dracuni. A jolt of shock passed through Kess to see Aishena laughing at something Dashiel had said. Laughing? Kess didn't think the woman had more than one emotion.

Even Benjin, a few steps away, was staring open-mouthed at the sight.

Riony took a step to follow Zeina, and Kess's heart caught in her throat.

Then another figure came jogging out of the base entrance, a skip in her step as hazel hair tumbled around her neat and new delver's armor.

"Nisk? What are you doing here?" Riony met her with a tight hug.

Niskina pulled out of the hug and raised her eyebrows at Riony's still flushed cheeks.

"I got your message about moving the gateway, and the Rebel Riders actually being *the* Rebel Riders, and I was going to reply with a note, but thought I'd just come through and give you my report in person, since you've moved the gateway here."

"I'm pretty sure our note also said that the gateways could run out of charge and would need to be used less." Riony had sent their last message through when the gateway was still at the shrine, before they brought it to the base. It hadn't been used since then.

Niskina waved that away. "By then we had also moved the depths gateway up into the undercity. I was getting ready to start using it all the time, setting up trade with the shrine enclaves. I suppose we're going to have to use the one down the hill instead now. But it is good to know rather than find out."

"And it is good to see you, but this will have to be the last time," Riony said.

Kess hoped so. Niskina still looked at her as though she were the vilest scum to walk the earth. Kess knew enough of her own guilt. She didn't need another reminder.

"Of course." Niskina nodded distractedly and craned her neck, taking in everyone there and waving to the others.

"So, where are they? I saw Zeina on my way out, and oh my stars, *Riony*! But where is *he*?"

Riony chuckled and pointed to the distant end of the empty field allocated to the dragonkeep, where Kess had sent Jaym to hunt his pocket-hawk, far away from Riony. He cut a fine, heroic silhouette in the distance, and Niskina sighed melodramatically.

"I know we're not using the gateways again now except for emergencies. But wanting to sleep with a Rebel Rider counts as an emergency, right?" Niskina looked longingly toward Rider Jaym.

"I would scold you but I'm feeling a very high level of emergency myself." Riony also had her eyes locked on the entrance to the base.

From it, the Alderkin stepped out into the light as well, squinting at the sun.

"Zeina?" Niskina pointed to Riony's still red cheeks. "Were you ... did I interrupt something?"

"Hopefully something that can be picked up again soon." Riony shook herself and focused on Niskina. "Come on, let us know what you came to say."

Niskina gave Riony a long knowing smile. "Only a couple of things to report. We've been hearing rumors of some dragonlords leaving Elundrae entirely, by ship."

"Leaving?" Aishena stepped in to join them. There was a hard edge to her voice. "Do we know which families?"

The Alderkin had reached them now too, standing

a little to the side to listen. Eslinde, still on Viska, had propped herself up to give the report her attention as well. Even Jaym meandered back their way. Only Lyrrin remained focused on her own activity.

Kess climbed back onto Griskin, moving to intercept Jaym before he brought his little bird close to Riony again.

"No. We only know the 'rats from a sinking ship' impression that the stories are giving." Niskina grimaced. "And there's worse news. A couple of the gateways, from shrines that we haven't taken Dracuni to for the longest, have gone dark."

Riony frowned deeply and lifted her sword over her shoulder to sheath it. "So soon? I thought they would last longer. How is the gateway in the depths still working but the others are running out of charge already?"

After a few shared glances between the Alderkin, Shael spoke up. "It's the living dead. When they move around the shrines, they drain the magic faster through the barrier protection magic. This happened to us as well during the war. Anywhere the living dead were nearby, magic disappeared for us, too fast, once the unicorns were gone."

"What can we do?" Riony asked.

"It's too much of a risk taking Dracuni through to any of the shrines to recharge them now," Aishena said.

"I can send out messages," Niskina offered. "Get any communities at risk of losing their protection to move along to enclaves where Dracuni has been more often and more recently."

"Have you heard from Myrwa? Are they okay?" Riony's voice was strained with worry.

Kess lingered behind her for a moment, wishing she could protect Riony from even the hurt of such worry.

"They're fine. All good for now. I did invite them to the undercity to keep everyone safe there, but Kellae said she wasn't letting her brother and baby grow up underground. None of them wanted to."

Riony's shoulders drooped. "Yeah, I get that."

"It's not so bad," Niskina said. "You could all come and join us. Even in the last week, we've been able to organize so much. The delvers have taken me back in and I'm also working with other groups. But having you there could help so much. And I'd love to have you with me. Well ... not all of you."

Niskina met Kess's eyes. Kess turned away.

Riony's voice followed Kess as she moved away from the conversation. "I'd love to, but I think we're safer here, especially with Dracuni. At least there's only a handful of people I have to keep an eye on here, rather than the entire undercity."

Am I still one of the people she needs to keep an eye on?

Kess tried to swallow the feeling away, but it felt stuck in her dry throat.

Stalking Griskin forward, Kess stepped into Jaym's path. He greeted her with a charming smile and stroked a finger down his hawk's neck. It cheeped, and Kess smiled softly at it. The sleek dark-eyed bird of prey was beautiful.

Jaym angled to watch the conversation continuing behind them.

"Who's the newcomer?" he asked.

"An ally," Kess replied. "From the undercity. To where she's returning soon."

He watched Niskina with smiling eyes, especially when she noticed he'd come closer and was fluttering long lashes his way. "Such interesting allies you have."

Niskina stepped away then, giving Jaym one last long, lingering glance before leaving. But his attention had turned to Dracuni.

"This one still can't fly? Rather strange for its age."

"Is it?" Kess sidestepped Griskin to put herself between Jaym and the unidragon.

He moved as well, keeping assessing eyes on Dracuni. "What breed is she? I haven't seen anything like her before."

"She's wild born." Kess remembered Eslinde saying she wasn't as good at lying as she thought she was, so she tried to keep to the truth, a truth that wouldn't raise any further suspicions. "No idea of the father. A seasong mother, but one that wasn't typical either. So we don't know."

"Hmm. A mystery then." Jaym shrugged, then moved as though to join Riony and Aishena where they chatted behind Kess.

"No. Take that bird of yours away. I told you before

to keep your distance."

Jaym laughed and scratched the bird's cheeks and it leaned into his fingers. "But why? My little hawk? How could anyone be frightened of her?"

Kess growled. "It doesn't matter. What matters is that you keep it away from Riony or you'll lose the arm you use to perch your bird."

Only smiling wider, Jaym lifted his free hand in surrender. "Yes, Mestra!"

He offered a mocking salute, then jogged off toward the base entrance.

"It's inspiring, you know," a soft voice murmured from Kess's side.

She turned to find Dashiel there, smiling with closed lips and a slight sadness to their eyes.

"What is?"

Dashiel leaned in and whispered, "How protective you are of her."

They indicated Riony with their eyes.

"It's what she deserves. The least she deserves."

Kess had spoken with Dashiel about how she and Riony knew each other a couple of nights ago during a quiet moment. Dashiel had broached the subject by asking which of the people in their life now were ones who wanted to kill Kess. Just so they could be prepared.

Kess explained she couldn't be sure but did explain the different relationships with each of them.

Staring across at Riony now, Dashiel sighed. "You know ... I do like you, Kess."

Kess choked on her words. "Like me? Like ... how like?"

Dashiel shrugged, smile growing. Their voice remained low. "But I really didn't realize the level of competition I was up against. I can't compete with her."

Opening her mouth, Kess found she didn't know what to say. Because no, nobody, in Kess's eyes, could match Riony. She was all Kess could think of, all she dreamed of, all she wanted to look at, all she wanted ... All she wanted.

Dashiel's lips twisted up cheekily. "Maybe I'll compete with you for Riony."

Kess scoffed. "You're senseless if you think I have any part in that contest. No, but you would be up against Rider Zeina. And maybe Aishena. Good luck."

"Aishena Hjelzahn." Dashiel turned glittering eyes toward the grayglim woman. "Impressive rivals indeed. Do you think I'd have a chance?"

Kess smirked, but before she could reply, a strange, tortured roar split the air.

Dracuni lifted her head high, her cry piercing the air. Then Shiff echoed her.

Kess turned Griskin toward them, but there was no sign of their distress. Nothing attacked them, there was no ambush, no invaders.

"Dracuni?" Riony bellowed, racing toward the unidragon.

Dracuni leaped down from the wall recklessly, the ground cracking beneath her where she landed. Her body swayed strangely as she stalked across the field.

Shiff followed, gliding down and prowling the same direction.

Viska remained motionless, glittering gold like a statue.

Eslinde, in Viska's saddle, yelled, "I don't know what happened."

"Shiff? What is it?" Dashiel called out. "She's not replying. She feels so ... I don't know, defensive?"

Riony chased to catch up with the smaller dragons. "Dracuni isn't responding either. What are they doing?"

Both dragons growled, eyes wild and furious.

Ahead of them, right in line of their path, Lyrrin sat on her stack of stones, eyes wide and shaking.

Ten

Lyrrin wanted to toss the stupid crystal down from the stack of stones she was sitting on and shatter it on the ground.

If it was to work for you, it would sing to you.

Lyrrin grunted through gritted teeth. The ten-stroke rune did sing to her. At least a little. Maybe she just wasn't listening hard enough.

She just had to keep trying, and then she could show the Alderkin that she was like them. But she'd been sitting under the blazing sun, and although the air was crisp, the heat had built up under the heavy hood she wore.

She tossed it back, glaring out across the field. Niskina was there, and as much as it was nice to see her, Lyrrin couldn't offer more than a frustrated wave. Riony and the others were all busy flirting with each other like idiots. Lyrrin didn't understand why all of them had been so silly lately.

Even the rustle of bantam ferrets scurrying around in the weedy brush that poked out between paving and unfinished foundations didn't brighten Lyrrin's mood.

Dracuni still hadn't learned to fly either, so at least Lyrrin wasn't the only one failing.

No. I'm not failing today.

It took countless more attempts before Lyrrin traced down the last curved line of the rune, and the crystal lit up in a deep green.

She was about to leap down from her perch and run to show everyone what she'd done—whatever it was—when Dracuni and Shiff roared and charged toward her, and everyone was yelling.

And the Alderkin's eyes all turned toward Lyrrin.

"The dragon summoning rune, she's activated it!" Shael said.

Lyrrin gasped, scrubbing her trembling fingers speedily across the rune surface, trying to remember the sequence she'd just worked out to deactivate the magic again.

It took three tries as Dracuni and Shiff breathed down on her, teeth bared, before the glow of magic went out.

Everyone stared at her. But at least they were all okay. At least she'd deactivated it before anything bad had happened.

Neither young dragon seemed ready to harm her, but

they were drawn in, compelled, fierce with determination. Lyrrin continued to shake.

A dragon summoning rune? What did that even mean? What were the dragons going to do?

Only Dracuni and Shiff had come toward her. Viska remained where she was, with Eslinde seated on top.

Lyrrin opened her mouth to apologize, to ask the Alderkin what she'd just done, but another roaring howl carried through the air.

One that didn't come from their dragons nearby. Not from any of the dragons within the base. Not from the two on patrol, high above.

Another dragon swooped in, drawn in, screaming and furious.

A dusky purple etherdart. The same dragon that had filled Lyrrin's nightmares for weeks as Kife and Kess relentlessly pursued them from its saddle.

"Sparks, no!" Riony screamed, rushing to Dracuni's side.

"There's no rider on him!" Kess circled Griskin around, out of the path of the incoming beast.

"As much of a relief as that is, I still never wanted to see that dragon again and it doesn't exactly look friendly."

The purple dragon scanned across the ground and all the targets before him. Then like an arrow through the air, he shot toward Viska.

"Watch out!" Vance scrambled down the half-formed

wall, racing for his dragon.

Shiff moved to follow, but eyeing the full-grown dragons again, backed up and hid behind an outcrop of wall.

Eslinde twisted in the saddle, reaching to control the gold dragon, but Kife's etherdart was already upon them.

The purple crashed down over Viska's head, pinning her to the ground beneath long talons. Dusky wings swept and fluttered, keeping his balance as he clawed viciously against the tamed dragon's skull.

One of his wingtips swiped across Viska's back, catching Eslinde in its path and flinging her off the saddle and across the field. She screamed through the air. The sound cut off as she thumped to the ground.

Lyrrin cried out in her stead. Hands on the crystals at her belt, she moved to help, but Dracuni, herself again, blocked her path, keeping her away from the wild dragon attacking Viska.

Caught between Viska and Eslinde, Vance growled almost as loud as the dragons, then ran for Lyrrin's mother.

Kife's etherdart howled and grumbled, claws raking into golden scales, and then leaning down to close sharp teeth around Viska's forehead. The tamed dragon whimpered and twitched, unable to defend herself.

Purple light streaked through the field as Riony charged in, sword glowing bright.

Lashing his head back, a spray of blood followed the

etherdart's clenched snout. Within its teeth was a sharp spike of metal. The taming stake.

Viska slumped. Blood poured from the open wound on her forehead.

The purple dragon spat the spike, and it clattered on the ground, a streak of crimson on the gray stone.

"Get away from her!" Riony bellowed, swinging her sword warningly through the air at the wild dragon.

Hissing, the purple turned all his attention to her. The spark of flame glittered between the dragon's teeth.

Lyrrin whimpered, fighting against Dracuni who had her hood grasped in a claw. Viska, Eslinde, Riony ... was her mistake going to cost all of them?

She couldn't throw far enough to get any of her crystals there to help.

The dragon's mouth opened, and Riony was knocked sideways by the heavy flank of a leaping wolf.

Kess and Griskin stood in Riony's place, glaring wordlessly up into the dragon's fiery maw.

"Kess!" Riony spat from where she lay sprawled across to the side, being dragged farther out of fireball range by Aishena.

Benjin bounded on his toes beside them, as though ready to race in too, but a sharp word from his sister kept him back.

Kess lifted her chin, daring. "I watched you hatch and I freed you. Don't make me your enemy."

The purple's mouth slammed closed again, eyes narrowing over Kess. And then Kess gasped, clutching at her head and slumping over Griskin.

"Get out of the way," Dashiel yelled. "The patrol is coming in!"

Thallan and Norallei, on their bronze and white dragons, were diving down from the clouds above. And from the entrance to the base, Zeina, on Gleem, Jaym on his red dragon, and Samor on his flamesong rushed out.

The purple's head whipped around to take in his enemies, then he bellowed out an earth-shaking roar. Hot air blasted over Kess and Griskin, gusting their hair and fur. The dragon spun in place, tail flicking out. It struck Kess across the chest, sending her off the wolf and rolling across the ground.

The purple etherdart took off, swirling the dust behind it, speeding away from the riders coming in.

Riony was back on her feet, breathing heavily as she watched the purple flee for a few seconds before turning her eyes toward Lyrrin. There was so much disappointment in her expression it made Lyrrin crumble.

Then Riony was in action again.

She took a few steps toward Kess. "Are you—"

"Fine ... Winded ..." Kess wheezed as she lifted herself on her elbows.

Griskin rushed to her. He licked her face, whining.

"Eslinde?" Riony yelled across the field.

Lyrrin couldn't see where her mother had fallen, behind stacks of rusted steel. She held her breath.

"I've got her," Vance called back. "She's coming around."

Dracuni had let Lyrrin go, but she couldn't seem to get her feet to work.

Her eyes were on the golden dragon, lying with the hole in her head, blood still tricking out. Dashiel was beside her, pressing their hands to the wound.

"Viska's still alive. But won't be for long," the pain in their voice was eye-watering.

Aishena rushed over beside them, lending her help to stem the bleeding. Shiff emerged from her hiding spot and scampered worriedly at Dashiel's side.

With two matching *thwumps*, Thallan and Norallei landed beside the other Rebel Riders.

"What happened?" Thallan asked, eyeing the wounded dragon. "We had our eyes on the horizon, but that dragon came out of the nearby woods, got to you before we could. Was it some kind of ambush?"

"It was something," Riony growled, stalking up to the Alderkin. "What was that? A dragon summoning rune?"

Yrik set his face firm and didn't reply.

Shael stepped between them, her icy-blue hair shimmering in the sunlight. "It's magic only meant for use in protecting unicorns."

Riony swung her arm in the direction the purple

dragon fled. "Then why did it send that dragon into a dragon murdering rage?"

Shael pressed her hands together before her face, then opened them palm outward. "I do not know. It is only meant to summon nearby dragons to a location, when a unicorn was under threat, so they could protect it."

Benjin gave the sky a thoughtful look. "That's what happened at the first taming, isn't it? Why a dragon was there, after Yeonard Draekhan attacked the unicorn?"

Shael bowed her head silently.

"Is that why Gleem, Hux, and Shani just went over all strange?" Zeina stroked her dragon's neck.

"Our steeds had no change," Thallan said from the back of the bronze dragon.

Priyune flicked a withering look his way. "It has no effect on tamed dragons, they have no mind to compel."

"Dracuni says she felt like she had to go to the source of the call, that she couldn't fight it. It scared her to lose control like that," Riony said.

"It should not have happened. The child shouldn't have invoked the magic," Yrik muttered.

Lyrrin's eyes filled with hot tears.

Riony pointed her finger aggressively toward the Alderkin. "Don't you dare blame this on her. Aren't you supposed to be teaching her? You wouldn't even tell her what the stone did."

Lyrrin held the unlit crystal so tight that it bit into her

palm. If she'd known, would she have kept trying, just to prove she could?

I just wanted to show them I could do it, that the crystals sang to me too. But if they'd told me, if they shared it with me because I'm Alderkin like them, I would have had nothing to prove.

And now Viska was mortally injured and Lyrrin's mother hurt.

Yrik caught her eye, the sapphire hue shared between them, then he looked down at his feet.

"Viska's fading," Dashiel's voice broke.

Their hands were slick with crimson. The wounds all around Viska's forehead were too large for them to hold together.

Looking to Riony, Dashiel pleaded, "Is there anything we can do for her?"

Dracuni sidestepped closer and closer to Viska, lilac eyes tilted in worry.

Riony dropped her sword and jogged over beside the unidragon. "No. I *know*. But ..."

Lyrrin didn't need to hear Dracuni's mind-speak to understand. Dracuni wanted to help. Dracuni always wanted to help.

But all the Rebel Riders were watching.

Still lying on her back, Kess struggled up into a sitting position. Her voice came out broken and husky, "No. Eslinde ..."

"It sounds like Eslinde's okay. And maybe Viska will get through this on her own?" Riony offered, her voice high and desperate.

Dashiel growled, "She has a gaping hole in her brain, and she's almost gone."

Dracuni snorted at Riony, then pushed past her to stand beside Viska. The gold dragon's head was half as big as the smaller dragon, and broken scales were scattered around the ground between splatters of blood.

Riony cursed under her breath and ran back to grab her sword. She muttered, "And of course all our new witnesses are on their dragons right now too."

Lyrrin took in the scene, as Aishena and Benjin moved in beside Riony. Kess was clawing her way back up onto Griskin.

Finding her feet again, Lyrrin rushed over to her sister's side. She pulled a flash crystal from her belt, ready just in case. She wondered about throwing it then and there, hiding what the riders were about to see. But she couldn't explain that, couldn't explain how Viska would magically be healed afterward.

Thallan squinted at the scene before him. "What's going on? What's your dragon doing?"

Riony cricked her neck. "Something that we're not going to have any issue from you about, agreed?"

Dracuni lifted a talon and raked it over the back of her other hand. She raised it to press against Viska's cheek.

Hobbling toward them, supported by Vance, Eslinde gasped. "No, wait!"

Then Viska glowed. Dracuni's healing blood absorbed into her and flushed through her like moonlight spilling between clouds, shining out through her wounds and the gaps of her scales.

And a swirling shadow drifted from the skies, floating down over the golden dragon. She stirred.

Lyrrin swallowed. Now they had a newly wild dragon at their backs, and five awestruck riders facing them.

Five more people who knew about Dracuni's blood.

ELEVEN

Riony and her companions formed a line between the newly untamed gold dragon and the Rebel Riders who were staring aghast at what they'd just witnessed.

"I'm sorry," Lyrrin whispered.

Riony bumped an elbow against her sister's shoulder. "It's not your fault, you couldn't have known."

Also sorry, Dracuni thought, slinking up behind Riony.

"It's okay. You did what you had to, to save Viska. Now we just have to see what this lot think of it." Riony tightened her grip on the hilt of her sword and addressed the riders. "Everyone's going to be calm and make good decisions about this, right?"

If the five riders on their dragons chose to attack them

then and there, Riony didn't like their odds. But Aishena and Benjin stood prepared to fight, and Lyrrin had a flash crystal ready.

Their presence settled Riony. With them at her side, she felt as though she could face anything, and even having Kess lurking at her shoulder with a throwing knife in each hand didn't detract from that.

Riony swallowed, as she felt the shocking realization that Kess's presence actually added to her sense of comfort and confidence.

She took my place in front of Kife's dragon.

For all Kess's promises and words, for all her little shows of loyalty, Riony still hadn't truly believed that Kess had meant it. That she wasn't still a selfish little gremlin plotting foul deeds.

But that moment with Kife's dragon was life or death. Kess had, without hesitation, put herself and Griskin in Riony's place when a fiery death was the likely outcome.

That wasn't some game or manipulation.

Kess had been ready to die to protect Riony.

What do I sparking do with that?

Kess still breathed unevenly and rubbed at the place on her chest where the tail had struck.

Under the heat of the sun and the crisp winter breeze, Riony felt feverish. She shook off all the confusing thoughts and feelings of that revelation and focused on the situation before her.

Still, as she glared up at the Rebel Riders, it made a world of difference knowing—*really* knowing—that Kess's blades were meant for her enemies and not for her.

Thallan stared back at Riony, taking his time in his own thoughts, but no doubt very different ones.

Finally, he said, "Your dragon bleeds silvernix?"

"So what if she does?" There was no point denying it with the way Viska had been magically healed in clear sight. "Do I need to also see what you bleed?"

The golden dragon raised herself gingerly off the ground, her head swaying.

Vance and Dashiel closed in on her cautiously, speaking to her in soft words and trying to keep the dragon's attention. But the snap of terse words between Riony and Thallan caused Viska's yellow eyes to narrow on them. She growled wildly.

Eslinde leaned heavily against a block of stone to the side. "Inside, all of you! You're going to overwhelm Viska."

Dracuni nudged Riony on the shoulder. ***She's right. Viska knows those two, but she's really confused. She needs space.***

Riony's nose twitched, and she gestured to the riders. "You first."

Zeina's expression was intense, but she gave Riony a single nod and led the way, in quiet conversation with her aqua seasong.

The four other riders followed after only a short

hesitation and a barked command from Thallan.

Once the riders and their dragons had disappeared into the entrance, Riony gestured for her friends and the Alderkin to follow.

Lyrrin hung back, her eyes on Eslinde.

"I'm fine, really." Eslinde offered a smile with a smudge of blood on her lip. "Go inside with your sister."

The princess tilted her head as she looked to Riony.

Leave Lyrrin outside with a newly re-wilded dragon or bring her in with me to face people who might want to kill us for Dracuni?

Riony wasn't sure either which was the best option, but she nodded to Eslinde and pulled her sister along with her.

Benjin glanced back at Viska and the Zarram siblings before stepping into the tunnel. "Why did he do that? Why did Kife's dragon pull Viska's stake out?"

"Is it because he was summoned?" Lyrrin asked in a small voice.

She still held the summoning crystal tight in one hand and flash stone in the other, as though her hands had fused closed around them.

The Alderkin shared glances and then shrugs that were some of the more human motions Riony had seen them make.

Yrik caught up to Lyrrin in a few long strides and spoke with his head slightly bowed. "The summoning magic lured the purple dragon in, but it wasn't the cause of the

violence. The dragon chose that himself."

Lyrrin turned wide eyes up toward him. "Are you sure? None of the other wild dragons have wanted to pull other dragon's stakes out."

"Maybe because none of those other wild dragons have experienced being tamed before themselves," Aishena said thoughtfully.

"You think he was trying to help? But he was so violent." Lyrrin's voice trembled.

A cold stone of old pain shifted heavily inside of Riony. "Maybe he didn't know whether pulling the stake out would cure or kill Viska, but maybe it didn't matter. Maybe he thought even death was preferable to enslavement."

Silence followed them the rest of the way into the base. They reached the stables where the riders were settling their dragons in. The purple glow of Riony's sword merged with the orange light of the torches crackling along the walls.

There should have been two dragons still on patrol, but with Kife's etherdart still out there and Viska currently a liability, nobody seemed willing to take their dragons up again right now.

Yensen came in after them. His silky hair was disheveled, awoken from a rest after his night, then morning shift. "What happened?"

Riony gave him a quick rundown, and with a nod, he rushed off to check on Eslinde.

Thallan guided his bronze dragon into a stall and left it

there, sitting dully. "You can put that giant sword of yours away, girl. We aren't going to fight you for your dragon."

Riony deactivated the rune but kept the sword in her hands.

Thallan shook his head roughly. "But don't think we aren't annoyed you kept this from us. All the bickering about what we could do, how we were going to untame enough dragons instead of killing them, while there you were sitting on the means to do what needs to be done."

Is that what I am? The means to an end? Dracuni sat down close to Riony, her tail tucked tightly around her.

No, Riony thought firmly.

Then to Thallan, she asked, "If our roles were reversed, and you had Dracuni, would you have told us?"

Thallan's mouth opened, then closed. He lifted his chin and huffed. "We'll never know, I suppose."

Jaym strolled over, sighing as he looked over Dracuni. "All that silvernix ..."

"Back it up," Riony snapped.

Jaym froze, grinned, and took two large steps back. His pocket-hawk was currently nowhere in sight, and Riony hoped it stayed that way.

He sighed audibly. "It's just incredible, though! And she's alive, hasn't withered away like the unicorns in captivity did. You've got all the silvernix you could ever want."

"She's not in captivity and no, we haven't. Dracuni's

blood is her own. How she uses it and when is up to her. She belongs to herself."

Samor reached a hand up to stroke the cheek of his black and gold flamesong. "As she should."

Jaym shrugged, which caused a smoky huff of disapproval from his dragon, followed by a flurry of apologies from Jaym.

Zeina leaned up against Gleem's aqua scales. "I suppose I'd feel the same way if it were Gleem with the precious blood."

Thallan and Norallei seemed less convinced. The leader and his partner stood shoulder to shoulder, the Taen woman on edge like a petite bodyguard at his side.

Glancing back, almost guiltily at his tamed dragon, Thallan scoffed. "It's one thing to look after your steeds, but it's another to put the feelings of a wild beast ahead of the salvation of our world."

"Using the resource is worth thinking about," Norallei added. "We need all the help we can get."

"And instead, we're losing dragons." Thallan gestured toward the exit. "If you had the silvernix, you should have put Viska's stake back in too. Now she's gone."

Dracuni tossed her snout up and huffed. *Viska isn't gone. She's waking up, for the first time since she was a baby. She's confused and hurt. But she recognizes the two who raised her.*

Riony translated that along, and the three riders with

wild dragons were in instant agreement. Their own dragons were agitated, eager, and worried, huddled together in silent communication.

Kess stepped Griskin forward to be beside Riony rather than behind. "Vance and Dashiel had spoken a number of times about wanting to untame Viska. I'm sure this isn't how they wanted it to happen, but I don't know if anyone would have been willing to put the spike back in again."

"We'll see how that plays out when those riders out there get roasted," Thallan scoffed.

Through the huge, arched doorway, Eslinde limped in, supported by Yensen. She waved away any concern. "Nobody has been roasted yet. If anyone can get Viska under control again, it's the Zarrams."

"What are we even doing here? Why did you bring us in, when you have all these resources"—Thallan flung one arm toward Dracuni and another toward the Alderkin—"but refuse to share them, refuse to even use them yourself."

A deep, angry heat rose within Riony, scorching her mouth dry. "Use them for what? Going out and waging war on the king and the curse and every other dragonrider in the land? There are times for fighting back and times for protecting what's important. I'm just trying to protect what we have."

In a low, mocking voice, Jaym said, "And you suggested we were the ones acting like dragonlords."

Eslinde's gaze was painfully disappointed. "For how

long? How long can we look after only what is important to us when the rest of the world burns?"

I could ... if it would help everyone—

"No!" Riony snapped.

Her head swirled with visions of Dracuni bleeding, stuck with knives, tied to bottles and drained. All for the cause. All to save a world and the dragon enslaving people in it who weren't doing a thing to save themselves.

Thallan watched her for a long moment, then in a voice like one would use to calm a wild animal, he said, "I'm not going to push you, because I can see that trying to use Dracuni against her will is a sure way to set you against us, and we don't want that."

Thallan sounded terrifically begrudging on that point. Zeina, however, nodded earnestly.

"So we aren't using Dracuni, but what if there was another one?" Jaym asked.

Riony squinted in confusion. "Another what?"

He waved a hand in Dracuni's direction. "Unicorn ... dragon thing? How did you come across this one, anyway?"

Pushing away her anger, Riony said, "I didn't just come across her. She was changed, in her egg, by silvernix."

"That's what you did?" Kess coughed a harsh laugh. Then looking at the ceiling, she muttered in barely a whisper, "Typical sympathetic fool."

Between Riony and Aishena, they explained the situation with the broken dragon eggs.

Dracuni's feelings washing through to Riony had an edge of heartbreak. She knew the story already, but it was never a fun one to recount. For Dracuni to hear again about her dead siblings. About her mother's rejection.

"I only ended up keeping Dracuni, and finding out about her blood, because her own mother attacked and disowned her because she was different," Riony concluded.

At her side, Kess turned her face away, hiding it behind her hair, and Griskin stepped back.

Having listened with great interest, Thallan asked, "If you made her, couldn't we make more?"

More like me? Dracuni blinked her large eyes.

Riony threw her hand up in the air. "Oh, there's a good idea. We've got one creature that the Dragon King would pursue us to the ends of the earth for. Why don't we have more of those? That's got to be the answer!"

Eslinde, however, perked up from where she leaned heavily against Yensen. "No, no, it might be worth considering."

Riony gaped. "Is it? How fair is that for the creatures you create? I didn't mean for this to happen to Dracuni, for her very blood to be something people would hunt her for, would kill for."

The Alderkin had moved forward into the conversation, circling around where Dracuni sat.

Priyune spoke with the cadence of a poet. "How can it be right to create a life knowing that is the fate you've given

it? That it will be seen only as a resource to be coveted?"

Shael tutted. "Seems like the very way humans ended up where they are currently."

Eslinde tilted her head. "Cruel as it may seem, having more living creatures with silvernix blood is an opportunity we can't ignore."

Aishena leaned in, speaking just for Riony. "It has its issues, but if there were more unidragons, smaller ones, that the Dragon King didn't know about, we could keep the shrines activated without risking Dracuni."

Riony's chest heaved. All she had done and suffered to protect Dracuni seemed to crash over her at once, a weight set against every life she'd tried to save and improve by giving them shelter at those shrines. Shrines that would soon have no magic left to keep them safe.

She only wanted to protect people, protect lives. Her shoulders slumped.

She didn't know what to do.

Thallan, however, spoke with a confidence as though he had already made his plans. "One of our other groups who keep to the west have eggs at the moment. They've been focused on trying to breed more dragons into our cause. I'm sure they could spare one for us to try."

"It's worth trying," Eslinde said. "At least then we'll know if the process is repeatable and can plan accordingly."

"It won't be a long trip to collect an egg," Zeina said, like a peace offering. "We can also gather the food we need along the way to bring back as well."

At Riony's shoulder, Aishena whispered, "You could go with them again, make sure they aren't plotting against us. We can keep Dracuni safe here."

Riony ran a hand down her face. She pictured Myrwa, and Kellae, and the baby Riony had helped bring into the world. If they could create even one more unidragon, who could keep the magic of the shrines alive a little longer, wasn't that worth it?

Mouth dry, Riony nodded her agreement. Although the way the others were already planning the journey, she wasn't sure they needed it. Eslinde and the Rebel Riders moved away to the meeting room, with Lyrrin chasing after, checking on her mother after the fall she had.

The Alderkin drifted away together, and Aishena and Benjin followed.

Kess hovered for a moment. She turned to Riony as though about to say something. Riony's own mouth opened, words of thanks for what Kess had done sticking in her throat. A raw graze marred Kess's cheek below the constellation of dark spots and the shadows of bruising spread on her jaw.

Anything Riony had meant to say came out as a rough grunt.

Kess flinched, barely perceptibly, nodded once, and left.

Riony dropped down onto her haunches and leaned her forehead into Dracuni's side. "Why has everything become so hard?"

Dracuni didn't answer, but the emotions she shared with Riony were laden with sadness.

"Because you're trying to do everything yourself to keep everyone safe."

The voice startled Riony, who thought she was alone except the dragons. She looked up to see Yensen there.

Razing, sneaky grayglim.

"How quickly everything turned dangerous today. I wasn't even there ..." Yensen's gaze went toward where Eslinde had gone, and his hands clenched into fists. "And it wasn't even a trained dragon. Just some wild beast causing chaos. What if it had been one of the Dragon King's riders?"

Riony sighed and stood back up. "Believe me, I thought it was when I first saw it and all of those what-ifs are still burning holes in my head."

Yensen walked by the stalls with the tamed dragons and watched the untamed ones moving freely together farther down the stables. "Such as, what if you were gone, and those of us remaining here were besieged, trapped with Dracuni?"

"That's what the gateway is here for."

Yensen strode to Riony's side, his mouth and eyes strained with worry. "But what if there's no one here who knows how to open it? I want you to teach me how. If the rest of you are gone on some mission, I want a way to keep everyone safe here too. To keep Eslinde safe."

Riony swallowed, shaken at seeing the stoic grayglim expressing emotion. "It won't happen. We'll make sure there's always someone here who can use the gateway."

Another layer to the hay, lamb, wolf, farmer riddle. A lamb that knows the gateway rune. Riony's head hurt.

"It would be easier if more of us knew how to do it. It would be safer. Teach me."

"I can't. That's not my knowledge to share." Now that the Alderkin were with them, and what Lyrrin had told her about them and her father, it didn't seem right to be sharing something that wasn't hers.

Yensen laughed bitterly. "The Alderkin aren't going to teach me. They are as closed off and unsharing as the tales always said."

After the events of the morning, Riony couldn't argue. But keeping the shrine rune secret was about more than just respect to the Alderkin. It was about keeping the way of fleeing with Dracuni safe among Riony and those she trusted.

She said, "We haven't even shared the gateway rune with our friends living at the shrines."

Yensen's eyes narrowed and he looked over Riony in a way that made her want to shrivel away to nothing.

"I feel as though if you truly cared for them, you would have, as if you truly cared for Eslinde. Keeping that knowledge secret is only leaving all of us in danger."

TWELVE

The aqua dragon cut to the right so swiftly Riony lifted from the saddle. She hung in the air, her brain sending desperate signals to her body to *grab something, grab on to something now before you fall to your death!*

A strong arm snaked around her middle, pulling her back into the seat. Zeina leaned in, pressing up close to Riony's back and speaking into her ear.

"I've got you. Don't panic."

"Who's panicking?" Riony replied in a high, panicked voice.

The rushing air whipped her hair around her face as they rose higher into the clouds at a blistering pace. The flickers of red around her flight goggles looked like licks of flame.

While Gleem wove and spun in the air, nearby Samor flew his immense flamesong dragon. Aishena and Kess rode with him, and Thallan was on his bronze dragon along with Norallei. Both glided calmly through the smoke-tinted sky on their way back to Eslindekeep.

Their mission had been surprisingly quick and easy. Half a day's flight out to find the other Rebel Rider group, a short conversation in which Thallan convinced them to relinquish one of their soon-to-hatch eggs, and some hunting on the way home. A refreshing lack of betrayal or infighting.

Riony was pleased.

The hardest part had been leaving Eslindekeep to start with. Kife's purple dragon had remained hanging around and ambushed Thallan's tamed dragon on their way out.

They'd left it behind after a short chase, but there were worries that it would be there waiting for them again when they returned. They were going to have to be more careful with their tamed dragons.

At least Jaym had stayed behind with his wild dragon to do patrols. Viska still wasn't allowing a rider but wasn't showing signs of aggression and had given in to pleas to move inside.

The second hardest part of the trip was when Zeina convinced Riony to fly up front.

A growl rumbled through the aqua dragon's neck and through Riony.

"I don't think your dragon likes me!" Riony yelled over her shoulder.

Through the layers of armor between the two of them, Riony felt Zeina chuckle.

"She likes you just fine. Just relax. Gleem knows what she's doing."

"But to counter that, I *don't* know what I'm doing."

"You're doing fine. Gleem's not some tamed dragon who's going to drop out of the sky if you stop giving her direction. You just need to get used to being in the rider's seat. So you can ride Dracuni one day, if she ever gets off the ground."

They dove then, shooting down in a way that felt like the whole world was coming up to smack Riony in the face. She yelped, and Gleem rumbled again.

She's doing this on purpose!

The way Zeina pulled Riony in closer, she wondered if they both were, and she flushed hot all over in a way that warded off all the chill of the winter flight.

Thanks to the dragon summoning rune, she hadn't managed to follow Zeina that day to find out just how not-disappointed she might have been.

And as much as she wanted to know, Riony had to admit to herself she was palm-sweatingly nervous about the entire situation.

Zeina was a *Rebel Rider*, and stories or not, Riony could

easily believe the audacious woman had known plenty of romantic encounters.

While Riony's only experience came down to a few fumbling kisses. One with a girl in the village she'd grown up in after leaving Heithorn estate, another with a young man in the undercity—just in case, but no—and her first kiss. The one with Kess, that had somehow been so terrible it left everyone in tears.

But 'so terrible it left everyone in tears' perfectly described most of Riony and Kess's relationship.

At least until everything had changed. Riony wasn't sure what their relationship was now, what she wanted it to be, or if she could ever get over all of the *terrible* and *tears* of their past.

Riony glanced across to where Kess rode on the black and gold dragon nearby, and Kess was already looking back. Riony turned away.

The way Kess had watched her recently felt ... different. Lyrrin's voice reentered her head, saying *I think she likes you.*

Riony shivered. *That selfish gremlin only likes whatever gets her closer to what she wants.*

Riony just didn't know anymore what that was.

Gleem curved beneath her, angling up as though ready to loop around entirely upside down.

Riony cried, "You do know this is only the third time I've ever been in the sky?"

Zeina leaned back a little. "Really? I would have thought ..."

She clicked her tongue and Gleem promptly evened out, coming back up into a soothingly smooth glide.

"Sorry, the way you were taking it, I thought you'd been up more. It took me a dozen times flying before I didn't feed the birds with the contents of my stomach. Do you want to switch places and I'll take over again?"

Riony laughed. "I think we all know you're already in control here."

All of the riders with untamed dragons could speak with them much the same as Riony could with Dracuni. They'd explained that only a person the dragon has bonded with can hear them speak, which is why most humans thought dragons were mindless beasts for so long.

Zeina didn't need to nudge and command her dragon into action the way riders with tamed dragons did. Gleem flew freely on her own, any discussion about where and how she flew was silent between her and Zeina.

Until recently, Riony had thought Dracuni was unique in her ability to communicate. But learning that all dragons spoke to bonded humans and each other left her wondering about the old Rolanian myth, that dragons were born from the tortured souls of the dead who got lost on their path to the stars.

Riony had loved listening to her mother sharing those stories at bedtime with her and Lyrrin, and after all that had changed, all she'd learned since, those stories now felt so childish. But childish in a way that she longed for and wished she could capture again in a world that now felt so hard.

"How long have you been with Gleem?" Riony asked around the lump in her throat.

"I found her as a hatchling when I was fifteen. Her mother had been downed by a patrol of dragonriders out near the dragonlord estate I was indentured to. And all of a sudden I found myself on the run with her."

Riony turned and smirked. "I know a little something about that. Sounds like an adventure."

Zeina beamed back. "It's quite the story. I could tell you all of it, if you like. Maybe ... tonight? Come to my room."

Riony had mistaken words and looks for flirtation in the past, but there was no mistaking the raw hunger in Zeina's gaze.

Heat flushed Riony's cheeks, and she cleared her throat. "Yeah. That sounds"—another throat clearing—"good."

Riony had already been anxious to get back, worried about those she'd left behind. Normally, Aishena would be there to keep everyone safe, but she came along on the mission when Lyrrin and Benjin demanded that they wanted to look after Dracuni themselves.

Not allowing it would be an insult to their capability. They had been adamant, in the way preteens excelled at.

The level of trust for Eslinde and her group had grown

as well, so the only person Riony wasn't sure of yet that was left behind was Jaym, and of all the Rebel Riders, he seemed the most harmless. Apart from his bird.

Lyrrin's heartbeat transferring through the paired crystals was steady, but Riony knew she'd remain worried until she saw them all again.

And Zeina's proposal only added another layer of anxiety to returning home.

The heavy beat of wings sounded loudly as Thallan and Samor brought their dragons in close by Gleem's side.

Aishena signaled and gestured down to the dry and cracked plains below.

A swath of darkness lay across the ground, undulating like ink spilling in slow motion, with two red glowing points—eyes like burning coals within a form of dripping gloom.

The shadow dragon.

It roared, and the air seemed to ripple and distort. A sharp pang of anguish ached through Riony and her eyes watered.

Now that she knew what the being was, what had created it, the sadness it emanated broke her heart even more.

Its roar also broke the hard-baked dirt beneath it, as long dead creatures clawed their way up through the ground.

"Glad we're up here," Zeina muttered.

Riony nodded and was about to turn away when she noticed more movement, from beneath where the shadow dragon's wings gusted as it raised itself away into the sky.

Small figures, insect-like from their distance, moved in a scattered pattern. People, running from the raised revenants. Leaving behind carts and belongings.

Riony's flesh pinched all over with goosebumps. She scanned the horizon to get her bearings.

They weren't far from one of the shrine enclaves. One that had run out of magic.

They must be traveling to find somewhere safe. Because we've been hiding. Keeping Dracuni away.

"We have to go help them," Riony said.

Zeina's expression was grim, but she nodded and made a few hand gestures to Thallan.

Thallan shook his head as he swiped a signal with his arm.

"He says we're going to continue on," Zeina translated.

"No, we sparking aren't. There are people down there. I'm going to help, one way or another." Riony pulled her sword from its sheath and activated the float rune.

Staring down, she set her jaw. She hadn't ever fallen quite that far before but had made some big jumps with the float rune and was fairly confident the magic would cushion her landing.

Catching Aishena's eye, Riony pointed down, hoping she was understood. The Hjelzahn girl nodded and began

barking orders toward Samor, with Kess backing her up. The quiet giant of a man hunched over, beset.

Zeina grabbed Riony's arm. "You want to risk getting ripped up by revs to save a handful of people? Our plans are bigger than that, and we need to stay in one piece if we're going to save the world. We're safe up here and should stay safe."

Riony tugged free of her grip. "And you'd be okay with just flying past and letting all those people die?"

"No, but—"

"But what? They can't stay safe up on dragon wings. Take me down lower or I'm taking myself down lower." Riony swung one of her legs around to sit sideways in the saddle, ready to jump.

"Fine," Zeina snapped, and Gleem snorted a huff and dove. "But you know my dragon's a seasong, right? She's got no fire attack to burn those revs."

"That's fine," Riony snapped back. "I have my own."

Gleem swooped in low, where the tree line would have been, if there were anything more than the odd charred stick and scratchy bush covering the ground.

Riony swiped her finger along the second rune on her sword, and pink flames cracked up the blade.

Then she jumped.

Winter-frosted mud cracked under Riony's boots as she landed.

A baby-faced woman screamed as Riony appeared

before her, sword blazing. She screamed again when she turned from the strange, burning, sky-fallen woman back toward the gnashing human revenant that had been chasing her.

"Duck!" Riony yelled.

The woman squealed a third time as she crouched down below grasping claws and the swing of a solid crystal sword, swirling with flames.

Riony hit the rev straight through the head, knocking the age-bleached skull into the air. But the undead abomination kept moving.

The headless body took a twitching step forward, and Riony rammed her sword through its tattered rib cage. The remnants of ancient flesh smoldered, then caught alight.

Angling her sword up and putting all her strength into the motion, Riony cut the rev through the middle, shattering its chest into jagged, burning chunks, then brought it smashing back down again to cleave through between its hips.

Disturbingly, the pieces of destroyed rev still moved, but there wasn't much it could do split in twain.

Riony stretched a hand for the woman and pulled her back to her feet. "Find somewhere to hide."

The woman stared back, wide-eyed and panting. "Where?"

Taking in a view of the battlefield, Riony had to concede it had been a dumb suggestion.

The plains were flat and almost bare as far as the eye could see. There was no cover, nowhere to hide, and the revenants were everywhere. The people dodged around them, running back and forth between carts and abandoned belongings.

A gust of wind stirred up dried grass and broken sticks as the other dragons came in close, but no undead-cleansing fire followed. The humans and revs on the ground were all too closely mixed.

Many riders wouldn't consider that a reason not to burn everything in their quest to destroy revenants, but the Rebel Riders didn't start raining fire on everyone and that raised their esteem in Riony's eyes.

A boar revenant ran for Riony. She spun to the side, thrusting her flaming blade into its flank as it charged by. She was still extracting her sword from the juddering remains when the flightless carcass of a massive carrion bird lunged for her, twiglike wings flapping as though it still had feathers.

The hooked beak struck for Riony's neck, then a flash of charcoal fur rushed by and it was gone.

Bones cracked and splintered in Griskin's jaws.

Shimmering gold and blue dragonrider armor came into view as Aishena twirled through the fray to Riony's side, athames slicing glowing arcs through the air as she went.

"You decided to join me!" Riony called over.

"Of course. Watch you back, tamebrain!"

Riony whipped around to see another human revenant dashing her way. Then two pale darts swished through the air. A bone dagger hit into each of the revs hip joints. The revenant's steps became stiff and awkward, slowing it down to a jolting march.

Still, it reached rotten claws for Riony, until another volley of daggers hit its shoulders, and its arms dropped like a lifeless puppet.

Riony's sword made short work of finishing off the incapacitated creature.

Kess and Griskin appeared at Riony's side. The wild girl's black-and-white hair had been detangled during her time spent with a princess, but the gusting air from circling dragons gave her a windswept look.

It paired with a fierce expression and flush of pink on her cheeks as her chest rose and fell, staring back at Riony.

As Riony realized she'd been staring in return.

"Are you okay?" Kess asked, frowning at her apparent dumbfoundedness.

Riony nodded mutely.

Aishena, moving in from ahead, raised her eyebrows at Kess. "Nice trick with the knives."

"Are you kidding me?" Riony huffed. "Nice trick? Do you know how long it took you to start complimenting me, and you're already impressed by her?"

Aishena's expression returned to normal and she

shrugged. "It was impressive."

"It's not enough to clear these revs, though," Kess said. "We need fire. And even that might not keep them down."

"I have an idea about that," Aishena replied, casually stamping a heel onto a small slithering snake skeleton. "I've already shared it with the riders. They're ready. We've got to let everyone here alive know to drop to the ground at the same time. And hold on."

Riony nodded once and got moving. She didn't need the details—if Aishena planned it, she trusted it. And they didn't have any more time to spare. Screams of pain sounded from all around and the three of them, even with their impressive tricks, weren't enough to save everyone there.

Dodging between ravenous undead, Riony vaulted up onto an abandoned cart and waved her flaming sword in the air.

She hollered out the instructions twice, hoping everybody heard through their panic and screaming.

Aishena and Kess both called out the same instructions from their positions as well, and on the count of three, bodies dropped to the muddy ground all across the field.

Okay, so far so good ... Except, across to one side, a young girl, smaller than Lyrrin, was still running. A ghastly bear revenant galloped after her.

To the side of the carnage, Zeina brought Gleem in to land, and the dragon's chest lifted, puffing up as it

prepared to breathe.

"Oh sparks."

Riony leaped across the field, coming down on top of the running girl. She brought both of them crashing to the ground. The girl screamed and whimpered beneath her. The revenant bear thumped down on top of them both.

And Gleem breathed.

It was like a hurricane being birthed from the dragon's maw and spreading across the land. So much more powerful than Dracuni's starved mother had been when her breath had flung Riony across the ice cave.

Riony dug her fingers into the dirt as air blasted over them. Revenants, unable to fathom what was happening, didn't slow their chase or hold on. They cartwheeled in the wind like tumbleweed away from the prone humans.

And once they were clear of the people, the fire hit.

Thallan brought his bronze etherdart sweeping over them, shooting fireballs at individual revs that were thrown beyond the main group.

But where the majority of the boney blights landed in a tangled mass, there was Samor and his flamesong.

Riony had never seen a flamesong breathe fire before.

When it did, she could feel the heat scorching her face from across the field. A constant raging jet of flames erupted around the revenants. The glow of fire lit the dragon's gold and black scales from within, all across her chest and neck, as though the inferno was more than it could contain.

Even with the intensity of that burn, some revenants still moved within it.

But between the rushing air blasting the revenants back and the roaring inferno they hit on the other side, the revenants were mostly gone.

Once the last few stubborn revenants were blown away, Gleem could stop and the humans could make a clear run for it. But there were a few revs that managed to hold on.

Like the bear. On Riony's back.

Its claws dug into Riony's armor, and the weight of its ragged bones threatened to squash the child beneath them both. Riony pressed up onto her elbows to give the girl space, and the wind caught beneath her, threatening to tear her free from her grip on the ground.

Huge teeth clamped down, crunching Riony's backplate and yanking at it with a growl. She cried out at the pressure as it pulled, ripping the leather straps free. The mangled steel clattered down beside them as the bear snapped again.

Fabric tore as it took a mouthful of her padded shirt and ripped it free. The chill of the air blasting over them cut across her bare back.

She had to move, do something, or the rev was going to kill her with its next bite.

Riony roared as she pressed her body upward and to the side, taking the weight of the skeletal bear with her. A curved claw scraped down her arm as they twisted together in the air, then the bear lost its grip and tumbled away from her in the wind.

But up off the ground, the air caught Riony as well. She reached out, dragging her fingers through the mud but not finding any purchase.

"Whoa, no, no, no!"

Air buffeted her on all sides as she flipped and rolled, skidding straight toward the burning wall of dragonfire.

THIRTEEN

Kess stared into the flames, aghast, as the heat intensified. "More wood?" she asked.

Riony had an old, half-burnt trunk over one shoulder, then dropped it onto the bonfire. "Yup. It must be *bigger*!"

"Bigger! Bigger!" Lyrrin chanted as she threw a bundle of sticks in as well.

The orange light glittered over Dracuni's scales as she and Shiff sat side by side, watching.

Kess thought considering how close Riony had been that afternoon to being cooked alive, she might have shied away from flame. But she built the bonfire with utter, fearless glee.

Kess had only caught Riony with seconds to spare. She and Griskin raced across the field when they saw Riony tumbling toward the flamesong's fiery breath. Kess swung off her saddle to grab her, falling free herself in the wind.

She grasped Riony's hand, then Griskin grabbed Kess's boot in his mouth, and the three of them held tight to each other and the ground until Gleem stopped gusting a tornado around them.

Sitting to the side as every Rolanian in their group threw anything that would burn onto the growing fire, Kess rubbed her ankle. But her heart ached more.

Every time she closed her eyes, she was met with a vivid image of Riony's bare back, where the rev had ripped her armor away.

Of the crosshatch of old scars wrinkling her skin.

The one time Kess had struck Riony herself, she never even broke the skin. But it didn't matter. She might as well have inflicted every single wound Riony had suffered.

Kess had never seen the results of those beatings before. The painting of cruelty made indelible upon Riony's skin. Now, it was all Kess could see.

Once the threat of being blown into dragonflame had passed, Riony had helped Kess back up onto Griskin and then thanked her. Actually thanked her. With her words.

It was an act that shattered something inside Kess, and it had been hard for her not to break down crying then and there. She didn't want or expect or deserve gratitude, not from Riony. That wasn't why she was doing any of it.

Maybe, *maybe* if she saved Riony's life one thousand

more times, she might feel as though she had come close to repaying the debts of all her mistakes. Beyond that, Kess doubted she could ever do enough to be worthy of Riony's *gratitude*.

But right now, Riony was still alive and even seemed happy, and Kess would do anything to keep things that way.

They hadn't managed to outright kill many of the revs, which was concerning considering the flamesong firepower applied, but they had managed to keep them burning and at bay long enough for the people to get their belongings and escape.

They considered that a win, and an air of celebration filled their camp as the bonfire grew.

Stars twinkled down from a clear, crisp night sky like a blanket of diamonds. Dashiel loped over to Kess, brushing their hands down from soot and smelling like woodsmoke.

"It's looking pretty good, isn't it?"

"Does it need to be so big?" Kess asked, wary of drawing attention to their location.

"Of course it does. It's Midwinter's Eve! Don't worry. There'll be fires all over Elundrae tonight." Dashiel grinned, and the light of the fire glowed through their blond hair. "I'm glad you got back in time for this."

Kess nodded, as though she understood, but Midwinter's Eve was a Rolanian custom, and one she'd never experienced. Taens considered the longest night of the year a more solemn affair.

Once, when she was little, she saw the slaves on Heithorn estate building a similar bonfire for their celebration. Her father sent one of their riders on a dragon out into the field. They destroyed the fire and all the decorations the slaves had made from fabric scraps and straw.

Kess didn't understand why. Their celebration wasn't going to hurt anyone.

Her father told her otherwise. "If we let them have one thing, they will think themselves capable of more. They might start to think they don't need us, our protection. They might think they could organize against us. They can't forget who they belong to."

Kess never did see a Midwinter's Eve celebration after that.

"What ... do we do with this?" Kess gestured weakly toward the fire.

Dashiel beamed. "Oh, you'll see. It's a lot of fun. I haven't done this in years. Not since my father banned it."

Their smile faded then.

Kess's voice came out rough. "I know you didn't exactly choose to leave your home and that things ended badly there, but I'm glad you are free to be who you want to be now."

Dashiel's shoulders lifted. They looked out over the fire again, watching Riony and Aishena, who were arguing about how much of their fuel reserves were going toward the bonfire. Riony had taken up the chant of *bigger, bigger*.

Dashiel returned smiling eyes to Kess. "I'm glad I ended up here, too."

Kess grinned crookedly. "So, how have you found life out here in the big bad world, after growing up as a spoiled dragonlord?"

Dashiel's jaw dropped in mock indignation, but their eyes remained smiling.

"What? I'm asking from experience." Kess laughed wryly. "I know there are still some things I miss."

Dashiel raised both hands as though weighing something between them. "Some burning sticks out in the middle of nowhere or going to parties at the Dragon King's palace ...?"

"Dash!" Vance called out. He was dragging in a very large log he'd found somewhere. "Give me a hand with this."

"Never mind. This is going to be amazing." Grinning again, Dashiel ran off.

Across the paved area, Aishena and Benjin were staring at the fire with as much confusion as Kess. Eslinde moved around, cheerily handing out bowls of steaming curry. The Alderkin took the food gratefully and Eslinde remained to speak with them.

Gleem lay resting near the fire, taking up all the space on that side, and the other two wild dragons were up on patrol with Samor and Jaym.

Kife's purple dragon had been seen again on their

return that afternoon, making another attempt on Thallan's bronze etherdart, so they kept all the tamed dragons inside. The purple dragon didn't seem interested at all in the wild dragons.

The Rebel Riders who weren't on patrol were on their way out of the base tunnel, carrying with them the dragon egg they'd retrieved.

Thallan placed it down on a cube of cut stone. "We're ready to make our attempt."

The bonfire was abandoned as everyone grouped around to watch. Kess climbed back onto Griskin and moved in closer as well.

Dracuni rested her head over Riony's shoulder, and Riony patted her cheek.

Warily, she said, "We never did agree on where you were getting your silvernix from."

"We have our own," Thallan replied gruffly. "How big did you say the crack was?"

The man drew his sword, aiming the pommel toward the head-sized egg. Riony explained, and he struck the shell.

The sound of it cracking echoed in the silence. Aishena flinched and turned away. He hit it one more time, splitting it down the middle so the inner membrane was visible.

Lyrrin gasped, and Riony pulled her in beside her. "It'll be okay."

"Here's hoping it is," Thallan said and opened a tiny vial of iridescent fluid.

"Here's hoping for more than okay," Norallei added, dark eyes gleaming in the firelight.

Thallan grunted in agreement, and he let the drop fall onto the egg.

A shimmer of moonbeam glow grew from within the broken shell, brightening as the immature creature inside wriggled and squirmed.

Kess turned away from the magical illumination, watching Riony instead. Imagining how she'd done the same for Dracuni's egg, after the others had been smashed beyond hope.

Remembering how she'd left Riony there to die when she could have saved her but had been too hurt, too angry, too selfish in the moment.

When Riony glanced her way, hand around the acorn pendant, Kess wondered if Riony was remembering the same thing.

With one final crackling tear, the shell fell open entirely, and the hatchling within mewled, fighting its way free of the membrane.

Everyone drew a collective breath. The Alderkin drew symbols in the air as they often did. Some form of prayer, Kess assumed.

The hatchling's scales were velvety and a bright silver, brushed with the light tint of rainbow hue. Just like Dracuni's.

It had a few horns around its head, and one central

one too, like Dracuni's.

Less fur, but still a small tuft at the end of its tail. Like Dracuni.

"Did it work?" Riony asked in a hushed tone.

"Only one way to find out." Thallan turned his sword in his hands with one swift motion and ran the blade across the hatchling's thigh.

The baby dragon bleated a scream.

Lyrrin matched it. "No! What are you doing?"

She ran forward, throwing her arms around the dragonling.

Driven by furious impulse, Kess's hands squeezed around Griskin, pushing him forward in a pounce to put them between the man and the hatchling.

Thallan raised his hands and scowled back. "Calm down. How else were we supposed to know if it worked?"

He held up the sword, tilting the blade in the low light. A soft line of red ran along its edge. "Which it didn't anyway, by the looks of it."

"You didn't have to be so violent about it," Kess growled. "It's a newborn."

Sneering at his sword, Thallan lowered it. "Some violence is necessary."

Lyrrin made low, comforting sounds to the hatchling and worked on dabbing the red blood away from its wound.

"What a waste," Norallei said flatly.

"We did everything right though." Zeina kicked a

rock, then turned toward Riony. "Was there anything else? Anything different the first time?"

Shrugging, Riony moved closer to the hatchling, looking it over. "Lyrrin had scratched a few patterns into the vial, after moving to the undercity and seeing runes for the first time. I didn't think much of them at the time, but now that we know what she is ..."

Eslinde gave the Alderkin a hopeful look. "Could the magic have worked that way?"

Yrik, Shael, and Priyune whispered between each other in their language for a moment before Yrik shook his head. "We don't know of any runes which would work that way. Do you remember what you drew?"

Lyrrin's lips pulled in. "No. It was years ago. I didn't know proper runes then. I just liked how they looked and drew my own."

"The vial is gone, too," Riony added.

"Regardless, it shouldn't work on glass either," Yrik said.

Thallan sheathed his sword with a harsh thrust. "So it may be impossible to replicate! That would have been nice to know before spending silvernix on *this*."

He gestured to the diminutive, floppy hatchling. Smaller still than Dracuni had been when Kess first saw her. "It's not worth the resources to be raising another hatchling right now, not something so small and strange."

Kess's finger's tensed, and Griskin growled.

Thallan raised his voice. "Am I wrong? The thing has

taken on only the worst aspects of a unidragon, and even this one still can't fly."

"Shh!" Lyrrin snapped. "You're scaring him. Can't you feel how scared he is?"

Riony's eyes closed and she swore softly.

Zeina released a breath that grew into a chuckle. "Well, Thallan, it looks like it's not your choice anyway what becomes of the hatchling. He's bonded with the little one."

"Bonded?" Lyrrin gasped.

Zeina smiled. "Pretty easy to do when a newborn has been hurt and you're the first creature to comfort him. Thallan might have realized that if he'd ever bonded with a hatchling himself."

Riony groaned a long sigh. "Didn't I say no more pets?"

Kess's heart raced, and she kept her face turned away from the group around the hatchling.

Was it so easy to bond with a dragonling?

And she'd missed yet another chance. Because her first instinct was to attack, rather than comfort. Because she had as much violence within her as the man she'd rebuked.

As much as Kess knew now that there were more important things than having her own dragon, knowing that the thing she had spent most of her life yearning for had been right there and she didn't get it, left her shaking with overwrought feelings.

It doesn't matter. I am by Riony's side, and I've been allowed to fly among friends. That's enough. That's so much

more than I deserve.

She swallowed away the ache inside her that longed for more.

Thallan gave the baby dragon a long, disappointed stare, then marched off in a huff, Norallei close at his back.

Dashiel helped Lyrrin take the newborn hatchling inside, followed by Dracuni, Shiff, and the Alderkin. Vance, Benjin, and Zeina returned to the fire.

Eslinde sounded tired as she said, "Another unidragon could have helped our cause so much. If we had a way to keep the shrine enclaves activated, you'd never have had to risk yourselves as you did for those travelers today."

"Sharing how to use the gateways would have helped save those people too," Yensen said. "They could have traveled to another enclave when there were signs theirs was failing."

Aishena and Riony moved into the conversation.

Riony pulled her coat tighter around her. She'd changed into an untorn shirt when they'd returned and wore no armor now. Away from the fire where they were, the chill was biting.

She sighed. "It could be worth sharing, but I feel like the Alderkin would be angry about that."

"We may have to risk angering them," Aishena replied. "Niskina's last message sounded worried about the enclaves, not just for them running out of magic. They've been using the gateway down the hill from the undercity to trade and grow the settlements, but it seems to be attracting dragonrider attention."

Kess was about to leave, when Riony called over, "What do you think?"

"What do I ... think?" Kess blinked back in surprise.

"Do we share the gateway rune with everyone? As someone who we only escaped from because we could use the gateways and you couldn't, I feel like you might have some insight." Riony smirked, but there didn't seem to be any malice in her tone.

She wants my opinion? Kess desperately wanted to give one that made Riony happy, to show she was on her side, but as she opened her mouth, she knew she owed Riony the truth.

"The gateways were the only thing that kept you out of our reach. And we were just two idiots with one dragon. With the Dragon King after you, the risk is so much more. The priority now is to keep Dracuni safe."

Which then keeps Riony safe, Kess thought.

"And if the wrong people found out how to use the gateways, we'd have no hope." Kess held Riony's gaze as she spoke. "But what is hope for us could be the condemnation of others. If you decide to share the knowledge, I'm behind your decision."

Riony's forehead wrinkled, and her mouth worked into a faint smile.

"Come on!" Zeina yelled from near the fire. "The

moon is up! It's time!"

A full grin broke over Riony then and she rushed away to Zeina's side. Everyone followed, leaving Kess alone and cold at the edge of the firelight.

Griskin whined softly as Kess rubbed his ears. He fidgeted beneath her as he often did when he'd spent all day inside or strapped to a dragon's back.

"Alright, boy. Go for a run." She pushed herself off his back and sat down against the block of stone that still had the dragon egg remains on top.

Griskin licked her face once, then bounded away across the empty roads and flat foundations of Eslindekeep, chasing rodents in the dark.

From this angle, the fire had two large peaks like burning columns, with a gap between. Kess inhaled sharply as Riony ran straight into the flames.

With one large leap, Riony passed through the gap in the fire and landed on the other side, whooping and laughing.

Zeina was the next to follow, and soon everyone was taking turns jumping through the flames. Even Aishena and Benjin had a go.

A low, long note reverberated through the air, lifting in a slow warbling melody. It took a moment for Kess to realize the sound came from Gleem.

She sat there, mesmerized by the singing dragon.

No seasongs in captivity ever sang. Even in all the time

Kess had tracked Dracuni's mother, she'd never sung. The sound was beautiful and sad all at once.

"Hey! Are you going to have a go?" Riony jogged up to Kess's side, face flushed and breathing heavily.

"A go?"

"It's tradition for Midwinter's Eve. Jump through the fire, be cleansed and reborn through an act of courage. It's a whole thing. You should do it."

"I would, but ..." Kess's eyelids fluttered as she stared back blankly. She gestured to her legs.

"I mean on Griskin, of course." Riony looked around for where the wolf had gone.

"No! It might singe his fur. Absolutely not."

Riony scoffed. "You ran him toward dragonfire this very afternoon."

"That was different. I'd never risk him for something frivolous."

A cheer went up from around the fire as Eslinde landed her first jump through the flames and stumbled into Vance's awaiting arms.

Even the princess is doing it. Kess stared at the ground.

Riony turned as though to leave, then turned back again. She ran a hand through her hair and frowned, struggling with something. Her wild red locks weren't tied back in the usual thin pigtail she wore and they curled around her neck.

She shifted her weight from one foot to the other a

couple of times, then made a sound between a sigh and a groan.

"Alright. Come on, then." She leaned down to Kess with her arms out.

Kess balked. "What are you doing?"

Riony paused where she was. "Unless you *don't* want to jump through fire, like some kind of fire-hating non-courageous non-jumper."

"If that was meant to provoke me it was a terrible attempt. The quality of your insults has dropped drastically."

"It's a lot harder to rip you up with words when you aren't being the living incarnation of nastiness." Riony shrugged. "So do you want to jump or not?"

Kess exhaled slowly. She could see in the deep furrows in Riony's forehead that her offer was costing her something. That carrying Kess for any reason was something that probably sickened her.

But still she stood there, arms out, waiting.

Still, she had followed a wolf across the blighted land to save someone who had hurt her, whom she hated.

She just couldn't help herself from helping others.

"Okay."

"Okay, then." Riony brought her arms down around Kess's shoulders and legs and scooped her up with ease.

Kess's chilled limbs pressed against Riony's warmed chest, and she wondered if the woman could feel how

fast her heart was beating. She swallowed down the way Riony's touch made her lips gasp and her eyes water from an overwhelm of raw emotions.

Dashiel whistled and cheered as they approached the fire, and before Kess knew it, Riony was running.

She kept Kess held tight in her arms, and the flicker of heat grew hotter, and then they were jumping, passing between the pillars of fire.

There was a moment where they hung in the air, free from gravity and surrounded by the glow of flames, and all Kess could feel was warmth and the press of Riony's body and the air imprisoned in her lungs.

Golden light touched the outline of Riony's neck and cheeks, sheened in sweat, and lit her hair up as bright as the flames themselves.

They hit the ground on the other side with a thud and Riony stumbled, giggling as she readjusted to account for Kess's weight, bringing them back upright at the last moment.

They breathed in time with each other, and for a moment, their eyes locked, and it felt as though Riony pulled Kess a little closer.

Then she leaned over to put Kess down beside a stone block where a couple of bowls and cups had been left.

"And not singed at all." Riony half smiled.

Kess wanted to disagree. It felt as though she were burning all over.

She just swallowed and said with a crackly voice, "Thank you."

She expected Riony to leave her alone again then, but instead, Riony pulled off her coat, grabbed a bowl of half-eaten curry and rice, and sat down against the rock beside Kess.

"I need a rest to cool off a bit," Riony said breathily.

Over at the fire, Aishena and Dashiel seemed to be taking turns, one-upping each other and measuring how far they could jump each time.

Kess glanced at Riony as the woman scooped food into her mouth with her fingers. The dark lines of the tattoo on her arm contrasted with the gleam of firelight highlighting her skin.

Clearing her throat twice before her words would work, Kess asked, "What does it mean? Your tattoo."

A sad smile lifted on Riony's lips.

"My mother." She pointed to the four rings.

"Aishena's brother." She pointed to the two blades.

"Niskina's father." She pointed to the candle.

"We all got the same tattoo. Sharing our pain." She returned to eating.

"Niskina too? I thought it was something special, between you and Aishena."

Riony side-eyed Kess.

"Because of your relationship." Kess blushed.

"My relationship with Aish is the same as with Nisk.

We're family. That's what this tattoo means. Why we all have it. But they chickened out of getting the other ones."

"You have more?"

Riony smirked. "Not any you'll be seeing."

Kess's breath rattled between the chill of the stone at her back and the warmth of the fire before her.

Aishena was taking another jump while Dashiel goaded her from the side. She vaulted through the flames with the elegance of flight, landing a body's length farther than where Dashiel marked their best attempt. Dashiel howled with faux outrage.

"I wouldn't mind ..." Kess licked her dry lips. "If you and Aishena were together. She's someone who would be worthy of you."

Riony choked on her food. "I'm sorry. In what world do you think I need your approval for who I'm with?"

Kess lifted one shoulder in a casual shrug. "Maybe you do need it considering you've spent so long with someone like Aishena and *haven't* gone there."

Riony dropped her bowl on the ground, staring at Kess. Then laughter burbled out, shaking her chest. "You are full of surprises lately."

"Got to keep you on your toes." Kess returned the smile but couldn't keep the sadness out of it as she watched Aishena and Benjin celebrating her win.

"You know, I met the Hjelzahns once before, when I was very young." Kess lowered her eyes, drawing aimlessly

in the dirt as the memory returned. "My parents took me to their dragonkeep while chasing a cure for my legs."

"I don't remember that," Riony said.

"It was before you came to me. We went to Hjelzahnkeep's palace to meet an experimental surgeon in the Hjelzahn's employ who said he was interested in my special case. He spoke of all the wonders his surgery could achieve beyond what silvernix alone could do. We had been so hopeful."

Riony leaned her head back, then rolled it Kess's way. "I already know this story doesn't end in a happily ever after. But I'll admit I'm a little scared about how it gets there."

Kess scrubbed out the lines she'd drawn. "It turned out when he said surgeon, he meant that he was employed as a torturer. He was interested in me because he wanted to learn how he could inflict my disability onto others."

Riony exhaled a breath that puffed into mist around them. "What? Why?"

"People who were immobile but could still feel every pain? I was perfect in his eyes. And the way he learned was by cutting into people."

Riony didn't say anything then, only stared at Kess with a deep furrow between her brows and those indescribable eyes.

"Four times he butchered me, then healed me with silvernix, only to open me up again, exploring my bones and muscles and sinew with his instruments. He used no

sedative. He wanted to see every effect upon me while he worked."

Kess took a trembling breath and closed her eyes, only to see the scars on Riony's back. She opened them again, shaking her head to clear it.

"I was ... I don't know, five? Six years old at the time? My parents stopped him when it became clear he was only working to his benefit and wasn't going to fix me. I still have nightmares sometimes ... that I'm back there."

Riony slumped slightly, moving in so that her shoulder touched Kess's. "I'm sorry that your parents were such utter, deplorable shits."

"Me too."

"Stars, how did we survive that place?" Riony stared up at the sky.

Kess waited until she looked down again, and she held Riony's gaze. "You survived because you're strong. I only survived because I latched on to your strength. And I'm sorry. I'm sorry that I hurt you. I'm sorry I let anyone ever hurt you."

Riony's head shook in the smallest motion, and she opened her mouth.

Then Zeina strolled by in front of them. The beautiful warrior woman had her hair out of its normal braids, and the deep-brown locks curled around golden eyes that watched Riony with a heavy warmth. She tilted her head ever so slightly as she gave Riony a pointed look, then

headed away into the base entrance.

Riony's throat pumped as she swallowed. She moved as though to get up.

Kess nodded to herself and stared at the ground.

Leaning forward, Riony pulled her coat back on and shivered, then settled back in beside Kess. "Have you eaten tonight?"

Unable to speak, Kess shook her head.

"I'll get you something."

"I don't need—"

"I know," Riony said firmly. "But isn't it nice sometimes to let other people look after you anyway? Like the way you've had my back lately. I appreciate that and I just ... I wanted to—"

A cloaked figure dashing out of the base entrance cut off Riony's words.

Aishena called out, "Niskina?"

Riony was on her feet in seconds, running to meet the woman. Kess whistled for Griskin.

Niskina grasped Riony for support. She gasped out her words around heaving breaths.

"Myrwa's enclave ... they're being attacked!"

FOURTEEN

Riony's sword glowed in one hand while Aishena helped buckle the side straps of the scale mail vest she'd thrown on.

"It'll do," Riony snapped, pushing past her toward the gateway.

"*Riony*," Aishena scolded back.

With Riony's own armor ruined earlier that day, and in the rush, the chest armor was all she had over her clothing. It was ill-fitting and without proper padding, but Myrwa's enclave was under attack *right now* and there wasn't any time.

"I was going to join them for Midwinter's Eve." Niskina spoke between gulping breaths. "When I went through, it was chaos. I got a couple of kids out who were hiding in the shrine building, then came right away for help."

Weapons were grabbed and they all assembled near the gateway, attaching what armor they could in the moments they had.

You should have more armor on. Dracuni's thoughts felt like a hailstorm of worry.

"Open it," Riony ordered Benjin, who waited with his crystal-studded staff near the activation rune.

He glanced to Aishena for confirmation, then the gateway magic flickered and glowed. He selected the symbol for Myrwa's shrine, and the light turned red.

It took a moment for Riony to realize what she was seeing through the shimmering window.

The glow of fire.

She ran.

The hot sting of smoke met her eyes and lungs as she broke through to the other side. Half the shrine structure around the gateway had been smashed away, opening it to the destruction.

The ground crunched beneath Riony's feet as she ran on, the footsteps of Aishena, Dashiel, Vance, Niskina, and the Rebel Riders fanning out behind her. Kess and Griskin bounded away through the smoke.

A charred, acrid stench clogged each breath, and Riony threw an arm up in front of her face as a burst of embers flew at her.

Everything was on fire. Riony pushed through between

the burning shelters, scanning for movement. There was only fire, and a single, gurgling scream that cut off before Riony could trace it.

"Where are they? Where is everyone?"

Her foot hit a lump and she stumbled. A burnt log, she thought at first. But it was too soft.

Bile stung her throat as the body became clear. Seared beyond recognition, their face was blackened and blistered. But someone Riony had known.

She had been looking to the skies and at eye level for any attackers or survivors. But as she turned her eyes to the ground, she saw the people who were missing.

Bodies smoldered amid the roaring flames. Everywhere Riony turned were faces and bodies and clothing she recognized. Emra, with her pretty doe eyes. The gaunt man she'd carried when they first ran from the revenant army together.

Kellae. Her legs burned away and body curled around two smaller ones. All gone.

Riony's face crumpled and twisted and she bellowed wordlessly.

Aishena appeared beside her, then barked through the smoke, "Keep the kids away!"

At the collapsed shrine, Eslinde and Yensen held Lyrrin and Benjin in place. Dracuni was squeezing her way through the gateway as well.

"No, go back!" Riony yelled.

I want to help too. I could save people.

Riony's knees felt ready to give way. She wasn't sure there was anyone left to save.

"Myrwa?" Riony cupped her hands around her mouth, calling the woman's name again and again.

Through a gust of smoke, Kess appeared on Griskin.

"There are some survivors hiding out in the forest. Not many. I saw two." Her words were crackly and forced. "They wouldn't come with me."

Griskin whined and licked his paws.

"Myrwa? I haven't seen her."

Kess's lips pulled in and she shook her head.

As everyone converged beside Riony, faces grim, it was clear nobody had found any more survivors.

Niskina let out an animalistic wail. "I should have stayed. I should have tried to get more people out. But I couldn't see, couldn't get out of the shrine ... There was no one else nearby, only fire ..."

"It looks like it was already almost over by the time you arrived," Aishena said. "The few you saved might have been the last."

Riony took another step and it crackled beneath her feet, crunching in an all too familiar way. She bent down, brushed her hand through the ash, and came upon something sharp.

She sifted it out in her fingers. Broken glass. Shards of shattered glass, all over the ground.

There was no reason for it to be there, no reason but one.

"Kife." The word was a guttural growl.

Glass collected from the nearby factory.

Did he scatter it before or after he killed everyone? Riony couldn't fathom the cruelty either way.

She held up the shard and it glinted in the flames. "This is a message from *your brother*."

Kess turned two shades paler. "He ... he knows the enclaves are important to you."

Hit with an awful realization, Riony had to fight back the urge to be sick. She ran back to the gateway.

What is it? Dracuni moved out of her way, but even from a distance Riony was sharing every heart-aching, anguished emotion with the unidragon.

She couldn't reply. Her fingers trembled as she activated the gateway again and chose the symbol for another enclave at random, smashing her palm against it.

The gateway rippled and glowed—flaming red.

"It's all of them! They're attacking all of them!"

Eslinde covered her mouth with her hands.

Through the rippling image, she saw movement. The flap of dragon wings. People running through the hazy red light.

There was still time.

Aishena grabbed Riony by the back of her armor as she tried to charge through. "We have to get to as many shrines as we can, as fast as we can."

"What do you think I'm trying to do?" Riony shook her grip off.

"We have to be smart about it if we want to save as many people as possible." She stepped up onto a fallen stone and pointed between everyone. "Three rescue groups. Bring the Alderkin through, one with each group to run the gateways. Riony with Yensen and Kess. Vance with Dash and Thallan. Benjin, you're with me and Norallei."

"I want to help too, I can," Lyrrin said, then was pulled in closer to Eslinde.

Aishena shook her head. "We need a place to bring and heal survivors. Eslinde, Lyrrin, and Dracuni will go back to Eslindekeep. Dracuni?"

Dracuni nodded forcefully. ***I'm going to help.***

Aishena couldn't hear her, but the intent was clear. "Eslinde is going to tell everyone that she's using her royal supply of silvernix to heal people, so we don't get questions. Lyrrin, you're going to help Dracuni provide the silvernix where it's private and safe."

"And us?" Zeina asked, pointing to herself, Jaym, and Samor.

"Get your dragons in the air and to the any shrines you can reach. Try to clear off the attacking dragons. We aren't going to be able to keep everyone at Eslindekeep with us, so Niskina, you're going back to the undercity to prepare."

Benjin pushed Riony out of the way and reset the

gateway to Eslindekeep, and the riders with wild dragons rushed through, followed by Dracuni at a slower, squeezing speed.

Riony's every muscle twitched and ached, needing to move, to take action. She couldn't even think clearly through what Aishena was saying, whether any of it would work, be safe, or if anything could ever be right ever again after what she'd just seen.

They're dead. They're all dead.

"Are we all set?" Aishena called across the remaining group.

"No." Yensen stepped closer to Eslinde. "I'm going back to Eslindekeep too. I have to make sure Eslinde and Lyrrin stay safe."

Riony found herself nodding, but Aishena swiped a hand through the air, cutting off the request.

"We need our best fighters out there protecting people and helping survivors escape. You're with Riony." Aishena's tone was final.

Yensen's jaw set, but Eslinde put a hand on his arm. "We'll be fine, Yen. Stay with Riony. That's an order."

But what if they're not fine? What if someone gets to them while I'm not there?

A buzzing hum of emotions built in Riony's skull.

How, how am I going to keep everyone safe?

Riony's mouth was dry, her voice harsh from the smoke. "Kess, will you stay back with them?"

"You ... don't want me with you?" Kess's face pinched in the way it did when she was fighting down emotions.

Riony shook her head. "I need someone I can trust to keep Lyrrin and Dracuni safe. Can I trust you?"

"You can," Kess said firmly.

"What about you?" Niskina asked, looking between Riony and Yensen. "It will just be the two of you."

"We'll be fine," Riony replied.

Kess locked eyes with her, nodded once, then followed Eslinde and Lyrrin through the gateway.

The Alderkin came through then, and the magical passageway to Eslindekeep closed and reopened again to a fiery scene. Dashiel, Vance, and Thallan went through with Priyune.

Riony held her breath as they opened the gateway again. Maybe it had just been that one other enclave ...

But as the magic rippled again, more fire shone through. She and Yensen stepped through. Yrik went with them, remaining at the gateway as Riony and the grayglim ran out into the flaming devastation.

It was like Myrwa's enclave all over again. Everything burned, including bodies on the ground. But here there was movement. Here there were still screams.

Here, Riony could fight back.

Silhouetted through the smoke, an armored figure raised a sword to strike a body beneath them. Riony barreled forward, colliding with the dragonrider and

bringing them down beneath her. She held her sword, glowing purple in one hand, but struck down hard with her bare fist against the man's face again and then again. Her knuckles cracked and split, and the rider fell still.

Seeking her next target, she caught her breath when dragons became visible through the haze. But they were grounded. Stationary. Sitting around the edges of the camp beside the standing stones.

She could see their riders, all off their tamed steeds, wandering through the burning enclave to finish off anyone their dragonfire had missed.

Everything was red through Riony's eyes, and her blood felt molten in her veins.

Whimpering behind her shot her around. The young man there, who had almost been ended at the blade of the rider, stared at Riony's feral expression.

She blinked at him, then snapped, "Get to the gateway!"

He ran, and Riony rose to her feet in time to block the swing of an incoming sword. She swept her blade around, roaring as she brought it hammering across the rider's helmeted head.

She struck with the flat of her sword. Some part of her, deep inside, cringed away from killing. But it was almost entirely lost within the mindless rage boiling through her. When the rider collapsed beneath her assault, she didn't know whether he was alive or dead.

She stalked up and down between the burning huts

like a beast of prey, cutting down the few dragonriders who strayed into her path, finding survivors to be even fewer.

Each body she stepped over, she checked for signs of life with trembling fingers. Each one who proved too still for life left a scar on her heart like a hot brand.

Ahead of her, the smoke parted briefly, and a rider stood there, motionless, staring at Riony. Her eyes streamed from the sting of smoke, and she wiped them with the back of her arm to clear them. The man's dark hair was braided thickly along the top of his head, and he laughed in a gut-twisting, familiar way.

"Kife!" Riony roared.

He laughed even louder and stepped back into the haze.

Riony ran for him. Smoke blew so thickly across her path that she couldn't see.

"Yensen? Over here! We have to catch him!"

Riony pushed farther through, chasing around the back of a burning hut.

"Yensen! Where are you?"

No reply.

Rounding the corner, Riony's face was met with the swing of a burning block of wood.

Sparks sprayed around her, singeing her eyes and hair. She choked on the puff of ash and stumbled back. Her body crashed into another, scale mail clattering against scale mail. Arms came up and grabbed her under the shoulders, pinning her to her captor.

The dragonrider in front of her—not Kife—kicked her sword from her hand.

Hot liquid ran from her stinging nose, and she tasted blood. "Yensen!"

She flexed her shoulders, pulling forward to free herself of the grapple. The rider holding her grunted. A woman. She held tight.

Sparks. Where's Kife?

A searing gust of wind blew around them and the sound of dragon wings beat through the dark night above.

"How'd we miss this one with our burn?" the rider in front of her said.

Sword in one hand and charred wood in the other, he swung the wood like a bat into Riony's stomach. The flexible scale mail offered little protection for the blunt blow.

Riony wheezed and spat blood at the rider. "The same way you're going to miss your asses when I've beaten them clear off you."

"The only thing coming off is that rider armor you've stolen." The man angled his sword point above her shoulder, slipping it under the straps of the vest. "How dare you wear it, peasant?"

With a tearing slice, he cut through and the scale mail fell free from Riony's shoulder on that side, slumping and clattering over her chest.

"Come on, finish her off. The others are leaving." The

female rider readjusted her hold.

"Yeah, yeah." The rider aimed his sword forward lazily, as though Riony were any of the defenseless civilians they'd just been murdering.

He pressed the tip against her unprotected chest where the armor had fallen away, then lunged.

She wrenched to the side, and the sword thrust across her instead of through. The edge scraped along her exposed collarbone. She overestimated the female rider's hold on her and turned too far, pulling out of the rider's grasp and putting her arm into the slicing sword.

The blade bit deep into her bare bicep.

The rider swore and readjusted their attack.

Gritting her teeth, Riony ducked the next swing, scooping her own sword up in the same motion. Grasping it in both hands, Riony stalked toward the riders, face and body dripping with blood.

The woman took one look at her and bolted, disappearing into the smoke.

A mad ringing in Riony's ears blocked out all other sound. The clash of her sword against the man's. His cries as she cut through his armor, knocking him to his knees. The useless pleas rambling from his lips as he crawled backward away from her.

Riony only saw a monster. How was he any better than the revs she smashed to pieces? How was the thing in front of her different than those cruel beings of destruction? *They*

killed them. They burned them all as though they were nothing.

Riony's whole face was wet as she raised her sword for a final blow.

The ringing sound shifted, cleared. The buzzing tone resolved into a long, high-pitched scream. Riony's chest heaved, scorched dry from smoke, and she turned away from the cowering rider.

The fury that overwhelmed her iced over as a toddler, hair smoking, staggered toward her, arms up. Their face was blackened with soot.

And Riony remembered why she was there.

Jamming her sword away in its sheath at her back, she gathered the child in her arms.

"It's okay. It's okay, I've got you." Riony glanced back at the rider, reassured to find him gone.

All the dragons were airborne now, and Riony expected to run from another volley of dragonfire. Then an even larger dragon came diving in through the dark sky, scattering the riders. There was a flicker of gold scales between others so dark they were lost in the night. Samor and his flamesong, Shani.

Riony steadied her breath. She'd missed her chance at Kife, but there was still more to do.

"Amma. *Ammaaaaaa.*" The infant sobbed, pointing a chubby finger toward the burning hut.

Holding the infant close to her, Riony moved sideways,

shielding the child from the radiant heat as she moved to the remains of the structure.

A body lay in the doorway. Riony squatted down and felt for a pulse on the blond woman's wrist. Still alive, but no amount of shaking would rouse her.

Riony dragged her away from the flames, balancing the squirming child in her other arm. "Yensen! Where are you?"

Still, he didn't come.

"Stars, damn it," Riony muttered. Her sliced arm throbbed, and every part of her head felt like it had been assaulted by lightning hornets.

With a pained grunt, she placed the child down for long enough to haul the mother over one shoulder, then pulled the child back in with her bleeding arm again and brought them all up to standing.

She carried them both back to the gateway.

Yrik, waiting there, activated the magic when he saw her approach.

"Where's that depths-cursed grayglim?" she growled.

"He took a survivor through a while ago."

"Why hasn't he come back yet?"

The shimmering window of the gateway glowed the cool blue of crystal light, and as though summoned, Yensen stepped through. His sweeping eyes were narrowed and lips thin.

Kess followed close behind on Griskin.

When she saw Riony in front of her, her eyes traveled

up and down Riony, taking in the dripping blood and bodies she carried, and her face pinched in violently.

Despite all the raging heat inside and out, Riony shivered. "What happened, is everyone—?"

"They're fine. Everyone's okay. We came back to help you." Kess's words trembled slightly. "We should have come sooner."

Movement on Riony's shoulder startled her. The woman there shifted, then moaned. Then in a rush she began struggling.

"Slow down, it's alright!" Riony bent forward and put her on her feet.

The woman wobbled, unsteady. She coughed desperately, but when she saw her child, she straightened and pulled the infant into her arms.

Wiping the blood off her mouth with the back of her good arm, Riony tilted her head to the woman. "There are people to help you through there. Can you walk?"

Nodding, the mother stroked her baby's ashy hair. "Thank you."

Her steps were faltering, but she made it through. Yrik closed the portal after her.

Even before the woman had left, Kess was at Riony's side, binding the gash in her arm with a bandage. "This will have to do until we go back. I'm assuming that's not yet."

"No. I still heard more survivors. The riders were chased off before they could get everyone." Riony didn't mention

Kife as she stared at the careful work of Kess's fingers as she tied the bandage.

Yensen grunted, then dashed away to continue the search.

Kess's hand lingered on Riony's arm.

Riony's breathing became hard. "You're ... You're supposed to be looking after Lyrrin and Dracuni, that's what I asked you to do."

Kess flinched slightly. "Aishena and Benjin are with them now. They cleared the smaller camps already. When we realized you were alone ... They agreed to stay so I could find you."

"Why was I alone? What was Yensen doing?"

"He came through with a survivor, but then he went to get a dragon. He said you needed more air support. But we knew Samor was already coming this way, so I made the grayglim come back through with me."

Riony frowned, her head still spinning with a sickening mix of grief and rage. Why would Yensen think she needed air support? To catch Kife?

Kess licked her lips and her voice cracked. "Was that okay? I know you told me to stay with Lyrrin and Dracuni. I'm sorry. I just ..."

The air sighed out of Riony. "No. That's okay. It's ... good you're here. We still have a lot to do."

Riony only said the words out of some sense of wanting to offer comfort to anyone she could when everything had

been razed all around them.

But as she and Kess worked together to clear the rest of that enclave, then moved to the next and the next, Kess's presence at her back was the only thing that kept Riony from falling apart.

The cool light of early morning filled the sky by the time they stumbled back to the gateway and Yrik informed them that there were no more shrines left to go to. They'd saved everyone they could save.

Yensen went back to Eslindekeep then, where everyone else was gathering to recover.

"I'm going back to Myrwa's first," Riony said as Kess moved to follow the grayglim.

Her voice came out jittery. She didn't want to ask. She couldn't speak the words aloud. But she didn't want to go alone.

But she didn't need to ask.

"I'm with you." Kess bowed her head in a slow nod and stepped back from the gateway.

Yrik waved to the passage through to Eslindekeep. "We should go back. I'm worried how much we've used the gateways tonight. They might not last much longer. I don't want to be stuck out here."

"You go. I can get us where we need to be." Riony patted him on the shoulder. "Thank you."

The Alderkin paused, then scribed a symbol in the air and pressed his hand to Riony's shoulder as well, before

disappearing through the portal.

Riony closed it after him, then reopened the way to Myrwa's.

Only low fires and hot coals remained of the earlier inferno.

Riony moved through them slowly on legs aching with fatigue. She worked systematically, checking every body within the ring of the standing stones. Kess remained at her back, silent, as a spill of orange light swathed the sky.

The bloodred-tinted sun came up over the mountains, reflecting over the smoky clouds, as Riony found what she was looking for but wished she'd never find.

A single, aged arm, reaching out from below the fallen wall of the destroyed shrine.

Riony held Myrwa's cold hand as daylight spread over them. She pulled the beautiful, wise woman's shawl free and clutched it to her face as though to dry tears.

But no tears came. They had all been burned away.

All that was left was pure blood-and-ash-stained rage.

FIFTEEN

The impact jarred through Riony's forearm and up the bone to her shoulder, aching deep in contrast to her knuckles that had long since gone numb. She ignored the pain and struck out again. Her lips twisted mirthlessly as the thin sheet of metal buckled and dented beneath her blows.

The storeroom—the farthest from anyone else in Eslindekeep that Riony could find—was dark. Only a trembling glow from a torch in the hall outside reached in to where Riony pummeled the steel crates with her fists.

A shadow passed between her and the flame and Riony's entire body tensed.

She didn't turn around. "What is it? Did something happen?"

"No. Everyone is fine." Kess's voice was low and cautious. "Are you ... okay?"

Every nerve inside Riony hummed, refusing any truth in Kess's words.

Everybody *wasn't* fine.

Myrwa was dead. Kellae, dead. Her brother and child, dead. Hundreds dead.

And any moment could bring more death. And Riony couldn't work out how to be strong enough to save everybody.

"I'm *fine*," Riony spat back. She struck out again, her fist hitting the metal crate like a gong. "I'm just training. *Alone.*"

How long had she been there? She couldn't even remember. It felt like forever since the burning enclaves, but at the same time the images filling her head were so fresh and new she could be seeing them for the first time.

On return to Eslindekeep, she'd made her way down a whole extra level to where narrow corridors led to an empty dungeon and more storage. She went as far as she could go without leaving the underground base. She didn't want anyone to see her like this.

Trust razing Kess and her wolf to find her.

"Okay." Kess and Griskin's shadow that cast over Riony shifted.

Loosing a shrieking grunt, Riony cracked her knuckles against the crate again. She blinked weary eyes at her hands.

They looked so dark.

Covered in blood, it soaked into every joint and stuck to the layer of ash Riony hadn't cleaned away. She hadn't healed, hadn't changed, hadn't washed, hadn't slept, hadn't eaten. The scale mail vest hung crooked over her, clattering as she stared at her trembling hands.

"Kess?" Her voice was a broken, tiny plea.

The shadow returned.

Riony remained still, her back to the wolf and creature who rode him. Her chest heaved as her fury rekindled.

"Why did you listen to me? Why did you stay with Eslinde and Lyrrin instead of helping save people?"

"I ... I wanted to do what you needed of me."

"You shouldn't have! Whatever this pledge of yours is, it's stupid." And Riony was stupidest of all for letting herself use it, for trying to take what she wanted from Kess instead of what should have been done.

Guilt burbled in Riony, shaking her words. "You could have saved more people. You and Griskin, you're fast and deadly. If you were there, we could have gotten to Kife. We could have stopped him!"

We could have cut him through to the core and pulled every pain of vengeance from him for killing them, for killing them all. Riony wanted to scream the words, but they stuck in her throat.

"He was there?"

Riony turned, locking Kess in her burning gaze.

"Sparking *Kife*. You brought him into this! How did you ever think letting a sadist like him know about Dracuni was a good idea? Biggest mistake of your life, Kess, with no small competition."

Kess's shoulders shook but she didn't look away. "I know. I'm sorry."

Riony roared, "Sorry doesn't cut it! Kife killed all of those people because of you! And I couldn't save them!"

Griskin lowered his head and growled.

Kess ran a hand over his ear, hushing him. "I know. All of this is on me. Not you."

Riony's lips pulled away from her teeth, feral. She wanted Kess to argue, to fight back. She wanted someone to scream at her in return and blame her in the same way the voices in her head did.

How dare Kessara Heithorn look me in the eye and just ... take the blame?

It made Riony feel as though there was something deeper within Kess's confession of guilt, that her admissions were easy because they were covering something far worse.

And that the something far worse was something Riony couldn't guard against or anticipate because she just wasn't smart enough to handle any of this.

Riony's body gave in, and she slumped, her back clattering against the metal crate behind her. She slid down to the ground.

"I can't deal with your games, Kess. I can't. Not now."

Riony pressed her palms against her eyes.

Griskin padded closer.

Kess's voice was low and thick. "I won't ask you to trust me. I know trust is something earned. All I can do is continue trying to earn it from you."

Riony laughed dryly. "And I'll be the idiot giving you a chance right up until you stab me in the back. Why can't I ever be smart about things?"

"Do you know what I've noticed?" Kess climbed down from Griskin in slow, cautious motions and sat against the crate beside Riony.

"How you never could respect personal space?"

Kess rolled her eyes in the gentlest way Riony had ever seen. "How every time you talk about yourself not being smart, it's when what you're really being is *compassionate*. Giving me another chance was your compassion. Coming back for me and facing a nightmare of conglomerated revs was your compassion. Not stupidity."

"It can be both."

"No." Kess leaned in, a bright fervor in her eyes. "Your compassion is not just smart, it's *powerful*. It affects those around you in ways you don't even comprehend. It's why everybody looks to you for your strength and guidance and love."

Riony let her head hang between her knees, shaking it.

"Do you remember, at Heithorn estate, when the barn cat got burned by Kife's dragon?" Kess asked.

Riony convulsed, the memory an unwanted sting among the fresher memories of fiery death.

Kess continued. "I was sad for the creature, but thought it was the way it was and there was nothing that could be done. But you ... you fought for it. You would have pulled the sun from the sky to save a barn cat if you could have."

"I was just a dumb kid." Riony's voice was heavy with pain.

"Your compassion inspired me. I spent that whole afternoon sneaking around, wearing my hands and gown raw crawling through the estate on my own, trying to find where my parents kept the silvernix."

Riony lifted her head and gave Kess a long, questioning look. "You did? But the cat ..."

Kess's expression hardened. "I didn't find it in time. I never told you because I was ashamed of having failed ... of my uselessness."

Riony swallowed a sob that pushed through her throat. She had been the one who had spent the day wailing and crying to her parents. Kess, the girl she always thought of as a cruel, selfish gremlin, was the one who had taken action, as futile as it had been.

She was still staring at Kess, unable to shift her eyes. And there was pain there, hidden beneath the hard pinch of her expression.

Feigning a light tone, Riony said, "Probably for the best. Can you imagine the whipping I would have had if your parents discovered silvernix missing and the cat magically healed? One I wouldn't have survived, I'm sure. All I'm hearing right now is that my stupidity inspires further stupidity."

Kess tutted. "Then you're not listening."

"Then I'm deaf and dumb."

"Stop it."

Silence fell over them. Griskin grumbled and curled up beside Kess and she stared at the floor with some deep, ferocious thoughtfulness.

Riony watched her mutely as the chill of the room cooled her fury and burning muscles.

"I'm sorry," Kess said. "For our life together back then. For ever treating you as though I owned you. For all the cruelty you suffered because of me."

There had been so many nights when she was young when Riony had lain awake, dreaming of the day Kessara would profess her apologies to her and how she would laugh and laugh in the girl's face when she did.

Riony's voice shivered out. "You were only a child. And you didn't exactly have it easy either."

"It's no excuse."

Riony shrugged. "It does mean a lot, though. That you've grown into someone who can acknowledge the harm you've done."

"And how do you think I got here? You. Only you. How else could I have ever learned kindness except from

the only person who has shown it to me, even in the face of my dreadful selfishness?"

Kess reached a hand forward as though to touch Riony, but pulled back again and pressed it to her chest. "You are a beacon, and we around you just moths, fated to follow your radiance in the hopes we could ever one day glow as bright."

Riony felt heat creep up her neck. "Overly dramatic, Kess."

Kess ignored the interruption. "You change me in ways I never dreamed I could be worthy of. You inspire people."

Anger rose in Riony again and she wrapped her arms around her middle. The scale mail points bit into her bare skin.

"Maybe I wish I didn't. I *inspired* those people to live around the shrines, to build homes there. I told them they would be safe there." The words growled out. "How many died because of *me*?"

Kess shook her head. "You lost friends out there last night, didn't you?"

"I lost family. I lost people who trusted me and paid for it." A great tearing pain filled Riony's chest, and she squeezed her arms tight as though holding herself together.

"I'm so sorry. It's not your fault, but I know you can't believe it right now. I can't imagine how much it hurts."

Kess frowned, watching Riony's dry eyes and the ragged breaths spilling from her lips. "This is different though, to

last time. When you ... I mean, at the waterfall. I thought you'd lost someone then ..."

"You *were* there. I knew it." Riony turned on Kess, facing her fully. "Why ...?"

Her voice stuttered out, remembering just how broken and vulnerable and *naked* she had been.

"You could have killed me then and there, and I couldn't have done a thing to stop you. Why didn't you?"

"Do you think me so dishonorable?"

Riony's gaze roamed over Kess's pale face. "I did."

Kess's head bowed, a sad motion of agreement, as though she felt the same about who she used to be. Then tentatively she asked, "What happened that day, that left you so ... hurt?"

Hurt? Kess chose a kind word. More like destroyed. Shattered. Ripped right in half in a way that still didn't feel mended.

"Are you intent on bringing up every painful memory for me right now?"

"I'm sorry. You don't have to answer."

Riony scrubbed her hands over her face as a sharp sting ran between her nose and eyes. But she found the words coming out anyway. "It was my amma. It was my dead mother. She'd risen as a revenant and ..."

Kess drew a sharp breath and covered her mouth with one hand.

Riony laughed, harsh and hysterical. "Oh, it gets worse.

Dracuni managed to heal her, but not really. Only in body, not in soul. So I got to watch her die in front of me. A second time."

Despite her efforts to pass it off as the world's most tragic joke, Riony's voice shook with sobs by the end of her sentence, and she barely got the last words out.

A tentative touch of chilled fingers pressed to her shoulder. Kess's hand, small and gentle, imbued with a crushing weight of comfort that cracked Riony right through.

With a strangled sob, Riony's arms lashed out and wrapped around Kess. Choking on her tears, she drew the girl's body into her own, right onto her lap. Kess let out a tiny yelp but remained still as Riony squeezed her as though she were a childhood doll that could ease all her suffering with a tight enough embrace.

Riony cried. She couldn't cry like that around anyone else, but with Kess, with all the pain they'd shared between them already, it didn't feel so hard.

And Kess made not a single other sound or movement until Riony could breathe again.

Snuffling into Kess's shoulder, Riony spoke wetly. "Sometimes I ... I wish the guest, Eslinde, never came to Heithorn estate. That I hadn't stabbed that guard, hadn't taken Lyrrin. And me and my parents would still have been slaves, but I would have still *had them*."

Kess's hips shifted, pressing into Riony's thighs, but

she didn't attempt to push free of the cage of Riony's arms. Instead, she lifted her own hands, placing them around Riony's back.

"It wouldn't have worked out. We'd all have died to the revs along with my parents."

The ruins of the estate when they'd last been there had been scattered with the remains of all those who hadn't survived that attack.

Had Kess seen the bodies of her parents too?

"I'm sorry you lost them that way. That's how I lost mine, the first time."

"Eylin and Farrad were good people. It's their loss that should be mourned. My parents can get razed in life and in death."

Riony huffed in surprise. "You remember their names? You couldn't even remember mine for most of your life."

"I was being willfully spiteful. I'm sorry. I won't ever call you that awful epithet again. I'll only call you what you wish to be called."

Riony's fury had eased in the warmth of their embrace, but her heartbeat still hammered as she remembered Kess bowing low, stumbling over how to address Riony for her pledge. "It's Eyfarr. That's my last name now. Lyrrin and I made it when we stopped being Uf'Heithorn."

"I like that," Kess whispered. "Maybe I need to change my name too. I'm not sure I ever was a Heithorn. If you think things were bad while you were around, they got far

worse for me once you were gone."

"Oh, I'm sorry," Riony scoffed. "How dare I emancipate myself and my family from slavery and a death sentence?"

Kess's forehead dropped onto Riony's shoulder. "If anything, you should have far sooner. I only mean that your absence made it clear you were the only good thing in my life."

A shiver rattled up Riony's back. She didn't know how to take this new version of Kess, so forthright and earnest.

But truthfully, Kess had always been forthright and earnest when it came to the things she cared about. She would tell anyone who would listen with her full heart how she would be the best dragonrider in the world one day, no matter how her claims were met with scorn.

Riony only had to believe that the thing Kess cared about had shifted.

Do I? And if I do, does that mean I'm the thing Kess now cares about above everything else?

Her closeness to Kess and press of their bodies together suddenly felt awkward. Riony swallowed roughly but didn't move.

"I'm not sure how good I ever was or what good I've ever done," Riony whispered. "All the mistakes I've made ... Even my compassion, that you're saying is my strength, has only screwed me up at every turn."

If she hadn't saved Kess in the cave, Brishan might still be alive, they could have stayed in the undercity, never

suffered the losses of everyone in the enclaves. But Riony found she couldn't speak that weight onto Kess's shoulders.

Instead, she said, "We shouldn't have freed Kife's dragon. If it wasn't lurking around, attacking the tamed dragons, Thallan and Norallei could have gone out by air and stopped more of the attacks. Every good thing I try to do comes back to hurt me."

Kess stiffened in Riony's hold, and then she slowly pulled away.

Riony's grasp involuntarily tightened for a second before she let go. Cold air rushed into the space Kess had been.

Eyes averted, Kess reached a hand for Griskin and he came to her.

"Then it's clear I'm failing at doing all I need to do to protect you." She half turned back to Riony. "Will you be okay?"

Riony nodded dumbly.

Kess pulled herself up onto the wolf's back and left.

Riony remained frozen in place for a long while, breathing through another short round of tears. The dark chill of the room felt so much deeper than before. Composing herself, Riony cleaned her hands off as well as she could, wincing at the deep splits on her knuckles, then wandered back toward the main living area.

She was met by Yensen, waiting within a passageway. His eyes narrowed over her face, and Riony wondered how

swollen it must look.

"Are you well?" he asked with stilted care.

"I'd be a whole lot weller if I hadn't been left alone out there last night."

Yensen lowered his eyes and bowed. "Forgive me. I felt I had to return to Eslinde to ensure her safety."

"And why did you *feel* that strongly enough to abandon your orders?" Riony figured the newcomers might not consider Aishena to be higher ranking than them, but she sure did.

The grayglim tilted his head, silky black hair curtaining the sides of his face. He sounded apologetic as he replied, "Because I don't trust Kessara Heithorn."

Riony's blank stare became a chuckle, and she began moving again. "Man, are you late to the party. I'm not even sure the party is still going."

Yensen walked at her side. "I've seen how she's manipulated herself into your favor, but I beg you to remain wary. Has she told you how she had a private meeting with the Dragon King not long before our escape?"

Riony's steps faltered. "No, but—"

"I fear they created a plot then, one that we have all been playing our parts out in since."

Riony picked up her pace as though she could leave Yensen and his accusations behind. "That doesn't make sense."

Yensen kept up without any sign of effort. "Doesn't it? Who knew the most about you and your connection to the shrine enclaves, specifically to Myrwa and how important they were to you?"

Pain bloomed fresh in Riony's chest, and she wrinkled her nose. Timelines and motivations flashed through her head. Had the Dragon King already known about Dracuni, the enclaves, everything, before she and Kess escaped Zarram dragonhold that night?

The riders who came for them then, maybe they'd waited for Kess to take a dragon and followed her, all part of the plan. When that didn't work out, Kess could have arranged the attacks on the enclaves, somehow. She'd been out flying patrols alone once or twice, could have taken a dragon and sent messages.

Riony's stomach roiled, and she shook it off. "No. Kess is smarter than that. If she'd really been plotting to hurt us, she'd have struck the undercity, not the enclaves. And thankfully that refuge is still safe from the dragonlords. The attacks last night were all Kife."

"You admit she's clever but underestimate the level of plotting she's capable—" Yensen cut off as figure marched toward them.

Aishena had her hands at the athames on her belt and her expression was dark. The torches along the corridor flickered from her brisk pace.

"Aish? What is it?" Riony jogged to meet her.

Aishena's lips pulled in. "It's Kess."

Riony and Yensen's gaze locked.

Aishena continued. "She's stolen the Zarrams' orange dragon and left."

Riony's heart froze into a solid stone.

SIXTEEN

Kife's untamed dragon was on Kess faster than she expected. She'd barely gotten Ambri into the air before the purple etherdart came shooting out of the nearby woods toward them.

"Come on, then. Let's do this."

Her heartbeat thundered as she aimed Ambri into the sky as fast as the orange dragon could fly. But it had been thundering like that for every second since Riony pulled her into her grieving embrace. The simple thrill of chasing dragons through biting winter air was a relief to her enflamed emotions.

The bright burst of fire gusted over Kess's shoulder, and she gasped away from it. The purple was on their tail, mouth snapping. Kess angled her dragon sharply away before the jagged maw could close on Ambri's wing.

Waves and waves of wailing anger washed over Kess and she felt faint with the disconcerting inability to distinguish her own feelings from those invading her.

She'd experienced similar the other times she'd been near the purple dragon since he was freed. He had screamed wordlessly in her mind when he'd been untamed and when she'd placed herself between him and Riony.

Dragons only communicated with those they were bonded with, but Kess wouldn't fool herself into thinking this was communication. The blare of anger and upset felt more like a psychic attack.

She didn't know what it meant. She only knew the dragon was furious, and ready to take that anger out on her.

He snapped at the orange dragon again.

As agile and free as he was, Kess wasn't sure she and her modest ability to control the tamed dragon were going to be enough to escape his attacks. But she had to try. She had to fix at least one thing for Riony.

At least I didn't bring Griskin into this.

Samor was out on patrol on his flamesong, and once Kess spotted the silhouette of them in the distance, she took Ambri and the purple dragon the other direction. She wanted to keep everyone else out of this as long as she could.

The faint echo of shouting rose from far below. Tiny figures emerged from the tunnel to Eslindekeep. Only one

could be identified at this distance by the bright glow of her red hair.

She's going to be angry. I should have explained myself.

But Kess knew if she had, she'd never have gotten away with Ambri.

With her eyes off the purple, Kess almost missed the claws angling for Ambri's head. She pulled away at the last moment. With teeth gritted, she leaned into the orange scales, pushing the dragon to fly faster, higher and higher.

The air felt thin up there, and the ground so, so far down.

They were above the purple dragon now, and Kess held her breath, awaiting the perfect moment. There. She was directly over Kife's dragon, flying in line as it came up toward them.

And Kess was no longer afraid to fall.

She gave Ambri one final order to glide in slow circles and then dropped from the saddle.

She kept her eyes open as she fell, the flight goggles protecting them as she aimed herself as best she could. Three heartbeats passed of nothing but the air whipping through Kess's hair and clothes and pummeling her ears and then came the hard impact against purple scales.

Too high near the dragon's head, Kess narrowly avoided skewering herself right through with one of his horns. She twisted and slid between the double row of spikes down its neck. Both her arms flung out, grasping for purchase.

She'd just gotten her hands around one of those spines and brought herself into a sitting position on the dragon's shoulders when he was upon the orange dragon again.

"No!" Kess commanded, wrenching the spike she held to her left with all her strength.

Kife's dragon turned, his stomach clipping the orange's wings, and he roared, inside and out.

A violent buck of his shoulders left Kess gasping as she lifted into the air, fingertips slipping along to the tip of the spike. She clutched on to the very end and pulled herself back in, thumping onto the purple scales again as the bucking continued.

His emotions ached through her, clearer than ever as she pressed herself to his back.

Angry. Angry. Angry. And also, deeper, **Hurt.**

Kess screwed her eyes closed at the barrage.

She screamed over the wind. "I'm sorry. You should be angry! You have been hurt. I should have saved you, right at the very beginning. When you first hatched and I wished you were mine. I should have kept you safe from Kife and all his cruelty."

A shiver of recognition intertwined with the violent feelings. The purple gave another, smaller wriggle of his shoulders in his attempts to dislodge his unwelcome rider.

His scales shimmered in the midday light. They had brightened since he'd been freed. Still dusky in tone, but not the dulled cloudy gray they had become under Kife's

ownership.

"I shouldn't have freed you from the taming when I did. You should have always been free, to have the life you deserved right from the start."

From the start. The words seemed to echo back at Kess with another wave of recognition. The dragon growled.

"From the start," Kess said again.

In the gap of time between Kife's cruelty in choosing the dragon Kess had wanted, and before the dragonhandler had come through to tame it, Kess had sat with the purple hatchling, telling him all about the life they would have had together if he were her dragon.

And after he had been tamed until Riony had come and found her there late at night, Kess had sat beside the hatchling and cried tears she couldn't explain, because the vibrant life she'd sensed in the newborn dragon, that had attracted her to it, felt as though it had all gone away.

The dragon's bucking and squirming stilled. The violent levels of anger reduced to a simmering rage.

"Do you ... do you remember me?"

The purple hissed suddenly and veered as two swift shapes shot their way. The red of Hux and aqua of Gleem cut through the air.

A growl rippled down the purple etherdart's neck to Kess.

From Gleem's back, Zeina waved the hand signals for, "Are you okay?"

Kess waved her own in return. "Back off, I've got this."

Gleem keened and flicked her snout toward the purple, who responded with bared teeth and low grumble. ***Confusion. Disdain ... Envy.***

The sensations tugged at Kess's nerves.

Zeina shrugged, pulling Gleem in to glide a respectful distance below. Hux came up and over them, carrying Jaym and Dashiel.

As they passed, Dashiel cupped both hands near their face and mouthed, "Wow."

They continued upward to rescue the riderless orange dragon.

Kess shook her head at Dashiel's awe. She felt no more accomplished than a flea on a wolf's back.

She'd come into the air with the goal of somehow convincing this creature to stop attacking them, but now she wanted so much more for it.

Her heart ached with every version of her life where she'd made better choices. Where the magnificent creature beneath her had never had his freedom and soul stripped away for so many years.

"I didn't know then what I know now. I wasn't someone then who could have made the right choice, who had the power to save you even if I did." Kess ran her hands over the purple scales.

"But when the chance came to me to free you, I'm glad I did. It's one of the few things I've done that I'm proud of."

She leaned in, pressing her forehead to the back of the dragon's neck. "So please don't make me regret it by continuing to attack us."

The storm of emotions blowing through Kess had cleared of anger now. Only the hurt remained within Kife's dragon ...

No. Kess refused to think of him as that anymore. Kife had never named him, never seen him as anything more than a simple tool.

Kess had once thought of a name for him, in the moment she'd seen the hatchling for the first time. It had just come to her and felt so right.

What was it again?

Lyomir. *That was it.* The memory of the name reverberated in Kess's mind. That's what she would call him now.

Lyomir ducked and wove away from the two Rebel Riders' dragons who coasted through the air on each side at a safe distance. The orange dragon descended quickly toward Eslindekeep with Dashiel in control.

Lyomir snarled their way but didn't try to chase the tamed dragon again.

Kess still breathed a little easier once they were both away and safe underground again.

Now she just needed to get herself safely on the ground again.

"Lyomir, will you stop attacking us?"

The purple dragon loosed a long, snarling growl, and Kess braced to be thrown off his back. And then ...

I'll stop.

Kess's breath stuck. Those were words. Kess hadn't been sure before, the way the thoughts had echoed her own. But those were words coming to her from the dragon. Begrudging, seething, irritable words.

Her eyes welled up and she couldn't wipe them because of the goggles.

To hear a dragon speak even once was a sun-born blessing greater than Kess had ever known. Even if the tone sounded like Lyomir hated Kess and everything about the situation right to his fiery core.

She leaned against his scales. "And if there's anything, anything I can do for you, I will. If there's any way I can help you through your pain, I want to."

As I learn to work through mine too.

They were slowly coming to land. The bare flat slabs of Eslindekeep were blocked out like a chessboard beneath them. It was through no effort on Kess's part, but rather the guidance of Gleem and Hux.

Both the seasong and etherflame were significantly larger than the etherdart, and Kess wondered whether anything she'd said or done had an impact on Lyomir or if he was just playing nice to avoid aggression from them.

They landed in the icy sludge that was all that remained from a light dusting of snow that morning. And then, as to make a point of what he thought of having a human on his back, Lyomir gave one whiplike buck and threw Kess off. She landed with a squelch in a puddle.

With one final growl, Lyomir rushed fluidly into the air again with a powerful flap of his wings and flew out of sight.

Kess levered herself up off her back with a groan as footsteps raced her way. A shadow cut the glare of the high sun as Riony bent over her and pulled her free of the mud.

"What were you thinking?" Every feature on Riony's face blazed with fury.

But her hands were gentle as they brought Kess up into her arms. Griskin had reached them as well, circling and prowling beside them, but Riony continued to carry Kess herself.

"I wanted to solve a problem for you."

"By killing yourself?"

"I'm still alive, aren't I?"

"I have no sparking idea how."

The sounds of Gleem and Hux coming to land whomped behind them.

Kess ringed one hand around her other wrist and rubbed it. She'd strained it somewhere along the way. She wouldn't be surprised if her entire body ached tomorrow.

Under Riony's glare, she tried to explain herself. "I only took Ambri out to lure the purple dragon in. I needed a way to get to him, attempt to communicate with him."

"I saw. I thought ... Why did you even think you could do that?"

Kess shrugged. "The day Lyrrin used the dragon summoning rune, I felt something. His emotions. I knew he wasn't just attacking mindlessly. He was hurting. I thought if I could do something, it might lessen the hurt for him and for you."

She could still feel that pain, even now. Although the dragon had flown out of view, she could still feel the lingering touch of his emotions within her. She knew he remained nearby.

Riony's jaw clenched. "You didn't ... You don't have to risk yourself for me like that."

They marched toward the tunnel entrance. Eslinde, Yensen, and Aishena stood there, waiting and watching, a range of scolding and concerned expressions across their faces. Riony took Kess straight past them.

There was a waver in her step, the kind of slight stagger that came from exhaustion, but she kept Kess held tight in her bandaged arms.

Dashiel jogged up the tunnel to join them. "Kess? Kess! That was incredible! You just flew on a wild dragon. Do you know how few people have done that?"

"And who do you razing think we are?" Zeina barked as she and Jaym strolled up beside them.

Dashiel's full lips pouted. "You know what I mean. A

full-grown wild dragon, not one she's bonded with. Not that you aren't impressive in your own right, of course."

"Of course." Zeina gave Dashiel a sly wink.

"So are we going to have a problem with the purple again? Or did our fierce little wolf rider scare him off?" Jaym eyed Kess as though he were ready to write her up into one of his stories.

"He said he'll stop."

Dashiel's steps bounced. "He spoke to you? Are you bonded?"

"No. No, I don't think it was like that, at all." Kess flicked at some of the mud on her leg.

Zeina and Jaym shared a look but said nothing else.

They reached an intersection as the tunnel split off into the various chambers and private rooms. Riony stopped, seeming unsure where she was going and why she was taking Kess along with her. Griskin grumbled and yapped, nudging up against Riony's side.

"You can put me down now," Kess said softly.

Blinking a couple of times, Riony nodded vaguely and placed Kess onto Griskin's saddle.

"I'm ... going to check on Dracuni," Riony stumbled the words out and turned away.

Kess wanted to tell Riony to get some rest, to look after herself. Dracuni was weakened from the blood spent on the injured the night before, but she was okay. She knew

Riony wasn't going to listen to her, though.

Which is why Kess strengthened her resolve to do anything she could to lighten Riony's load.

If Lyomir stopped attacking them as he said, that was one small problem solved. But only one of many so much larger.

What if we can't solve the others?

Kess didn't know what that would mean. Only that Riony wouldn't give up. She'd never give up. Even if it killed her.

SEVENTEEN

Riony dropped into the saddle behind Zeina, adjusting the tightness of the strap she'd just added around her wrist.

"This is utter foolishness," Eslinde's strained voice came from below.

The silver-haired princess skirted around Gleem as though she could block the dragon's way.

"It's been decided." Riony didn't look at her or any of the others they were leaving behind.

She focused instead on triple-checking her weapons and new armor were all in order. Being kitted head to toe in the blue and gold scale mail from Eslinde's supplies rather than her dinted and rusty hodge-podge of reclaimed steel armor had been one of Aishena's requirements for agreeing to the mission.

The only variation to the gleaming scales was the faded, dried-blood red of Myrwa's shawl, tied around her waist. A reminder of why she was doing this.

"I never decided it," Lyrrin snapped back. "You can't just go and attack a *dragonkeep*! That's ... utter foolishness."

Riony flicked an annoyed gaze Lyrrin's way. Siding with Eslinde instead of her, now?

She probably wouldn't have liked this even if Eslinde wasn't here, a deeper voice of reason told Riony. But Riony wasn't in a mood to listen to reason. Reason could go die in a ditch.

Turning her eyes back to her armor, she muttered, "Utter foolishness would be letting Kife and the Dragon King and all those riders who burned the enclaves think they can do that with no consequences."

So, you're going to be as violent as them? Dracuni sat across the space, tail flicking.

Riony ignored her.

"It's been a while since we bit back," Thallan said from atop his bronze dragon. "We let the dragonlords grow too bold. But with more numbers now, it's as good a time as any to attack."

He pushed his tamed dragon into motion and headed out of the stables first. Yensen rode with him, glowering. He'd wanted to remain with Eslinde again, but Riony insisted. She had a plan for him.

Norallei followed, with Kess riding as her second. Griskin remained behind. They had no intention of being out of the air until they came home triumphant.

"I don't know why you want to attack at all." Lyrrin's voice grew higher. "How is that going to protect anyone? I thought that's what we did."

Riony's eye twitched as Jaym walked through with his pocket-hawk on his arm and climbed onto Samor's dragon behind him.

"Did we? Did we protect Myrwa and Kellae? We haven't protected *anybody*. Nothing we did made a difference. Nothing is going to end the dragonlords cruelty unless we make it stop. And *you* ..." Riony turned to face Eslinde. "I thought you'd be all for this. Didn't you want us on the offensive? Taking out the Dragon King himself?"

"Ready?" Zeina asked softly.

You shouldn't go. Dracuni snorted. ***Not without me.***

Riony ignored the unidragon again. Even if Dracuni could fly, there was no way Riony would bring her along. That would be *utter foolishness*.

Riony nodded to Zeina, and Gleem carried them out of the stables. Dashiel and Aishena followed on Ambri.

Jaym sighed in a dramatic way. "I doubt Yeonard Draekhan will be there today for us to assassinate, most unfortunately, but taking out even a few tamed dragons should weaken the shadow dragon, so that's something."

Eslinde jogged to keep up beside them. "It's not so

much the method as the timing and the target. Striking Gerichkeep is a distraction, a bait you are taking. The attacks on the enclaves were clearly on purpose to draw us out and look what is happening!"

Eslinde waved her arm at the five dragons in a line, making their way along the long corridor to the exit.

"If they planned to draw us out, we were drawn out that night and they didn't take their advantage." Riony blinked for too long, and flashes of fire and bodies filled her vision. "I don't believe there was any plan greater than Kife's cruelty."

"I think there was more," Kess said. She spoke with a heavy thickness of guilt. "The dragonlords couldn't allow the enclaves to keep thriving."

Riony knew how the enclaves were thought of. Dens of criminals and cannibals. The riders probably thought they were doing the right thing exterminating everybody.

Kess continued. "They couldn't allow a place where people could live freely outside of the keeps, without the control and ownership of masters, without needing the protection of dragons. It was a threat to their power, and they will destroy anything that threatens their power."

Riony twisted around in her seat, holding Kess's gaze. She had easily agreed to come along, but these days Kess might jump into a vat of molten glass if Riony asked her to. She didn't seem happy about it, though. Deep lines of concern wrinkled her narrow face.

Am I making a mistake?

All voices of doubt were buried beneath a haze of anger and memories falling like ash.

Daylight temporarily blinded Riony as the dragons moved outside. The five formed a rough circle, awaiting the order to go.

Eslinde moved into the center, turning on the spot as she pleaded with them. "If our enemies seek to crush us, then all the more reason to play it safe for a while."

Lyrrin stood beside her, fingers clenched around the paired heart stone hanging from a string at her neck. "You could at least take me with you! You know I can help. I'm sick of sitting back here, feeling your heart straining through battle, unable to do anything! You have no idea how that feels!"

Eslinde's hand went out almost reflexively and pulled Lyrrin closer to her.

Riony checked her sword was secure one last time. "You haven't flown on a dragon before and you aren't starting now."

Dracuni, remaining in the shadow of the tunnel, said nothing else, only watched Riony with sorrowful eyes.

Riony's jaw twitched.

She turned away from those on the ground and addressed the ones riding with her. "We have to take a stand."

"You don't." Eslinde's voice had become soft. "You're

just a child—"

"Hiding away while the world burns is what dragonlords do," Riony raised her voice.

Vance joined Eslinde. He placed a hand on her shoulder, but it seemed not so much in support as consolation. Riony nodded to him. He was their best rider remaining behind with Jaym's dragon—who they'd been assured had agreed to allow Vance as a rider.

"We're not going to keep hiding while others suffer. We're taking the fight to those causing the suffering."

"Hear! Hear!" Zeina bellowed.

Thallan gave Riony a slow, firm nod, then flew into the air.

Samor's face remained grim, but behind him, Jaym thumped a fist to his chest, saluted Riony, then they were next off the ground.

Moments later they were all flying far above Eslindekeep, and Riony fought off a shiver, feeling as though she'd left her heart behind.

The dragons arranged in a V-shaped formation, with Thallan at the lead, and glided northeast toward Gerichkeep.

It had been chosen as their target for three reasons.

First, it was a smaller keep and would have fewer defenses.

Second, it was a long way away from other dragonkeeps, so it would take a while before backup arrived.

And third, the reason that had warmed Riony to the plan, the riders who had attacked Myrwa's enclave wore Gerich's colors.

Riony and her team took the flight there easy, making sure not to tire the dragons before the attack.

Eslinde had provided what information she had on the keep in their earlier planning stages, before it became clear they were moving from planning to doing.

Gerichkeep had twenty-five dragonriders in their ranks, now twenty-three after Samor and Shani took out two during the attacks on the enclaves.

Riony had balked at the madness of going five against twenty-three, but it was likely only a few riders would be on patrol when they first struck, with a few more sitting in preparation for if they were needed. Most wouldn't even be in the rider's dragonhold.

They could take down the ones in the air fast and not get overwhelmed by more as they came out in waves. At least, that's how Thallan said it was when they used to harry keeps.

"Besides, most of the kids they put on dragons these days are only trained to burn revs from the air. They have no idea how to handle attacks from other riders," Jaym had added.

Checking over her sword and armor for the dozenth time, Riony stifled the anxiety jittering through her nerves.

In front of her, Zeina shifted suddenly, then yelled

back to Riony, "Behind us and up."

Riony looked over her shoulder, squinting through the ashy air. A dusky shape followed at a distance.

Kife's sparking dragon.

Riony wasn't sure how she felt about the thing. It was a reminder of all she'd suffered while Kess and Kife had hunted them, and Viska was still out of action thanks to it.

But after the stunt Kess had pulled, however she'd managed to communicate with the purple dragon, it had no longer attacked the tamed dragons within their group.

"Is it going to be a problem?" Riony asked.

Zeina shook her head. "Gleem doesn't think so. The poor thing is confused, mostly. Angry, but not sure who to be angry at."

Riony bit her lip. "As long as it doesn't take any more of that anger out on us."

They settled into silence for the rest of the flight. Zeina didn't chat or flirt or invite Riony to her bed again since the two times Riony hadn't followed through.

Maybe she would when they got home again, triumphant after the mission.

Riony wasn't even sure she wanted that anymore.

If they got home again.

It felt far too soon when Thallan signaled Gerichkeep was within sight. They lifted higher into the sky then, hiding within the smoke-tainted clouds in order to get closer without causing alarm too soon.

Riony counted four dragons out on patrol. It seemed like a lot for a smaller keep, based on the information Eslinde provided.

But Riony didn't doubt they could deal with four tamed beasts.

They were almost directly over the keep when one of Gerich's riders changed course suddenly, aiming their way.

Across their five dragons, Riony's companions signaled their readiness and dove from the clouds.

Zeina hung back slightly as Samor and Norallei brought their dragons into a swift chase with two of the keep's riders. All four of Gerich's riders wore her colors—green and black—and even their dragons stayed on theme as well, foresty toned treedarts and etherdarts.

Thallan and Dashiel took their dragons even farther down, shooting fast right to the rooftops of the dragonkeep, to the large open flight deck of the rider's dragonhold.

They unloaded their cargo of the two grayglims there and took off again.

Riony held her breath as Yensen and Aishena disappeared from view. That part had been Riony's contribution to the plan. She wanted the grayglims to hit the riders in their barracks before they had a chance to reach their dragons.

Even Yensen, who'd been arguing blue in the face that he wanted to remain with Eslinde, had turned around at the proposal. He'd agreed it was a good plan and could

make the whole mission work.

"Do I have to kill them?" Aishena had asked.

"They didn't think twice about killing innocent people at the enclaves," Riony reminded her.

Aishena had stared back with her stony expression and midnight eyes.

Riony flinched first. "Do what you think is best."

"I will."

Now, Riony just hoped Aishena would make it out of there alive.

Samor had already taken down one rider and turned his massive flamesong to another. Norallei's white shimmerdart, Iffyr, sped circles around it as well, and thin white blades flashed through the air. One of Kess's daggers hit the target and another rider fell.

Zeina evaded sharply as a bolt of flame shot by. A grass-green dragon chased close behind.

Riony grunted. "Quit running. The thing is half Gleem's size."

A moment later there was no need, as Thallan and Dashiel brought their dragons back into the battle, chasing the spring-toned dragon off.

A small speck flew from Jaym's wrist toward the fourth rider, hitting them in the face in a puff of feathers. The rider's cries carried across the sky as the small hawk ripped at their goggles and face.

Riony stared, horrified at the bird.

The harassed rider's dragon veered sideways, dropping the rider right off its back.

"One of Jaym's favorite tricks," Zeina said.

"Wow. I hate it." Riony shuddered and looked away. "But that's four down already."

From the city below, a cacophony of bells sounded. The alarm was well and truly raised.

"By the stars ..." Zeina waved her arms in broad signals to the other riders. "Ten more! Ten coming out now!"

"What? There shouldn't be that many!" Riony followed the woman's gaze and confirmed the numbers.

Maybe they had been wary of retaliation after all. Maybe they were ready and waiting for this attack that had been lured in, like Eslinde had said.

Aishena and Yensen must not have been able to stop that wave. Riony only hoped they could stop the next.

She bared her teeth at the incoming dragons.

If they want a fight, that's exactly what we came for.

Dashiel cut Ambri right across Gleem's path as three of the new riders went after them. They ducked and wove through the air, leading those three away. Norallei and Thallan brought their two dragons close, flying them in a matching evasion pattern as Kess downed the first of the ten new attackers.

Samor and Shani didn't run. He and his massive dragon barreled headfirst toward the largest two of the incoming riders.

"Not scared of much, are they?" Riony laughed out the words.

"Yeah, well." Zeina's tone was flat. "Neither of them has cared much about anything in life since they both lost their partners."

Riony's breath stuck. "Oh."

She didn't have long to dwell on that, though, as a speckled green and black treedart crashed into Gleem's back, claws first.

Gleem roared a high-pitched cry as the smaller dragon grasped onto her hips and began climbing up toward Riony and Zeina.

"I've got it!" Riony yelled and unsheathed her sword.

With one hand she activated the float rune and then quickly buckled the hilt to the end of the strap she'd attached to her wrist. She wasn't dropping her weapon midair ever again.

Riony ducked a thin dart of fire as she shifted around into a crouched position. Wind buffeted her on all sides as Gleem's wings beat hard. Trying to stand still was harder than remaining in motion so she could adjust to the movement of flight.

She stood up and marched toward the small dragon climbing Gleem's back.

The rider on the speckled dragon wore an astonished expression as though that were the last thing they expected to see.

Surprise jolted Riony too.

She's so young.

Riony swung her sword toward the rider, but the girl was already backing their treedart off Gleem. They pulled back awkwardly, jarring sideways to dodge the sword, and the rider yelped as she lost grip of her dragon.

Her scream as she fell free entirely pierced right through Riony. The tamed treedart, without instruction, continued its awkward sideways flutter and followed the falling girl toward the ground below.

Riony's breath came hard, and her nerves rattled. She returned to the seat behind Zeina as they dove suddenly beneath another attack.

There were still eight after them, and they were staying in groups, keeping the Rebel Riders on the back foot.

Yensen and Aishena better keep any more riders from coming out or we're done.

Both of Gleem's wings snapped in beside her chest as Thallan and Norallei flew down each side with a Gerichkeep rider close after them. Riony followed Kess with her eyes as Norallei's dragon went past. The intensity in her expression seemed filled with pain, and the scream of the young rider who fell echoed in Riony's mind again.

She hadn't even touched the girl, but Riony knew her death was going to haunt her for a long time.

How many had Kess killed directly with her knives? How much did it cost her each time? What had Riony

asked of her?

Bile burned the back of Riony's throat.

That's what we came here for, isn't it? To fight? To kill?

Some violence is necessary.

Thallan and Norallei's dragons separated then, and the two riders diverted all attention to Norallei. They were almost on her and Kess when a dark shape came rushing down from the clouds.

Kife's purple etherdart screamed a roar as he grasped one of the small dragon's head within his talons. They wrestled midair, and the rider was thrown moments before the purple pulled the smaller dragon's taming stake free.

Riony gasped. They had no silvernix to complete the untaming, even if they could get to the groundward tumbling dragon in time. It didn't have a chance.

The purple spun on one wing and aimed next for Norallei's dragon, and Riony yelled wordlessly for Zeina to turn their way.

But Kife's dragon didn't attack Iffyr. He went instead for the next rider chasing after them.

Well, damn. That might help turn the tables a bit.

Swooping back up again, Zeina headed Gleem up into the ashy clouds.

"What are you doing?" Riony yelled.

"There's too many of them!"

"There wouldn't be if you'd actually attack!"

They were too far away from the rest of the battle, and

none of the riders had followed them up there, meaning all the remaining riders were focused on the rest of their group. Another two chased Norallei and Kess again, sending a volley of fireballs their way.

Riony's head filled with fire again. Burnt bodies. Burnt friends. Riony shook off a disturbing vision of Kess lying still in ashes.

Nerves jangled through Riony. Zeina was being too cautious, and Riony had run out of patience.

Dashiel brought Ambri not far beneath Gleem as they tried to shake the enemy on their tail. And Riony didn't hesitate to take her chance.

She launched herself toward the dark-green dragon chasing Ambri. With her glowing sword in hand, she came down fast, but not bone-breakingly so, right between the dragon's wings.

She didn't let the rider turn around, didn't want to see their face. She struck hard, batting the rider with the flat of her sword across the back of the head. They slumped in the saddle and the dragon spiraled, spinning groundward.

Grunting and breathing in sharp pants, Riony leaped again. Norallei's shimmerdart was the next closest island in the air, and Riony landed on Iffyr's outstretched wing as he glided by. She ran lightly along the thick leather.

"What are you ...?" Norallei snapped in shock.

"Be careful!" Kess reached out an arm almost as though to catch Riony as she ran across the dragon's back and sent

herself flying toward the treedart chasing after them.

Riony overshot her jump to the small dragon and struck her sword out at the last moment, catching the dragon's pale-green wing. It sliced through the membrane without slowing Riony's momentum at all.

The resistance of sword through leather was enough to jerk the hilt out of Riony's hand, but she caught onto the strap and pulled it back into her palm before gravity took her entirely.

Still, she was falling, with no other dragon in her path.

I guess I'm going to see just how far I can fall with this float magic.

As the wind rushed up around her, Riony had a clear view down to the dragonkeep below, where a gleaming shimmerdart came racing out of the dragonhold faster than a shooting star.

Thallan took his dragon after it, but it was far too fast.

Riony's vision filled with aqua scales and she thumped onto Gleem's back.

"What kind of stunt was that?" Zeina rasped and swore under her breath a long string of curses. "Never mind. That messenger dragon was our cue to finish up and get out of here before reinforcements come in."

Zeina began signaling to Thallan, and him back.

"No, we're not done here," Riony growled.

Someone else had taken out another two riders. Only three remained. If they could rid Gerichkeep of all its riders, all those who had rained fire on Myrwa's enclave, Riony would call it a good day.

Zeina smacked her hands down onto the front of her saddle and yelled both at Thallan and Riony. "Stars! We're done! We should go before things get worse!"

Thallan signaled what Riony had learned was a negative and pointed toward the remaining three riders.

Riony grinned viciously and her lips trembled.

Zeina only grunted and Gleem curved to join Dashiel and Ambri in chase of a fast etherdart.

A shrieking roar scraped through the air. A larger Gerichkeep rider had latched their dragon onto the wild purple's neck from above. They twisted and wrestled, but the talons of the green etherdart were latched tight.

Norallei and Kess swooped in on the white shimmerdart, snapping at the air near the attacker's wings. As they flew a tight loop to come after them again, the Gerichkeep rider backed off, letting the purple go.

Iffyr's second pass looped around again, white blades flicked through the sky like the shimmer of flying fish.

One hit the rider. He fell from his saddle and his dragon lurched, wings twitching wildly in a way that left it tumbling from the air, blocking Iffyr's path. With less than seconds to spare, Norallei pushed her dragon down in an attempt to dodge the falling beast.

Riony's breath caught. *No. Go over. OVER.*

The weight of the mindless dragon crashed across Iffyr's

back, wings tangling against wings with a whipping crack.

A moment later the dragons separated again. And another body fell.

"No!" Riony cried. She grasped Zeina's back. "Quick, that way!"

She knew they were too far away. Everyone was too far away.

The white shimmerdart had carried two small women with dark hair wearing the same blue and gold armor, and from this distance Riony couldn't tell whether it was Norallei or Kess who was falling.

The remaining rider seemed dazed, injured, but quickly regained control of the tamed dragon.

Riony held her breath as it dove and caught the falling body in its talons.

Samor brought his flamesong in a moment later and then continued through to beside Gleem.

"It's Norallei," he bellowed across the gap of air.

Riony found herself able to breathe again. But then—

Samor shook his head with a dreadful finality.

Dead? Riony's hand clenched around the acorn at her neck.

Zeina shrieked. "We should have gone! We should already be gone, all of us ..."

Riony kept staring at the shimmerdart circling below. Norallei and Kess had been sitting as close as Riony and Zeina were now. It could have been either of them. It had

been so close ...

The last of the Gerichkeep riders was gone and Thallan brought his bronze dragon up into a smooth glide beside them.

"Thallan," Zeina's voice broke over the word.

"I know," he barked back. "It doesn't change the plan."

"But ... *Norallei*! She's ... you ..." It sounded as though Zeina was crying.

Thallan stared back, still and grim. "Norallei would want us to finish this. We're winning. The grayglims have kept the remaining dragonriders grounded. We should push our advantage now. We could burn down the whole keep!"

"That wasn't part of the plan. Riders only," Riony said, but her voice had become small, too small to carry across the noise of flight.

"No," Jaym bellowed from behind Samor. "We're done. We're leaving."

With a dully sad look, Samor nodded. He signaled to Dashiel, who nodded in reply.

Ambri loosed three loud, piercing wails on Dashiel's command, and they dove together toward the dragonhold. Thallan sneered at the other Rebel Riders but turned his dragon to follow.

With the end of their attack signaled, Riony kept her eyes on the building below and as far away as possible from Kess and the dragon she rode and the body that dragon carried. And she waited to see the grayglims emerge, ready to be picked up so they could leave.

Come on, Aish. Time to get out of here.

Riony had given them clear instructions. Don't go too far in. Stay close to an exit so they could leave as soon as the signal was given. But as Thallan and Dashiel circled the dragonhold, it felt like an eternity, and neither Yensen or Aishena came out.

Then there was movement. On a balcony on the far side, Yensen stepped out into view, carrying Aishena, limp in his arms.

EIGHTEEN

Riony cradled Aishena's body as they rode behind Dashiel back toward Eslindekeep. The moment she'd seen Aishena slumped in the grayglim's arms, she'd leaped from Zeina's dragon, far and fast enough that her knees felt like they were ready to pop right out of their sockets.

She was trying to rub the pain out of them as Aishena finally stirred.

"Hey, welcome back," Riony said softly.

Aishena's face scrunched and she groaned.

"She's awake?" Dashiel asked.

"She just reached for her weapons so I'd say that's a good sign." Riony made a hushing sound and wrapped her free hand around Aishena's fingers that were clasped around an athame.

Her other arm remained supporting Aishena against her chest.

"Where are we?" Aishena's voice was woozy and drawling.

"Yensen found you unconscious and got you out."

"Mmph." Aishena reached a trembling hand to her windblown hair, touching tentatively around her head and wincing.

Riony pulled her a little closer. "Careful, just stay still. We'll get you back and I'm sure Dracuni will make you all better."

She'd already checked Aishena's wounds. One growing lump on the back of her head from a blow that thankfully didn't break the skin, and a graze on one cheek—probably where she'd fallen.

Having had her own head cracked like an egg before, Riony didn't feel much relief from Aishena being awake. She wanted Aishena healed, and cursed herself that she didn't bring silvernix with them.

It still felt wrong to her, somehow, asking Dracuni to bleed into a bottle for them. Probably because she knew Dracuni would do it, and once they started asking that of her, where would they stop?

"I'm fine," Aishena mumbled. "Must have gotten blindsided by one of the riders in the barracks. Surprised they didn't finish me when I was down considering what I'd done to their friends."

The sky seemed touched by fire as sunset fell early over the end of the short winter's day. They would be back at Eslindekeep soon, and Riony looked forward to being somewhere warm and out of the relentless cold wind. She couldn't stop shaking.

"What did you do to their friends?" she asked gently.

"Made sure they couldn't get into the air. They should live though, if that's what you're asking, depending on how soon they are treated. Although they won't be flying for some time depending on what treatment is spent on them."

Riony felt a low swell of sadness fill her chest, thinking about those who silvernix wouldn't have the chance to save. Up ahead, Kess flew Norallei's tamed shimmerdart alone, Norallei's body still carried within its claws.

She felt a pang of bitter gratefulness that Iffyr was a tamed dragon, that he wouldn't be mourning his rider too.

"You did good, keeping them from joining the fight. We would have been ruined if more riders showed up."

Aishena scoffed, then winced. "I'd have done better if I wasn't unconscious so long. I thought I'd cleared my area. I don't know where my attacker came from."

"I'm just glad you're still here with us, thanks to Yensen. How would we replace you if you died? How could we ever find someone as hot as you to fill that hole? Impossible."

A thin smile spread on Aishena's lips. "Are we back to this again? Must I once more crush your hopes of a relationship?"

Riony rolled forward and bent to rest her forehead against Aishena's. "No. You know how I feel about you. We're family."

And I almost lost you. Like the Rebel Riders lost Norallei.

Zeina, Samor, and Jaym flew in a tight group farther ahead. Thallan hung back behind everyone. Riony knew he and Norallei were in some sort of relationship, but they were private about it. She was glad at least Yensen was with Thallan on his dragon in case he needed someone.

Riony wasn't scared of taking risks herself, but seeing other people suffer the consequences left her questioning whether the entire mission had been a mistake.

"Almost there. Hold on," Dashiel said from up front, and they descended toward the blocky slabs and bare ground of Eslindekeep.

There was some maneuvering and tense communication as Samor and Jaym received Norallei's body midair so that Kess could land.

Dashiel got Ambri to the ground first and headed them toward the tunnel into the base.

"Can you look after Aishena for a moment for me? I want to check on the others." Riony shifted Aishena into a more upright position.

"I'm okay," Aishena said, sitting at a slight angle.

Dashiel pulled Aishena closer to them, holding her with one arm to help keep her from slipping off. "I've got her."

"Thanks." Riony jumped down and opened the

entrance for them.

The heavy doors slid open, and Eslinde stood there waiting.

Riony hesitated as the princess cast shrewd eyes over those who returned, and those who hadn't. "Casualties?"

Blood rushed away from Riony's face as she choked on Norallei's name.

"I'm surprised there weren't more," Eslinde said coldly.

A spark of anger warmed within Riony. "The mission was a success, overall. We cleared fourteen dragons and more riders from that keep."

"And one of our friends is dead. You call that a success?" Eslinde gestured to where Gleem and Shani were landing in the clearing where they had the bonfire on Midwinter's Eve.

"Fourteen dragons," Riony said again. "And only one—"

"You're prepared to lose someone every time you launch an attack? Only the blessed sun knows how you've kept Lyrrin alive so long with that approach."

Riony's hands curled into fists.

Eslinde lifted her chin, staring up at Riony unflinchingly. "Who, exactly, are you prepared to lose next?"

Riony's words caught in her throat, and then Thallan came through on his dragon, pushing Riony and Eslinde apart as he took himself, Yensen, and his dragon straight into the base.

Riony tried to get his attention but was thoroughly

ignored in a way that felt like a hot knife to the gut. Eslinde turned and followed them into the dark tunnel.

Fuming, Riony returned her attention to the Rebel Riders.

Samor carried Norallei's broken body down from his flamesong over his shoulder, then laid her gently on the ground.

Parts of the small Taenish woman were bent in the ways they shouldn't have been and her head hung limp.

Zeina came to stand beside Samor and Jaym. Her face was drawn in a long frown and her eyes sharp. They flashed toward Riony as she approached, followed by a small shake of the head.

Riony's steps faltered. She wasn't welcome.

Do they blame me?

It had been Thallan who had suggested retaliation, who mentioned how they could do some damage to a dragonkeep the way they used to.

But it had been Riony who ran with the idea of attacking the keep and riders. Who pushed for it until everyone who needed to be was on board.

She stood there, separated from the tight huddle of Rebel Riders as the night darkened and then grew suddenly bright as Shani breathed her powerful flamesong breath.

No pyre for Norallei. She would have a rider's funeral of dragonfire.

Kess appeared on Griskin by Riony's side. She hadn't

even noticed Kess take Iffyr away into the base and return with her wolf.

Staring into the blazing fire, Riony whispered, "Was it all a mistake? Should we have never attacked the keep?"

Kess turned shadowed eyes her way. "What happened wasn't your fault. You had a good plan. Everybody involved knew the risks. We all considered it worth it."

The gentle wariness in Kess's tone made Riony's hackles rise.

"Don't bovinshit me, Kess. Of anybody, I don't want you telling me what I want to hear." Riony pointed toward the burning body. "That was almost *you*."

Kess held her stare, chin set as though she were going to argue. Then she exhaled deeply and rubbed where a deep bruise was forming around one wrist.

"You inspire people, Riony. With your compassion and desire to protect others."

"You've done this speech already," Riony growled.

"But you aren't the only inspiring person around here," Kess continued, undeterred. "People like Thallan, they inspire people too. But they inspire people to violence."

Riony shook her head, still feeling like she was being coddled. "The mission was my idea."

"Inspired by who? No. I recognize people like him because I grew up surrounded by them." Kess turned away to face the fire. The flame flickered in her eyes and glowed across her spotted cheekbone.

Her voice became faraway and dreamlike. "I grew up torn between a family that knew only violence and cruelty, and you and the resilient kindness you showed when you had every right not to. Torn on who to become, caught between all those confused desires and loyalties."

The depth of emotion, of thinly concealed fury merged with longing, had Riony transfixed. She watched Kess's lips as she spoke.

"I only wish I'd chosen kindness sooner. If I could start over, I would have chosen you, and the kindness you inspire, right from the start, over any dragonrider or dragonlord or Dragon King in the land."

Kess turned back to her then, eyes like burning stars. "That's the Riony I love. Not the one that the violence and cruelty of others is creating."

A weak crackle of sound emerged from Riony's throat as her breath cut off midway.

Of all the words that might have come out of Kessara Heithorn's mouth, Riony never expected those. Even with Kess's recent turnaround in attitude, Riony would have found it more likely for her to say, 'excuse me while I go and feed Griskin to a dragon' or 'you know what, you're right about Aishena being the hottest in the land.'

But Kess had used the words *Riony* and *I* and *Love* in a combination that made Riony's head ring like a struck bell. And Kess said it like it was the simplest, easiest thing, as natural as breathing.

Sparks. What the sparking WHAT?

She wanted to throw back something about how a vile little gremlin such as her shouldn't use words she didn't understand, but she could only stare back as some great and terrible emotion released and unfurled within her chest like a blossom from beneath snow.

Kess didn't wait for any kind of reply. She bowed her head and left, slinking away on Griskin into the base.

Riony remained shaken and numb in the winter night as she watched Zeina and Samor and Jaym console each other and the funeral fire burned down, and then she stumbled her way in to sleep on the floor beside Dracuni.

Her dreams were all of death and fire and Kess.

Big sister, wake up.

Riony groaned as Dracuni nudged her with a claw. "What is it?"

"Vance saw smoke while out on patrol." Eslinde's voice came from somewhere above.

Riony's eyes felt swollen, and she peeled them open to squint at the princess. "So it's a normal day in Elundrae."

"A large tower of smoke, from the direction of Gerichkeep," Eslinde clarified.

Pulling herself up into a sitting position on her thin blanket, Riony stretched out sore muscles in her arms. "What? Why? We explicitly didn't leave the place burning."

"We don't know. Vance was on patrol all night and the other riders are mourning. So Dashiel and Kess are

preparing to go and see what is happening. I was hoping you'd go with them. Keep them safe."

Riony nodded, her exhausted mind still trying to catch up.

You need more rest. Stay. You don't have to take orders from her.

Riony patted her on the end of her snout. "I know. But I do want to make sure everyone stays safe. And I want to see what this smoke business is about."

Riony had dumped her armor around the floor of the stables beside her when she'd gone to sleep, so she scooped up just the basics. She put them on and met Kess and Dashiel beside Ambri as they prepared for the three of them to go.

The trip back to Gerichkeep was fast as they didn't need to conserve energy this time.

And the pillar of smoke was clear from the moment they were in the air. They followed it like a beacon. The dark column rose swaying into the sky, thick and clogged with ash, and then rained those burned-out embers across the land.

Dashiel kept Ambri up high within that smoke at first, hidden in case of any other riders on wing.

But they were alone in the sky. Coming down closer to the dragonkeep, the source of the billowing blackness was clear. The entire city was ablaze. Between the glowing patches of flame, the streets churned with dark shapes.

"Revs," Kess called out, pointing.

"What? How did they—?" Riony choked on her words.

The revs got in because there was nothing left to keep them out. Revs could, given the chance, scale a dragonkeep's walls. It was up to the riders protecting the keep to burn them before they went over the top.

But Gerichkeep had just lost most of its riders.

"There are so many." Dashiel's voice was low, awed with fear. "I'd heard rumors of a revenant army, but I never thought ... I didn't think it would be like *this*."

Riony shivered. She'd seen something like it before, the night Kellae gave birth, and when they had flown to find the Rebel Riders, but even then, it wasn't that many. Had it just been growing and growing all this time?

Kess half turned around to Riony behind her. "Even if the keep had all its riders, they might not have withstood—"

"Don't." Riony swallowed hard. "Is anyone down there still alive? Can we save anyone?"

She pulled a seeing stone from her belt pouch and activated it but couldn't bring herself to look. She handed it forward to Kess.

Kess took a few seconds to get the angle right on the clear crystal, then scanned over the city below.

"I don't think so. I can only see revs and fire."

Their fingers touched as Kess handed the crystal back.

Dashiel shook their head. "The fires must have been from people's attempts to stop the revs, from what

remaining dragons there were. But the revs don't seem to care."

Riony felt a wave of sickness, imagining all of those people in their last moments, trying to fight the revs back with fire only to find that they wouldn't burn.

Her heart broke into a separate piece for every soul that had been lost in the keep below.

"A messenger dragon got out. Why didn't it bring help from other keeps?" Kess asked.

The words warbled emptily in Riony's mind. She was unable to make sense of anything anymore through the morass of grief and pain.

Dashiel circled them around to the far side of the keep, where the main road went off to the east. Like ants swarming over abandoned cake, revenants poured out of the dragonkeep, creating a thick blanket on the ground as the army headed east.

Now one dragonkeep's worth of corpses larger again.

Riony feared for anything in its path.

NINETEEN

Lyrrin held the silvernix-changed hatchling on her lap, stroking his soft scales. Her sister's room, where she waited, was practically bare. Bags remained unpacked to one side of the simple cot that looked like it hadn't been slept in once. The mattress was cold and firm beneath Lyrrin.

A few items of armor and clothing lay strewn around from hasty changes. Many of them crusted with dried blood.

Lyrrin wiped her nose and squeezed Elumon closer. "Lyrrin?"

She startled, and Elumon's emotions matched hers, sending a streak of *scared, scared* through her head.

She whispered, "Hush, it's just big sister."

Riony stood frozen in the doorway. "Are you here to say 'I told you so' as well?"

Lyrrin had heard Riony tell the others the fate of the dragonkeep. She'd also seen the crushed spirit and exhaustion in the dark lines and red stain around Riony's eyes.

"I'm not."

"I wouldn't blame you if you were." Riony unbuckled the vest of scale mail and dropped it unceremoniously to the floor.

"I'm *not*," Lyrrin repeated. "But maybe if you'd listen to me—"

"I know, okay? I know things aren't going well. I know I'm screwing everything up. But I don't know what to do." Riony leaned her back against the wall and clasped her hands behind her head, squeezing it between her arms.

Lyrrin bit her lip. Things had been going so well for a while. Lyrrin had been so happy spending time with Eslinde and the Alderkin and all her friends and family at the base, that it had been easy to forget the problems of the outside world.

Up until the enclaves were attacked. Lyrrin could hardly fathom that all those people they knew were gone. She couldn't look too closely at that truth or the pain it caused, or she began feeling like the world was broken right through and could never be better.

But she could see how Riony couldn't look away. How

her sister took on every weight and trouble of the world as though they were her fault.

Lyrrin knew it wasn't Riony's fault though. That lay only on those who caused the harm. Those who attacked the enclaves. The revenants who brought down the keep. Only those causing the harm could take that blame.

She cleared her throat softly. "Do you know how jealous I was of you and Dracuni?"

Riony shook her head, still pressed between her arms. "You don't need to be. Dracuni loves you, and you've spent almost as much time raising her as I have."

"But you bonded with her. You can speak with her. And I used to get so upset that I couldn't share that connection."

Riony slumped a little farther down the wall. "I'm sorry."

"But now I have Elumon—"

"You decided on a name?"

"Yes, Elumon Opalscales."

The hatchling blinked up to Lyrrin and thrummed happily at the sound of his name.

Riony raised her eyebrows. "Not Sir Elumon Opalscales?"

"Why would he be a sir? Now stop interrupting me for once!"

Elumon had a full stomach, but still sleepily chewed on one of Lyrrin's thumbs with his gummy mouth. She patted him and sighed.

"Now that I have Elumon, I've started to understand how big of a responsibility it is. And Elumon doesn't even have silvernix blood, but I'm still worried about him *all the time*."

Riony's arms dropped to her sides, and she huffed wryly. "You're good with animals. You'll be fine."

"Shush!" Lyrrin snapped. "You're still not listening. Come and sit down and be quiet for once."

Lyrrin shuffled over and patted the spot on the mattress beside her.

Riony grumbled under her breath, "Been spending lots of time with the princess I see."

But she still slouched across the room and sat beside Lyrrin.

Facing her sister, Lyrrin locked her with a serious stare. "What I'm saying, is that I know you have so many responsibilities, and you're doing your best to look after all of them. But even with good intentions, things can go wrong."

Riony shivered, but her mouth remained firmly closed.

Softening her voice, Lyrrin said, "You couldn't have known the revenants were going to attack the dragonkeep."

Riony shook her head as though fighting the words, but they came out in a rush. "But if we hadn't weakened their defenses, they might have been able to keep the revs out."

"And if they hadn't attacked the enclaves first, you wouldn't have weakened their defenses," Lyrrin countered.

"And they might not have attacked the enclaves if we weren't in hiding," Riony's voice went higher.

"How far back do you want to keep chasing the blame? All the way back to the first taming? There would be no revenants at all if the king hadn't begun taming dragons. Or perhaps we go back earlier? Was it the Alderkin's fault? Or maybe unicorns fault for the very blood they were born with?"

"That's ridiculous."

Lyrrin gestured wildly with her hands at the point floating between them.

Sleepy. Be still. Elumon grumbled and tucked his head under his tail.

Lyrrin calmed herself and said, "Of course it's ridiculous. So why are you happy to take the blame back just so far that it lands on you?"

Riony shook her head and stared at the floor. "Because I can't keep making mistakes that hurt people."

"And it's because you feel that way that I know you're a good person. Because you care. About all those people. About everyone." Lyrrin grasped her sister's hand in hers and squeezed it gently in her sharp fingers.

"Caring doesn't keep people alive." Her voice came out husky and broken. "And fighting back ... I don't know if I can ..."

Lyrrin reached her other hand to Riony's as well. Elumon snorted, disturbed by her movement, and hopped

off her lap to go and sniff Riony's discarded armor.

Lyrrin watched him, still unable to believe he was hers, that they were bonded, that his egg had been brought in by Rebel Riders who had become their friends.

She could hardly believe, even now, that her mother was here with her, and an Alderkin family, and all these people who had come together to help Dracuni and Elundrae.

She offered her sister a gentle smile. "I wish we could fix the world just by making friends. And I still think we can, in a way. We were, with the enclaves."

Riony flinched as though struck but remained silent.

"*They weren't a mistake.* The mistake was that we didn't realize that there are people and forces out there who don't want the world to change, and who are going to do anything to stop us. And those are the ones we need to fight back against."

"It hasn't helped. I don't know ..."

Lyrrin pulled Riony's hand in tighter. "Sometimes we do have to fight. And kick the asses of everyone who gets in our way. And nobody is better at that than you. And I know it's a big responsibility. That's why we're going to change the world *together*."

Riony's hand squeezed back, and she finally looked up and met Lyrrin's gaze. "Big dreams, bold deeds, right?"

It hurt Lyrrin to see how much pain filled her sister's eyes. But there was still fire there too.

She smiled and nodded. "Big dreams, bold deeds."

"If we left when I signaled it, we'd still have Norallei." Zeina's voice carried through the meeting room. She stood, leaning with both hands palm down on the table, staring down Thallan on the other side.

Eslinde had called the meeting, after giving the riders some time to grieve, but it seemed those few days weren't enough to cool tempers. Riony could see the raw pain in all of them, except Samor who as always held his feelings close.

"You pushed it too far, old friend. As you always do." Jaym sat beside her, hunched in his chair.

Thallan's battle-worn features had roughened over the last few days. His neatly trimmed beard grew long and patchy and his hair hung unbraided. He paced behind Riony's chair.

But he seemed to take no worry in his companion's words. "Too far? Look at the win we've struck. Not just a dozen or so dragons, but an entire keep, gone."

"A win?" Riony balked at the word, one she'd come so close to using with Eslinde herself.

She'd called it a success. But time and the fall of the entire keep had stolen that word from her mouth.

"Thousands were lost in that keep. Families. People who loved and cared for one another," Eslinde spoke with the ringing eloquence of restrained emotion.

"Dragonlords," Thallan spat. "Our enemy. And the enemy to our land. So many have now been removed, will no longer keep taming dragons for their factories or defenses. This *is* a win."

Zeina dropped into her chair, mouth hanging open. "But we lost Norallei. Don't you even care?"

"Don't you dare assume how I feel." Thallan paused his pacing to glare across the room where everyone had gathered except the Zarram siblings who were on patrol.

Riony glanced to Aishena on her one side and Lyrrin on the other. She couldn't assume how Thallan was feeling, but she could imagine too clearly her own reaction if she lost someone she loved.

She'd almost lost Aishena. And it had been a close call for Kess.

That's the Riony I love. A jolt rattled down her spine like an icy avalanche at the memory of the words.

She turned, casting a surreptitious glance over her shoulder. The table had been filled by the time Kess arrived, and she remained on Griskin, by the wall at Riony's back. Pale eyes met hers from the shadows, and Riony hastily turned away again.

Thallan batted a hand in the air and paced again. "Beyond any pain, I refuse to have her loss count for nothing. If anything, we should ramp up attacks. We defeated fourteen dragons with ease. Do that a few more times and surely that would weaken the shadow dragon

277

noticeably. Isn't that what we want?"

Silence. Benjin opened and closed his mouth a few times without finding his words. The Alderkin leaned toward each other, whispering in their language.

Riony locked eyes with Eslinde for a moment, and then she stood slowly, facing Thallan.

"We were lucky to only lose one during our attack of Gerichkeep. How many are you willing to lose each time?"

His fiery expression didn't waver. "As many as necessary."

Riony moved to block his pacing and hold his attention. "We hardly have the numbers as it is! Which of us should die next?"

Thallan moved around her, waving her away. "Any sacrifice is worth destroying our enemy!"

Sparks, was this how I sounded? Riony was mortified, and anger brewed in her, twitching the tendons in her hands.

Thallan paused his pacing again, turning to Riony with a dark fervor in his eyes.

"Don't you see? We could have the upper hand if we keep the pressure on. We could follow the revenant horde and weaken any keep in its path. The revs would do the work for—"

Riony's fist cracked against Thallan's nose.

Chairs scraped around the room as everyone shot to their feet.

Thallan stumbled backward, more shocked than hurt. "How dare you?"

"You're lucky I held back," Riony growled. "What you're saying, what you're planning, it's not okay, and it's not going to happen. We will fight when we need to, but we will not get drawn into the kind of rampant cruelty the dragonlords deal out."

Aishena, Kess, Lyrrin, and Benjin lined up beside Riony. Yensen had Eslinde and the Alderkin moved into a corner and behind his guard.

A twinge of scolding emotion reached Riony from Dracuni in the stables.

Are you punching people?

Only those who deserve it.

Thallan scowled back at Riony, flicking his chin toward the other Rebel Riders for support.

Riony shook out her hand and pulled it into a fist again with the crack of knuckles. "Do we have an understanding? Or do you need me to hit you hard enough that you understand that unnecessary violence isn't the answer?"

Zeina and Jaym strolled over, almost warily. They moved to join the group standing beside Riony.

Only Samor stood beside Thallan.

The leader of the riders breathed heavily as he looked Zeina and Jaym up and down. "You'd stand with them? Those you've only known a few weeks?"

Jaym shrugged and shook his head at Samor. "I'm more

surprised you're sticking with him. Sam ... after everything. After it was Thallan's plans that got Gerlinda killed."

Samor folded his arms, looming behind Thallan. "We stuck together then. We stick together now. This is all I have left. And it's all Thallan has left now too. Taking out as many dragonlords as possible in the time we have left sounds good to me."

Zeina's face remained still and fierce, but her eyes glistened. "I will not put myself nor Gleem into another of your suicide missions."

Jaym nodded. "Not Hux either. They have their own say in this too, unlike your dragon."

Thallan's jaw twitched. "So we are separating, then. Fine. Samor and I will go and find one of our other groups that might be more worthy of action."

"Oh no. I don't think that's going to be possible." Eslinde stepped out from behind her grayglim.

"What do you mean? I'm sure our true friends will take us in." Thallan seemed genuinely confused.

"I mean that we can't exactly allow those who know about Dracuni to leave and go about their own business." Eslinde's expression was apologetic, but firm.

Riony's lips shifted into an *O* shape. Eslinde was right, and as usual at least a full step or two ahead of Riony.

Thallan's lips turned up on one side. "What are you going to do? Imprison us here?"

"If we must." Eslinde bowed her head. "Or we could

stop the infighting and come to an agreement again."

Thallan barked a laugh. "Yes, tell me how you will imprison us and then how you'd like to be agreeable again in the same breath."

Kess moved forward on Griskin and whispered in Riony's ear, "Something is happening. Griskin hears people in the base."

"What?" Riony wished she'd brought her sword with her. "Everyone, quiet!"

There was a muttering of continued argument before the intensity of Riony's glare silenced everyone.

Then she heard it too. Whimpering. Crying. Stumbling feet.

"It's coming from the gateway." Riony moved fast, vaulting over the table to get to the exit and out into the hall. Her friends followed close behind.

The first person who wobbled out of the long shadows between torches was a teenage boy, wide-eyed and confused. He backed up against the wall and held his arms up to protect himself as Riony barreled toward him.

"Where did you come from?" She tried to sound calm and kind, but urgency raised her voice.

"The ... the undercity. It's under attack. There were dragons."

"An attack on the undercity?" Aishena repeated in a rasp.

And one bad enough that Niskina is evacuating people

here.

A woman hovering over a clutch of small children tumbled up the hallway next, and Riony moved again, running for the gateway.

"Niskina?" Riony yelled as the crowd grew thicker the closer she got.

An old man stumbled past, shirt smoldering as he gasped in pain.

A surge of people pushed through the gateway as Riony reached the room, brightened by the light of the rippling magic. And then that light stuttered, faltered, then faded entirely.

TWENTY

The urgency of panic overlaid Riony's movements as she traced over the rune to reopen the gateway.

"Oh, blessed sun, it's still working." Eslinde sighed from behind her as the symbols around the geode stone glowed to life.

"No, it's not." Riony pointed to the one for the undercity gateway, and it hadn't lit up like the other active options.

"My husband is still on the other side. Please open it again," a woman's voice came from the back of the crowd, and more murmurs followed with the soft crying of children.

Riony ran her hand over the sharp edge of the geode slice. "We can't. We could maybe go through to the shrine down the hill, if people can get out to there ..."

"The exits were all blocked off by the riders. They have dragons, small ones, but a lot of them."

"City guard dragons, likely," Eslinde added. "Treedarts."

"What about the delvers and Niskina?" Riony turned to the crowd, seeking the wide-eyed escapees for answers.

A couple of them shrugged, but a child Riony knew from the Orphans' Den piped up. "Niskina opened the gateway for us. She was right there on the other side."

Riony grunted, then selected the symbol for the shrine down the hill from the undercity. She stepped through briefly, but it was abandoned as it had been since they'd evacuated the small enclave there on the night of the attacks.

Coming back through, she blinked as her vision went dark. A few gasps and whimpers came from the crowd, and Eslinde moved through them, comforting people.

Riony turned on the spot to find the gateway dark again.

"Did someone deactivate it?" She crouched down to trace the rune again.

"No, it just went out." Aishena stared at the crystal window, her expression grim.

Riony finished the sequence, but nothing happened. Maybe she got it wrong in her rush. She tried again. No sign of magic.

"It's run out of charge," Lyrrin said.

"Are you sure?" Yensen moved closer to Riony.

Lyrrin craned her neck, as though looking for someone.

Of their group, only the Alderkin didn't come in to where the refugees had fled. It would have been good to get their confirmation of what was happening with the Alderkin artifact, but they were keeping hidden from the newcomers.

Riony slapped her palm against the rune. There were maybe twenty or thirty people who made it through. Out of thousands. What were the dragonriders going to do to them all? To Niskina?

Aishena and Benjin whispered to each other, then approached the squirrelly boy who had known Niskina.

"Cammi, can you tell us more about what you saw?" Aishena asked.

His jaw dropped when he saw Aishena and Benjin standing before him. Using one hand to swipe his dirty-blond hair back, he stood at attention.

He delivered a report in a confident, high voice. "The dragonriders came in through the main entrances, then started rounding up delvers and anyone they thought looked dangerous. Pretty much anyone young and healthy. Someone called Kife was in charge, and he was making sure everyone knew who he was."

Riony and Kess's eyes met.

Kess shook her head warningly but didn't look away. "It's a trap. He wants us to know he's there. He wants to lure us into those horrible caves, kill us all, and take Dracuni."

"We still have to do something. They could be doing what they did in the enclaves ..." Riony's voice trailed away as her heart clenched painfully.

She shook herself and stood from where she'd knelt in front of the gateway. "If Kife is using himself as bait, I'm going to take it. The thing about bait is that even if the fish gets hooked, it's the worm that has no chance of making it out alive."

Aishena raised an eyebrow. "What do we consider our chances of the fish making it off the hook?"

Riony shrugged. "The best. Excellent. One hundred percent."

Aishena smirked. "You never were good with numbers."

"Because I put all my effort into staying alive. We can do this. We must do this. And we'll do it in a way we survive and that doesn't hand over Dracuni."

"You're determined?" Eslinde asked.

"Nothing will stop me. I'll go alone if I have to," Riony replied.

Lyrrin's lips pulled in. "No, you won't."

"Whatever you decide, I'm with you," Kess said from her side.

"Come on then, we must prepare." Eslinde gestured for them to move. "I'll see to our new guests, then join you in the meeting room. Yensen, fetch the Zarrams."

The grayglim nodded and was first to move. Riony and her friends followed, meeting the Rebel Riders where

they had waited in the hall. Even Thallan and Samor had remained, watching the darkened gateway and refugees with frowns.

As they walked back to the meeting room, Aishena spoke in a clipped beat. "With the gateway out, we'll have to fly there. We won't be able to go in through the main entrances either if they are held by the Dragonriders."

A little farther down the hallway, they found the Alderkin, tucked into the shadows, having observed from a distance. They fell into the group as well.

"We'll go in through the ice cave in the mountain." Riony marched ahead, her mind racing, playing through their options.

What's happening? Dracuni's thoughts played through into hers.

Trouble. I'll explain everything soon.

You're going without me again, aren't you?

Riony pressed on, trying to ignore the pain in Dracuni's thoughts.

Aishena's face shifted only slightly, but Riony could tell she didn't like her suggestion. "We won't be able to take any dragons in that way. Even Dracuni won't fit down those tunnels."

Benjin trotted to keep up with his sister. "What about Shiff? She's still small, but even a little dragon's fire is better than nothing."

"That will be up to her and Dash," Kess said from

behind.

"Elumon could come, but he's not breathing fire yet," Lyrrin added.

Riony pushed through the door into the meeting room. "Which is why he's staying here with you."

"Excuse me?" Lyrrin snapped.

Riony turned to Zeina, glancing at Jaym as well. "Will you fly us there? You only need to get us close, drop us off near the peak."

"You don't want us to join you inside?" Zeina didn't sit down, instead leaning on the back of one of the chairs.

"I want people to stay with the dragons in case we need a quick escape. We can work to clear one of the larger entrances, then signal you to come in that way."

Yensen returned then with Dashiel and Vance, talking them through what had happened.

Aishena nodded to Dashiel. "We need to get there fast, not weigh the dragons down too much. We'll take Ambri too, if that's okay."

"However we can help," Dashiel said.

Aishena took that opportunity to broach the idea of taking Shiff in.

Dashiel was already in full armor from being on patrol and paused for a moment, their face thoughtful. "Shiff is in, but I'm going with her."

Vance grunted softly. "I don't like the sounds of any of this."

Aishena nodded and looked around their group. "Jaym, will Hux let me fly with him? I want you on Ambri. We can't have a tamed dragon without a rider once we head into the depths."

Jaym gave a roguish smile. "I'm sure he could be persuaded."

Eslinde floated back into the room then, watching keenly as they planned.

"Good." Aishena nodded, then pointed around the group. "I want Benjin and myself on Hux."

Benjin quietly pumped his fist behind her.

Aishena continued. "Jaym, you can take Dashiel and Shiff on Ambri. Riony, Kess, and Griskin go with Zeina on Gleem."

"What about me?" Lyrrin's face had turned a deep red.

Aishena tilted her head slightly toward Riony. "We could take one other, if you agree."

Riony looked at her little sister for a long moment. The fierce child who had saved her life possibly more times than Riony had saved hers.

"She could—"

"You can't possibly be considering taking Lyrrin into that trap?" Eslinde placed her hands on Lyrrin's shoulders and squared up to Aishena and Riony.

Riony met her gaze. "She's capable."

Lyrrin seemed to grow visibly taller at the words.

Eslinde gaped, looking between her daughter and Riony. Her fingers were white around Lyrrin, but she began nodding slowly. "Maybe we could all go."

Yensen leaned in toward her. "You cannot. And we need people here to keep Dracuni safe. If Lyrrin is capable, then she's another capable protector who should remain here with us."

"I will stay with you as well," Vance said.

"No!" Lyrrin cried in a high-pitched whine. She tried to move closer to Riony, but Eslinde held her back.

Lyrrin's bright-blue eyes glistened with tears. "There will be enough people here with Dracuni. I should go with you. We're supposed to do things together, remember?"

Yrik took the opportunity to step into the silence. "She's right in that we should act together, but we must all act for the unidragon's well-being. None of you should be going."

"Dracuni will be fine. Our enemies don't know where we are, and it's worth going to do what we can for all those people. Sometimes we have to fight." Riony looked to Lyrrin as she spoke instead of the Alderkin.

The guilt of leaving weighed heavy on her, but Lyrrin gave a single small nod at her words. "It is worth it. Which is why I should go too."

Riony didn't want to admit the relief she'd felt when Yensen suggested Lyrrin should stay. Knowing her sister

remained safe was one less thing for her to worry about.

She turned away from Lyrrin's seeking gaze and spoke to Eslinde. "I trust you will keep her safe."

"Of course," the princess replied.

Lyrrin's jaw dropped, and she let out a shriek of utter disgust. She shook Eslinde's hands off her and ran to the corner where the Alderkin stood, hiding among them.

Riony looked over the separating groups again. She didn't like taking so many of the dragons with them, especially with Dracuni still unable to fly, and Viska uncooperative.

Norallei's dragon, Iffyr, still remained, ghostlike and motionless in her stall, but nobody seemed willing to fly her or even mention her, out of respect for her lost rider.

"And you—" Riony turned to where Thallan and Samor remained, although begrudgingly, beside the other Rebel Riders. "Can we trust you to remain, just until our return? If you would stay on patrol for us while we're gone, you will be free to go after that."

Thallan folded his arms. "We are free to go now if we—"

Samor cleared his throat.

"Fine. Yes. We will do our duty here until you return. But then we part ways."

"Then we leave shortly," Aishena said.

Riony moved quickly, unable to look at Lyrrin. She left the meeting room and headed to the stables where she'd

left her armor and weapons where she and Dracuni slept.

The unidragon lay with her snout on her front claws and lifted her head at Riony's approach.

I want to go too.

Riony looked away, focusing on the armor strewn around the floor. "You can't fly. How would you get there?"

Shani can carry me. She agreed.

"Shani and Samor are staying here, to keep watch here while we're away, to keep you and Lyrrin and everyone else safe." Riony pulled the scale mail vest on and began buckling it. "And what isn't safe, is taking you into a trap. You're too important."

Dracuni lifted her head and snorted roughly.

Maybe I don't want to be. Maybe I'm tired of being so important that everyone else can get hurt except for me. You always say I can make my own decisions, but then you don't let me!

"I ..." Riony froze, bent halfway to retrieve a pauldron. "I'm sorry."

She dropped the mail with a clatter and moved to kneel so she was eye to eye with the seated unidragon.

Dracuni had gotten so big, her head as long as Riony's torso. Riony leaned into her, hugging her with her shoulder just below the golden horn on her forehead.

"I wish you could have had a normal life. As normal as any of our lives could be. And I know it was my fault you were born how you were, in a way that meant you never

could have that."

You didn't know this would happen. Dracuni's words seemed to thrum between them.

"Stars, you were so tiny back then. I just wanted to protect you. I couldn't bear it if you were captured. What Kife did to you last time ... it would only be the beginning."

Dracuni exhaled deeply, the warmth of her breath gusting around Riony's body.

Fine. You can go. But only if you do one thing for me.

Riony argued a little longer. She didn't like it, but in the greater scheme of all she didn't like, the gesture was small, and it made Dracuni feel better.

She spent what remaining time she had strapping on her armor and sitting with Dracuni, stroking the silky tufts of hair that emerged between the scales down her neck, trying to reassure her and herself that she would come back safe.

Then Kess and Griskin appeared in front of her. "Everyone's ready."

Riony leaned into Dracuni for one more hug. "We'll see each other soon."

We better.

When she turned around again, Kess was staring at Dracuni with an expression Riony couldn't read.

Yensen's warnings teased the edges of her thoughts,

but as Riony and Kess fell into pace beside each other, Griskin's paws silent on the cold floor, Riony felt no threat.

Who would have ever believed Kessara Heithorn could change?

The idea still made Riony's insides feel strange and rattly, but she did believe it. She wanted to believe it.

If Kess could change, become someone she could trust, someone who was kind and caring, it gave Riony hope for the greater change they wished to bring to the world.

Kess fussed with the bone daggers sheathed in her bracers, but remained silent, her slim body swaying in the saddle as Griskin stalked out of the stables.

"Here." Riony reached to the side of her belt. "I want you to have this."

She thrust her arm out and kept her eyes ahead as she handed Kess the pointed shard of crystal.

"Is that ...?"

"A cutting athame. You've used it before. I'll show you how it activates on the way."

"And you want me to have it?" Kess still hadn't reached to take the crystal.

"I just thought you should have something ... a better weapon. I'd give you a return athame, but Aishena has claimed all of them. This is the only good weapon I have except my sword—especially since *somebody* made me lose my dragonguard sword."

Kess made a stuttering sound that wasn't quite a word. Riony thrust the athame handle toward her again, and finally, she took it.

"Thank you."

Riony cricked her neck and picked up her pace. "It's no big deal."

The others had their dragons outside near the entrance to the underground base. A cold wind blew over the bare roads and empty foundations of the unfinished keep. A dark smudge of soot marked the clearing nearby where Norallei's body had been burned.

It was only midafternoon, but somehow Riony already felt exhausted as she said her goodbyes to Eslinde, Vance, and Yensen.

Lyrrin and the Alderkin hadn't come out to bid the group farewell.

It's okay. We'll be back soon. Once the undercity is safe again. And Kife is dead.

Everyone else was on the three dragons that would be leaving, with Thallan and Samor already circling far above on patrol.

Kess was still tying Griskin and herself in as Riony began climbing up Gleem's aqua scales.

"Wait!"

Lyrrin's voice caused Riony to spin around.

She opened her mouth, ready to try to explain again why her sister couldn't come, but couldn't find her words.

Lyrrin ran up to her, cheeks and eyes pink.

"Activate your heart stone," she demanded, tapping her chest where hers hung on a string.

Riony reached to her neck, pulling at the necklaces there, revealing the acorn pendant and the flat paired crystal. She activated it and tucked both treasures back away against her chest.

Lyrrin's small heartbeat fluttered against her own.

"And take this." Lyrrin stuck her arm out.

Riony reached for the crystal in her hand. The ten-stroke rune she'd spent so long working out, until she finally did. The dragon summoning rune.

Her voice was low with confusion and the desire not to enrage her sister any further. "What's this for?"

Lyrrin moved in close beside her, pointing at the carved lines on the crystal. "We've altered it. Me and the Alderkin. See here?"

Riony looked closer, counting out the lines. Eleven now.

"Is this going to explode?" Riony asked.

"Not everything has to explode to be useful."

"Wise words. I wonder where you heard them?" Riony smirked.

"Actually, I can't say for sure it won't explode," Lyrrin admitted.

"Wonderful."

"But we think we did it right. We've altered it so it

should work on tamed dragons now." Lyrrin held Riony's hand that held the crystal, lifting it up where they both could see and gesturing to show Riony the sequence.

Riony smiled at her sister and a rush of pride made her eyes water. "Now that could be very useful. Show me again."

Lyrrin grinned back and showed Riony the sequence two more times.

Once she thought she had it memorized, Riony tucked the crystal away in a belt pouch, then bent down to crush her sister in a tight embrace.

"You will be back, won't you?" Lyrrin mumbled into Riony's shoulder. "I hate watching you leave. It always feels like it will be the last time I see you."

Riony stepped back, gave Lyrrin her most bravado-laden smirk, and ruffled the kid's blue-and-brown hair.

But as she climbed up onto Gleem behind the others and they lifted into the sky, Riony watched Lyrrin grow smaller and smaller and couldn't tear her eyes away until Eslindekeep had disappeared from sight entirely.

TWENTY-ONE

High in the mountains above the undercity, a fresh powder of fluffy snow drifted in the brisk wind, and gray clouds lay smotheringly low, blocking the sun.

Kess kept Griskin close beside Riony. Worry seared her insides like acid and kept her face pinched into a tight frown.

They would be facing Kife today. And Kess knew exactly how cruel her brother enjoyed being.

Her hand idly touched the cutting athame in her belt as she waited for everyone to climb down from the dragons.

Nearby, Riony showed Aishena the new crystal her little sister had provided. Kess could almost see the cogs turning in the Hjelzahn woman's head, working the new resource into their plans.

Benjin stood on tiptoes to watch the information being shared as well.

From atop Gleem, Zeina was giving Riony a long look. "We'll keep out of sight and watch for your signal. Stay safe."

"Happy hunting!" Jaym called from his seat on Ambri.

Hux stalked through the snow, freely on his own. The red dragon was the first back into the sky, but soon they were all gone, high in the clouds.

"This way," Aishena said, marching toward a cliff face sheeted in ice.

Riony turned on the spot. All around them was white.

"Wasn't it that way? Nope. No, you're right." She jogged through the thick snow to catch up.

Griskin grumbled a warbling growl.

Kess leaned close to his neck and patted his ears. "Don't worry. We won't be out in the cold as long as we were last time."

"Shiff isn't enjoying the snow either," Dashiel said cheerfully.

The pale blue and purple dragon stomped grumpily at their side, hot breath streaming out in clouds. Shiff was only a little smaller than Griskin now, and the shimmerdart had been showing off how good her ball lightning breath was getting.

They reached the cliff, and Aishena ran her hands over the flow of frozen water. "It should be around here."

299

Riony bent down, peering through a glassy section. "Through here. It's iced up even more than before. Hang on a second."

Riony pulled her sword and looked ready to take a swing.

Kess winced. "Careful. It'll be harder than you think."

"Oh, I know. I've done this before." Riony turned her sword so the unicorn horn-shaped hilt pointed to the frozen wall.

She jabbed it deep into the ice in a few places, then spun the sword around and thrust the thicker blade between the fracture points.

It split through, and with a grunt of effort, Riony wrenched it out again, then kicked in the shattered ice until the hole was big enough for them to pass through. She sheathed her sword, never having activated its magic, and waved for Aishena to step through first.

Riony had always been strong. Kess knew that from the duties she'd been expected to perform as Kess's servant, little more than a beast of burden most of the time. As they spent so many hours together as children, Kess had seen Riony's other qualities as well, how she was so much more than a vital body.

But still, seeing just how strong Riony had gotten left Kess flushed.

Like a gentleman holding a door, Riony gestured everyone through, then followed in behind Kess.

The temperature was already warmer in the cave, sheltered from the gusting wind. Bats and owlettes overhead chittered at the intruders. Aishena and Benjin lit the way with the cyan light of glow stones, but the darkness and weight of the mountain above still seemed to crush in around Kess.

She shivered. "Didn't really want to come back to this cursed place."

Riony traced the rune on her glow stone and let it dangle in the netted pouch on her belt. "You just never saw the best parts."

"You mean swarms of cave spiders and a giant tangled conglomeration of revenants aren't highlights?"

Dashiel called back, "I thought we were only up against some riders with treedarts."

"We are," Riony confirmed. "Kess is exaggerating."

"Yes, just exaggerating," Kess said sweetly.

Riony cracked a half smile and gave Kess a small wink.

"Quiet now," Aishena hissed. "We're nearing the inhabited areas."

A hushed tension spread as they stepped from the natural caves into the Alderkin-carved tunnel through a broken wall. Griskin whined softly and licked his nose. The spores of the mushroom farms were already bothering him.

Each of their group was fully armored in Eslinde's colors and wore a plain cloak over the top. Griskin and Shiff were harder to conceal, but the undercity was large. Kess had managed to move through it before unseen, sticking to roofs and dark alleys.

As they reached the end of the tunnel and it opened out into the occupied cavern, Aishena signaled them all still, and those with glow stones deactivated their light.

From her perch on Griskin, Kess watched as a dragonrider on a dull-brown treedart stalked through an empty street. The soldier yelled when a boy stepped out of an alley, then froze at the sight of a dragon.

The guard prowled toward the child, bringing his dragon's snout right up to the boy's face. He backed up against the wall, shaking his head and crying.

Soft sounds of crystal sliding through hard leather echoed in the tunnel as Riony drew her sword.

"No," Aishena hissed back. "We can't be seen until we get to a more central area. We need to reach somewhere Lyrrin's dragon rune can get the best effect."

Riony snorted air out her nose and took a step forward.

A door opened on the street beside the dragonrider and boy, and an old woman bustled out. She grasped the boy's arm and dragged him out from under the dragon and into her home, slamming the door behind her.

The sound of the rider chuckling carried through the deserted area.

Riony still looked ready to ambush the soldier. "We should have helped."

"We need to keep as much element of surprise as we

can," Aishena replied.

Once the rider had moved on, she beckoned them forward again.

"Surprise? This is a trap, remember. They know we're coming." Riony moved up beside Aishena, pointing to a narrow alleyway.

Aishena nodded and they all scurried that way. "All the more reason we need to get as close to Kife and those in command before we strike."

A thick stench of garbage filled the narrow path and things moved in the shadows ahead around a pile of refuse. Each as large as a person, the fluid forms squirmed and tumbled around each other in a pile, fighting to get to the food scraps.

"What under all the stars are they?" Dashiel whispered.

"Just cave otters. Don't worry, they won't bother us," Riony said.

At their approach, the creatures scattered. All except for one, who stood up on its hind legs, sniffed the air, and then raced toward Riony.

The collision left Riony stumbling, and the furry critter snuffled her neck as she steadied herself.

"Butterfur?" Riony gasped.

"Is that the little furry sausage that you tried to follow out of the depths?" Kess asked.

"Thought you said they wouldn't bother us," Dashiel had a hand on their sword, ready to draw.

Shiff gave the otter a low growl.

"No, but this is Sir Butterfur Spelunkychunks."

At Dashiel's blank expression, Riony continued. "He was Lyrrin's pet for a while, and no, I don't have the treats!"

Butterfur had his snout tucked under Riony's cloak and paws trying to get into her belt pouches. Whiskers twitching, he backed off, looking around behind Riony and giving each of the party a quick sniff.

He turned back to Riony with a parted mouth and a tilt to his head.

Riony frowned. "Lyrrin's not with us."

A long, low whistle from above sent the otter skittering away and the rest of them pressing further into the shadows.

Seeking the source of the sound, Kess saw shadows moving behind a gauzy curtain a few stories up.

The fabric shifted, and a familiar voice whispered down, "In here, quick. Another patrol is on the way. Bottom floor is barricaded, come in through the second."

"Was that Niskina?" Benjin whispered.

"Should have known she wouldn't let Kife's goons catch her. Let's go." Grinning widely, Riony put her hands out, fingers woven together in front of her.

Benjin stepped into them first and she boosted the boy up to the flat roof of the tiered building that had been carved from a massive stalagmite.

She helped Aishena and Dashiel reach the second floor the same way, then gave Shiff a concerned look and tried

to offer her a hand climbing as well, but the small dragon managed to scramble up the limestone wall alone with a little help from sharp talons and fluttering wings.

Griskin took Kess up with a short run and bounding leap. She looked back over the edge. "You need a hand?"

"I'm good." Taking a short run up, Riony kicked up the wall and grasped the lip at the top. A satisfied, but also somehow sad smile played on her lips as she pulled herself up with the others.

The flat rooftop held a washbasin and a littering of toys. The group ducked below a line of hanging laundry, and the door ahead of them opened.

"Riony, Aish!" Niskina beckoned them in, hugging each briefly and firmly along the way.

Until she got to Kess.

"What is she doing here?" Niskina snapped.

"She's here to help," Riony said, voice low as she scanned the dark interior. "And she's been doing a remarkable job of not betraying us lately. Best streak ever."

Holding Kess in her stare for a moment, Niskina finally huffed and turned away.

She muttered under her breath, "Yeah, we'll see how long that lasts."

Closing the door behind them, Niskina got moving again, taking them through the darkened room. "This way. There's more room up here."

From the walls and corners of what looked like a family

home, gasps and whispering spread as their group moved through, with wolf and dragonling in tow.

"When the gateway went out, those of us who were trying to evacuate managed to get back here to hide." Niskina nodded toward the people huddling in the dark. "I wasn't sure what to do next. I'm so glad to see you all. We might have a chance now."

They reached a flight of carved stone stairs, and in a flutter of whispers, a figure stood up before them.

"Here, please take this." An older man with age-paled red hair handed something that looked like a dirty stick to Riony.

She pushed back at his hands. "No, you should keep it. I'm not hungry."

He grasped her about the wrist with wiry fingers and placed the item into her palm. "I want you to have it. I know it's not much, but you saved my life on Midwinter's Eve."

Riony blinked at the man as though trying to remember. "I did?"

A few of the other faces huddled in the shadows nodded.

"Thank you." Riony's hand closed around the brown object and she brought it to her mouth, tearing a chunk off between her teeth.

She continued following Niskina up the stairs and made a low sound in the back of her throat. "Sparks, it's good. I can't believe how much I missed this."

Kess just raised her eyebrows.

"Shroom jerky." Riony took another bite and then almost absentmindedly handed the remaining piece to Kess.

And Kess was too startled by the gesture to refuse. She nibbled on a corner of the leathery strap. It wasn't half as bad as she expected. An almost meaty texture, salty and rich. But far too fungus-flavored for Kess's liking.

She mumbled, "Not bad." And then tucked the rest away in her pocket.

Riony rolled her eyes at her. "Maybe it's an acquired taste."

They reached a room where only a few people sat, but with a short word from Niskina, they left. The curvy young woman had her tumbles of hair bundled up in a messy knot and wore the same sort of armor Riony had been wearing when they were in the depths last—soft leather covered in harnesses and steel rings.

Once they were alone, Niskina looked them over. "So, do you have a plan?"

It didn't take long to catch Niskina up on what plan they had, which made Kess worry that it wasn't enough of a plan. They explained the dragon summoning stone, although none of them knew exactly what it would do, if it worked at all after its alterations.

Niskina paced and rubbed her chin with her thumb. "Kife and his riders have taken all of Upslope and set up command on the platform overlooking Sinking Stream

Lake. There are a lot of them. Even if this new rune of yours works, I just don't think we have the numbers."

"That's why we were hoping to get to Kife first, to get rid of him so the riders are without a leader." Riony's voice rattled over Kess's brother's name.

There was a day, a while ago, when Riony and Eslinde had been speaking, then Riony stormed out, glowering like a storm. When Kess asked what happened, the princess had only said she told Riony how she and Kess had met.

"Oh, is that why you're going after him?" Niskina gave Riony a skeptical glare, then shook her head. "No. The riders will have a chain of command in place. Getting rid of Kife isn't enough."

Aishena nodded at this.

Niskina continued. "We need the other delvers. I know where they are imprisoned. If we can free them, get everyone their weapons again, we could beat the invaders. As long as nobody turns on us before then."

Kess narrowed her eyes. "You think the delvers will be enough to give us the advantage? When they were imprisoned so easily already?"

Niskina took a slow, threatening step Kess's way. "They were taken by surprise. I only got away because I'm more of an honorary delver these days. I wasn't with the rest of them. The delvers will help."

"It's a good idea," Aishena agreed. "Not many in the undercity are trained the way the delvers are. They're the

closest we have to a fighting force."

"So, what do we do?" Riony looked to Aishena, Niskina, and Benjin.

The Hjelzahn siblings opened their mouths at the same time, and Aishena gave way to her brother.

Benjin puffed up as he said, "Shiff is around the size of a treedart now. If we can capture one of the other riders and take their uniform, Dashiel and Shiff could disguise themselves and get through to free the delvers."

"Shiff isn't the right color," Kess muttered. "It's not going to work."

But nobody seemed to be listening to her.

They worked through a few more details, then decided they were ready to go ahead.

Kess didn't feel ready.

As they moved back down through the home and out onto the rooftop again, all Kess could think about was what would happen if something went wrong? What would happen if Kife got his hands on Riony?

I can't let that happen. No matter what.

Riony led the way then, taking them at a run across the rooftops. Most of the flat-topped structures butted up against each other with only a small jump to the next. It was an easy run as the group left the side cavern which held the mushroom farms and reached the larger main cavern.

Kess wasn't clear on all the location names the others had been rattling off, but *Upslope* and *Downslope* at least

were descriptive enough for her to follow. They came into the main cavern at the lower end, but not far from where the large central lake pooled in ascending tiers to the higher level.

Griskin's ears twitched, and Kess rasped, "Dragons, up ahead."

Riony slowed, bringing them to the edge of the next rooftop in a low crouch.

Below, a baker's stall was tipped on its side, loaves scattered and crushed into crumbs on the ground. A long line of men, women, and children knelt along the middle of the street.

The same rider as before on the dull-brown treedart strolled up and down beside them. "I'm getting tired of bringing your criminals in. Maybe I'll have my dragon burn you all where you are instead."

Aishena pointed to their left and whispered, "We can go around this way."

Riony didn't move.

"Riony?" Kess questioned softly.

"We wanted to capture a rider for their uniform, didn't we?" Her eyes remained locked on the man below.

"Not here." Aishena took another step, beckoning the others to follow. "It's too exposed."

A cry echoed from below. One of the kneeling men was pushed down beneath the front claw of the dragon.

Riony stood to full height.

"Riony!" Aishena, still crouching, whispered the warning.

"We're here to save people, aren't we? To save everyone we can save. That's the whole point." Riony shook her head, her jaw clenched.

"There's only one rider," Benjin offered. "We could take them, easily."

Riony gave Aishena a pleading look. "We'll still get the uniform, still go after the delvers. We'll just save who we can along the way as well. We have to."

Aishena didn't seem convinced, but another wail came from below.

The rider had his steed's mouth open, laughing as he angled it around the skull of the man beneath him. Sparks flickered around the dragon's teeth.

Riony dropped her cloak and drew her sword, lighting it up in a purple glow. She caught Kess's eye.

Without waiting for any reply, she launched off the side of the building toward the rider below.

And without a second thought, Kess followed. She was no longer afraid to fall. Not afraid to burn. Only one thing scared her now. Seeing Riony come to harm. And the fear she wouldn't be able to stop it.

TWENTY-TWO

Riony's elbow cracked across the rider's helmeted head before her feet hit the ground. The man swung in his saddle, falling with her the rest of the way. The blow dislodged his helmet and it flew off, rolling about in a clatter on the limestone street.

Without the rider's instructions, the treedart stilled with its mouth hanging open around the civilian's head. He whimpered once and then crawled his way free.

Riony landed easily, standing above the rider.

She glared down at him. "You can consider that a warning. But I'm brimming with the desire to continue beating you to a pulp if you feel the need to fight back."

The rider returned her glare from where he'd fallen. The wideness of surprise and insult in his eyes shifted.

They narrowed with recognition as he took in Riony's defiant stance, her glowing sword, her wild red hair. His gaze flickered to Kess at her back, mounted on her wolf. A smirk twisted his lips.

He bellowed, "Edvin! Kase! It's them. The ones the commander has been waiting for!"

Riony coiled an arm to punch the man into silence, but his voice already echoed through the street.

She turned on the spot to find two more riders emerging from the broken doorways of nearby buildings, their dragons' eyes gleaming in the low light. They spread out, forming a loose circle around Riony and Kess. A ripple of cries spread through the kneeling prisoners.

All three riders wore full armor in silver and red—the king's colors. In the air, riders normally went without helmets, wearing flight goggles only, but both the newcomers had a full head helmet and neck protection. All vulnerable parts of their body were covered.

Riony's eyebrows raised, and she glanced at Kess and the throwing daggers in her hands.

Her reputation precedes her, it seems.

A clatter of scraping and thumping behind Riony signaled the rest of her team descending to street level to join them.

"So much for just one rider." Dashiel didn't sound too upset by the change and pulled a wide, single-edged sword into one hand and a viciously pointy push dagger into their other.

"That's them alright. I'll get backup!" One of the riders broke from the circle, spurring her dragon into a sprint down the street.

"Oh no. We don't want that. Kess?"

A dagger was already flying, but the additional armor proved too effective. The bone plinked away off the rider's back.

Swearing, Riony dashed forward. She grabbed the end of the retreating dragon's tail with one hand. Then she tucked her sword under her arm and latched her other hand on to the dragon's scales as well.

The dragon kept marching forward and Riony dug her feet in against the gutter of the limestone street and strained back the other way. With a fierce growl of effort, she pulled the creature to a stop.

"What the razing—?" The female rider turned back.

With every muscle locked into the hold, Riony saw the second new rider charging toward her too late. A wide maw of pointed teeth moved in, eager to meet with her flesh.

Sailing in from the right, a wall of fur and fury hit the side of the dragon's head, sending it off target.

Riony's breath caught as she watched, and there was a moment when Kess and Griskin hung in midair, a deadly pairing, expressions sharp with fierce determination. Kess's lightning-streaked stormy hair flew back and the constellation on her cheek highlighted the icy beauty of her eyes.

Pulse pounding, Riony's own eyes widened in horror. She swore a steady stream of curses in her head as though she could scold her confused heartbeat back to normal.

Did I just find Kessara Heithorn attractive?

Her heart replied with an even larger *ka-thump* within her chest.

Oooooooh, sparks.

The full-grown gray wolf and the treedart were of similar size, and Griskin wrestled the tamed dragon's head down and away with his teeth around its neck.

The female rider pushed her steed, and the tail slipped. Riony adjusted her grip and held firm again. Sweat trickled down her neck and her muscles burned.

She glanced back, hoping for Aishena or someone to come and deal with the dragon she had by the tail. But the first rider had managed to remount and Aishena, Dashiel, Niskina, and Benjin were occupied with him.

And once that rider's attention was refocused, his victims decided it was time to escape.

Seizing their opportunity, the crowd scattered, running up and down the street. Dodging between Riony's team and the riders, they bumped and scrambled.

A lanky teen tripped over a swiping dragon's tail and slammed into Riony's side. The impact broke Riony's grip and her sword fell to the ground. It was all she could do to catch herself and the crying kid before they ended up hitting the stone street as well.

Now freed, the dragon Riony had been holding back barreled down the road, out of reach, and a moment later, out of sight.

Panting hard, Riony's lips curled. Their chance at keeping their presence quiet just rode away, and they were going to have more trouble any moment now.

A scream filled the air, and Riony hunted for the source. The first rider's dragon had its mouth clamped around Dashiel's arm. Aishena swept in like a hurricane of glowing blades, sending the rider into retreat.

Shiff hung back to the side, mouth glowing with the shimmer of lightning, but unable to get a clear shot.

A burst of fire shot through the crowd, forcing Riony to drop flat onto her stomach to dodge it.

"Careful. Our commander wants them alive." The second rider had a weighted net swinging in one hand as he faced off against Kess and Griskin.

The first rider scoffed. "Capturing them alive was a preference, not an order."

Kess held her knives but didn't send them flying against the near impenetrable armor. She and Griskin stood between her enemy and a clutch of civilians who had been cornered against a wall.

The rider threw the net. Kess met the throw with her own, daggers *thwacking* against the balled weights at the edges, redirecting them enough to tangle the net midair and send it spinning the wrong way to the ground.

Benjin and Shiff tried to move in, but a dart of fire whistled through the air from the treedart's mouth, sending them back again.

It was only two small dragons and riders, but the treedarts were nimble on the ground, harder to pin down and relieve of their riders than the flying riders of Gerichkeep were, especially while trying to keep the innocent people around them safe.

And there would be more on their way soon.

Scooping up her sword, Riony seethed with the feeling she'd made another mistake. But this one wasn't too late to fix.

Aishena had Dashiel behind her and moved as though ready to strike again. Riony ran in between her and the rider she faced, drawing his attention with a swipe of her glowing sword.

"Aish! Take the others and get out of here! I'll stay—"

"I'm not leaving you. I'm with you. Always," Kess snapped.

Huffing, Riony continued. "*Kess and I* will stay to help the remaining people. You know what you have to do."

Niskina shook her head. "Ri—"

"No, I'm not leaving these people."

The air brightened as another dart of fire flew, bursting against the wall above the heads of the huddled crowd. They crouched, crying out as sparks rained over them. Kess

swatted at a singed patch of her hair as Griskin bounced side to side in front of the dragon, looking for an opening.

Drawing the summoning stone from her pocket, Riony tossed it back to Aishena.

Hissing in a low voice, she said, "Take it. We'll try to deal with this and catch up. But if we can't ... we'll be the distraction you'll need to make your plan work."

Aishena nodded, her face drawn but resolute.

Supporting Dashiel with one arm, she grabbed Niskina with the other and barked an order to Benjin and Shiff. Then the five of them ran for the shadows.

Neither of the two riders attempted to chase after them. It was clear Riony and Kess were their only targets of value.

Riony backed away from the first rider, bringing herself toward Kess. They faced the two dragons and their riders side by side.

Kess gave Riony a worried glance that made something in her chest twang sharply.

Riony forced a crooked smile. "Come on, we can take these two, easy."

Tutting, Kess turned her eyes back to their enemy. "Maybe, if you can do something smarter than throw yourself and your sword directly at your foe for once."

Riony leaned in closer and said huskily, "Are you calling me ... a *one trick Pony*?"

A fierce grin spread across Kess's face. "Wouldn't dream of it."

The cruel first rider had his helmet back on. He kept one hand on his dragon, keeping it under control, and held a long rapier with his other. The second seemed to have given up on his goal of capturing them and now held a spear. Neither seemed to hold enough sense to turn around and run.

Narrowing her eyes on her opponents, Riony shrugged. "I could show you a few new moves."

Bursting into motion again, the rider with the spear rushed Riony. She dove over the swing of his long weapon and rolled to come back up to her feet, her body light with the magic of her sword.

Another *tink* as a bone blade bounced off the other rider's helmet, close to the narrow eye slit. No damage, but enough of a scare to back the man and his dragon away a few steps. Griskin pressed the advantage, snarling and snapping and the two creatures danced around each other.

That gave the people pushed into the corner enough room to run, and in a huddle of helping hands and supportive embraces, the last of them made it free.

Riony's breath grew steadier.

Just us and the riders now.

As the soldier with the spear rounded on her again, Riony took in all the details of his armor. It was almost the same as what she wore, but with the additional neck protection and helmet added as an afterthought. She could see the mismatched buckles over the top of the finer scale mail chest piece.

Riony flicked her crystal blade out, keeping the movement as precise as she could. The crystal sang as it sheered across the rider's shoulder on one side, then she spun and sliced it across on the other as well.

The tip caught under the shoulder guard, popping it off, and then the gorget fell free, leaving the rider's neck exposed.

"All yours," Riony called, ducking under a swing of the man's spear.

White bone blades passed by the side of Riony's face. They pierced the man's padded clothing, side by side above his collarbone. He juddered to a stop, wavered in his saddle, then slumped over his treedart's neck.

The tamed beast continued in its last order, turning on the spot, over and over, with no new order coming to stop it.

A short jet of fire lanced toward Kess as she pulled two new blades. Riony stepped into it, swatting the splash of flame with the flat of her sword. It licked around the edges, heating her face.

"Edvin?" Panic rose in the rider's voice as he noticed his downed companion.

In a swift movement, Riony sheathed her sword, still glowing, and rushed the distracted soldier. Using the float magic of the sword pressed at her back, she leaped across the treedart's back. As she passed the rider, she grabbed

him by two fistfuls of scale mail.

She twisted her body in midair and wrenched him from his seat and slammed his body to the ground beneath hers. His helmet clanged as his head hit hard against the stone street.

He coughed one rough, wheezing breath, then stilled.

Blood welled between Riony's fingers where they remained clamped around his dragon scale armor. She gave the man a gentle shake, but he didn't move again. A glazed, bloodshot stare met hers through the thin slit of his helmet.

She jumped up to her feet, backing away until she came up against warm fur and a small body.

Spinning around, she found herself nose to nose with Kess.

"Are you ...?" Kess searched Riony's face, glancing between her and the downed rider. "It's okay. Just breathe. You're okay."

"I didn't mean to ..."

The circling dragon, turning around and around on the spot without its rider, drew Riony's eye. Both riders were just as dead. As all who had faced them at Gerichkeep were.

It wasn't getting any easier, knowing she had become a killer. That this was what the world had made her. That part of her wanted it, relished in paying back the pain to those who inflicted it on others. Her thoughts spiraled and collided painfully in a racket of screaming confusion.

The touch of warm fingers to her cheek drew Riony back to reality, and to Kess.

Kess held her stare. "We did what we had to."

Riony pressed her lips firmly together, took a shaky breath, and nodded once. "Come on. Let's catch up to the others."

It took one more long breath as she stared into Kess's eyes before Riony found she could move again.

When she turned away and took a step to leave, another form slithered in around the corner. A dragon, larger than any of the treedarts they just faced.

Its scales glistened with an eerie frost-like sheen.

Riony and Kess exchanged a grim look, their sides pressed together as more riders emerged, blocking both ends of the street and guarding every rooftop. There was no way out.

The white dragon strode into the space it was too large for. Its wings scraped the buildings on either side as it thumped heavy claws on the ground.

Riony tightened her grip around the hilt of her sword and pointed it at the dragon's chest. It came to a stop.

From atop the snowflame, the helmeted rider spread his arms wide in a welcoming gesture. "And here you both are."

There was no mistaking the voice of Kife Heithorn.

Riony shot a look at Kess. "Have we found ourselves at an impasse? Because I'm looking at someone who is both an imp and an ass."

Kife snapped back, "What you're looking at is your overdue ending, slave."

"You're overdue to go eat a flaming dick, Kife."

Kife's voice sounded so satisfied Riony wished she could scrub it out of his throat with a wire brush. "I knew you idiots would take the bait, but I didn't expect it to be this entertaining."

Rolling her shoulders, Riony glared back. "We always knew it was a trap. You're the one who never realized that you're a worm."

Kife pushed his snow-white dragon so that it lowered its belly to the ground and brought him close in front of Riony's eyes.

He crooned. "Oh, it was a trap alright. But it wasn't a trap *for you*."

TWENTY-THREE

"What do you mean, gone?" Despite being a hushed whisper, Eslinde's voice carried over to where Lyrrin sat with Elumon, having just calmed the little hatchling to sleep. Curled up within the same stall, Dracuni lifted her head at the sounds of the conversation. It seemed both her and Lyrrin were straining to listen in.

Yensen leaned close to his princess's ear. "Thallan and Samor are nowhere within sight."

"They gave us their word they would stay on watch until the others returned. You don't think they ...?" Fury flashed in Eslinde's silver eyes. Then she shook her head. "Maybe they saw something, danger they needed to go and assess or lead away? Surely, they wouldn't leave Norallei's dragon behind. Or leave us in such a precarious situation without reason."

Yensen made a noncommittal sound, eyes narrowing. "Whatever the reason, they are gone. Leaving us with only Iffyr, Dracuni, who can't and shouldn't be out flying, and Viska, who is still refusing a rider."

Vance moved away from Viska's stall, where he had been in a tense, silent conversation with the newly untamed gold dragon, as he spent most of his time recently. "Given the way she feels, we're lucky she's chosen to remain with us at all. I'll take Iffyr out on watch."

Eslinde nodded and touched her hand to his arm as he passed her to mount the white shimmerdart. "Thank you. Hopefully what you'll see is Thallan and Samor returning safe."

Vance returned a thin-lipped smile. Pushing the tamed dragon into motion, he left, followed by Yensen, sent by the princess to check on the new refugees from the undercity.

Lyrrin pressed a hand to her chest where the paired heart stone hung under her clothes. She knew she should be worried about the two Rebel Riders leaving and that they no longer had a working gateway to escape from if they ended up penned in.

But all she could think about was the pounding, rampant beat of her sister's heart.

She's fighting. She's fighting hard.

Lyrrin could only imagine what Riony might be facing, but she tried not to because it always became too terrible.

She imagined her sister and friends burned in dragonfire. She imagined them rounded up and captured by an army of one hundred riders. She imagined that the altered dragon summoning rune she'd given them didn't work or, worse, backfired in some way which hurt her family.

She hadn't had time to test it, and despite reassurances from the Alderkin that it should only effect tamed dragons, exactly what it would do was unknown and created a deep well of worry in Lyrrin.

Screwing her eyes closed, Lyrrin focused on the pulse beating through the stone. It was still beating. That's what mattered.

Soft scales bumped up against her cheek.

Dracuni nudged her and made a soft thrumming sound.

"You're worried too, aren't you?" she replied, patting the unidragon's cheek.

"I'm sure it will all be okay." Eslinde floated over, back straight and smiling, but her thin fingers tangled and fidgeted in front of her.

She wore her gown today, the only one she had left her palace home with. Some days she wore the plain military uniforms available in the stores, but most often, she had remained in that same dress. The shimmering silver fabric looked more gray and flat now, as was the princess's tone.

Lyrrin's lips twisted at her mother's empty words. She had felt like this when the others had helped the enclaves and attacked the dragonkeep. Left behind to wait on news of whether those she loved survived.

But now she felt even worse. Riony and the others would be in an enclosed space, underground, with no dragons of their own but up against who knows how many others. And also up against Kife and his cruelty.

Her clawed fingers formed a fist. "You don't know that things will be okay. You don't know what Kife is like. He has no honor or goodness at all. He was more than happy to try to burn me or Benjin with his dragon's fire the first time we met!"

Eslinde knelt in front of Lyrrin and reached out to touch her cheek. "He tried to burn children? You shouldn't have even been in such a situation. How you've even remained alive, I don't know."

Lyrrin pulled away from her touch. "I'm not just a child. I was the one who saved the others that time. And now I'm not getting the chance to help at all. Not since *you* arrived."

Eslinde gasped. "I'm just trying to keep you safe."

"We're supposed to keep each other safe! That's how we've stayed alive so long, because we protect each other and trust each other. All of us."

Eslinde withdrew her hand, staring at Lyrrin with saddened eyes for a long moment. She shifted backward, sitting on her heels.

When she spoke again, her voice was low. "I'm sorry.

I suppose I've never known that sort of trust. I grew up surrounded by lies and cunning."

Lyrrin swallowed her anger at the sight of her mother's pain. The few times she had tried to find out what life had been like for her as a princess, her questions had been waved away with a polite smile and a response of, "Much as you'd expect."

Eslinde's head tilted to the side, and she smiled, although without joy, her gaze on the ground.

"For a long while I thought myself clever, good at reading when someone was lying to me or not. But the truth was all I needed to do was assume everyone was lying about something, and it was always true."

When she looked back up at Lyrrin, her silver irises were flooded with a wash of tears. She reached out for Lyrrin's ungloved hands, and Lyrrin didn't pull away.

Eslinde squeezed her fingers gently in her own.

"Even now, with more allies than I've ever had at my side, I feel as though anyone could betray me at any moment and all I want is for you to be safe, for you to have a world you can live safely in. I'm sorry if I've been overprotective. But I grieved you as dead for so many years, and I couldn't bear to lose you again."

Lyrrin's nose stung with the threat of tears, and she wrinkled it. "I don't want to lose you either."

Lyrrin reached up to hug her mother, but the thump of heavy claws on stone turned her away. Vance returned on the white dragon, racing into the stables.

He slid down from the saddle with a speed that cracked his prosthetic leg against the floor, and he winced as he staggered their way. The tamed dragon remained still in the center of the wide space.

Lyrrin liked Vance. He had let her carve a little swirl of runes and patterns into the wood of his leg, even though it would do nothing.

But she didn't like the look on his face as he rushed toward them.

"There are dragons, coming in to land now."

Carefully moving Elumon's sleepy head off her lap, Lyrrin stood up. "Is it Riony and the others? Are they back already?"

Dracuni perked up at that, lilac eyes bright as she awaited the answer.

Vance shook his head and gave Eslinde a dark look.

"Thallan and Samor returned?" she asked.

Vance grunted. "No. They came in from the east, directly our way. Ten dragons with riders. I hadn't even gotten off the ground before I saw them."

"Coming in to land? Now?" Eslinde lunged to her feet.

"I've already closed and locked the outer entrance from inside."

"We've been found? How? Even if Thallan or Samor had betrayed us, surely the attack wouldn't have come so soon."

Lyrrin looked from Dracuni to Elumon to Eslinde, Vance, and Viska. They had all feared this day since they fled the first round of the Dragon King's riders. But for it to be upon them now seemed unreal.

And for it to be upon them now, while Riony was gone, left Lyrrin shaking.

Eslinde pressed her hands to her temples and then smoothed down her pale hair. "The defenses are solid. That will buy us some time. But with no gateway ... And so many more people to feed now with those who came in from the undercity."

Lyrrin said, "The others might get back soon. They might be able to chase them away."

Eslinde sent a small, fluttering smile her way, then began moving, marching for the exit of the stables room. "We must barricade the entrance, build it up even stronger, and then make a list of our food and resources, begin rationing."

Lyrrin hurried to her side. She slipped her hand into her mother's.

As they reached the door, Yensen appeared there. His expression was flat and calculating.

Eslinde gave a small sigh of relief. "Yensen, there are dragons—"

"I know." The grayglim took two large steps forward, right into Lyrrin's path.

His arm lashed around her shoulders and pulled her with him. Surprised, Lyrrin's fingers slid free from Eslinde's

and she was turned around in the grayglim's rough grip.

He pinned her with her back against him and a blade pressed to her throat. "Get those hands of yours up and out in front of you, now."

Gasping, Lyrrin lifted her arms, holding them out.

"Yensen!" Eslinde shrieked his name. "What are you doing?"

"Following orders, Your Highness." He moved Lyrrin with him as he took careful steps toward the stalls holding the dragons.

Viska's golden eyes tracked them, confused and narrowed. In the middle of the room, the white dragon, tamed, gave no reaction at all.

"Orders? Who's orders? I ..." Eslinde's words trailed off and her face turned a sickly pale green.

"My orders have always come from a higher place." Yensen brought Lyrrin to a stop in front of the stall holding Dracuni and Elumon.

Dracuni growled long and low, waking the smaller dragon.

The hatchling blinked sleepy eyes, and his confusion and worry washed over Lyrrin.

Eslinde's head was shaking wildly, her usual composure completely gone. "But you've been with us all this time. You helped us escape."

"I did what had to be done to reach the target." He gave Lyrrin a sharp squeeze and she squeaked, making it

clear the target he meant.

"And when it became clear there was a secondary and more important target, I did what had to be done to bide my time until both were ready to be taken. And since my plan to remove your ability to flee through the gateway worked, the time has come."

Lyrrin's fear shifted into something darker. "You did that? You had the undercity attacked, just so the gateway would run out of charge?"

The grayglim ignored her. The knife came off her throat just long enough for it to be waved Dracuni's way. "You're coming with us."

Dracuni rose up to full height, her teeth bared as she took a lunging step forward. Lyrrin edged her hands in toward her belt and the crystals it held.

But the blade was already back against Lyrrin's flesh, and it pressed closer. The bite of the sharp edge made her flinch, and she put her hands up again.

Yensen's voice above Lyrrin's head was emotionless. "Behave, both of you. And the rest of you stay back too, or the child's blood is on you."

Eslinde clutched Vance's arm for support. "Yensen, please. She's my daughter."

"She's the target and has been since I was assigned to you. Be grateful that my orders as to what to do with the target changed. Now you will let me leave with her and the silvernix dragon."

Yensen skirted around, dragging Lyrrin with him and with Dracuni following afterward. The unidragon stalked slowly, worried eyes locked on Lyrrin.

Vance and Eslinde backed away as they reached the door. Yensen leaned his head through the threshold, checking the way ahead.

And Vance rushed at them. He cleared the few steps' gap in one giant stride. Lyrrin tugged at Yensen's hold, trying to get clear, but he held tight.

Only his blade moved, flashing in the torchlight as it struck out.

Vance stilled, hanging there from the end of Yensen's arm for a moment before he stumbled backward.

"Vance!" Eslinde grasped for him, and as his weight hit hers, she fell along with him to the floor.

He groaned and curled on his side, blood pooling beneath him.

Then a larger growl overtook the room. Behind Vance, Viska loomed over him and Eslinde, golden scales shimmering and a hot glow building in her throat.

"No, she'll burn them all." Eslinde tugged at her dress, pinned beneath Vance's bulk.

Vance coughed once, then rolled onto his hands and knees. He slipped, coming back onto his stomach.

He cried out in pain, then bellowed, "Viska, no!"

The golden dragon hissed, teeth bared and eyes sharp with fury. But the glow of her flame receded.

But a rush of rage hit Lyrrin, and for a moment she wondered if it was from Viska herself. Until Elumon charged in. The hatchling snapped and bit at Yensen's ankles, small teeth pinching at the leather of his boots.

With a grumble of annoyance, Yensen kicked the dragonling away.

Pain, pain! Elumon whimpered, curling up against a wall.

Lyrrin screamed and lashed her own hands at the man. Her sharp claws met his cheek and drew four red lines along it. He glared back, unwavering as he locked her neck in his hand and aimed the tip of his bloodied blade up under her chin.

"Enough! You're only my secondary target now, child. Don't test me again!"

Eslinde sat with Vance's head on her lap, lolling lifelessly. Her shoulders shook. She was mouthing Lyrrin's name, but no sound came out.

With a harsh tug, Yensen pulled Lyrrin toward Norallei's dragon, but Viska moved between them and the tamed dragon with a warning snarl.

Yensen stilled for a moment, then muttered, "We've our own dragons waiting outside anyway."

He backed away out into the hall and barked at Dracuni to keep following them.

The unidragon's chest heaved as she trailed after them toward the exit.

Reaching the final barrier, Yensen turned to work the locks. Lyrrin looked back down the tunnel, to where Vance might die without Dracuni's help, to where the dragonling she was responsible for lay hurt. To where her mother would be left, grieving for her again.

All because she was a target? She didn't even know what that meant or why.

Figures moved in the low light at the other end of the hall. The three Alderkin, walking toward them, and then slowing as they took in the situation.

Yensen made a show of the dagger at Lyrrin's neck, and the Alderkin stilled. Then the grayglim took Lyrrin and Dracuni out into the open air, where ten dragons surrounded the entrance, awaiting them.

TWENTY-FOUR

Through their rush to arrive at the undercity and the fighting since, Riony hadn't spared a thought for the paired crystal hanging at her chest. She had barely felt the pulse of her sister's small heartbeat below the raging drum of her own.

But as Kife's words settled over her, the flutter against her chest grew and grew, thumping in panic. The stone rattled where it hung from her necklace next to the acorn pendant.

It wasn't a trap for you.

Now she understood what it had been like for Lyrrin all those times, feeling a loved one's fear from a distance, knowing they were in danger and unable to reach them.

Riony didn't know something could hurt so much.

"What have you done?" Riony roared.

Kife touched a gloved hand to his chest. "Me? All I'm doing is collecting my reward—you two, and anything I want to do with you. Another close ally of our king, sun bless him, came up with this wonderful plan and will probably be capturing the real prize right now."

The real prize. Dracuni. *I never should have left them.*

Another close ally of the king ... Riony's mind raced, trying to work out who would betray them. It could be anyone. She cursed herself for how trusting she'd been.

The hairs up the back of her neck twinged and she shot a glance back at Kess, half expecting her to declare it was her plan, then go and join her awful brother again. But Kess held firm at Riony's back.

And Lyrrin's heart beat like a trapped rabbit through the stone.

At Riony's desperate expression, Kife only laughed, a muted echo from under his helmet. The sound demolished all of Riony's restraint. She rushed at the vile man.

He shifted, bringing his dragon standing tall again, and Riony came up against the hard plates of the snowflame's chest. She dodged to the side to avoid colliding into the bulk of the beast, ducking under its trunk-like neck.

Riony knew this was a fight she couldn't win, but that last scrap of sense was buried deep under a desire to inflict a mountain of pain upon Kife for having any part in what was happening to Dracuni and Lyrrin.

There were too many dragons, too many riders, all too well armored. Fighting back was reckless and stupid and utterly a terrible idea in all ways and Kess followed Riony right into the brawl without hesitation.

Riony surged forward again. Maybe they could at least hold Kife and his riders' attention long enough for the others to free the delvers and regain control of the undercity.

She pounced to the side, stepping onto the forearm of Kife's snowflame and vaulting up its shoulder.

Her weightless leap brought her eye level with Kife, and as her sword arced toward him, his eyes widened through the narrow slit of his helmet.

Then pain shot up Riony's leg and she was tugged away, her sword tip passing a hair's breadth in front of Kife's face.

Sharp teeth clamped around her ankle and Riony was pulled from the air and thrown to the ground like a wet rag. She cried out as her back hit the street, armor clattering.

One treedart had her foot in its mouth, and another two were approaching from her sides. With her free leg, she kicked the small dragon in the snout with all her strength. Once, twice, and then its teeth slipped free, tearing along her boot as they went.

Riony rolled left as the dragon on one side snapped its jaw at her sword hand, then rolled right as the dragon on the other side bit for her shoulder. She scrambled backward, gritting her teeth at the sharp zings of pain shooting from her bleeding ankle.

Riony rose crookedly to her feet to face the three soldiers on treedarts bearing down on her. Her eyes wildly sought Kess, sought the comfort of knowing the wolf rider had her back.

But Kess was busy with her own assault.

She and Griskin were on the other side of the large snowflame and surrounded by five smaller dragons and riders. The wolf dodged and danced between the snapping jaws on all sides. Kess kept herself low to his back, churning through her supply of throwing knives in a hail of attacks.

Bone blades flew, clinked against armor, and scattered on the ground. Then one of the riders and dragons suddenly stilled, the white end of a blade protruding from the thin slit in the helmet.

That fine shot gave Kess some more room as the other riders surrounding her and Griskin hesitated and backed off.

But Kife on his snowflame did not. The white dragon's chest heaved and its head swung toward the wolf rider.

Riony's heart rammed against her chest as Kife's dragon ejected a river of white-hot liquid flame across the street where Griskin had been.

"Kess!" Riony raised an arm over her face to block the wave of heat and glare of the lightning-bright inferno.

She could only look for a moment before using her sword to block the next attack from the treedarts in front of her. She couldn't see whether those liquid flames had

swallowed Kess within them. Jaws snapped the air around her and she roared ferally as she batted their snouts away, desperate to see signs of life beyond the fire.

Through the flickering burn, shadows moved. Someone screamed—a man's voice. A treedart and rider stumbled out, globs of molten liquid searing them all over, as they gurgled in pain through their last moments.

Kess had been there, right in there as well. Is she ...?

The shadows shifted again, then Griskin leaped free, over the wall of shimmering white flame. Kess remained safe on his back.

Riony felt no relief. Only a heavy, suffocating realization of how much she didn't want to lose Kess and how there was still far too much risk of that happening.

Kife kept his dragon's head aimed for his sister who was pushed into a corner with a fall of limestone curtain blocking behind her.

The snowflame opened its mouth wide again, but nothing happened.

"Come on, get her!" Kife snapped, slapping his hands against the tamed dragon's neck.

It convulsed as though breathing but no more liquid flame emerged. It moved sluggishly, pain and weakness clear in the droop of its neck, wings, and shoulders. The snowflame made a wheezing, hacking sound and shook its head, spattering droplets of liquid flame across the street.

One landed on Riony's hand and seared right through

the leather of the glove. She hissed, trying to wipe it away.

Kess glared up at Kife with raw disdain. "You've already burned your dragon out? You never did deserve to be a rider."

"Still a better rider than you'll ever be." Kife growled, and his dragon spun in a tight, swift circle beneath him.

The tail lashed out, swiping through the air. It caught Kess in the chest and sent her flying off Griskin. She rolled along the stone street, each bump knocking a gasping cry from her.

She tumbled to a stop right up beside the wall of fire and didn't move. The roasting heat caused thin trails of smoke to rise from Kess as she lay alongside it.

"Kess!" Riony willed Kess to move. She had to get away from there or she was going to be cooked.

Why isn't she moving? She can't be ... She's only here because of me. She's only hurt because of me.

Riony pressed her attack against the three dragons keeping her busy, trying to push past them and get to Kess. She thrust through a gap and struck one rider with her sword, but another sent a jet of orange flame her way. It scorched along the side of her head and Riony smelled burnt hair.

Griskin howled, jumping between the treedarts that penned him in, also pushing in Kess's direction.

"Kill that damned mutt already," Kife ordered lazily.

Kess stirred then, lifting onto her elbows.

She rasped. "Gris, run. Run! Go find the others."

The wolf's growl lightened to a whimper. A hot dart of fire shot his way and he skittered clear of it, gave Kess one more look, then switched direction and pounced clear over the heads of the riders on that side.

A couple of them chased him down the street.

Kess coughed and rolled herself away from the baking dragonflame. But she was down and injured, with only a few knives left on her.

The stench of singed hair filled Riony's nose, her temple and cheek hot, blobby flares of light burning in her vision. She turned in a wide swing to bring another rider off their steed, then lunged through the gap.

Dashing between swiping tails and snapping jaws, Riony reached Kess's side just as another burst of flame splashed across her back. Her scale armor heated but kept her flesh protected from the treedart's fire.

Still, the impact stunned her enough that she tripped on her injured foot. She was staggering when Kife brought his dragon around again and its tail knocked her sword from her hand. It clinked and rolled out of reach.

Riony grunted out her frustration and pain and turned around to square up against Kife and the army of dragons around her. She raised her empty hands and closed them into fists.

"What are you doing? Get out of here!" Kess hissed up from the ground.

She breathed in short, clipped breaths and blood dripped from her lips.

Riony scanned around, but there wasn't a single opening she could break through as the dragons closed in tighter. Not with her injured ankle. Not without her sword.

And even if she could, there was no way she was leaving Kess behind.

Kife lifted his helmet off, smiling down with glittering eyes at his prey. "On your knees."

Riony returned a brash smile. "I would never kneel for someone who looks like they cry when they masturbate."

With a flick of the chin from Kife, the rider closest swung the flat of his sword into the backs of Riony's legs and they folded. She cracked down onto her knees with an *oomph*.

Kife said, "Get these two in chains. We've only just begun having our fun with them."

Four riders dismounted and drew manacles from their saddlebags. One approached where Kess lay on her side, dodging a flying knife before stilling her with a swift boot to the stomach.

The other three came for Riony. She tried to stand back up but her knees had hit the stone in a way that they weren't happy about at all.

It was all she could do to land one last punch. She hit square into one rider's chest, sending him stumbling back, before the other two caught her arms and brought them

in front of her.

The heavy, cold steel clicked closed around her wrists.

Riony set her jaw, glaring at the soldiers as they patted her and Kess down, taking away all remaining daggers and weapons.

Riony's eyes narrowed as she looked at the pile of discarded bone daggers on the ground. The cutting athame she'd given Kess wasn't there.

She must have it hidden somewhere. Riony tried to hide how impressed she was by that.

It was pretty easy when Kife was watching her with a smug smile and her face could only twist in disgust in response.

He flicked his head, gesturing from Riony to Kess. "You. *Carry her.*"

Riony snorted hot air from her nose. She'd carried Kess a few times recently, voluntarily even—which still felt weird. But to be ordered to do so by a Heithorn left her skin crawling.

But she feared Kess's treatment in someone else's hands more than she hated following Kife's orders.

Groaning, Riony brought one aching knee up. She leaned over where Kess was still balled up from the kick she'd taken.

"No. You don't have to," Kess whispered.

"I know," Riony whispered back and scooped her manacled hands under Kess.

Kess had always been much smaller than Riony, even though only a year younger. But she'd always seemed too heavy when she was a weight Riony was forced to carry.

Now, as Riony lifted her in her arms, she didn't seem to weigh a thing.

Both of them tensed, sore and bloodied, as Riony brought them painfully to her feet.

Kife beamed. "Good girl, just like the dumb beast you are."

Through blood-tinted teeth, Kess said softly, "Don't listen to him."

Riony smirked. "Listen to what? I can't hear dead men."

Kife rattled out orders, sending half his troops off to find the rest of Riony's friends and the other half to march with him, flanking their prisoners.

The point of a sword at her back got Riony moving as Kife led them through the empty streets.

Riony's body hummed with the hammering of three heartbeats. Her own, Lyrrin's through the paired stone, and Kess's where they pressed together.

Every step was a lesson in how much pain she could withstand, as her knees howled and ankle stung and wrists twisted awkwardly within the sharp-edged manacles to keep Kess supported.

Riony settled into that agony, embraced it, because no matter what Kife's plans for them were, she knew it would only get worse.

Their slow parade moved out from the narrow pathways into the Grand Arch markets where stalls and carts had been upended. Broken crystals lay scattered amid a burst sack of flour and tangled fabric.

A hushed murmur came from ahead, and people came into view. A huge crowd, tightly packed into a clear area at the lower side of Sinking Stream Lake.

It seemed as though half the undercity community kneeled there, surrounded by dragons. They seemed tired and overwrought, as though they'd been trapped there under threat of dragonfire since the initial attack.

As Kife led them around the edges of the crowd and up the stairs, almost all eyes tracked Riony.

They were faces she knew. Some from her time in the undercity and those she'd helped reach the undercity from her time aboveground. Those who came here for refuge after the enclaves were attacked.

The dour-faced man from the Orphans' Den who had given Riony candy after she'd returned the stolen kids. A red-bearded man who had given Riony an extra serving of rice at Myrwa's camp. The small, craggy woman and her children who Riony had warned away from the rough settlement.

I've failed them all. None of them found safety.

It wasn't judgment, though, that filled the people's eyes. But worry. And beneath that, a simmering flicker of rage.

"I brought a little something from home. What do

you think?"

Kife's voice turned Riony's attention away from the crowd, and her blood went cold.

Along the central platform—the flat-topped limestone plateau beside the tiered wall of the lake, where market-day performances were often held—stood the Heithorn estate whipping post.

The thick beam of wood was charred black up one side, but still appeared solid. Riony could imagine exactly how solid it was. She knew. She could remember. She'd bucked and pulled against that timber so many times trying to free herself from the lash of a whip, but it never granted her mercy.

"Hook them up," Kife commanded, looking like a child on a gifting day. "We are all going to enjoy the public execution of these criminals today."

Riony could only stare back. Could only hope Aishena and the others would put a stop to what was going to be a humiliating and painful death.

Kife's dragon slinked closer, and he lowered his voice. "But I think I'm going to enjoy it the most. You were always the most fun of all our slaves to whip. How you could take a lashing! And I always wondered just how many strikes it would take before you broke. Before your body simply gave in and died. Now we're going to find out."

TWENTY-FIVE

Lyrrin lifted her chin and scowled defiantly at the king's riders surrounding the entrance to Eslindekeep's underground base. Her arms ached as she kept her hands lifted in front of her, but anytime they dropped, the blade at her neck pressed closer.

Dracuni stood back at a distance specified by the grayglim, so that he remained out of reach of her claws or bite. Her nostrils flared as she growled. But Lyrrin knew there was little the unidragon could do from that distance. Her breath did not burn; it only healed.

Low clouds darkened the day and a light fall of snow left Lyrrin chilled. She wasn't dressed to be outside. She had her hooded coat on, but no shoes, and hadn't been wearing her gloves for a while. Her fingers already ached from the cold, and she didn't know what Yensen intended to do with her next.

The grayglim marched forward, his grip ironclad on Lyrrin's arm.

"I have the ones our king wants. All has gone as promised," he announced.

One of the riders, with intricately braided black hair and dark, calculating eyes, replied, "Not quite. You said there would be no dragons left here when we came in, but we had to lure off a couple that were on patrol with two of our own. I thought grayglims were supposed to be better than allowing a mistake like that."

Yensen stilled, and his voice had the brittle sharpness of someone unable to believe their authority would be challenged. "My plan has still succeeded. You'd have had no luck digging our quarry out of its hole without me."

The rider, sitting atop a huge yellow dragon, only huffed. He squinted at Dracuni. "What sort of strange dragon is that anyway?"

"One our king will be pleased to receive. Now, give me your steed."

The two men locked gazes for a long moment, then the rider sniffed lazily and climbed down from the saddle. "Of course. I'll ride with another."

One of the other riders tossed Yensen some flight goggles, then Yensen yanked Lyrrin toward the yellow dragon.

He was really going to take her away. Away from her friends, her mother, from any chance of seeing Riony return safe from whatever was making her heart beat a manic percussion.

Yensen pulled the knife away and readjusted his hold, grasping Lyrrin under the armpits to push her up onto the dragon's saddle.

"No!" she shrieked.

Feral panic ignited within her and she bucked and screamed, writhing in his grip. She arched her back and kicked her feet into Yensen's legs. His hold didn't falter.

She cried, her voice raw with desperation, "Dracuni, run! Fly! You've got to get away!"

Dracuni spread her wings and ran. Penned in as she was by the ring of larger dragons, there was nowhere to go, and her wings flapped helplessly, unable to catch the wind. She remained grounded, panting and cowering between the larger beasts.

Ignoring her struggles, Yensen hoisted Lyrrin onto the dragon and secured her in front of him on the saddle. He took the reins and signaled the dragon to take off. With a powerful beat of wide, leathery wings, the dragon lifted from the ground.

Hovering there amid a swirl of snowflakes and dust, the yellow beast snatched Dracuni in its talons, lifting her effortlessly along with them. Dracuni whined and her tail whipped, but she was pinned within the cage of claws.

Yensen leaned over Lyrrin from behind and undid her belt. He pulled it free with a sharp tug, then tossed it and all of the crystals it contained away into the air.

Lyrrin wriggled but his hold on her remained firm. He grasped her with one hand as he pulled his goggles on with the other.

"There's nowhere for you to run now, child. Stop squirming. Consider yourself lucky you're wanted alive."

Lyrrin growled, "You're the one who'll be lucky to be alive when Riony finds out what you've done. She's going to smash you into jelly!"

Around them, the other nine dragons lifted from the ground as well, following them skyward.

"Best if you give up hopes of seeing your sister again now. I doubt she'll survive the trap laid for her."

Lyrrin refused to believe that, and the man's assumption only made her angry. "A trap you helped lay! We trusted you. How could you?"

"I'm following my king's orders, and there is no higher honor. I only remained with Eslinde so that if and when she ever found you again, I could finish the job of killing her child."

She tried to stay strong, but knowing her death had been wanted for so long wasn't a good feeling.

She whimpered, "Why?"

Yensen pulled a length of cord from a pocket and bound Lyrrin's wrists together, then fastened them to the front of the saddle. "Because you're a half-breed abomination that the king wanted erased."

Tears reappeared in Lyrrin's eyes, freezing there in the blast of the icy wind. She felt chilled right through in her thin clothes as they ascended higher.

With Lyrrin secure, Yensen took the reins again. "But after I reported back about the silvernix dragon, the king had me watching you both and holding my cover. Lucky for you he decided having someone who could perform Alderkin magic but pass as human was more valuable than cleaning up Eslinde's mess."

Lyrrin wrenched at her bound hands, trying to curl her sharp fingers into the twine, but she was stuck fast. They had lifted directly upward toward the gray clouds, and Eslindekeep was a small stamp of patchwork beneath them.

Yensen turned the yellow dragon to the east, when something flashed far below.

A golden streak, bursting at speed from the base tunnel.

Viska emerged and rushed into the sky, roaring with fury. Dracuni cried a sad yelp in return.

Yensen swore, then muttered, "I didn't think that sulking beast would be a problem."

"Looks like you made her angry." Wind buffeted Lyrrin's eyes, making it hard to see, and she squinted, tracking the shooting-star of golden scales.

Not just Viska, but Viska with riders. They shot vertically toward them, closing space quickly. Five figures rode together along her back.

Lyrrin's heart jolted with the spark of hope.

Unless any of the undercity refugees could fly, that was Vance, Eslinde, and the Alderkin. Considering Viska hadn't even allowed Vance to ride her since she was untamed, Lyrrin doubted it could be anyone else.

Vance is okay!

Lyrrin didn't know how but was happy to see him still alive and able to fly, and they were coming after her.

Yensen gestured a few signals to the other king's riders, and they peeled off from their positions around the grayglim's dragon, heading back toward Viska. Yensen pushed the yellow to fly faster and kept to their eastward heading.

Lyrrin angled around to watch behind them, holding her breath.

Viska's golden scales blazed against the pale backdrop. She roared as the riders reached her, blocking her path. The sky became a tangle of tails and wings, weaving, darting, chasing.

Viska had the advantage. She was fast and nimble and able to react with her own mind, compared to the slower tamed dragons that relied on orders from their riders. But with nine versus one, Viska was harried from every angle, unable to break through.

A burst of bright light cut through the battle, and two riders backed off.

Flash stones. The Alderkin are helping!

The battle of dragons shimmered and swirled in the air like colorful flags buffeted by wind. Viska flamed, catching a rider off guard and sending them spiraling. Then another rider caught Viska's tail in their dragon's claws, pulling her away from the group.

Another bright flash of a midair explosion went off. A burst stone shattered, showering the air with ember-hot shards. It echoed like thunder and Viska broke free.

But all the while Yensen took Lyrrin and Dracuni farther and farther away.

Then, from the horizon, two more dragons appeared. Thallan, riding his bronze etherdart Brunzell, and Samor on his black and gold flamesong Shani, dove into the fray.

Brunzell moved at an incredible speed and reached the battle first, his shooting fireballs scattering the enemy.

Lyrrin smiled. The Rebel Riders hadn't abandoned them. They'd only been led away by the king's riders, who they must have defeated. And they'd come back to help. But her smile faltered as Samor and Shani joined the fight as well.

The flamesong unleashed her massive torrents of flame against the king's riders, taking three of them out in one blast. Both riders and dragons fell to the earth, burning. Lyrrin gasped, mouth hanging open, the horrific sight scorched into her eyes.

The sky was clearer now, and the two new riders had

balanced the battle, but neither of them seemed interested in pursuing Yensen.

They focused their attack on the king's riders.

Only Viska separated out, chasing after the yellow dragon, bringing the fight with her.

The crisp air filled with the smell of smoke and charred flesh and Yensen grunted, pushing the yellow to fly faster, but with its burden of Dracuni, it seemed to have reached its limit.

One of the swifter king's riders caught up to Viska again, causing the gold dragon to loop around and backtrack to get away from a volley of fireballs.

Yensen turned to watch too then, a grim look on his face as a woman's scream reached them through the air.

Lyrrin bit her lip, and Yensen sucked in a sharp breath too.

He had spent so long pretending to be working to keep the princess alive, maybe he cared more than he thought?

"It's not too late to turn around. We could go back, help them. They would forgive you," Lyrrin said.

Yensen's reply was dry and rough. "They made their own decision to come after us into the fight. They will face the consequences."

Lyrrin wrenched her arms against where they were tied, trying to break free so she could show the grayglim some of his own consequences, but the bindings remained tight. Her fingers grew cold and numb.

Viska flew like a streak of lightning, leading the dragon on her tail in a race through the clouds.

Come on, come on! You can beat them.

Thallan and Brunzell kept occupied trading blasts of fireballs between them and the king's riders, and Samor and Shani had been forced downward by a pair of blue dragons working together.

In a move more elegant than any of the tamed dragon's could achieve, Shani arched upward in a full loop, coming up over the battle and back in behind her pursuers, catching them in her enormous jet of flame.

But one of Thallan's combatants had broken off from his group and snuck up behind them.

Lyrrin gasped as a fireball struck directly onto Shani's back, between her wings. The black and gold scales came away singed, but otherwise unhurt.

But Samor, who had been riding on that back, fell.

His arms and legs waved limply as his body tumbled in the air, trailing smoke, and Shani dived for him. The flamesong dragon caught her rider in her claws.

There was a moment of stillness as Shani glided clear of the rest of the battle.

Then Shani roared. The sound filled the air, a terrible wailing howl of grief that seemed to reach from horizon to horizon. It started low, then turned high and pitiful with the pain of mourning.

Lyrrin let out her own small whimper, her mouth open

and eyes watering.

Then Shani's roar changed again, growing stronger, and she launched herself back into the center of the battle. There were four king's riders remaining, swerving between Brunzell and Viska, and Shani brought herself to hover in the middle.

She bellowed a deep, painful, grumbling sound, and her chest seemed to expand. She barked that noise again, growing larger, glowing brighter, the shimmer of flames showing around her neck and chest but not emerging from her throat.

Viska seemed to understand what was coming and turned to flee. But too slow.

Shani exploded.

Lyrrin's mouth snapped wide open and her whole face stung with the anguish of what she'd just seen. The explosion was blinding, a churning mass of rushing flame that filled the sky and blew apart clouds. Even from their distance away, the shock wave smacked Lyrrin like a physical blow.

And somewhere within that explosion was Viska and those she carried.

Twenty-Six

Kess had become so still in Riony's arms that she had to look down to see if she was still breathing.

Kess stared back with eyes round and pale as a full moon. Filled with a kind of fear Riony had never seen the stubborn young woman express before.

"Hey, it's okay," Riony whispered through a half smile. "This isn't my first time, you know. I'm an old hand at this. I'll be fine."

Kess's head shook in a small jittery motion.

The intensity of Kess's expression made Riony frown. "Don't worry. I'll handle it as long as I have to handle it. You just focus on being ready when the others show up to save the day."

"No." Kess's voice trembled, and her breath came fast.

"I can't see you hurt like that again. I won't."

Riony's mouth opened to reply, but her throat felt like it had been clogged by her heart. She managed a weak, "Kess ..."

Then a soldier pulled Kess out of Riony's arms. Riony tried to hold on, but her manacled wrists had no purchase and had left her fingers deadened.

Two more soldiers came up behind Riony and grabbed her arms, lifting them up to hang the manacles over one of the steel hooks at the top of the post.

She resisted, straining against them, and they shoved her face-first into the whipping post. Her shoulders twisted badly as the familiar click of the locking bolt slid home. Then they released their grip on her, knowing there was nowhere she could go.

Riony tested the hold of her bonds, tugging with all her strength. She was bigger now, older, stronger than the last time she'd been bound to that post. But it remained just as solid. The wooden beam had been mounted onto a heavy steel plate beneath them, and Riony tried to rock the entire construction, but it stayed steady.

On the opposite side, the soldier who had taken Kess struggled as she snarled and writhed in his arms, her legs hanging limp beneath her. He ended up using the full length of his body to pin Kess against the post as he lifted her arms high to hook her to the post.

Once she was attached, she remained hanging with her

face pressed against the charred timber. Her feet wobbled weakly but couldn't support her weight.

Riony stretched around to the side to move closer.

Kess's cheeks were red from anger and black from soot and she stared blankly at the crowd as though she were already gone.

Riony wanted to touch her chin, lift her face up and look into those piercing eyes so much that her bound hands ached.

"Hey, Kessara, look at me. We're going to be okay. I can take whatever your weak-ass brother has in mind. I'll bet you his noodle arms simply fall right off long before I break."

Kess remained still and didn't look up. And murmurs arose from the watching crowd.

Riony followed her gaze then. Over the lip of the platform, across the lake below, through the middle of the crowd, another parade of dragonriders approached.

They had three prisoners in tow. Niskina, Dashiel, and Benjin.

So much for our escape plan. Riony swore long and loud, inside her own head only so as not to give Kife the satisfaction of her panic.

He watched her with shrewd pleasure regardless. Riony glared back. They didn't have Aishena yet. Griskin and Shiff were still out there somewhere too. Riony refused to give up hope while she was still breathing.

Kife climbed down from his dragon. He landed lightly and strode to the edge of the platform, right beside the whipping post. Small pieces of limestone crystal from the plateau's lip crunched as he put one boot onto it.

"People of the caves." He addressed the crowd in a booming voice. "My riders and I have come to liberate you from the fear you've lived in all these years."

As he spoke, the soldiers who had locked them to the post pulled daggers and were working them between all the joins and buckles of Riony and Kess's chest armor. Riony's body jostled as the last fastening was cut and her scale mail clattered to the ground at her feet.

Next, they cut away her under-padding. Soon she was left in just a shirt that had been drenched in sweat from the earlier fight and now clung cold to her skin.

Kess's armor and gambeson followed shortly after, and the soldiers took it away.

Kife continued. "We will free you from the fear of the world above, of the shadow dragon and revenant curse, and fear of dangerous criminals such as these two here."

He swung an arm back toward Riony and Kess where they were bound.

Kife paused as though expecting some kind of reaction, but the crowd remained silent.

"They aren't buying your bovinshit, Kife." Riony leaned back casually, creating a triangle between her arms, body, and post.

Kife unsubtly ignored her and raised his voice again. "We are here to turn this place from a mess of cowering pitiables, into a flourishing city, under the protection of dragonriders and the wing of our Dragon King himself. You will become great under our care and under our control."

A solitary voice in the crowd booed, loud and sharp. Dragonriders at the perimeter of the group descended upon the woman and dragged her away.

Mutters and whimpering spread, then was silenced again as Kife yelled, "You will see there is no room for dissent. You will see exactly what happens to those who go against me and my rule, and you will learn who is in control."

Kife reached an arm straight out to one side, palm up and waiting.

"Are you hoping for someone to hand you a spine, a heart, or some other vital organ you're missing?" Riony heckled, eyeing his pants pointedly.

Kife kept his arm out and his smile broad. "I did consider gagging that big mouth of yours, but I so look forward to hearing you scream."

A soldier approached carrying a lash. Riony's skin shivered into rough goosebumps at the sight of it. The whipping post Kife had brought from home, but the lash was something new.

Back at Heithorn estate, they had always used simple leather whips. Enough to welt and sometimes tear the

skin. Enough to make the recipient wish to never feel that pain again.

But the knotted, hooked lash of stiff hide being placed into Kife's hand was something altogether different.

Riony wondered if it was Kife's own design. She wondered whether he'd whipped anyone else with it before, and whether they survived. She wondered how much it was going to hurt.

"It's fine. I can do this. Don't worry." She whispered the words toward the beam of wood in front of her, but it wasn't clear whether she spoke them to Kess or herself.

Kife stepped up behind Riony, arm lifted.

"I enjoyed it, you know." Kess's voice rang strong and clear from the other side of the post.

Kife stilled. "Enjoyed what?"

"Freeing your dragon." Kess sighed out the words. She shifted her torso and leaned her side into the post, lifting her head. "Just as I enjoyed freeing your pretty slave back at Skaellakeep."

"What are you doing?" Riony whispered, but Kess ignored her.

Kife's forehead creased, then he shook his head in dismissal and raised his arm higher.

A wild chuckle emerged from Kess. "How she ran when I gave her the option to! I think that was when I realized that you and I are more alike than I ever imagined."

"We are nothing alike!" Kife snapped. He took a

lurching step her way.

"But, brother, we are," Kess crooned the words, with all the sly, nasty energy she used to hold. "Because no human or creature would ever want to remain by your side unless forced to. Because in the end, even as able-bodied as you are, you're even more unwanted than *I* am."

Kife bared his teeth and air hissed out between them. He straightened up and marched over behind his sister. "I'll show you exactly how unwanted you are."

Riony's indrawn gasp was only halfway through her throat when the lash hit. It cracked across Kess's back with a blistering sound.

The broken, wailing scream that followed felt like it split Riony deeper than the lash could have. Her mouth opened as though the cry were her own, then she bit it closed, teeth grinding against each other.

"No! What are you doing?" she growled through her locked jaw. "It's meant to be me."

Riony had been prepared for a beating. She'd been prepared for it for half her life. To bleed at the hands of others had become her normal and for all she wished she could live free of pain, she could *handle* it. She was used to it.

But when she'd thought feeling Lyrrin's panic through the paired stone and being so far away was a torture greater than she'd ever known, she hadn't imagined this. Seeing the pain that should have been hers inflicted onto someone else. Someone she cared about. Unable to make it stop.

Kife pulled back the knotted lash and struck again. Droplets of red sprayed across the air.

Kess's scream was lost under the roaring that filled Riony's ears. White-hot fury scorched her every nerve ending. She bucked against her bindings like a wild animal.

"Somebody do something!" Riony shrieked desperately toward the crowd.

She sought her friends, lined up at the front of the crowd below, bound in their own heavy manacles. Niskina's face had gone pale, watching with her jaw set. Benjin looked away. Dashiel cried.

Everyone else's expressions were a mix of the same. Some eyed the dragons surrounding them warily.

"Do something!" Riony pleaded again. "There are more of you than there are of them. You can stop this! Somebody stop this!"

Kife lifted his arm again. Kess's body heaved with sobs that were more like short, rasping screams.

"Don't do it, Kife. Touch her again and you are dead!" Riony bellowed, straining against her bonds.

He smiled in reply. "Why ever would I stop? As though you have anything to offer me other than this beautiful display. And this is so much better than I'd originally planned. Far more entertaining."

He struck again, and Kess's neck arched back, her face turned up to the cavern ceiling and mouth open in

a silent scream.

Riony screamed in her place, and hot tears spilled as Kess's head lolled down against the post.

"Stop, please stop," Kess whimpered.

"Ah, the begging begins already." Kife toyed with the lash, inspecting the bloodied ends. "I knew you wouldn't last long. But let's keep going anyway."

He raised the lash, and Kess screamed before it even hit, then the sound shifted into a low moan.

Riony couldn't feel or think anything anymore except blurring, burning, roaring rage. She was barely aware of the feral grunts she made and the wild thrashing of her body.

Kess's voice was a screaming whisper. "Please. No more. I'll do anything. Anything."

Kife laughed. "Then keep on begging."

"I can do more!" Kess rushed the words out. "I have something more valuable to offer."

Scoffing, Kife brought the lash swinging toward her again.

"I know how they made Dracuni. I know how to make more!" The words flew from Kess's mouth faster than the lash.

Kife pulled back at the last moment.

Riony stilled, blinking the fury from her eyes. "Kess?"

Kife's eyes shot to Riony, assessing her, then back to his sister. He moved closer to the whipping post, standing between the two of them.

With his voice low, he said, "More? You can make more? Tell me how."

Kess wobbled where she hung from the hook, her face wet with tears and spattered red. "I will. Once you free me. Please. It hurts."

What is she doing? We never worked it out. Not really. Unless she's just desperate enough to lie, or unless she has some other plan. Riony's mouth had gone dry and all she could do was stare between the Heithorn brother and sister and pray to all the stars far above them that Kess wasn't betraying her again.

Kife tutted. "Four lashes? I'm disappointed that's all it took to have you giving up such wealth of knowledge. I'm disappointed to share our family name."

"Then free me *and* promise me a place as a dragonrider. You know that's all I want. All I've ever wanted."

Riony's blood turned cold at Kess's words, and all the fight left her.

Kess didn't meet her eyes as she continued. "Promise me that, then I will tell you. Then you will have more, be richer than any lord or king in the land."

Rubbing his thumb over his chin, Kife paced. "No, no, that seems too easy. You've always had too much of a soft spot for this redheaded beast. If I'm going to believe you've turned on her again, I need a show of loyalty from you before you can rejoin the winning side, sis."

"I'll do anything," Kess replied.

Riony knew what Kife was going to ask before he spoke. She and Kess locked eyes, a swirl of unspoken emotions pleading through red-rimmed lashes and determined, steady gaze.

Kife dangled the cruel lash in the air, letting it swing. Crimson painted the ends and dripped onto the pale limestone below.

"You never had the guts to whip your slave yourself. You're going to make up for that today."

Twenty-Seven

Kess closed her eyes for a few seconds, breathing through the pain of her shredded back.

Her flesh felt on fire and blood soaked what remained of her shirt, pooling around to the front. The lashing was both harder and easier than she'd expected. Harder for it being a different kind of pain than she'd ever known before, like fire and ice at war within her flesh. But easier because she wasn't watching it being inflicted on Riony.

She'd done her best to balance appearing to break at a realistic moment, while not being so hurt she couldn't move. But considering her brother's low estimation of her, she may have been able to stop even sooner and have him believe she couldn't take any more.

The agony far greater than her raw back was how Riony

was looking at her.

"You miserable, backstabbing goblin! I can't believe you'd turn on me *again*." Riony gave one sudden wrench against the hook, her face contorted with anger. "Actually, yes, I can. It's exactly the kind of thing a traitorous, malignant pest like you would do."

Kess's expression twisted into the sneering mask she'd worn most of her life. "I'll do anything I have to do to get what I want. You'd have learned that by now if you weren't such a tame-brained beast."

She loaded her words with bitterness, drawing on all her pain from every cruelty and heartbreak in her life to give them unquestionable sincerity.

She needed Kife to believe everything she said. And if Riony believed it too, it was a price Kess was willing to pay. It was a small cost, when what she planned to do had the biggest price of all.

Kife's broad smile showed he was lapping up every moment, as though watching his favorite stage play.

He stepped up onto the small platform with the whipping post and reached up to where Kess's heavy manacles were hooked. The soldier hadn't bothered locking the bolt in place for her as they had for Riony. Kess couldn't stand tall and lift the chains off the metal loop herself.

All eyes were on them as Kife hauled Kess up by the wrists and released her from the solid beam. The crowd below seemed confused, muttering between themselves.

And at the front, Riony's friends had no confusion. Niskina and Benjin looked ready for murder.

But it was Dashiel's expression that cracked Kess's heart in two. Wide-eyed and unbelieving, their head shook. Kess wanted to shout out, to explain herself, to banish the look of disappointment that cut deeper than Kife's lashings.

But she kept her expression set. They would all know her true intentions soon enough. And then it would be too late.

I just hope this works.

Kess had gone through dozens and dozens of plans and ideas and hopes in her mind since they were captured. She wanted to use the cutting athame, still hidden behind her belted waistband, to cut Riony free. But there was no way she could reach up high enough for that once her hands were free.

Aishena was still unaccounted for. And as terrifyingly skilled as the young woman was, Kess doubted she could take on all of the soldiers and their dragons alone. Kess hoped that, at best, Aishena would save Riony and her friends.

At least Griskin is already free.

All of Kess's planning came down to one final idea. One action she could take.

She could get rid of Kife, once and for all.

Her brother let her fall from the hook, and she folded roughly down to the ground. The motion pulled at her torn skin and she gasped in pain.

Riony wrenched at the whipping post again, making the metal sheet the beam was bolted to rattle.

Kife then pushed the handle of the lash into Kess's hands and dragged her by the arm around to behind Riony.

He looked at where Kess hunched over on her side on the ground and up at Riony's back. "We might need to bring a chair in for her!"

A chuckle rippled from the soldiers nearby.

Kess took a deep breath. *At least once Kife's gone, his cruelty will be gone with him.*

Maybe whoever is next in command will end this public display, treat their prisoners better, give Aishena more of a chance to free everyone. Kess knew it was a slim hope, but she had to hold on to something.

She knew it was worth it, either way, to remove Kife. As one of only two enemies who knew about Dracuni, he had to go. And since she was the one who told him, she would make that happen.

Kess's hands felt heavy in the manacles. Good. She dropped the lash, and the chain hanging between her wrists clattered as she moved her fingers toward her waistband. She flinched at the sound, but a sudden roaring covered her actions.

She froze, seeking the source of the howling, mourning screams that seemed to echo from every direction.

Every dragon in the room had lifted their heads, wailing

horribly.

Every *tamed* dragon. Kess scanned across the crowd and toward the back she saw a figure slinking through the shadows, lit by a sickly yellow-green glow from something in their hand.

The dragon summoning crystal. Aishena had activated it.

The result wasn't exactly as anticipated. The dragons weren't moving Aishena's way as the wild dragons had. But it was certainly doing something.

The dragons' distressed cries sounded so much like those of the shadow dragon that it left Kess shaking.

"What's going on? Get those dragons under control!" Kife barked.

A nearby rider called back, "It's not reacting to any commands!"

Kife took a step away, and Kess panicked. She needed him to remain close. She had to act fast.

Grasping for the athame at her belt, she fumbled it and it clattered loudly onto the metal square of the whipping platform below her.

Kife spun around, glaring down at it and her.

"Oh dear. Did you think you were going to catch me off guard with that little toothpick?"

Smirking, he bent down to where it lay, plucking it out of her weakly grasping fingers.

And Kess smiled back in return.

She flung both arms upward so fast that it made the wounds on her back ignite with agony, then dropped the chain around Kife's neck.

He swore and pushed back to his feet, taking her with him as she clung tight around his shoulders with her manacled hands.

"Let go of me, you useless wretch!"

He wavered on his feet as her weight unbalanced him, lurching to the side. Kess arched her back, swinging as much of her weight the same way, taking them both toppling over the lip of the limestone platform.

"Kess! *Kess*!" Riony's cries chased them from above.

And they fell, down the drapery of the limestone slope and into the lake below. The ice-cold water slapped against Kess's back, blinding her with pain, and she put everything she had into remaining conscious, keeping her grip.

The water was cloudy from churning silt. Kess wasn't sure how deep it was. It just had to be deep enough. Her brother kicked and writhed against her, but his own armor and the weight of Kess's body and chains fought against his efforts. They both went deeper, deeper, into the milky blue pit.

Stars filled Kess's closed eyes and her lungs swelled to bursting, but she kept her arms locked around her brother's fighting body.

She could do this. For Riony. To remove Kife as a danger from her life forever, she'd do anything. As her consciousness darkened, this seemed the easiest thing of all to do.

All she had to do was keep holding on. And sink.

Riony's shoulders strained as she angled to see over the lip of the platform to the lake below where Kess and Kife had just vanished.

"Kess?" Her cry was lost under the warbling screams of the dragons around the cavern.

Riony's face burned hot against cold streaks of tears.

Raze it, Kess. What did you do?

There was movement all around, cries and murmurs reaching through the periphery of Riony's vision and hearing, but all she could do was stare at the cloudy water below, where nobody re-emerged, where no reply came.

Riony tried to lean farther out, to see the edge of the lake closest to the drop from above. Maybe Kess had resurfaced there, out of her line of sight. But with her hands pinned above her head, she couldn't reach far enough.

"This depths-cursed, sparking post!" Riony kicked unhelpfully at the solid beam and rattled her cuffed hands against her bonds.

She still hasn't come up. I have to get to her.

In desperation, Riony wrapped her fingers around the chain between her manacles, then leaned back and put her

feet up against the beam of wood. She stretched her entire body out, pulling against the metal hook she was attached to, every muscle from head to toe screaming with effort.

The smallest bend in the weld holding the hook to the metal top casing rekindled her resolve, and she bellowed wordlessly, wrenching against her bonds. The steel groaned and warped and Riony's arms felt as though they did the same.

And then with a final crack, the hook snapped free.

Riony fell backward, hitting the ground and rolling from the momentum. She curled up and brought her knees under her, coming up into a crouching position.

The cries from below grew louder. No longer whimpering murmurs, but a chorus of confident, rousing shouts.

"She's free!"

"Move, now."

"Come on, together."

Breathing heavily, Riony watched the crowd below as she rose to her feet.

And they rose too.

Only a few at first. Faces Riony recognized. People she knew. People she had helped.

But more quickly followed, building like a wave of bodies. The fierce determination on every face made Riony's heart swell.

The dragonriders, still trying to get their screaming

dragons to respond, were caught unawares as the first of the crowd reached them. They were swarmed. Dragged from their steeds, they disappeared beneath the surge of bodies.

A flash at the corner of her eye turned Riony from the scene below and she leaned back to dodge an incoming swing of a sword. The few soldiers on foot who had guarded around the platform came for her.

Sparks flew as Riony blocked another strike with the chain between her wrists.

She yelled at them, "Back off! I don't sparking have time for this!"

Riony could swim well enough, but not with her hands chained. Not if she was trying to carry another body as well. The cutting athame Kess had dropped lay just behind the line of guards. If she could just get to it, then get to the water ...

Riony's pulse hammered.

It's been so long already.

Riony clasped her hands together as one and brought them and the heavy manacles hammering down over a guard's helmeted head. He stilled, swaying, and she kicked him in the chest, sending him bodily into the soldier next to him. Both went down.

In the breathing space that followed, Riony shot a look over the lake again, and the rioting population beyond. No movement in the water.

"Kess, come on, come back."

At the front of the crowd, Aishena came into view, her own glowing yellow athame brandished in one hand. In a flurry of elegant strikes, she downed the final guard beside Niskina, Dashiel, and Benjin, then freed them from their chains.

Riony lunged sideways to avoid being skewered by a sword, then ran across the platform to the nearest edge.

She stood tall and screamed, "Aish! I need help!"

"I'm coming!" The young grayglim woman vanished into the crowd again.

An almost gleeful growl came from behind Riony, and Shiff burst through into the middle of the remaining guards, snapping at their legs.

Griskin followed, leaping on soft paws toward the now abandoned whipping post. He sniffed around it, but his eyes and nose were running. Turning his face up, he looked desperately toward Riony.

"I'll get her. I'm going to get her!"

Aishena appeared by Riony's side, cropped hair swinging around her chin as she scanned for nearby threats. Shiff and Griskin had the closest guards at bay.

Riony held her arms out in front of her. "Quick!"

Aishena nodded once and sliced so swiftly through the cuffs of steel Riony thought she'd take her hands right off along with them and wasn't sure at that point she even cared as long as it was fast.

But the manacles were cut away with careful precision and clinked onto the ground.

Riony touched her fingers briefly to Aishena's shoulder, turned away, and dove off the high platform into the lake below.

The cold touch of the meltwater hit Riony like a slap to the face and she aimed her body down, kicking her aching legs hard until she reached the silty bottom. She swung her arms all around, finding nothing. A current pulled at her—the lake's waters flowing from this reservoir along to the next—and she worried how far Kess might have been drawn along.

But she didn't have enough breath to find out. She pushed off the bottom, speeding desperately to the surface to draw in air again.

She turned on the spot in the milky water, hoping to see that Kess had somehow returned on her own, as she gulped three deep breaths, then went under again.

Back and forth she swam, her body screaming from exertion as her armored legs weighed her down, and no other body met her searching fingers.

Again, she emerged to breathe.

Her face scrunched up and she squeezed her sodden hair in her hands. "No. No, no, no!"

Something approached her through the water, and Riony spun around to meet it, splashing water in her wake.

She wished to see Kess's face, but instead, a furry snout pushed up to sniff at her cheek.

She blinked water from her eyes, staring at the cave otter as her breaths heaved. She swiped a hand to push Butterfur away.

"Kess?" she cried desperately, as though her voice alone could bring her back from the watery depths. "Kess!"

Butterfur returned, undeterred, sniffing and nipping at Riony's shirt as his long, silky body sluiced through the water.

Riony lifted a hand again in frustration and then through her panic came a moment of clarity.

Her voice stuttered. "Kess ... *Kess has the treats.*"

The otter rolled in the water, sniffed once, then duck-dived away in a flash.

Riony clamped her mouth closed, holding back the gut-wrenching sobs that were building in her chest. Shaking her head, she gasped a frustrated breath and prepared to dive again, when a shadowed shape rose in the water toward her.

A pale face, veiled in a tangle of dark and light streaked hair broke the surface.

Riony cried out wordlessly. She splashed closer, and the top of Butterfur's head emerged as well, then his snout, biting closed around a mouthful of shirt. Kess's thin arms hung heavy on one side, hands heavy in the manacles, and the milky water around her tinted pink.

Riony clutched the unresponsive girl to her chest and leaned back, kicking toward the nearest shore as Butterfur followed, digging around one of Kess's pockets.

Riony's fingers pressed into the mangled flesh on Kess's back and she flinched, clenching her teeth.

"I'm sorry. I'm so sorry," she whispered, but there was no reply.

There was no sign Kess felt any pain, or anything at all.

Reaching the bank, Riony hauled herself out of the water, then pulled Kess up after her. The body was a dead weight, slumping bonelessly. Riony fell into a sitting position, shaking all over.

All around, fighting continued. But the sounds were muted in Riony's ears. Even when cheers went up in the crowd, they sounded like a distant humming.

She adjusted Kess's lifeless body and drew her onto her lap.

Riony pushed the matting of wet hair off Kess's face. Her skin was cold and still.

"Kess? Come on. I know you're tougher than this. I know you're still with me. You said you'd be with me, always."

Riony grasped for the string around her neck. Fishing the acorn pendant and heart stone from under her shirt, she yanked on the string, breaking it. Tucking the pulsing crystal back against her chest again, Riony took the acorn in trembling fingers and pulled it open.

Inside, in a small glass vial procured from Eslindekeep's stores, was the gift Dracuni had forced on her before she left.

A gift she now thanked all the stars she took.

She let the silvernix drop onto Kess's cheek. As she waited for it to take effect, wishing and praying that it would take effect, that it wasn't too late, she lifted Kess closer.

Cradling her in one arm, she pressed her forehead to Kess's. "Come on. You can't leave me. Not now. Now when ..."

A shimmering light sparkled through Riony's wet eyelashes. She sobbed in relief as that glow built, growing stronger, and Kess's body jerked and twitched in her arms. Riony held tight as Kess's lungs expelled water and torn skin knitted closed and the small body seized and gasped in pain.

Kess *gasped*. Kess *breathed*. And that was all Riony wanted to hear.

As pale eyes opened and stared up at Riony's, there was a moment of confusion. And then a flurry of words.

"Forgive me. I was never going to hurt you. I'd never whip you, ever again. I was only pretending to betray you again to get free, to get close enough to Kife so that—"

"I know." Riony cupped Kess's cheek and pressed a

thumb to her lips. "I'm not that big of a *tame-brained beast*, you know. I knew all along. Kind of nice to see you tricking someone who isn't me for once. Although I wish I knew what you really had planned."

"You knew? You trusted me?" This seemed to break something inside Kess more than the lashing had, and fat tears toppled from her eyes.

"Not actually dumb, remember? Just caring."

Kess's still shackled hands came up together, fingers still icy cold, and clutched around where Riony's were against her face. "I'd have done it anyway, even if you hated me for it. It's okay. It's okay if you hate me, as long as you're safe."

There was a soft ache to Kess's voice. A dreaminess, as though none of this were true, as though she couldn't believe she were still there and alive, that the fingers she squeezed within hers were real.

Riony pulled her closer again, pressing her cheek to Kess's.

Her lips moved against Kess's ear. "I ... I don't hate you."

An avalanche of sobs overtook Kess then, shaking them both with their ferocity, and Riony kept her held in their embrace as though they were the only two people in the world.

Two soon became three, as the warm bulk of Griskin's fur settled down against them. He whined softly, pressing his forehead against Kess's back.

Then another cheer went up, louder this time as the fear and fury and water had all drained from Riony's ears.

"The last rider is down!" Benjin's voice rang out over the crowd.

The dragons had stopped screaming at some point. Riony wasn't sure when. The effect the altered summoning stone had on them hadn't lasted long. Riony and her friends alone wouldn't have stood a chance defeating the soldiers without the help of the people of the undercity.

Butterfur sat on the bank a little way down, gnashing open-mouthed on the saturated piece of mushroom jerky he'd extracted from Kess's pocket.

And the creatures of the undercity too.

Niskina could be heard through the chattering of triumph, giving orders about what to do with the dragonrider prisoners and any remaining soldiers out within the city. Riony hadn't seen any other delvers around. Aishena must have never reached them. But everyone seemed to look to Niskina as a leader.

Dashiel came sliding down the slick limestone bank toward Riony and Kess.

"Is she okay? Oh, stars." Their approach slowed as they took in how Riony and Kess held each other.

"I'm okay." Kess wiped her face, now very red, and sat up, shifting out of Riony's lap.

"Wow. That was ... I can't believe we did it! I mean,

not that I did a lot, but look. We, they, everyone stood up against the dragonriders and won." Dashiel beamed.

Despite the smile, their face was pale, and they cradled one bloodied arm close to their chest.

"Yeah, I suppose we did." Riony wasn't sure either just how much she'd done.

You inspire people.

Riony found herself staring at Kess's lips as though she spoke the words again, but they were still.

Relief for the undercity being freed lasted only a moment for Riony. A cold, aching heaviness struck her, as though one of the mammoth stalactites from the ceiling above had cracked off and crushed her.

She clutched for her chest, panting with fear.

Halfway to climbing onto Griskin, Kess stilled. "What is it?"

Riony's hands closed around the paired heart stone, knuckles white and fingers cutting against the sharp edges.

It had gone entirely still.

TWENTY-EIGHT

The sky roiled with fire. A single mammoth ball of it, hissing and crackling where Shani had been moments before.

Lyrrin couldn't take her eyes off it. The sheer horror of it, of that poor dragon, driven to such a grave act by grief. Of the fear her mother, her Alderkin family, and her friends had also been caught in the explosion. That she might have just lost them all in one instant.

But as she watched, neck craned to look around Yensen, she noticed that Yensen also had his eyes locked on the tragic inferno.

Their dragon continued to glide forward, Dracuni still caught in its claws below. But Yensen was distracted.

And she couldn't waste that moment.

Lyrrin glanced down at where her belt usually was, with its array of crystals ready to blind or explode at a moment's notice. But it was long gone. And her hands were still bound together at the wrist and tied to the front of the saddle.

There was only one thing she had left.

She crumpled over, hunching onto her hands, wailing for her mother. The kind of bratty, tantrummy cry she'd recently outgrown.

Yensen ignored her, pointedly continuing to look away.

With her chest leaning over her bound hands, she plucked her fingers around her neck until one hooked on the string there, and she pulled the heart stone free. It jumped in her hands, beating so hard from her sister's heartbeat that it almost bounced free and fell from her grip.

Lyrrin clutched it hard with one hand and brought one of her sharp claws against it with the other, covering the action with her leaning body.

She paused. What to draw? She'd never tried recreating the paired heart rune. She'd never seen much point in creating more. There were only so many heartbeats she wanted to keep track of at one time, and feeling Riony's from a distance generally brought her more worry than comfort.

So she'd also never tested the rune with any others.

"What are you doing?" Yensen grumbled.

Lyrrin flinched and rushed out two quick runes. Her pointed nail screeched over the crystal surface.

Yensen grabbed the back of her shirt, pulling her up. His hands thrust to either side of her, grasping for the crystal in her hands. She ran her finger over the runes.

Light. Burst.

Lyrrin had considered using light and burn but didn't want to cause the kind of explosion that might send her or Dracuni falling from the sky. It was already risky enough adding her flash combination to an untested rune.

Riony's heart beat faster and wilder than Lyrrin had ever felt it, and the glow of the crystal built.

"Let go of that! What have you done?"

Lyrrin locked her fingers around the flat slice of translucent stone as Yensen tried to pry it free.

The light pulsed, flashing in time to the heartbeat, growing bright and strong, then brighter and stronger. Lyrrin squeezed her eyes closed and her eyelids flashed red, black, red, black as the blinding light shone right through.

Yensen leaned away, grunting, then forward again and the hard strike of blunt metal smashed against Lyrrin's fingers.

She cried out, and the crystal slipped free. She opened her eyes to try to grasp it again, but it was already out of reach of her tied hands.

The stone spun, flashing like a falling star as it tumbled from the sky. The power of its glow burned a wavering line into Lyrrin's vision, but she could still see around the edges.

Yensen, on the other hand, rubbed watering eyes with the palms of his hands, cursing. He held a dagger in one of them. He must have looked directly at the stone in order to strike it free from her grip.

Blinded. But not for long.

Lyrrin wrenched at the rope around her hands, wriggled and kicked in the saddle, but she remained stuck. But her thrashing seemed to send confusing signals to the tamed dragon they rode on.

It veered from their smooth glide, twisting sideways and flying a full, horizontal circle. Maybe if she could move the right way, she could make the dragon turn back toward Viska.

Riony should have let me fly with some of the riders before. I could have seen what to do.

But her movements did something, and that was all she had. Emboldened, Lyrrin leaned forward as far as she could, thrusting her hands through the rope so they stuck farther out up front. She pushed and slapped at the dragon's neck, wherever she could reach.

A short puff of fire emerged, then the dragon ascended higher.

"Stop it!" Yensen grasped the back of Lyrrin's neck in

a painful pincer grip and pulled her back.

Lyrrin twisted in the saddle, bringing her legs up for a final, reckless kick against the dragon's neck.

And Dracuni screamed.

No. Lyrrin's chest squeezed with the fear that she'd made the dragon crush her friend. But as she looked over the edge of the saddle, through the blurring streaks in her vision, she saw something almost as bad.

Dracuni was falling.

The dragon had let go, and Dracuni tumbled in a spiraling rush through the air.

"No!" Lyrrin yelled aloud.

"What did you do?" Yensen turned his head side to side, blinking unseeing eyes.

Dracuni howled again, more distant, and Yensen grunted.

He leaned over Lyrrin, taking control of the dragon again. He aimed the beast in the rough direction of the screaming unidragon and pushed it into a dive.

Lyrrin wriggled, jabbing her shoulders into the grayglim. Even without his sight, he was gaining on Dracuni simply from following her cries.

"You've got to fly! Dracuni, put your wings out. Stretch them out!" Lyrrin shouted with her whole chest.

Dracuni yelped again, passing through a low puff of cloud. Her wings fluttered and tangled around her spinning

body. And then she pushed them out.

One diaphanous wing caught the air but the other crumpled against the pressure, twisting up at a painful angle.

"Keep trying! You can do it," Lyrrin yelled. "Straight out, nice and strong!"

Pale scales glittered in the dim light as Dracuni turned over and over again. The ground came up fast beneath her and Yensen's dragon came down from above.

The unidragon's wings thrust out and wavered. Held, then failed. Thrust out again, billowed in the wind, and Dracuni stabilized.

"Good work! Now flap! Go! Get out of here!" Lyrrin's eyes flooded with tears and her mouth split in a fierce, proud smile.

With her eyes on Dracuni, making small careful motions of her shimmering wings, Lyrrin almost missed the oncoming field of grass and rocks.

She shrieked, high-pitched, "We're going to hit the ground!"

Yensen swore and adjusted his hand movements, and their dragon arched and swooped upward, skimming the earth, then rising back into the sky.

"Where is it? Where did the silvernix dragon go?" Yensen yelled in Lyrrin's ear.

Dracuni wasn't far below them now, flapping her small

wings frantically and hovering in a wobbly way. But as she remained silent, and Yensen's red eyes still searched blindly, she could have been anywhere.

"Gone! Flown away. You can't catch her."

Yensen brought their dragon to a slow glide. He rubbed his eyes again.

Dracuni's lilac eyes met Lyrrin's and her nostrils flared. Her wings pumped harder, moving their way, but even with all her effort, their own dragon's gentle soaring took them farther away.

Lyrrin shook her head fiercely. She mouthed the words, *No. Go!*

She wished once more she could communicate with Dracuni in her mind. Even at the now vast distance, Lyrrin could still feel a small tug of emotion from Elumon, twanging inside her.

Am I ever going to see him again? What will he do without me?

Lyrrin tried to send comforting emotions back to the hatchling. But all she could do for Dracuni was shake her head and hope the unidragon could read lips.

"Is that it? Over there?" Yensen squinted at Lyrrin and then in the direction she was looking.

His vision is clearing.

Dracuni still hovered, struggling to stay airborne. Not moving closer, but not fleeing either. She was an easy target

for a larger, faster dragon, even with a half-blinded rider.

Yensen turned their dragon back around. They had glided a fair distance away, but at full speed they would close that gap quickly.

Then another dragon appeared through a gust of gray cloud, rushing their way. Glinting gold against the ashy sky.

"Viska!" Lyrrin yelled, bouncing in the saddle.

She breathed deeply and leaned into the chilled wind, trying to see the faces of all who rode with her, to know they were still okay.

Yensen grumbled, eyes twitching as he wiped them dry again and looked between the shimmer of silver and sparkle of gold in the sky.

Behind Viska, two more dragons appeared. Thallan riding Brunzell, and one remaining king's rider. They dodged and chased each other in swirling arcs, all coming their way.

Muttering under his breath, Yensen leaned over Lyrrin again and pushed their dragon around, turning it away from the others and building its speed again.

He's running?

Lyrrin twisted her wrists within the rope, but it remained tight. Viska was moving a lot slower than she had before and wasn't gaining on them. They were going to leave them all behind.

Lyrrin turned in the saddle as far as she could, trying

to keep her eyes on the others. "No! Just let me go. You've lost. Dracuni's gone. You didn't get what you wanted. Let me go!"

Yensen pushed her shoulder out of his way. "Quiet!"

Lyrrin turned to the other side. Viska had caught up to Dracuni now and hovered beside her, assisting the struggling unidragon. They were so far away now they were just small, bright smudges in the air.

Lyrrin hadn't been able to see if Viska still carried everyone she had before.

She tried to use her most convincing voice as she pleaded, "You don't need me. Please. Just give up, give me back to them. Before it's too late."

"It's already too late." Yensen kept his eyes forward, on the eastern horizon. "We'll be lucky if the king doesn't take both our heads for failing to bring the silvernix dragon in after all this time, because of you."

"Then don't take me to him! Take me back to Eslinde. It doesn't matter what you've done. If you just take me back, we can work it all out." Lyrrin thought that might be a lie.

Still, they had forgiven Kess and brought her in as a friend, after all she had done. But at that moment Lyrrin hated the grayglim so much she couldn't make it sound true regardless.

"No. There'll be no other opportunity for me now. But at least I still have you. You might have been the secondary target, but my king still wants you. So that's where I'm taking you."

Lyrrin's voice broke. "To the Dragon King himself?"

Yensen's voice remained strong and low. "You're going to meet your grandfather. And pray that he decides you're worth keeping when you stole from him the prize he wanted most."

Lyrrin shivered. The blasting, icy wind felt as though it went straight through her. Her eyes watered from straining to stay open against it, and her eyelashes felt frosted. Hunching forward again, she wished she still had the heart stone to cling to as she tried to stay warm.

She ached as though she'd been punched in the belly.

She'd only just found her mother. Only just found the truth of who she was and met people like her. And now she was being taken away from everyone she loved to meet family that she never wanted to know.

TWENTY-NINE

Riony couldn't even remember how she'd gotten from the edge of the lake back to the platform with the whipping post. She gave it a single, resentful glance, then kicked at the chest armor that had been cut off her. The buckles were all ruined. It wasn't going back on.

I'll have to find something else. Or just go without.

Everything blurred in an anxious haze.

Riony didn't know what was happening. She only knew she had to get to her sister as fast as possible.

The crystal could have run out of charge. Or she left it behind somewhere. It doesn't mean her heart has stopped.

Please let it not mean that.

Riony's chest felt hollow without the additional pulse

beating beside it. But almost as though to fill that space, more worry and fear and guilt flowed in.

Her own ... and more? Even from such a vast distance, she shared those emotions with Dracuni. She had to get to them both.

What do I need? Armor. Sword ...

"Kess?" Riony turned on the spot, her mind whirling with worry.

Where did she go? The last time Riony saw her was a few moments ago when she'd explained how the paired crystal had stopped beating.

"I'm here," said Kess from her side. She carried Riony's sword, rested across both her arms.

Griskin panted from the run he'd just been on to retrieve it.

Behind them, Aishena bandaged Dashiel's arm as Shiff stood guard, and Benjin helped Niskina round up the defeated soldiers and catch up the newly freed delvers on what was happening.

Riony stared at her sword in Kess's hands for a long few seconds. Had she asked Kess to get it? She couldn't remember.

"Thank you." She grasped the hilt and took the still lit but fading weapon.

She hadn't been to a shrine with it in a while, and the charge seemed to be running out. After quickly deactivating

it, its true weight returned.

Riony winced as she took a step back.

"Your ankle ..." Kess said.

"It's fine." Riony leaned heavily on her other leg.

Her skin had swollen around the puncture holes from the dragon bite, tight inside her leather boot, and it throbbed hotly. But there was nothing to be done. Unless someone else had a precious family heirloom squirreled away in an acorn, Riony doubted there was a single drop of silvernix in the undercity.

Riony leaned on her sword like a crutch. "We'll head out the top way, flag down Zeina and Jaym, and get to Eslindekeep as quick as we can, then ..."

Another surge of emotion hit Riony. The same soup of worry, guilt, and fear from before, but stronger now, enough to make her guts ache and eyes water. How was she feeling Dracuni so intensely from so far away?

Big sister? Big sister!

Riony frowned. "Dracuni?"

"Dracuni?" Niskina echoed as she, Aishena, Benjin, and Dashiel joined them.

We're coming. Where are you?

Riony's eyes widened. "She's nearby. We have to get to one of the entrances."

"Stoneshield Gate is closest." Niskina raised her voice and gestured to the milling people in that direction. "Clear

a path!"

The crowd parted, and Riony broke into a loping, uneven sprint.

Griskin could have moved faster, and with her pounding ankle, Riony was sure Aishena, Benjin, and even Dashiel with their injured arm could have all moved faster than her. But they all kept pace, even Shiff at the back. Niskina remained behind.

Beyond the market area where the community had been gathered, the streets through Upslope were clear, and they reached the tunnel exit quickly.

Riony had never been out that way before, a passage normally reserved for delvers only, and she hadn't been one long enough for such perks. Soon the huge stone doorways loomed into sight, carved into an imposing shield design surrounded by crystals.

A couple of treedarts sat idly beside the gate, unresponsive due to their riders having been taken away. Aishena split off to an alcove at the side and worked the opening mechanism. The deep, gravelly grinding of stone against stone reverberated through the tunnel, and daylight cut through the dusty air.

I'm here, Dracuni. Can you hear me? Riony stepped out onto the rocky plateau, staring up at the low storm clouds that were tinted orange in the few gaps the afternoon sun reached.

"She's flying!" Benjin shouted and jumped once on the spot.

Riony followed his gaze and saw three dragons descending. Viska, Iffyr, and Dracuni. *Flying!*

Three others emerged from behind the snowy peak, red, orange, and aqua. Zeina and Jaym with their dragons plus Ambri, following the others in.

"What happened? Why did they come here?" Aishena asked, her expression grave.

Riony! The word was like a sob in Riony's mind, and then no more words followed, only torrents of crushing sadness.

Riony squinted to see the faces of the riders. Benjin had lost his crystal-encrusted staff when he was captured and it hadn't been returned to him yet, and none of them had a seeing stone on them, so they had to stand and wait as the dragons landed.

Dracuni came in first, a little too fast. Her claws clattered on the stones as her momentum tumbled her all the way along the plateau and right up to Riony's side.

Eslinde landed next on Iffyr, with the hatchling, Elumon, holding onto her lap. Viska had scorch marks down an entire side and one wing was torn. She carried Vance and the Alderkin. Only two of them. Yensen was missing as well. No Thallan. No Samor.

And no Lyrrin.

"Where is she?" Riony planted her feet firmly apart

to avoid crumbling.

Dracuni bowed her head and closed her lilac eyes. Her sides pumped like bellows, gasping deep breaths.

Silence only followed.

"WHERE IS SHE?"

Eslinde slid from the white shimmerdart dragon. She clutched Lyrrin's hatchling against one shoulder and landed heavily on the rocky ground. Elumon pushed out of her hold and jumped down, running over to hide between Dracuni and Shiff.

The princess took a few wavering steps toward Riony and then dropped down onto her knees. "I'm sorry. It's all my fault. Yensen ... he betrayed us."

Eslinde's face was swollen and red, dripping with tears.

Riony spoke through a mouth that felt filled with ash. "Is she ... did she ...?"

Vance approached Eslinde, standing above her. "The grayglim took her. Alive."

Riony's hand pressed against her chest, feeling the crystal below her shirt. "The paired heart stone stopped a while ago."

Dracuni lifted her head, and the sounds of her thoughts were laced with sorrow. *She used it. Blinded the rider with it so I could get away. But I couldn't fly well enough to help her too.*

Riony's legs could have been made of chalk, ready to crumble to dust, and she leaned onto Dracuni's neck,

holding her for both comfort and support.

But she was alive?

She was alive, and he took her away. I'm sorry.

"It's not your fault." Riony squeezed her tight.

"It's not. It's mine." Eslinde's voice cracked, and she bent forward, placing her forehead on the ground. "I won't ask your forgiveness, because I won't ever forgive myself for bringing a traitor with me."

Vance crouched beside Eslinde and put an arm over her shoulders. "We tried to catch up and get Lyrrin back, but with Viska injured, there was no chance. It was all we could do to get away safely."

The two Rebel Riders had landed now as well, and Jaym and Zeina looked at the charred golden dragon.

Zeina asked, "And the others?"

Vance shook his head. "All lost. With Eslindekeep compromised, we took Iffyr and Elumon and fled here. The refugees at the keep will make their way on foot to the nearest still active shrine."

All lost? Riony turned her eyes away from where Eslinde's thin shoulders shook. Behind her, Yrik and Priyune held each other, missing their third. Shael was gone. Thallan and Samor too. Zeina and Jaym shared heavy expressions.

Riony's fingers drifted over Dracuni's scales, and she stepped away. Hobbling forward, she reached down to Eslinde, pulling the princess reluctantly to her feet.

"We're going to get her back, okay? Our little spitfire is a survivor."

Eslinde squeezed Riony's fingers in hers, and fresh tears fell in heavy, fat drops.

Kess was giving Eslinde a sharp, scrutinizing stare. "You lost an earring, princess."

Riony noticed it then, how the spiraling silver jewelry dangled only on one side.

Eslinde's face crumpled, then reformed into an expression of solemnity. "We almost lost Vance, too."

Dashiel jogged to their brother. "What happened? You look fine. Is that *blood*?"

Vance patted Dashiel on the back and gave a more thorough rundown of Yensen's trap and what they had been through.

The fear and worry surging from Dracuni had eased now, but the guilt only grew stronger.

Little sister saved me. And I couldn't save her.

Riony shared in the heartbreak. Her sister had been taken away, and she knew that in every logical way, saving Dracuni came first and was the most important thing, but it didn't make the loss of Lyrrin hurt any less.

She wished she could go back and make different decisions but didn't know what she would change.

We did the right thing, helping free the undercity, helping save those people. Riony couldn't make herself choose between all of them and her family, even hypothetically.

She couldn't work out where the line fell, between what was right for the world and what she was willing to lose for that cause.

She would give up her life for all those around her, all who had become her family, and at the same time didn't want any of them to give up theirs.

With so much at stake, with so much against them, loss was inevitable.

But Riony refused to lose her sister.

Scanning across the faces of those around her, she knew they would stand with her. Aishena and Benjin stood side by side, with fierce, determined expressions. Dracuni had brought Elumon in closer, and she and Shiff both calmed the distraught hatchling.

The Rebel Riders looked eager for vengeance, and the Alderkin would protect Dracuni no matter what. Eslinde, Vance, and Dashiel looked to Riony expectantly.

And Kess sat on Griskin, close to Riony's shoulder, willing to do anything for her.

Between them all, they had six dragons and something to fight for.

Riony called out, "Is everyone ready to move? If we follow right away, we'll have an advantage of surprise. And the quicker we can get Lyrrin back, the better."

Eslinde's head shook in a wobbly way. "Yensen is taking her to my father, to the king. They're probably already there."

"Then that's where we are going too."

I'm ready. Dracuni took a step forward, chest still heaving and wings heavy at her sides.

Riony looked the unidragon over. "You can stay here with the Alderkin and recover."

I can fly again. I want to go too.

"I'm not sure if any of us are going anywhere," Aishena said, her eyes on the eastern horizon. "Look."

Riony turned, and for a moment she couldn't quite work out what she was seeing. Something like a strange flock of birds, but distant and too large to be birds, but too many to be anything else ... surely.

It couldn't be dragons. Not that many of them. Not hundreds of them.

But as much as Riony willed the truth away, dragons they were.

And they were coming directly toward the undercity, fast.

"Everyone inside, quick! Dragons too!" Aishena yelled.

Riony's head shook. *No. We need to go after Lyrrin.*

But there was no point in speaking those words. She knew there was no way forward as the sky between her and her sister had become a wall of flying beasts.

And as the dragons were within sight of them now, so were they within sight of the incoming dragons. A dozen broke ahead of the rest, shooting their way at a terrifying speed.

Despite Aishena's order, everyone had remained frozen.

"Go." Riony gave Eslinde a gentle push, and then yelled at Dracuni, "Inside, now!"

But little sister ...

I know.

They all moved. Vance supported Eslinde, and Dracuni and Shiff herded Elumon in front of them. The larger wild dragons followed after their riders, and the two tamed dragons were brought in by Aishena and Dashiel.

The Alderkin stared up in heartbroken awe at the opened doorway to a home they had been separated from for so long, then stepped inside as well.

Riony and Kess remained until the rest had made it inside, as the dragons above were close enough that their wing beats thundered like drums.

"Come on," Kess urged with a gentle press of her hand to Riony's shoulder.

Her face scrunched up and she shook her head heavily, then allowed herself to be guided inside.

The heavy stone doors of the undercity closed behind them, cutting off the roar of the first dragon to land where they had just been standing.

They were safe inside, for now. But those doors felt like a tomb closing them into their graves alive. With the full force of the Dragon King's army imprisoning them from outside.

THIRTY

Lyrrin's teeth chattered as Yensen marched her through the immense hallways of the Dragon King's palace. Her eyes bulged, both in fear and in awe.

She'd never set foot in a dragonkeep city before, let alone seen anything as grand and daunting as this place. She'd grown up in makeshift huts and limestone rooms small enough she and her sister were always stepping on each other.

The brutal vastness of the glossy, gilded space she walked through was overwhelming.

Slick black tiles reflected a strange, cold blue glow from the lamps. Sculptures of dragons in fierce, violent poses lined the hall. Their eyes seemed to follow Lyrrin's every move and made her feel small and vulnerable.

The floor gleamed like a polished mirror, every slapping step of her bare feet echoing in the cavernous space.

They passed by other guards and servants on duty, who cast curious looks their way, but nobody challenged what Yensen was doing with her, why the grayglim was pushing a trembling child along beside him.

He had pulled her hood over her blue hair and thrown a cloth over her bound hands, but that was more to hide her fingers than the fact she was bound up like a hostage.

A large glass and steel window framed the next intersection, offering a view out over the capital city, with all its jutting towers, shadowed by the high protective walls in the distance. The sun had nearly set.

Are the others okay? Does Riony know what happened to me by now? Will she come for me?

Riony probably would, but Lyrrin wasn't sure she wanted her to. Her sister would fight her way across half the kingdom if she had to. But here, in the slick marble hallways surrounded by high walls and guards and grayglims and dragonriders, Lyrrin feared what would become of anyone who tried to rescue her.

But she hadn't yet given up on trying to rescue herself.

Her eyes darted around, taking in the high ceilings adorned with chandeliers that sparkled like icy stars and the long corridors that seemed to stretch into infinity. She felt like a mouse in a maze, trying to spot a way out before the trap was sprung.

Lyrrin's heart pounded as they approached a grand pair of double doors, and Yensen whispered to the guard standing before them.

With a nod, the guard moved to open the entryway.

Lyrrin tried to steady her breathing, but the chill rattling her bones from their recent flight and the fear of what lay ahead made it impossible.

Her pace slowed, and she tried to turn back, but Yensen held her shoulder in an iron grip, as unyielding and cold as the palace itself.

The doors swung open, revealing the vast throne room beyond. Lyrrin's breath hitched as she took in the sight of the Dragon King.

He sat still as a statue, silver hair woven into an intricate net of braids that hung down to his waist. A large hooked nose gave him a commanding, predatory appearance emphasized further by the sharp, toothlike crown on his head.

To the side of his throne stood a young woman. Almost a match to Eslinde, but with black hair, streaked only with a few long lines of silver.

The look she gave Lyrrin as she was pushed in front of them was withering, as though Yensen had thrown the carcass of a mangled rat at her feet.

As they neared the throne, Lyrrin's stomach tightened. She couldn't help but glance at the grayglim, wondering if there was any trace of humanity left beneath his stony exterior. But his expression remained blank.

He'd long since stopped talking to her, refusing to even acknowledge her pleas or bargains.

Only the tremor in his fingers betrayed any emotion. *Is he scared too?*

The Dragon King turned then, casting terrifying eyes over Lyrrin and Yensen. They sparkled in all the wrong ways.

"I'm told you flew in alone, without the dragon I asked you to bring me." His voice filled the chamber in a way that made Lyrrin want to clutch her ears to block them.

Yensen knelt at the foot of the throne, tugging on Lyrrin to force her to do the same.

"Your Majesty, the dragon escaped in the last moments, due to the explosion of a rebel flamesong dragon." There was no pleading in the grayglim's voice, only a statement of fact.

Lyrrin shot him a glance, though, because it wasn't the whole truth. He had left out the part that it was her actions that helped Dracuni escape.

Lyrrin lifted her bowed head slightly so she could peer up at the king from under her hood. He looked younger than Lyrrin expected, but she'd heard the tales of how he

had become immortal through the copious amounts of silvernix he used.

He glared with those strange darkly bright eyes. "It would be an understatement to say I'm disappointed. After so long waiting for you to set your trap, all the resources spent, for you to return empty-handed now is unforgivable."

Unforgivable. Is Yensen going to be punished? Executed?

A deep, angry part of Lyrrin hoped for it.

Yensen only bowed lower, as though he'd already accepted this was his fate, and Lyrrin's eyes stung.

What was it Aishena used to say? *I am the hand and must act as the voice commands.* Lyrrin had seen how even an unfinished grayglim training left Aishena acting as though that was all she was. A tool for someone else's control, and the Dragon King was the one who controlled all the grayglims.

Yensen was nothing but a tool, utterly loyal to a king who seemed ready to discard him for his failure, and Lyrrin suddenly found herself scared for his life and what her life might become without him, there in a place where he was the only familiar face she had left.

Her voice felt scratchy and small in the echoing chamber. "He brought me in. I wouldn't call that empty-handed."

Yensen flashed her a confused look from the corner of his dark eyes.

Both the king and the woman beside him also turned to her then and Lyrrin flinched under their gaze.

"Are you even sure this is the right child? She looks ... almost normal," the woman said.

On her streaked hair, she wore a fine crown of thin silver and gold braided around what seemed to be a real dragon tooth at the front.

Is she the queen? Is she Eslinde's mother?

Yensen reached over and pulled Lyrrin's hood back and removed the cloth covering her hands.

The queen gagged as though she'd seen something horrific and fanned her face with one hand. "Why is it still alive? It should have been destroyed the moment you found it."

"Calm yourself, Vellira." The king raised a hand her way, holding it still in the air between them. "It was my decision to bring the half-breed in alive. Since Eslinde ran off with my other precious resources, I had to take something precious back. Stand, grayglim."

Yensen stood.

"You said in your reports this child can carve runes into crystal?"

Yensen flashed a dark look toward Lyrrin. She remained on her knees, unsure whether she should, or could, stand again.

He nodded once. "That she can."

"And she can, given the right costuming, pass as human," the king continued. "That will make things easier."

"My love, please," Queen Vellira knelt at the side of the throne, hanging on to the armrest on one side and staring up with pleading eyes. "You can't consider keeping this abomination. It never should have lived. We must erase our daughter's mistake before any more learn of it."

It. Abomination. Mistake. A face-flushing fury rose within Lyrrin. That woman was her *grandmother*. Her own grandmother wanted her dead, because of something Lyrrin had no way of changing about herself.

Lyrrin wanted to argue, to tell them she wasn't just some thing to be erased, but overwhelming emotions left her mute.

Vellira continued in a sweet, pleading tone. "We can recapture the Alderkin when your army captures that other rare dragon you're so interested in. You can keep those monsters for whatever you need them for, keep them locked up and hidden away as before, but don't keep this *thing*."

Yeonard Draekhan turned toward his wife, cupping her cheek in his hand. His head swayed in small motions as though considering, and then he nodded.

Lyrrin's shaking stopped as her body turned even colder.

The king opened his mouth to speak again, but Yensen's

voice came out faster.

"I hadn't been able to include the information in a report yet, but it was the child's actions that created the ... rare dragon. She may be able to assist in breeding more." There was an edge of panic in his words that hadn't been there before.

The king stilled, eyes widening slightly, and then he withdrew his hand from the queen's cheek.

"You know how it was created?" The king's voice lowered but seemed to boom even louder.

Yensen's lip twitched but he remained standing at attention and spoke clearly. "Partially."

"And this child knows the rest?" Yeonard Draekhan stood then. He loomed tall, backlit by the crackling blue lamps along the wall.

Yensen didn't confirm or deny the king's assumption. He locked eyes with Lyrrin, his expression urgent, and flicked his chin up.

Lyrrin rose shakily to her feet as the Dragon King strode toward her.

Staring down with narrowed eyes, he grasped her chin, his strong fingers in a pincerlike grip, and made her face him. "You will share with me what you know, child. We could become great allies, you and me, if you obey me. And you will obey me. For I am your king, and we are family."

Lyrrin knew her continued existence relied on being

useful to this man. On being obedient. She knew even if he allowed her to live that he could make that life as difficult and painful as he wished.

But for the king to command her obedience with the mention of *family* fired up every rebellious nerve inside her. Family was love. Family was protecting one another. Family was what Lyrrin had just been wrenched away from.

Lyrrin glared at the Dragon King through stinging, hot eyes. "We are *not* family."

TO BE CONTINUED
IN
SECRET OF THE DRAGON THRONE

GLOSSARY

Including pronunciation guide

CHARACTERS

Riony Eyfarr (Ree-OH-nee AY-far) – Rolanian, Daughter of Eylin and Farrad, born when servants to the Gyrstein Dragonlords, then sold on as a family to the Heithorn Dragonlords, and since living as fugitive slaves. Trained as a midwife and herbalist. Sword enthusiast.

Lyrrin Eyfarr (Li-rin AY-far) – Daughter of "The Guest", an unknown dragonlord woman, and an unknown father. Taen and Elgarthan? Has some unusual features. Likes animals and magic.

Kessara Heithorn (Kess-AH-ra High-thorn) – From the once wealthy Heithorn dragonlords with strong dragon riding traditions, estranged. Taen. Rides a wolf.

Kife Heithorn (K-eye-f High-thorn) – Elder brother to Kessara, dragonrider. Taen.

Dracuni (Drak-YOU-nee) – Unique hybrid between unicorn and dragon, created from the use of silvernix on a broken dragon egg, and something more?

Griskin (Griss-kin) – Large gray wolf, male, for some reason abides Kess's company.

Aishena Hjelzahn (AYSH-ena Hyel-zarn) – Delver, Middle sibling of three (remaining), fifth generation heir, grayglim in training. Taen.

Benjin Hjelzahn (BEN-jin Hyel-zarn) – Youngest sibling of three (remaining), fifth generation heir. Taen.

Kverra Hjelzahn (Kv-errar Hyel-zarn) – Grayglin warden and wife to Vori Hjelzan, fourth generation heir to the Dragon King. Taen.

Yeonard Draekhan (Yeh-nard DRAKE-arn) – Dragonking, ruler of Elundrae. Taen. First to tame a dragon.

Eslinde Draekhan (Ez-Lind-eh DRAKE-arn) – Last of the dragon-king's first generation heirs.

Alderkin (ALL-der-kin) – a secretive and powerful race of elven humanoids. Masters of rune crystal magic. Extinct.

Alderkin Depths – Massive underground cities once inhabited by the Alderkin. There are five known Alderkin Depths across Elundrae.

Alderkin Runes – Magical symbols carved into crystal items, which, when somehow charged, allow for a range of magical functions. The runes must be traced in the right sequence and direction of strokes in order to be activated and deactivated.

Alderkin War – A twenty-year war between the Alderkin and the Dragon King's forces, ending thirty years prior to the events in these books. Prompted by the human's slaughter of unicorns, and the Alderkin's attempts to protect them.

Athame (Ah-Thahm-Ay) – A dagger of varying size, made from crystal, and powered by various Alderkin runes for utility or combat.

Breachers – Undercity dwellers who brave the aboveground world to scavenge resources, highly dangerous but sometimes required.

Delvers – Undercity dwellers who brave the dangers of the Alderkin depths to salvage useful artifacts to be sold in the undercity. A risky but lucrative profession.

Dragon Glass – Glass manufactured with the use of dragon's fire to melt the base ingredients.

Dragon guards/riders – Those trained to ride dragons, generally for combat purposes. Either born to or hired by Dragonlord families who own the dragons.

Dragonhold – A building with multiple facilities for dragon keeping and raising, including hatchery, stables, and training areas.

Dragonkeeps – Walled in cities protected by dragons. The Dragon King has built and gifted a dragonkeep to each of his first generation heirs.

Dragonlords – Those who have the riches and resources to own their own dragons. Not necessarily royalty.

Elgarthans – A sea-faring race, pale skinned, they will visit and trade with Dragonkeeps for the riches of steel and glass provided through dragon labor, but rarely remain in

Elundrae due to the dangers.

Elundrae (Ell-Un-Dray) – The continent in which the story takes place. Nearest neighboring country being Elgartha, across the seas to the East.

Rebel Riders – Title of a popular serial fiction, published and distributed in chapters.

Revenant/Rev/Shadow Revenant – Any undead creature raised by the Shadow Dragon's curse. Generally defeated by fire or dismemberment.

Rolanians – Once ruling large cities throughout Elundrae, most Rolanian settlements were destroyed as the Shadow Dragon curse spread through the land. As very few Rolanians became dragonlords, they had to buy into protection from those who had dragons, often at the cost of their own freedom. Generally presenting with a warm array of darker skin tones, and hair ranging from blonde, through reds and browns.

Shadow Dragon – a cursed and mysterious creature of smoke and sadness that brings the undead blight to the land of Elundrae. Wherever the Shadow Dragon touches ground, the dead rise.

Silvernix – Unicorn blood. Miraculous healing qualities, a single drop can cure a body from near death. Can only

be stored in dragon glass, otherwise loses potency within minutes. Opalescent liquid.

Taens – Generally dark-haired and light-to-mid-brown skin-tones, Taens were once a warrior like clan of horse-riders, taking residence through the north-west of Elundrae. When the Dragonking rose to power, Taens became favored and more likely to become dragonlords, and soon became the dominant race across the land.

Taming – The ceremony in which all dragons are subjected to in order to be domesticated, similar to a lobotomy. Performed not long after birth on dragons bred in captivity. Utilizes silvernix in the process.

Undercity – A human settlement, established in the large upper cavern of the Central Alderkin Depths, as a refuge from the dangers of the aboveground world.

Unicorns – Ethereal, horned horse-like creatures. Driven to extinction in the race for the riches of their blood.

Herbs

Carrowmy – culinary.

Corpsefoot – used for contraception, dangerous in high doses.

Genjermint – sleeping tea.

Hennen – for hair dye.

Morass Mercy – powerful sedative with bad side effects.

Plumeberry – tart, seedy berries, poison detox.

Shillgrue – to condition leather.

Tinctoria – for hair dye.

Weftweed – a sticky (both in appearance and sap production) antiseptic.

Dragons
Natural subspecies

Etherflame – Plains dragons. Golds and reds, large size. Fire breathing for clearing grasslands/cooking herds, and big wings for hovering. Blood itself is flammable and is aerosolized in breath weapon. Most common dragonrider mount.

Seasong – Sea dragons. Silvers, greens, blacks, largest size, big lungs creates big surge of air/sound to stun schools of fish, and bigger mouth for feeding. There are tales they once sang, but never have in captivity or once tamed. Mostly used for interbreeding and beasts of burden.

Snowshimmer – Mountain dragons. Whites-blues, medium-sized, fast build for snatching up rare prey. Big talons, lightning breath attack, rare and solitary. Used in industry for power and interbreeding.

Treedart – Forest dragons. Yellows, browns, purples, camouflaged scales. Smallest type, with concentrated fire bolts for individual prey. Considered pretty basic by breeders and dragonlords, mostly used for interbreeding. Main/only dragon still in the wild because of size.

Dragons

Interbred selective breeding species

Etherdart – Etherflame/Treedart cross. Medium size, tough but slow, big fireballs. A basic combat dragon.

FlameSongs – Etherflame/Seasong cross. Largest size, high-capacity fire-breathers, used mostly for industrial uses, not used as mounts because they can spontaneously explode.

Seashimmer – Seasong/Snowshimmer cross. Large size, cold, icy breath used in ice making and food storage industry.

Shimmerdart – Snowshimmer/Treedart cross. Small size, with small ball lightning darts, dangerous for single targets but not great against mass undead, bred for speed as scouts/communications/assassinations.

Snowflame – Snowshimmer/Etherflame cross. Medium-large size, white "liquid" fire, fast, considered a great dragonrider mount, but short lifespan as breath weapon deteriorates their health fast.

Treedart/seasong – don't interbreed successfully.

ANIMALS

Bantam Ferrets – Mouse sized ferrets.

Bovin – A large (twice human height) buffalo or yak style creature, docile, used to be in large herds that supported wild dragons. Moved into farming for captive dragons.

Carrion Birds – Massive scavengers with a cry like a wolf's howl.

Cave Otters – A large sized otter with specially adapted claws that allow them to climb sheer walls easily, pale colors to match limestone surroundings.

Cave Spiders – Head-sized spiders, nonvenomous.

Dreer – Deer with Armadillo like scales, that grow as large as giraffes. Also popular prey for wild dragon populations in the past.

Glowflies – firefly-like bugs, finger sized, live in large swarms and light up when disturbed.

Mouse Deer – Cat sized deer with fangs.

Olm – Just like real olm, but larger than human size and carnivorous.

Owlettes – Cave dwelling owls that feed on small rodents and insects within the caves, the size of a small hand.

Rope Worms – Just a worm, but much larger. Delicious when fried.

ALDERKIN RUNES

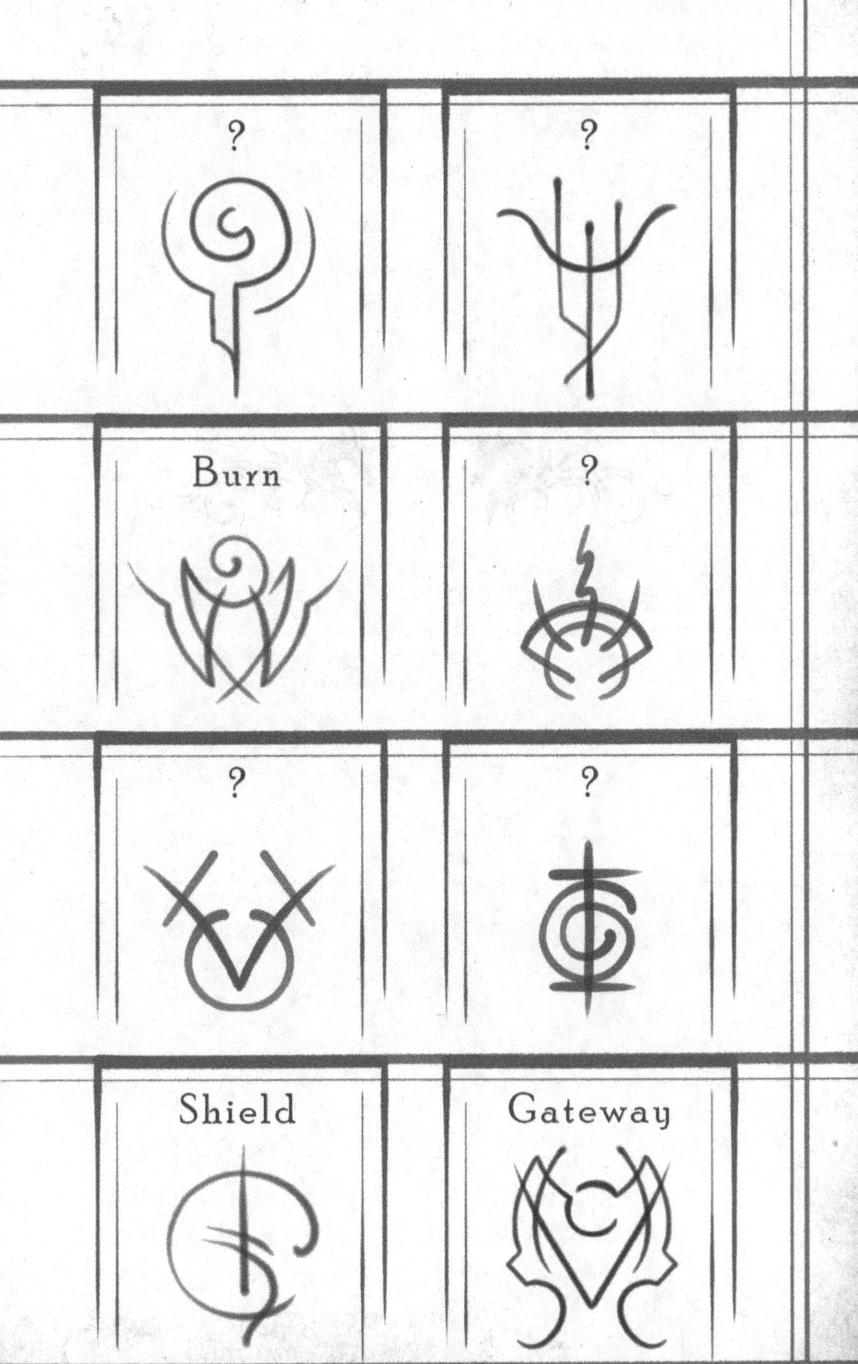
?
?
Burn
?
?
?
Shield
Gateway

Tree Dart
Sea Song
Snow Shimmer
Ether Flame

ABOUT THE AUTHOR

Professional daydreamer, Selina A. Fenech writes "adorably dark" Epic and Urban Fantasy for teens and adults. Filled with sweet and quirky characters, laugh out loud moments, and perilous adventures, her magical worlds are perfect for readers who love daring twists and happily ever afters.

A cancer survivor determined to live life to the fullest, she is an escape room enthusiast, avid gardener, foodie and self-proclaimed geek, residing in Australia.

In addition to literature, Selina applies her unique take on the dichotomy of light and dark as a professional fantasy artist working under the name Selina Fenech and has published many illustrated books, oracle decks, and colouring books.

FIND OUT MORE ABOUT SELINA

OFFICIAL WEBSITE: www.selinafenech.com

Memory's Wake Trilogy

A modern girl lost in and hunted in a fairy tale world.
An illustrated young adult portal fantasy with
Arthurian and Victorian themes.

Empath Chronicles

Teenagers with superpowers fueled by emotions ... what
could go wrong? A young adult superhero romance.

More Books by Selina A Fenech

Beshadowed

You have been lied to. Werewolves, vampires, ghosts … they aren't what you think. What is really lurking in the dark? A spooky urban fantasy.

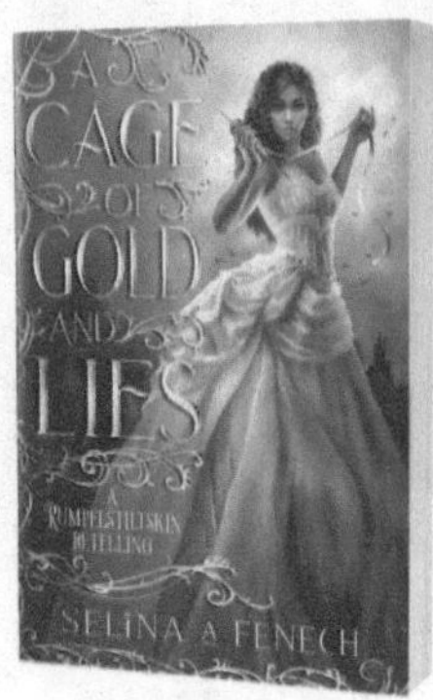

Fairy Tale Wishes

Enchanting and inclusive standalone fairy tale retellings.

9 781922 390882